ROBERT REED
MARROW

www.orbitbooks.net

ORBIT

First published in Great Britain by Orbit 2001
Reprinted 2002, 2004, 2005, 2007

Papers used by Orbit are natural, recyclable products made from
wood grown in sustainable forests and certified in accordance with
the rules of the Forest Stewardship Council.

Typeset in Bembo by
Palimpsest Book Production Limited, Polmont, Stirlingshire
Printed and bound in Great Britain by
Mackays of Chatham plc
Paper supplied by Hellefoss AS, Norway

Orbit
An imprint of
Little, Brown Book Group
Brettenham House
Lancaster Place
London WC2E 7EN

A Member of the Hachette Livre Group of Companies

www.orbitbooks.net

To the first artist in my life,
My grandfather,
Quentin 'Heinz' Moore

THE SHIP

. . . A SLEEP, SWEET as Death . . . time traversed, and an incalculable distance . . . and then a splash of light emerged from the dark and the cold, its warming touch slowly explaining itself to me, showing suns and little worlds and great swirls of colored gas and angry, roaring dust.

A barred spiral galaxy, this was.

Possessing such beauty, and a majesty, that I could not help but stare. And wrapped within that majesty, a frailty, ignorant and vast.

The galaxy's path and mine were plain.

Without question, we would collide.

My gaze was sure to be returned by many more gazes. I knew that, just as I had known that this day was inevitable. Yet when I saw that tiny first machine racing toward me, I was surprised. So soon! And yes, the machine could see me. I watched its mirrored eyes focus on my scarred old face. I watched it fire tiny rockets, exhausting itself in order to pass nearer to me. Then it spat out a minuscule device whose only duty was to collide with my face, undoubtedly followed by a trail of data and new questions. At nearly half the speed of light, we met. Only I survived. Then the mother machine swept past, turning its eyes, watching my trailing face, a part of me imagining its wondrous surprise.

My backside is adorned with rocket nozzles.

Bigger than worlds, and more ancient, my engines are as chilled and quiet as this ancient universe of ours.

Hello, I said.

Without a voice.

Brother machine, hello.

My friend continued on its way, and for a little while, I was alone again. Which was when I first sensed just how deep my loneliness had grown.

Ignoring caution, denying every duty, I began wishing for another visitor. What would be the harm? A little robotic companion, transitory and incompetent . . . how could a mere device present any hazard to me . . . ?

But it wasn't one probe sent to greet me. No, the machines came in flocks and fleets. Some serenely committed suicide, diving into my leading face. Others flew near enough to feel my tug, curling around my backside, enjoying a close quick look at my great engines. Their shape and basic design were the same as the first probe, implying a shared maker. Following their trajectories back through space and time, I discovered a telltale intersection. A single yellowish sun lay at the nexus. It and its neighboring suns had spawned the machines. I slowly accepted the unlikely answer that a single species had seen me before any other. But clearly, this galaxy was not a simple place. As time passed and the intervening distances shrank, other devices arrived from a multitude of places. I watched a parade of machines built of simple metals and sculpted gas and encased in hydrogen ice, and from hundreds of thousands of suns came every sort of electromagnetic noise, in soft squirts and squawks, elaborate songs and brazen shouts.

'Hello,' the voices shouted. 'And who are you, friend?'

Who I appear to be, I am.

'And what, friend, do you mean to us?'

Just what I appear to mean, I told them. With silence. In every way, what you see in me is most definitely what I am.

ANIMALS CAME FROM *someplace between me and that yellow-ish sun.*

Their first vessel was tiny, and simple, and extraordinarily frail. Enormous bravery must have taken them this far. The creatures had to leave the brightness of their own galaxy, and at midvoyage, they stopped themselves, turned and started home again, their little engines pushing and pushing, matching my terrific velocity at the perfect moment. Then they slowed again, just slightly, letting me catch up to them, and maintaining a smart cautious distance, they coaxed themselves into a useful orbit.

As I watched, a thousand automated machines descended on me.

Hovered, then set down.

My scars and my trajectory implied my age.

No galaxies lay behind me. Not even a dark, half-born galaxy of consequence. That kind of emptiness has few obstacles. Comets are rare, suns rarer, and even simple dusts are scarce. Yet my leading face was cratered and cracked, implying to the curious animals that I had come a terrific way, and I was as old as their home world.

At the very least.

'This ship is cold,' their machines reported. 'Most definitely asleep, and quite possibly dead.'

A derelict, in simple terms.

Between my leading face and the trailing face lay great ports, empty and closed, and securely locked. But smaller hatches and doorways could be opened with a determined push, and after begging for instructions, that was what several machines did. They eased open doors that had been closed almost forever, and behind them they found descending passageways and neat, unworn stairs perfectly suited for a humanoid's graceful, long-legged gait.

The animals themselves made their last little leap.

When feet had last descended my stairs, I could not recall. But here came the humans, in twos and tens, entering my interior with a cautious sense of purpose. At first, they wore bulky suits and carried weapons and spoke in soft radio voices, using elaborate codes. But as they moved deeper, the old air thickened around them, and tests showed oxygen left to breathe, a multitude of life-support systems still at work, coaxing my guests to remove their helmets, sniffing once, then breathing deeper, and in that human fashion, smiling.

The first voice said, 'Hello,' and heard only its own nervous echo in reply.

Beneath my armored hull was a vast cold ocean of stone laced with grand passageways and abrupt dead ends and rooms too vast to be absorbed in a single look, or even a lifetime. The darkness was thorough, relentless. But every wall and ceiling had its lamps and holoprojectors, their machinery transparently simple and easily ignited; plus there were armies of local reactors waiting to be brought from their slumber modes to furnish power.

In little places, then larger ones, I was awakened.

And still, I had no voice.

Did I ever possess the power of speech?

Perhaps not, I realized. Perhaps what I remember as my voice is actually another's. But whose? And how can any span of time rob such a basic, essential knowledge?

Most of the humans now boarded me.

With care and fondness, I counted them. Twelve to the fourth power, plus a few more. Which was a tiny, almost negligible number compared to my vastness.

But then more ships arrived — an armada coming from other suns, other human worlds. These newer vessels had more powerful, efficient engines. And I realized that even if these were animals, they could adapt quickly. Which had to be a good thing.

But why was it good?

With all of my new energies, I tried to shout at my innocent companions, begging them to please listen to me.

Yet I was mute.

Save a whispering wind, and the crackle of random energy in a granitic wall, and the dry clatter of gravel preceding the touch of a human foot, I could make no sound.

The human population increased another twelvefold.

And for a little while after that, nothing changed.

The explorers had all arrived. With a crisp efficiency, they mapped every tunnel and crevice, giving each a precise designation

Every large room and cavernous chamber was honored with a special name. Great seas of water and ammonia, methane and silicone, were found in my interior, at many depths. Banks of machinery could manipulate their chemistry, making them suitable for a wide range of life-forms. Understandably, the humans adjusted one of the water seas as an experiment, its salts and acidity made to their liking, its temperature warm on the surface and cold beneath; and with a bid toward permanence, they built a little city overlooking the sea's black-bouldered shore.

Whatever the humans discovered inside me, I discovered, too.

Until that moment, I had never fully comprehended my greatness, or my own glorious, well-worn beauty.

I wanted to thank my guests, and could not. Just as I couldn't make them hear my plaintive warnings. But I was growing more comfortable with my muteness. Everything has its reason, and no matter how great and glorious I am, I am nothing compared to the wise ones who created me . . . and who am I, a mere machine, to question their boundless wisdom . . . ?

BENEATH MY WATERY *seas were still larger oceans of liquid hydrogen.*

Fuel for my sleeping engines, no doubt.

Humans learned how to repair my pumps and giant reactors, and they managed to activate one of the great engines, an experimental burst of high-velocity plasmas proving hotter than expected, and more powerful.

By then, we were plunging into their galaxy.

It was named for a mother's secretions, this Milky Way.

I began to taste its dusts, and its feeble heat warmed my old skin. A quarter of a trillion suns were below me, plus a hundred trillion worlds, living and otherwise. From nothingness, I was falling into the cosmopolitan heart of the universe. Tens of thousands of species had seen my arrival, and naturally a few sent their own tiny ships, orbiting me at the usual respectful distance, using many voices as they asked to be allowed onboard, or bluntly demanded to be given possession of me.

The humans refused everyone. Politely at first, then less so.

I heard their cold officious words about interstellar law and the status of derelict ships. Then came a careful, calculated silence.

One of the interlopers decided on action. Without warning, it attacked, turning the human starships into light and pulverized debris.

Unprepared for war, most species made a graceless retreat. Only the most violent few remained, unleashing their weapons against my armored hull. But if I can withstand a giant comet impacting at a fat fraction of lightspeed, their tritium bombs and X-ray lasers could do nothing. Nothing. The humans, safely inside me, went about their lives, ignoring the bombardment, repairing and recalibrating my old guts while their enemies exhausted themselves against my great body.

One after another, the starships gave up the fight and left for home.

Desperate to establish any claim, the last species attempted a hard landing. Their captain plunged toward my leading face, dipping in and out of craters while streaking toward the nearest port. It was a brave and bold and foolhardy act. A network of shield generators and lasers and antimatter cannons lay inside deep bunkers. In some lost age, they must have worked to protect me from comets and other hazards. As they had with my other systems, the humans had discovered the machinery and made repairs. And with a mixture of retribution and charity, they used the lasers to destroy the attackers' engines, and their weapons, and they made prisoners out of the survivors.

Then with a roaring voice, they shouted at the Milky Way.

'This ship is ours!' they shouted.

'Ours!'

'Now, and always! The Ship belongs to us . . . !'

★ ★ ★

SET ON TOP of a great black boulder were black wooden chairs, and sitting on those chairs, enjoying the false sunshine, were the Master Captain and her closest staff, each dressed in his or her fanciest mirrored uniform.

'Now that we've won,' began the Master, 'what have we won?'

No one spoke.

'We've got title to the largest starship ever,' she continued, gesturing at a blue ceiling and the warm surf and the warmer basaltic rock. 'But governments and corporations paid for our mission here, and they aren't unreasonable to expect some return on their fat investments.'

Everyone nodded, and waited. They knew the Master well enough to hold tight to their opinions, at least until she looked at them and said their names.

'This ship is moving awfully fast,' she pointed out. 'Even if we could rotate one hundred and eighty degrees and fire its engines until the tanks are dry, we'd still be moving too fast to dock anywhere. You can't make twenty Earth masses dance for you. Can you?'

Silence.

She chose a narrow, coolly professional face. 'Miocene?'

Her assistant said, 'Yes, madam.'

'Ideas? Any?'

'We can't stop ourselves, madam. But we could use our engines to adjust our course.' Miocene was a tall, perpetually calm woman. She glanced at the compad on her lap, then let her walnut-colored eyes lift and meet the Master's impatient gaze. 'There is a white dwarf ahead of us. A three-day burn starting now would take us past it at relatively close range, and instead of slicing through the galaxy, we would be turned. The ship would pass through human space, then continue on into the heart of the galaxy.'

'But to what end?' asked the Master.

'To give us more time to study this technology. Madam.'

A few of her fellow captains risked little nods of agreement.

But for some reason, the Master wasn't convinced. With a sharp creaking of wood, she rose to her feet, towering over even the tallest of her subordinates. For a long while, she did nothing. She let them watch as she did nothing. Then she turned and stared across the open water, studying the wind-driven waves as they broke against the basalt, her colorless swift mind trying to distill what was best from everything that was possible.

Out in the surf, a whale appeared.

It was a tailored minke whale — a popular species on terraformed worlds — and riding the saddle on its dark broad back was a single child. A girl, judging by her build and the wind-thinned giggle. Quietly, the Master asked, 'Whose child is that?'

With the war finished, the captains and crew had produced the occasional child, setting roots deeper into the ship.

Miocene rose and squinted at the bright water, then admitted, 'I'm not sure about the parents. But the girl lives nearby. I'm sure that I've seen her.'

'Get her. Bring her to me.'

Captains are captains because they can accomplish any chore, and usually with a minimum of fuss. But the girl and her whale proved difficult to catch. She ignored the orders coming across her headset. When she saw the skimmer approaching, she gave a loud giggle, then made her friend dive, both using their hydrolizing gills to breathe, staying out of easy reach for another full hour.

Finally a parent was found, then convinced to coax his daughter to the surface, where she was captured and dressed in an oversized robe, her long black hair dried and tied before she was ushered to the top of the great boulder.

The Master rose, offering her captive her own enormous chair. Then she sat on a knob of basalt, her mirrored uniform brilliant in the afternoon light, her voice almost as friendly as it was firm.

'Darling,' she asked, 'why do you ride that whale?'

'For fun,' the younster replied instantly.

'But swimming is fun,' the Master countered. 'You can swim, can't you?'

'Better than you, ma'am. Probably.'

When the Master laughed, everyone else did as well. Except for Miocene, who watched this interrogation with a growing impatience.

'You'd rather ride than swim,' the Master said. 'Am I right?'

'Sometimes.'

'When you're clinging to your friend, do you feel safe?'

'I guess. Sure.'

'Safe.' The word was so important that it needed to be repeated. The Master said it a third time, then a fourth. Then again, she looked at the girl, smiled, and told her, 'Fine. Thank you. Go on off and play some more, darling.'

'Yes, madam.'

'By the way. What's your name?'

'Washen.'

'You're a beautiful young woman. Thank you, Washen.'

'For what?'

'For your help, of course,' the Master purred. 'You've been absolutely vital.'

Everyone was puzzled. The captains watched the girl walk away in that careful, slow way that children use when they know they are being watched. But before Washen had gone, Miocene blurted, 'What does all this mean, madam?'

'You know perfectly well. Interstellar travel is less than safe.' A broad, bright grin spread across the Master's golden face. 'Even our largest, most durable starship can be obliterated by a chunk of nothing no larger than my fist.'

True, of course. Always.

'But inside this great ship, the passenger is perfectly safe. Today and forever, she is protected by hundreds of kilometers of high-grade hyperfiber, and protected by lasers and shields, and served by a cadre of the finest captains anywhere.' The Master paused *for an instant, enjoying the drama. Then speaking over the rumble of the surf, she announced, 'We are going to sell passages on this great ship. Passages for a journey around the galaxy — a journey like no other — and every wealthy customer will be welcome. Human, alien, or machine!'*

Suddenly, the wind gusted.

The Master's empty chair was pushed over on its side.

A dozen captains fought for the privilege of righting the chair, while Miocene, knowing what was best, joined the Master instead, bowing and smiling as she said, 'What a fine and perfect and wonderful idea . . . madam . . . !'

One

WASHEN WAS A captain of consequence.

Fashionably tall, with an ageless strong body, she possessed handsome features wrapped around wise chocolate eyes. Her long obsidian hair was worn in a sensible bun, streaked with just enough white to lend authority. She conveyed a sense of easy confidence and relaxed competence, and with a little look or a gentle word, she lent her confidence to whoever deserved it. In public, she wore her mirrored captain's uniform with a regal bearing and gentle pride. Yet she had the rare gift of keeping others from feeling jealous of her station or intimidated by her presence. And even rarer was Washen's talent for embracing the instincts and customs of truly alien species, which was why, at the Master Captain's insistence, one of her duties was to greet their strangest passengers, explaining what *the ship* was and what it expected from its cherished guests.

Her day, like so many days, began at the bottom of Port Beta.

Washen adjusted the tilt of her cap, then gazed upward, watching as a kilometer-long taxi was lowered from the airlock. Stripped of its rockets, the bulky fuel tanks, and wide armored prow, the taxi resembled a great needle. Its hyperfiber hull glittered in the port's brilliant lights as skilled mates and their AIs controlled its descent with hair-thin cable and squid-limbs, bringing it down with the smoothness of a descending cap-car.

Which was a mistake. Through an implanted nexus, Washen called for the mates' boss. 'Let it drop,' she advised. 'Right now.'

An ice-white human face grimaced.

'But madam . . . ?'

'Now,' she demanded. 'Let it fall on its own.'

A captain's word weighed more than any mate's caution. Besides, the taxi's hull could absorb much worse abuse, and both of them knew it.

With a low crackle, the squid-limbs pulled free.

For an instant, the needle seemed unaffected. Then the ship's gravity – much more than earth-standard – took hold and yanked it down into the cone-shaped berth reserved for it. The impact was jarring, but muted by the hyperfiber floor and a heavy dose of antinoise. Washen felt the collision in her toes and knees, and she let herself smile for a moment, imagining the passengers' delicious surprise.

'I need to fill out an accident report,' growled the white face.

'Naturally,' she replied. 'And I'll accept all the blame you can give me. Agreed?'

'Thank you . . . Captain . . .'

'No. Thank you.'

Washen strolled toward the berth and taxi, her smile fading, replaced with a theatrical grimness appropriate to this job.

The passengers were disembarking.

Flounders, they had been dubbed.

At a glance, Flounders resembled thick woolly rugs carried on dozens of strong and very short legs. They came from a superterran world, accustomed to five times the port's gravity, and like many species from such worlds, they demanded a thicker, richer atmosphere than what they found here. Implanted compressors aided their quick, shallow breathing. Pairs of large, eerily human eyes were rooted at one end of each long body, staring up at Washen from what, for lack of a better term, was their heads.

'Welcome,' Washen announced.

Her translator made a low rumbling sound.

'I despise each of you,' she bellowed. Then, following the advice of exopsychologists, she bent over, making eye contact as she reminded these newcomers, 'You have no status here. None. A word from me, and you are crushed in the most horrible ways.'

Human politeness had no place in that alien society.

Flounders – whose real name was a series of poetic ticks – equated kindness with intimacy. And intimacy was afforded only family members, by blood or by ceremony. The exopsychologists were adamant. If Washen couldn't intimidate the Flounders, they would feel uneasy, much in the same way that a human would feel uneasy if a stranger approached, referred to her by a lover's nickname, then delivered a sloppy wet kiss.

'This is my ship,' she told her audience.

Several hundred aliens were in shouting range, tiny ears tilted high, absorbing her voice as well as the thunderous rumble of her translator.

'You have paid for my patience as well as a berth,' said Washen. 'Paid with new technologies, which we have already received, mastered, and improved upon.'

Long whiskers stroked each other, the aliens conversing by feel.

Again, she stared into a pair of eyes. Cobalt-blue, utterly alive. 'My rules are simple, little monster.'

Whiskers suddenly grew still.

Her audience held its collective breath.

'My ship is *the ship*,' she explained. 'It needs no other name. It is remarkable and enormous, but it is not infinite. Nor empty. Thousands of species share its labyrinths with you. And if you do not treat your fellow passengers with complete respect, you will be discarded. Evicted. Flung overboard, and forgotten.'

The breathing resumed, quicker than ever.

Was she playing this game too well?

But instead of holding back, Washen kept pressing. 'An empty chamber has been prepared for you. As you begged us to do. Sealed, and pressurized. With plenty of space, and your ugly foods in abundance. In this new home, you may do as you wish. Unless you wish to procreate, which requires permission from *me*. And fresh payments. Since children are passengers, their status is negotiable. And if I have reason, I will personally throw them overboard. Is that understood?'

Her translator asked the question, then with a soft, sexless voice, offered a sampling of the aliens' replies.

'Yes, Lord Captain.'

'Of course, Lord.'

'You scare me, Lord!'

'When does this show end, Mother? I am hungry!'

Washen strangled a laugh. Then after her own quick breaths, she admitted, 'It has been forever since I last threw anyone off *the ship*.'

Other captains did the banishing. In humane ways, naturally. Taxis or other starships would take the troublesome species home again, or more likely, to obscure worlds where they had a better than fair chance of survival.

'But make no mistake!' she roared. 'I love this ship. I was born here, and I will die here, and in the long time between I will do whatever I can to protect its ancient halls and noble stone, from anything or anyone that shows it less than perfect respect. Do you understand me, you little fools?'

'Yes, Your Lord.'

'Your Goddess!'

'But is she finished yet? My tongues are numb from hunger!'

'I am nearly finished,' she told the aliens. Then even louder, she said, 'But I will be watching. From this moment, I am hovering over you like Phantom Night.'

That brought a respectful silence.

Phantom Night was a Flounder god, the name translated into a rugged little squawk that brought a chill even to Washen's spine.

With a practiced haughtiness, she turned and strode away.

The quintessential captain.

One of the lords of the galaxy.

And now, for this blunt moment, she was a mythical monster who would steal the souls of those who dared sleep.

LONG AGO, WASHEN reached that age where the past is too large to embrace, where even the sharpest, most efficient memory has to slough off little details and entire centuries, and where even the most cherished childhood has been stripped down, nothing left but a series of fragmentary recollections and a few diamond-hard moments that no amount of time, not even ten million years, can dilute to any degree.

Washen's first aliens were dubbed the Phoenixes.

That was when the ship was still outside the Milky Way. Washen was more a child than not, and her parents – engineers who had come on board the first starship – were part of the large unhappy team who fashioned a habitat for the Phoenixes.

Those aliens were unwelcome. They had tried to conquer the ship, after all. It was an ineffectual invasion, but people found it difficult to forgive them anyway. Washen's father, usually charitable to a fault, openly stated that his work was a waste, and worse, it was a crime. 'Give the shits a tiny catacomb, enough water and some minimal food, then forget they're there. That's my little opinion.'

Washen couldn't recall her mother's precise opinion; even Washen's own early biases were lost to time. And she couldn't recall why she first visited the prison. Was she looking for her parents? Or was it later, after their work was finished, and youngsters like herself were pulled there by simple curiosity?

Whatever the reason, what she remembered today was the funeral.

Washen had never seen Death. In her short happy life, not one human had died on board the ship. Age and disease had been tamed, and the modern body could absorb even horrific injuries. If a person was cautious, and sober, she didn't need to die. Ever.

But Phoenixes embraced a different set of beliefs. They evolved on a small hot world. Gills augmented a trio of large, black-blooded lungs; their metabolisms were quick and fierce. Where most winged aliens were gliders or soarers, passive and efficient, the Phoenixes were the ecological equivalent of human-sized peregrines. Skilled hunters and determined warriors, they possessed a broad heritage older than any human culture. Yet despite a wealth of advanced technologies, they didn't approve of the immortalities that most species simply took for granted.

Inside a human mouth, their name was an unsingable string of notes.

'Phoenix' was pulled from some ancient Earth myth. Or was it a Martian myth? Either way, the name was only partly appropriate. They weren't birds, after all, and they didn't live for five hundred years. Thirty standards was too long for most of them, physical infirmities and senility leaving their elderly incapable of flight, or song, or the smallest dignity.

Upon death, the body and a ceremonial nest were burned. But instead of a sweet resurrection, the cold white ashes were carried high by family and friends, then released, winds and wingbeats spreading the soft remains to the ends of their enormous and lovely prison cell.

Their home wasn't built out of simple charity. The Master, taking her usual long aim, decided that if the ship was to attract alien passengers, her crew needed to know how to tweak and twist the ship's environmental controls, turning raw cavities into abodes where any sort of biology would feel at home. That's why she ordered her top engineers to make the attempt. And aeons later, when she came to understand the Master, Washen easily imagined the woman's impatience with someone like her father – a talented employee who dared grumble about his job, unable to appreciate the long-term benefits of this apparently misplaced beneficence.

The Phoenix habitat was once someone's magnetic bottle.

It could have been an antimatter containment tank, though at its best this remark was an authoritative, utterly wild guess.

Five kilometers in diameter and better than twenty kilometers deep, the prison was a column of dense warm air punctuated by thick clouds and masses of floating vegetation. Biological stocks from the Phoenix starship had been cultured, then adapted. Since the original tank lacked lights, ship-style sky lamps were built from scratch, their light tuned to the proper frequencies. Since there wasn't room for jet streams or typhoons, the air was assaulted with an array of hidden vents and other engineering tricks. And to hide the tall cylindrical walls, an illusion of endless clouds covered every surface – an illusion good enough to seem real to humans, but not to the Phoenixes who flew too close.

The prison was meant to hold the defeated and the evil, but both sorts of prisoners quickly grew old and passed away.

It was one of the old warriors whose funeral Washen saw. It seemed unlikely today, but she could remember standing on a platform built against that great round wall, herself and a thousand other humans with their hands locked on the railing, watching winged shapes rising toward them, then higher, flying with a wondrous precision and singing loudly enough to be heard over the constant whistle of wind.

When the ashes were dropped, the bereaved were too distant to be seen.

Intentionally, no doubt.

The young Washen contemplated the funeral. That next day, or perhaps next year, she proposed, 'We can let the rest of them go free, since the bad ones have died.'

Her father felt otherwise.

'If you haven't noticed, Phoenixes aren't human.' He warned his soft-hearted daughter, 'The creatures have a saying. "You inherit your direction before your wings." Which means, dearest, that the children and grandchildren are just as determined to slaughter us as their ancestors ever were.'

'If not more determined,' said Mother, with an unexpectedly dark tone.

'These creatures hold a grudge,' Father continued. 'Believe me, they can make their hatreds fester and grow.'

'Unlike humans,' said their sharp-witted daughter.

Her irony went unmentioned, and perhaps unrecognized. If there was more to that argument, it went unremembered. The modern brain is dense and extraordinarily durable — a composite of bioceramics and superconducting proteins and ancient fats and quantum microtubules. But like any reasonable brain, it has to simplify whatever it learns. It straightens. It streamlines. Instinct and habit are its allies, and even the wisest soul employs the art of extrapolation.

When she concentrated, Washen could recall dozens of fights with her parents. Childhood issues of freedom and responsibility never seemed to change, and she remembered enough of their politics and personalities to picture little spats and giant, ugly explosions — the sorts of emotional maelstroms that would make good engineers sit in the dark, quietly asking themselves how they had become such awful, ineffectual parents.

To Washen and her closest friends, the Phoenixes became a cause, a rallying point, and an extraordinarily useful thorn.

A ragged little political movement was born. Its bravest followers, including Washen, publically protested the prison. Their efforts culminated in a march to the Master's station. Hundreds chanted about freedom and decency. They held holosigns showing wingless Phoenixes bound up in black iron chains. It was a brave, remarkable event, and it ended in a small victory: little delegations were free to visit the prison, observe conditions firsthand, and speak to the pitiable aliens under the careful gaze of the captains.

That's where Washen met her first alien.

Phoenix males were always beautiful, but he was exceptionally so. What passed for feathers were a brilliant gold fringed with the darkest black, and an elegant, efficient face seemed to be all eyes and beak. The eyes were a lush coppery green, bright as polished gemstones. The beak was a vivid jade color, hard and obviously sharp. It was open when he sang, and it remained open afterward, always gulping down the liters of air that he required just to perch in one place and live.

The apparatus on his chest translated his elaborate song.

'Hello,' he said to Washen. Then he called her 'human egg-bearer.'

Several young humans were in the delegation, but Washen was their leader. Following Phoenix protocol, she fielded every question and spoke for the others, following a shopping list of subjects agreed upon weeks ago.

'We want to help you,' Washen promised.

Her translator sang those words in a half-moment, if that.

'We want you free to move and live wherever you wish on board the ship,' she told them. 'And until that can happen, we want to make your life here as comfortable as possible.'

The Phoenix sang his reply.

'Fuck comfort,' said his box.

A deep unease passed through the human delegation.

'What is your name, human egg-bearer?'

'Washen.'

There was no translation, which meant that it was an impossible sound. So the young Phoenix gulped a breath and sang a note that came out as 'Snowfeather.'

She liked the name, and said so. Then she thought to inquire, 'What's your name?'

'Supreme-example-of-manhood,' he replied.

Washen laughed, but only for a moment. Then quietly, carefully, she said, 'Manly. May I call you Manly?'

'Yes, Snowfeather. You may.' Then the feathers around the jade beak lifted – a Phoenix smile, she recalled – and he reached out with one of his long arms, reaching past Washen's shoulder, a strong little hand gently, ever so gently, caressing the leading edge of her own great wing.

* * *

EVERYONE IN THE delegation wore strap-ons.

Their wings were powered by thumb-sized reactors and guided both by the wearer's muscles, and more importantly, by elaborate sensors and embedded reflexes. For the next ten days, humantime, they were to live among the Phoenixes as observers and as delegates. Since no portion of the facility lay out of surveillance range, there wasn't any overt danger. Regardless how thick the intervening clouds or how loud the thunder, the children couldn't do anything that wasn't observed, and recorded, every one of their well-intended words spoken to a larger, infinitely suspicious audience.

Perhaps that's why Snowfeather took Manly as her lover.

It was a provocative and defiant and absolutely public act, and she could only hope that news of it slinked its way to her parents.

Or set aside the cynicism. Maybe it was something like love, or at least lust. Maybe it was stirred by the alien himself, and the gorgeous dreamy-strange scenery, and the sheer sensual joy that came with those powerful wings and the feel of wind slipping across your naked flesh.

Or deny love, leaving curiosity as the root cause.

Or put aside curiosity, and call it a deeply political act brought on by courage, or idealism, or the simplest, most wicked forms of naivety.

Whatever the reason, she seduced Manly.

On the summit of an airborne jungle, with her long back pressed against the warm and slick skin of a vegetable bladder, Snowfeather invited the alien's affections. Demanded them, even. He was quick to finish and quick to begin again, and he was tireless, his powerful, furnace-like body held over her with an impossible grace. Yet their geometries didn't mesh. In the end, she was the one who begged, 'Enough. Stop. Let me rest, all right . . . ?'

Her body was damaged, and not just a little bit damaged.

Curious but plainly untroubled, her lover watched the blood flow from between her exhausted legs, crimson at first but turning black in the hyper-oxygenated air. Then her blood clotted, and the ripped flesh began to heal. Without scars and with minimal pain, what would have been a mortal wound in an earlier age had simply vanished. Had never been.

Manly grinned in the Phoenix way, saying nothing.

Snowfeather wanted words. 'How old are you?' she blurted. And when there wasn't an answer, she asked it again. Louder this time. 'How old?'

He answered, using the Phoenix calendar.

Manly was a little more than twenty standards old. Which was middle-aged. Late middle-aged, in fact.

She grimaced, then told her lover, 'I can help you.'

He sang a reply, and his translator asked, 'In what fashion, help?'

'Medically. I can have your DNA replaced with better genetics. Your lipid membranes supplanted with more durable kinds. And so on.' She surprised herself more than him, telling him, 'The techniques are complicated, but proven. I have friends whose doctor-parents would adore the chance to reconfigure your flesh.'

The squawk meant, 'No.'

She recognized that defiant sound before the translator said, 'No,' with a cold, abrasive tone.

Then he roared, 'Never,' as those lovely golden feathers stood on end, making his face and great body appear even larger. 'I do not believe in your magic.'

'It's not magic,' she countered, 'and most species use it.'

'Most species are weak,' was his instant reply.

She knew she should let the topic drop. But with a

mixture of compassion and pity, plus a heavy dose of hopeful defiance, she warned her lover, 'Changes aren't coming soon. Unless you can extend your life, you'll never be anywhere but here, inside your little prison.'

Silence.

'You'll never fly on another world, much less your home world.'

There was a musical whine, feathers swirling in a Phoenix shrug.

'One home is enough for a true soul,' the translator reported. 'Even if that home is a tiny cage.'

Another whine.

Manly told her, 'Only the weak and the soulless need to live for aeons.'

Snowfeather didn't bristle, or complain. Her voice was steady and grave, remarking, 'By that logic, I'm weak.'

'And soulless,' he agreed. 'And doomed.'

'You could try to save me, couldn't you?'

The alien face was puzzled, if anything. The beak came close, the girl smelling the windlike breath, and for the first time, for a terrible instant, Washen was disgusted by that rich, meat-fed stink.

'Am I not worth saving?' she pressed.

The green eyes closed, supplying the answer.

She shook her head, human-fashion. Then she sat up and swirled her wings, her thick, aching voice asking, 'Don't you love me?'

A majestic song roared out of him.

The box fixed on his muscled chest efficiently reduced all that majesty and passion to simple words.

'The Great Nothingness conspired to make me,' he informed her. 'He intended me to live for a day. As He intends for each of us. I am a selfish, loud, arrogant, manly man, yes. But if I stay alive for two days, I am stealing another's life. Someone meant to be born but left without room. If I live for three days, I steal two lives. And if I lived as long as you wish . . . for a million days . . . how many nations would remain unborn . . . ?'

There was more to the speech, but she heard none of it.

She wasn't Snowfeather anymore; she was a young human again. Finding herself standing, she interrupted the translator's blather with a raucous laugh. Then scorn took hold, making her cry out, telling the Supreme-example-of-manhood, 'You know what you are? You're a stupid, self-absorbed turkey!'

His box hesitated, fighting for a translation.

Before it could speak, and without a backward glance, Washen leaped off the bladder, spreading the mechanical wings and plunging fast, her chest perilously close to the forest's blue-black face before a rising wind claimed her, helping carry her to the observation deck.

On her feet again, Washen unstrapped the almost-new wings and shoved them over the railing. Then she quietly returned home. That day, or sometime during those next few months, she approached her parents, asking what they would think of her if she applied to the captains' academy.

'That would be wonderful,' her father purred.

'Whatever you want,' said her mother, her feelings coming with a relieved smile.

No one mentioned the Phoenixes. What her parents knew, Washen never learned. But after her acceptance to the academy, and under the influence of a few celebratory drinks, Father gave her a squidlike hug, and with wisdom and a drunk's easy conviction, he told her, 'There are different ways to fly, darling.

'Different wings.

'And I think . . . I know . . . you're choosing the very best kind . . . !'

WASHEN HAD ALWAYS lived in the same apartment nestled deep inside one of the popular captains' districts. But that wasn't to say that her home hadn't changed during this great march of a life. Furniture. Artwork. Cultivated plants, and domesticated animals. With several hectares of climate-controlled, earth-gravity terrain to play with, and the resources of the ship at her full disposal, the danger was that she would make too many changes, inspiration ruling, never allowing herself enough time to appreciate each of her accomplishments.

While returning home from Port Beta, Washen composed her daily report, then studied the next passengers scheduled to board the ship: a race of machines, super-chilled and tiny, eager to build a new nation inside a volume smaller than most drawers.

Whenever she grew bored, Washen found herself dreaming up new ways to redecorate the rooms and gardens inside her home.

She would do the work soon, she told herself.

In a year, or ten.

The cap-car delivered her to her private door. Stepping out of the car, she decided that things had gone well today. A thousand centuries of steady practice had made her an expert in alien psychologies and the theatre that went into handling them, and like any good captain, Washen allowed herself to feel pride, knowing that what she did she did better than almost anyone else on board.

If there was anyone better, of course.

She wasn't consciously thinking about her long-dead lover, or the Phoenixes, or that fateful day that helped make her into a captain. But everything that she was now had been born then. The young Washen had no genuine feel for any alien species, much less for Manly. She never suspected what the Phoenixes were planning. Events had come as a complete surprise, and a revelation, and it was only luck and Washen's popularity that kept her from being tainted by the whole ugly business.

Several youngsters besides Washen had taken lovers. Or the Phoenixes had allowed themselves to be taken. Either way, emotional bonds were built on top of political hopes, and slowly, over the course of the next years, the humans helped their lovers in ways that were at first questionable, then illegal, and finally, treasonous.

Along a thousand conduits, forbidden machines entered the prison.

Under the watchful gaze of AI paranoids and suspicious captains, weapons were designed and built, then stored inside the floating bladders – invisible because the captains' sensors were sabotaged by the sympathizers.

When it came, the rebellion gave no warning. Five captains were murdered, along with nine hundred-plus mates and engineers and young humans, including many of Washen's one-time friends. Their bodies and bioceramic brains were obliterated by laser light, not a memory left to save. The Great Nothingness had reclaimed a few of its weakest children – an accomplishment that must have made Manly intensely proud – and for a moment in time, the ship itself seemed to be in peril.

Then the Master Captain took charge of the fight, and within minutes, the rebellion was finished. The war was won. Unrepentant prisoners were forced back into their chamber, and its ancient machinery was awakened for the first time in at least five billion years. The temperature inside the great cylinder dropped. Frost turned to hard ice, and numbed by the cold, the Phoenixes descended to the prison floor, huddling together for heat, cursing the Master with their beautiful songs, then with their next labored breath, their flesh turned into a rigid glassy solid, undead, and with an accidental vengeance, they were left glancingly immortal.

Millennia later, as the Great Ship passed near Phoenix space, those frozen warriors were loaded into a taxi like cargo, then delivered home.

Washen herself had overseen the transfer of the bodies. It wasn't an assignment that she had requested, but the Master, who surely possessed a record of the young woman's indiscretions, thought it would be a telling moment.

Maybe it had been.

The memory came like a rebellion. Stepping through her apartment door, she suddenly remembered that long-ago chore, and in particular, the look of a certain male Phoenix caught in mid-breath, his gills pulled wide and the blackness of the blood still apparent after thousands of years of dreamless sleep. Still lovely, Manly was. All of them were lovely. And just once, for an instant, Washen had touched the frozen feathers and the defiant beak with the sensitive glove of her lifesuit.

Washen tried to remember what she was thinking as she touched her lost love. There had to be some leftover sadness and an older person's acceptance of things that would never change, and there had to be a captain's genuine relief that she had survived the assault. The ship was a machine and a mystery, and it was filled with living souls who looked on her to keep them safe . . . And at that instant, stepping into the familiar back hallway of her apartment, her thoughts were interrupted by the apartment's voice.

'Message,' she heard.

The entranceway was footworn silk-marble, its walls currently wearing tapestries woven by a communal intelligence of antlike organisms. Before Washen could take a second step, she heard, 'A priority message. Coded. And urgent.'

She blinked, her attentions shifting.

'Black level,' she heard. 'Alpha protocols.'

This was a drill. Those protocols were intended only for the worst disasters and the gravest secrets. Washen nodded, engaging one of her internal nexus links. Then after several minutes of proving that she was herself, the message was decoded and delivered.

She read it in full, twice. Then she sent away for the essential confirmation, knowing this was an exercise, and the Master's office would thank her for her timely and efficient response. But the unthinkable occurred. After the briefest pause, the word 'Proceed' was delivered to her.

She said it aloud, then whispered the rest of those incredible words.

'Proceed with your mission, with utmost caution, beginning immediately.'

It took a lot to astonish an old woman. Yet here was one old woman who felt astonished to the point of numbness, and perhaps a little afraid, not to mention incandescently happy to have this abrupt, utterly unexpected challenge.

Two

REMORAS WORKED TIRELESSLY to make Miocene feel ill at ease, and without exception, their best efforts failed.

Today's attempt was utterly typical. She was making

one of the ritual tours of the outer hull. Her guide, a glancingly charming and notorious elder named Orleans, steered the skimmer across the ship's leading face, passing as many markers and statues and tiny memorials as physically possible. He did it without subtlety or apology. What passed for a mouth kept smiling at the Submaster, and a gloved hand would gesture at each site, the deep wet voice reporting how many had died at this place and how many had been his good friends or members of his enormous, cantankerous family.

Miocene made no comment.

Her spare face wore an expression that might be confused for compassion, while her thoughts centered on those matters where she could actually accomplish genuine good.

'Twelve died here,' Orleans reported.

Then later, 'Fifteen here. Including a great-grandson of mine.'

Miocene wasn't a fool. She knew Remoras lived a hard existence. She felt a measure of sympathy for their troubles. But there were many fine fat reasons not to waste a moment grieving for these supposed heroes.

'And here,' Orleans trumpeted, 'the Black Nebula killed three whole teams. Fifty-three dead, in the space of a single year.'

The hull beneath them was in good repair. Wide stretches of fresh hyperfiber formed a bright, almost mirrored surface, reflecting the swirling colors of the ship's shields. The three memorials were bone-colored spires no more than twenty meters tall – visible for an instant, then gone as the shuttle streaked past each one in the blink of an eye.

'We got too close to that nebula,' Orleans informed her.

Miocene showed her feelings by closing her eyes.

Brazen like all Remoras, her guide ignored the simple warning. 'I know the good reasons why,' he growled. 'A lot of wealthy worlds near that nebula, and inside. We needed to pass close enough to lure new customers. After all, we're a fifth of the way through our great voyage, and we still have empty berths and quotas to fill—'

'No,' Miocene interrupted. Then slowly, with a contemptuous sigh, she opened her eyes and stared at Orleans, telling him, 'There is no such monster as a quota. Not officially, and not otherwise.'

'My mistake,' said Orleans. 'Sorry.'

Yet the man's expression seemed doubtful.

Dismissive, even.

But what did any Remoran face mean? What she saw was intentionally gruesome: the broad forehead was a waxy white with thick beads of grease aligned in neat rows. Where human eyes should have returned her gaze, there were twin pits filled with hair; each hair, she assumed, was photosensitive, all joined together as a kind of compound eye. If there was a nose, it was hidden. But the mouth was a wide rubbery affair, never able to close entirely. It was hanging agape now, so large that Miocene could count the big pseudoteeth and two blue tongues, and in the back of that yawning mouth, what seemed to be the white image of an old-fashioned human skull was plainly visible.

The rest of the Remora's body was hidden inside his lifesuit.

What it looked like was a mystery without solution. Remoras never removed their suits, even when they were alone with each other.

Yet Orleans was human. By law, he was a treasured member of the crew, and in keeping with his station, this human male was entrusted with jobs that demanded skill and a self-sacrificing duty.

Again, with an intentional gravity, Miocene told her subordinate, 'There are no quotas.'

'My fault,' he replied. 'Entirely, and always.'

The great mouth seemed to smile. Or was it a toothy grimace?

'And,' the Submaster continued, 'there were future considerations at stake. A brief danger now is better than a prolonged distant one. Wouldn't you agree?'

The hairs of each eye pulled closer together, as if squinting. Then the deep voice said, 'No, frankly. I don't agree.'

She said nothing. Waiting.

'What would be best,' Orleans informed her, 'would be for us to get the fuck out of this spiral arm, and away from every damned obstacle. That's what would be best, sir. If you don't mind my saying.'

She didn't mind, no. By definition, an inconsequential sound can easily be ignored.

But this Remora was pressing her more than tradition allowed, and more than her nature could permit. She gazed across the bland landscape of hyperfiber, the very distant horizon perfectly flat, and the sky filled with swirling purples and magentas, the occasional burst of laser light visible as it passed through the ship's shields. Then with a quiet, calculating rage, she told the Remora what he already knew.

'It's your choice to live up here,' she said.

She said, 'It's your calling and your culture. You're Remoran by choice, as I recall, and if you don't want responsibility for your own decisions, perhaps I should take possession of your life for you. Is that what you want, Orleans?'

The hairy eyes pulled into hard little tufts. A dark voice asked, 'What if I let you, madam? What would you do to me?'

'Take you below, then cut you out of your lifesuit. To begin with. Rehabilitate your body and your mangled genetics until you could pass for human. And then, to make you especially miserable, I would turn you into a captain. I'd give you my uniform and some real authority, plus my massive responsibilities. Including these occasional tours of the hull.'

The gruesome face was furious.

An indignant voice assured her, 'It's true what they say. You've got the ugliest soul of any of *them*.'

Quietly and furiously, Miocene said, 'Enough.'

She informed Orleans, 'This tour is finished. Take me back to Port Erinidi. And in a straight line this time. If I see one more memorial, I promise, I'll carve you out of that suit myself. Here, and now.'

IN AN ACCIDENTAL fashion, the Remoras were Miocene's creation.

Ages ago, as the Great Ship reached the dusty edge of the Milky Way, there was a critical need to repair the aged hull and protect it from future impacts. The work swamped the available machinery – shipborn and human-built. It was Miocene who suggested sending the human crew out into the hull. The dangers were obvious, and fickle. After billions of years of neglect, the electromagnetic shields and laser arrays were in shambles; repair teams could expect no protection from impacts and precious little warning. But Miocene created a system where no one was asked to take larger risks than anyone else. Gifted engineers and the highest captains served their mandatory time, dying with a laudable regularity. Her hope was to patch the deepest craters with a single warlike *push*, then the surviving engineers would automate every system, making it unnecessary for people ever to walk the hull again.

But human nature subverted her meticulous plans.

A low-ranking crew member would earn negative marks. They might be minor violations of dress, or moments of clear insubordination. Either way, those offenders could clean up their files by serving extra time on the hull. Miocene looked on it as an absolution, and she gladly sent a few souls 'upstairs.' But a few captains confused the duty for a punishment, and over the course of a few centuries, they banished thousands of subordinates, sometimes for nothing worse than a surly word heard in passing.

There was a woman, a strange soul named Wune, who went up onto the hull and remained there. Not only did she accept her duties, she embraced them. She declared that she was living a morally pure life, full of contemplation and essential work. With a prophet's manipulative talents, she found converts to her newborn faith, and her converts became a small, unified population of philosophers who refused to leave the hull.

'Remora' began as an insult used by the captains. But the insult was stolen by the unexpected culture, becoming their own proud name.

A Remora never left his lifesuit. From conception until his eventual death, he was a world onto himself, elaborate recyke systems giving him water and food and fresh oxygen, his suit belonging to his body, his tough genetics constantly battered by the endless flux of radiations. Mutations were common on the hull, and cherished. What's more, a true Remora learned to direct his mutations, rapidly evolving new kinds of eyes and novel organs and mouths of every nightmarish shape.

Wune died early, and she died heroically.

But the prophet left behind thousands of believers. They invented ways to make children, and eventually they numbered in the millions, building their own cities and artforms and passions and, Miocene presumed, their own odd dreams. In some ways, she had to admire their culture, if not the individual believers. But as she watched Orleans piloting the skimmer, she wondered – not for the first time – if these people were too obstinate for the ship's good, and how she could tame them with a minimum of force and controversy.

That's what Miocene was thinking when the coded message arrived.

They were still a thousand kilometers from Port Erinidi, and the message had to be a test. Black level; Alpha protocols? Of course it was a test!

Yet she followed the ancient protocols. Without a word, she left Orleans, walking to the back of the cabin and closing the lavatory door, scanning the walls and ceiling, the floor and fixtures, making sure that not so much as a molecule-ear was present.

Through a nexus-link buried in her mind, Miocene downloaded the brief message, and within her mind's eye, she translated it. No emotion showed on her face. She wouldn't let any leak out. But her hands, more honest by a long ways, were wrestling in her long lap – two perfectly matched opponents, neither capable of winning their contest.

THE REMORA DELIVERED her to the port.

Sensing the importance of the moment, Miocene tried to leave Orleans with a few healing words. 'I'm sorry,' she lied. Then she placed a hand on the gray lifesuit, its psuedoneurons delivering the feel of her warm palm to his own odd flesh. Then quietly and firmly, she added, 'You made valid points. The next time I sit at the Master's table, I'll do more than mention today's conversation. That's a promise.'

'Is that what it's called?' said the blue tongues and rubbery mouth. 'A promise?'

The obnoxious shit.

Yet Miocene offered him a little stiff-backed bow, in feigned respect, then calmly slipped off into the port's useful chaos.

Passengers were rolling into a tall capsule-car. They were an alien species, each larger than a good-sized room, and judging by their wheeled, self-contained lifesuits, they were a low-gravity species. She nearly asked her nexuses about the species. But she thought better of it, lowering her gaze and moving at a crisp pace, appearing distracted as she slipped between two of them, barely hearing voices that sounded like much water pushed through a narrow pipe.

'A Submaster,' said her implanted translator.

'Look, see!'

'Smart as can be, that one!'

'Powerful!'

'Look, see!'

Miocene's private cap-car waited nearby. She passed it without a glance, stepping into one of the public cars that had brought the aliens up to Port Erinidi. It was a vast machine, empty and perfect. She gave it a destination and rented its loyalties with anonymous credits. Once she was moving, Miocene removed her cap and her uniform, habit making her lay them out on top of a padded bench. She couldn't help but stare at the uniform, examining her reflection, her face and long neck borrowing the folds and dents of that mirrored fabric.

'Look, see,' she whispered.

She accessed command accounts set up by and known only to her. The compliant cap-car found itself with a series of new destinations and odd little jobs. Waiting at one location was a small wardrobe of nondescript clothes.

Miocene left the clothes untouched for now. During the next hour and over the course of several thousand kilometers, she picked up a pair of sealed packages. The first package contained a small fortune in anonymous credits, while the other opened itself, revealing a scorpionlike robot free of manufacturer's codes or any official ID.

The robot leaped at the single passenger.

With a patient concern, the car asked, 'Is something wrong, madam? Do you need help?'

'No, no,' Miocene replied, trying to lie still on a long bench.

The scorpion's tail reached into her mouth, then shoved hard enough to split modern bone. Her naked body straightened, in shock. For an instant, in little ways, the Submaster died. Then her disaster genes woke, fixing the damage with a crisp efficiency. Bone and various neurological linkups were repaired. But the nexuses that had been buried inside Miocene, part of her for more than a hundred millennia, had been yanked free by the titanium hooks of that narrowly designed robot.

The robot ate the nexuses, digesting them in a plasma furnace.

It did the same with the Submaster's elaborate uniform.

Then the furnace turned itself inside out, and with a flash of purple-white light, what was metal turned to a cooling puddle and a persistent stink.

A tiny amount of spilled blood needed to be burned away. Once that chore was finished, Miocene dressed in a simple brown gown that could have belonged to any human tourist, and from the attached satchel, she pulled out bits of false flesh that quivered between her cool fingers, begging for the opportunity to change the appearance of her important face.

Three more times, the car stopped for its odd passenger.

It stopped inside a major arterial station, then at the center of a cavern filled with bowing yellowish trees and a perpetual wind. And finally, it eased into a quiet neighborhood of well-to-do apartments, the resident humans and aliens among the wealthiest entities in the galaxy, each owning at least a cubic kilometer of the great ship.

Where the passenger disembarked, the car didn't remember, much less care.

After that, it hurried toward its initial destination. But those coordinates had always been an impossibility, and the AI pilot was too impaired to realize that this was a foolhardy task. Empty and insane, it streaked down the longest, largest arterials, hard vacuums allowing enormous speeds. Circumnavigating the ship many times in the next days, the car stopped only when a security team crippled it with their weapons, then burst on board, ready for anything but the emptiness and an utter lack of clues.

A WEEK LATER, eating breakfast and watching passersby, Miocene asked herself why now, at this exact moment, was it so important for her to vanish?

What did the Master intend?

The basic plan was ancient and rigorously sensible. After the wars with the Phoenixes, the Master had ordered her captains to prepare routes into anonymity. If the ship was ever invaded, their enemies would naturally want to capture its captains, and probably kill them. But if each captain kept a permanent escape route, and if no one else knew the route – including the Master – then perhaps the brightest blood in the ship would remain free long enough to organize, then take back the ship in their own counter-invasion.

'A desperate precaution,' the Master had dubbed this plan.

Later, as life on board the ship turned routine, the emergency routes were kept for other robust reasons.

As a form of testing, for instance.

Young, inexperienced captains were sent a coded message from the Master's office. Were they loyal enough to obey the difficult order? Did they know the ship well enough to vanish for months or years? And most importantly, once they vanished, did they continue to act in responsible, captainly ways?

Simple bureaucratic inertia was another factor. Once established, escape routes were easily maintained. Miocene invested a few minutes each year to keep hers open, and she was probably much more thorough than most of her subordinates.

And the final reason was the unforeseen.

Since the Phoenixes, no one had tried to invade the Great Ship. But in a voyage that would circumnavigate the Milky Way, it didn't pay to throw away any tool that might, in some unexpected way, help the Master's hand.

What if the unforeseen had happened?

Miocene was sitting in a tiny cafe, safely disguised, when she noticed a dozen black-clad security officers interviewing the local foot traffic. A standard business in this kind of district, yes. But it made her wonder about the other captains. How many besides her had been called away by the Master's explicit orders?

There was a temptation to use secret tools to count the missing. But her probes might be noticed and tracked, and ignorance was infinitely more seemly than being caught in someone's clumsy net.

Half of the security team was working its way toward the cafe. They were perhaps two hundred meters away when a dose of paranoia took hold of Miocene. She left her sausage cakes and iced coffee unfinished, but she rose to her feet with a casual grace, then chose the most anonymous direction before slipping out of sight. In this district, every avenue was a touch less than a hundred kilometers long, and it was exactly one thousandth as wide and one ten-thousandth as tall. There were a thousand identical avenues setcarved into the local rock, aligned with a clean geometric precision.

The original guess, formulated by the first survey teams, was that these geometric relationships were fat with meaning. The ship's builders were at least as clever as the people who had discovered it, and an accurate map of every room and avenue, fuel tank and rocket nozzle, would reveal an ocean of mathematical clues. Perhaps a genuine language could be built from all those intricate proportions. In simple terms, the Great Ship supplied its own explanation . . . if only enough data and enough cunning could be applied to this wondrous and slippery problem . . .

Miocene had always doubted that logic.

Cleverness was an uneven talent at best. Imagination, she believed, was something that would fool its owner, luring her to waste her time chasing every wishful possibility. That's why she long ago predicted that no AI and no human, or any other sentient soul, would find anything particularly important in the ship's architecture. This was one of those circumstances where the boring and the unclever provided the best answers. These thousand avenues, plus every other hollow place within the Great Ship, had been chiseled out by sterile machines following equally sterile plans. That would explain the repetitive, insectlike patterns. And more importantly, it offered a telling clue as to why no expedition had ever found the tiniest trace of left-behind life.

Not one alien corpse.

Or unexplained microbe.

Or even a molecular knot that was once someone's once-dear protein.

Where imagination saw mystery, Miocene saw simplicity. Obviously, this ship was built not to travel between the stars, but to cross from galaxy to galaxy. Its designers, whoever they were, had employed sterile machines at every stage of construction. Then for reasons unknown, the builders never stepped on board their creation.

The easy guess was that some natural catastrophe had struck. Most likely it would be something vast, and horrific.

When the universe was young, and quite a bit denser, galaxies had the nagging habit of exploding. Seyferts. Quasars. Cascading series of supernovae. All were symptoms of a dangerous youth. There was ample evidence showing the Milky Way had a similar history. Life born in its youth was extinguished by the amoral pulse of gamma radiation: once, twice, or a thousand times.

What the dullest, most credible experts proposed – and what Miocene believed today without question – was that an intelligent species arose in the past, in some peaceful and extremely remote backwater. The species predicted the coming storm. A crash program of self-replicating machines were sent to a jovian-class world, probably a world drifting inside a dusty nebula, far from any sun. Following simple, buglike programs, that world was rebuilt. Its hydrogen atmosphere was burned to give it velocity. Slingshot flybys added still more. But by the time it came streaking past the homeworld, there was no one left to save. Empty avenues waited for humanoids already killed by a Seyfert's fire, and for the next several billion years, the ship waited, empty and patient, plying a blind course between galaxies, slowly degrading but managing to endure until it reached the Milky Way.

No one had ever indentified the parent galaxy.

Looking back along the ship's trajectory, one couldn't find so much as a dim dwarf galaxy that seemed a likely mother.

And there was also that nagging issue about the ship's age.

Five billion years was the official verdict. A huge span, but comfortably huge, demanding no great rewriting of the universe's early history.

The trouble was that the parent rock could be older than five billion years. Before it solidified, the granite and basalt were doctored. The telltale radionuclides had been harvested by some hyperefficient means. To mask its age, or for some less conspiratorial purpose? Either way, it left the rock cold and hard, and it was just one means by which the ship's builders had left behind a hard puzzle for today's scientists.

Earnest, imaginative people, filled with cocktails and braver drugs, liked to claim that eight or ten or twelve billion years was a more likely age for the ship. And twelve billion years wasn't the upper estimate, either. Enjoying the imponderables, they argued that this derelict had come from that fine distant sprinkle of little blue galaxies which covered the most distant skies, all born at the beginnings of time. How humanoids, or anything, could have evolved so early was left unanswered. But since mystery was their passion, they found this entire business more intoxicating than any drink.

Miocene didn't enjoy vast questions or ludicrous answers, particularly when neither were necessary.

She saw a simpler explanation: the ship was a youthful five billion years old, and somewhere between galaxies, probably soon after its birth, its course was deflected by an invisible black hole or some unmapped dark-matter mass. That explained why it was an orphan in every sense.

Thinking otherwise was to think too much and to do it in the wrong places.

This had been an orphan and a derelict, and then human beings had found it.

And now it was theirs; was Miocene's, at least in part.

Walking that long, long avenue, Miocene smelled a hundred worlds. Humanoids and aliens of other shapes were enjoying the false blue sky, and most were enjoying one another. She heard words and songs and sniffed the potent musks of pheromonal gossips, and occasionally, as the mood struck, she would wander into one of the tiny shops, browsing like anyone with nowhere else to be.

No, she wasn't as imaginative as some people.

In most circumstances, Miocene would make that confession, without hesitation. Yet in the next breath, always, she would add that she had imagination enough to revel in the ship's majesty, and its cosmopolitan appeal, and sufficient creativity to help rule this very original and precious society.

Nursing a well-deserved pride, she worked her way along the avenue.

Alien wares outnumbered human wares, even in human shops. Entering a likely doorway, she could always expect to be noticed. And when she wasn't, Miocene would recall that she wasn't a Submaster now. Out of uniform, free of responsibilities, she possessed an anonymity that seemed an endless surprise.

From a spidery machine intelligence, she purchased an encyclopedia written entirely about the Great Ship.

In a tiny grocery, she bought a harum-scarum's sin-fruit, its proteins and odd sugars reconfigured for human stomachs.

Eating one purchase, she skimmed over the other.

There was a slender hundred-tetrabit entry about

Miocene. She read portions, smiling more than not, making mental notes about half a hundred points that the author needed to correct.

From a monkeyish Yik Yik clerk, she bought a mild drug.

Then later, reconsidering this indulgence, she sold it at a profit to a human male who referred to her as 'lady' and left her with the advice, 'You look tired. Get laid, then get yourself some good sleep.'

He seemed to be offering a service, which she chose to ignore.

Afterward, Miocene spotted another security team. Humans and harum-scarums were disguised as passengers. But what's more obvious than a police officer on the job? No passenger is that watchful, ever. Yet they never saw Miocene as she slipped into one of the very narrow, very dark passageways leading to a parallel avenue.

Invisible demon doors made the skin tingle. She strolled into a colder climate, the air having a delicious mountain thinness about it.

Another spidery machine was renting dreams and the rooms to use them. Miocene took one of each, then slept for twelve straight hours, dreaming about the ship when it was first discovered, and empty, her dream-self strolling along these darkened avenues, her eyes first to see the polished green olivine walls that would soon be laced with rooms that would become, in a geologic blink, thriving shops.

It was the rented dream, at first.

Then Miocene's own memories were building images. How many tunnels and rooms had she seen first? No one knew. Not the encyclopedia's author, or even Miocene herself. And that brought a lingering joy that made her smile the next morning while she sipped icy coffee and ate spiced blubbercakes for breakfast.

Her secret orders had included a destination.

And a loose timetable.

Presumably her questions would be answered. But sometimes, particularly in quietly happy moments like now, Miocene wondered if this business was nothing but the Master's clever way of giving her favorite Submaster a good rest.

A vacation: that was a simple, boring explanation.

And compelling.

Of course this was a vacation!

Miocene rose to her feet, a thousand faces in easy view, and she began to hunt for yesterday's boy, reasoning:

My first vacation after a thousand centuries of devotion.

Why not . . . ?

Three

IT WAS AN expensive vegetable, particularly when you paid for quality. But Washen knew her audience. She was certain that her old friend would appreciate the voices rising from the plant's many mouths, the voices filling the empty, almost darkened cavity with a serene, deepest-space melody that his particular ear would find lovely.

Her friend wasn't here just now.

But wherever he was, he would hear the llano-vibra singing about blackness and emptiness and the glorious cold between the galaxies.

In another life, her friend raised the llano-vibra as a hobby, mastering the species' complex genetics, twisting its elaborate genes to where it sang melodies even more serene than this specimen, and on the open market, infinitely more precious.

But he would never sell his companions.

Then his life and peculiar interests moved in even stranger directions, and he lost interest in his once precious hobby.

Eventually, he lost his post as a rising captain.

Crimes had occurred. Charges were filed. Using the escape route that the Master herself ordered her captains to create, the man went into hiding. The only contact Washen had had with him since was a cryptic note telling her that if she ever wanted to reach him, she should plant a llano-vibra in this empty and very dark corner of the ship, then plant herself in a comfortable seat in the nearest human tavern.

Which for the next two days was what Washen did.

The tavern was dark and mostly empty, but considerably warmer than deep space. She sat in back, in a booth carved from a single pertified oak, and she drank an ocean of various cocktails, thinking about everything, and nothing, finally concluding that it was too much to expect anyone to remember you after this many centuries . . . deciding that it was time to get on with her mission . . .

A man appeared, squinting into the cheap darkness, and Washen knew it was him. He was large, just as she remembered. The face was changed, but it was still pleasantly homely. His bearing had lost that captainly arrogance, and he wore civilian clothes with an ease that Washen could only envy. Who knew what name he went by? But ignoring the risks, she cupped a hand against her mouth, shouting across the gloom:

'Hey, Pamir! Over here!'

★ ★ ★

THEY HAD BEEN lovers, but they weren't well suited as a couple. Captains rarely were. The man was headstrong and confident, and he was smart, and in most circumstances, he was perfectly self-reliant. Yet those qualities that made him a successful captain had also weighed down his career. Pamir had no skill or interest in saying the proper words or giving little gifts to people in higher stations. If it hadn't been for his considerable talent for being right more than most, the Master would have cut off his professional legs at the beginning, leaving him with a minimal rank and next to no responsibilities. Which might have been for the best, as it turned out.

The big man sat and ordered a pain-of-tears, and staring at the homely face, Washen replayed his tragic fall.

When he was a captain, Pamir befriended a very strange alien. And on this ship, strangeness took some doing. It was a Gaian entity – a small, deceptively ordinary humanoid body with a secret capacity to cover any world with its own self. Its flesh could grow rapidly, forming trees and animals and fungal masses, all linked by a single consciousness. The creature was a refugee. It had lost its home world to a second Gaian. And when that archenemy came on board, a full-scale war erupted, eventually destroying an expensive facility as well as the remains of Pamir's career.

The Gaians fought to an exhausted draw, but their hatred still burned.

On his best day, Pamir was a difficult man, but he had a gift for seeing what was best inside any hopeless mess. He turned a laser on both Gaians, saving just enough of their tissue to let them begin again. Then he used his own flesh to make a child that embraced what was best in both aliens. And because Washen was Pamir's friend, and because it was the right thing to do, she raised the Child. That was her name for it. The Child. Like any mother, she kept it safe and taught it what it needed to know, and when it grew too powerful to remain on board the Great Ship, she hugged it and kissed it and sent it off to an empty planet where it could live alone, making ancient wrongs right again.

It seemed as if the Child were sitting with them now, listening as its mother told proud stories and happy stories; and hopefully it could sense how very remarkable it was to see its father weep with joy.

Pamir wept like a captain. Quietly, and always under control. Then he wiped his eyes dry with heavy fingers and summoned up a grim smile, looking at his old friend for too long, reading her clothes and face and how she sat with her back against the backmost wall of this dingy pub.

Finally, he asked, 'Are you like me?'

She volunteered nothing.

A thick, effortlessly strong hand reached out, touching her through the sleeve of her silk blouse. Then he quietly, and firmly, and with certainty said, 'No. You aren't like me. That's pretty obvious.'

She shook her head. 'I'm not a wanted felon, if that's what you mean.'

'Who is?' he asked. Then he laughed, adding, 'I've never met a genuine criminal. Ask the worst sociopath if he is, and he says he isn't. He talks a lot about good reasons and bad circumstances and the unfairness of his luck.'

'Is that what you talk about?' she inquired.

The grin strengthened. 'Perpetually.'

'Have you heard?' she went on. 'Have any other captains vanished?'

'No,' he replied. 'No, I haven't heard.'

She watched his hands.

'Do you know if they have, Washen?'

Carefully, she gave away nothing with her eyes.

'But all of you could vanish, and we wouldn't notice.' He said it, then gave a low laugh, adding, 'And we wouldn't care. At all.'

'Wouldn't you?'

A softer laugh. Then he explained. 'Living any life but a captain's teaches you. Among all the good lessons, you learn that captains aren't as important as they tell yourselves they are. Not in the day-to-day business of running this ship, or even in the big, slow, massive matters, either.'

'I'm crushed,' she replied, and laughed.

He shrugged and said, 'You don't believe me.'

'You'd be astonished if I did believe you.' Washen shook her newest drink – a reliable narcotic exploded with the carbon dioxide bubbles – and after sniffing her fill, she suggested, 'You just wish that we were unimportant. But without us doing our important work, everything would collapse. In less than a century. Maybe less than a decade.'

The one-time captain shrugged his shoulders again. The subject bored him; it was time to move on.

Washen agreed. She emptied her glass, then let the silence last for as long as her old friend could stand it.

For almost an hour, as it happened.

Then with a delicate caution, he asked, 'Is something wrong? You've gone underground . . . so is there some sort of disaster looming . . . ?'

She shook her head with confidence.

And Pamir, bless him, was still enough of a captain not to ask anything else, or even look too deeply into her wide chocolate eyes.

THEY SPENT TWO full days together, and as many nights. Wanting privacy, they rented a shelter inside an alien habitat, filling their days hiking through a dense violet jungle, special boots allowing them to keep their feet since the only pathways were the thick and slippery slime ribbons left by the passing landlords. During their second night, as something massive dragged itself past their little front door, Washen moved into Pamir's bed, and with a mixture of nervousness and bawdy zest, they made love until they could fall into a deep sleep.

Washen hugged the Child in her dreams. She hugged it ferociously, and sadly. But when she woke again, she realized that it wasn't the Child that she'd held in her dream arms. It was the ship itself. She had reached around that great and beautiful body of hyperfiber and metal and stone and machinery, begging it not to leave her. For absolutely no good reason, she hurt enough to ache now, and in a captainly way, she wept.

Pamir sat up in bed, watching without comment. A sloppy gaze would have missed the empathy in his eyes and in his pressed-together lips.

Washen wasn't sloppy. She sniffed and wiped at her face with the backs of both hands, then calmly admitted, 'I need to be somewhere. I should be there already, honestly.'

Pamir nodded. Then after a deep, bracing breath, he asked, 'How long would it take?'

'Would what take?'

'If I happened to turn myself over to the Master, bent low and begged for her forgiveness . . . how long would she keep me locked up . . . and how soon could I get back to being some sort of captain . . . ?'

In her mind's eye, Washen saw the rigid, colder-than-death Phoenix.

Remembering its punishment and appreciating the Master's quixotic moods, she touched her newest lover on his lips, pressing down as she told him, 'Whatever you do, don't do that.'

'She'd keep me locked up forever. Is that it?'

Washen said, 'I don't know. But let's not test the woman, all right? Promise me?'

Yet Pamir was too stubborn even to offer a comforting lie. He just pulled away from her hand, and smiled at a faraway point, and said to Washen, or himself, 'I still haven't made my mind up. And maybe I never will.'

Four

THERE WERE SIX primary fuel tanks, each as large as a good-sized moon, set in a balanced configuration deep inside the ship – spheres of hyperfiber and shaped-vacuum insulation far beneath the hull and the inhabited districts, below even the sewage plants and giant reactors and the deepest stomachs of the great engines.

Every tank was a wilderness.

Only the occasional maintenance crew or adventurer would visit them. In boats carved from aerogels, they would voyage across the liquid hydrogen, nothing to see but their own cold lights, the frigid and glassy ocean, and beyond, a seamless, soul-searing night that left most visitors feeling profoundly uneasy.

Aliens occasionally asked permission to live inside one of the fuel tanks.

The leech were an obscure species. Ascetic and pathologically secretive, they had built their settlement where they could be alone. Weaving together thick plastics and diamond threads, they dangled their home from the tank's ceiling. It was a large structure, yet following leech logic, its interior was a single room. The room stretched on forever in two dimensions while the glowing gray ceiling was near enough to touch. Washen would do just that from time to time. She would stop walking and lay both hands against the plastic's surprising warmth, and she would breathe, shaking off the worst of her claustrophobia.

Voices lured her on.

She couldn't count all the voices, and they were too cluttered to make sense or even tell her which species was speaking.

Washen had never met the leech.

Not directly, she hadn't.

But she had been part of the delegation of captains who spoke to the leech's bravest diplomats, nothing between the parties but a windowless slab of hyperfiber. The aliens spoke with clicks and squeals, neither of which she could hear now. But if it wasn't the leech, who was it? A dim memory was triggered. At one of the Master's annual dinners – how many years ago now? – some fellow captain had mentioned in passing that the leech had abandoned their habitat.

Why?

For the moment, she couldn't recall any reason, or even if she had asked for one.

Washen hoped that the leech had reached their destination, disembarking without incident. Or perhaps they had simply found a more isolated home, if that was possible. But there was always the sad chance that some great disaster had struck, and the poor exophobes had perished.

Shipboard extinctions were more common than the captains admitted in public, or admitted to themselves. Some passengers proved too frail to endure long voyages. Mass suicides and private wars claimed others. Yet as Washen liked to remind herself, for every failed guest there were a hundred species that thrived, or at least managed to etch out a life in some little part of this glorious machine.

To herself, in a whisper, she asked, 'Who are you?'

An hour had passed since Washen stepped from the simple elevator. She had begun walking in the habitat's center, passing first through a necklace of cleansing chambers meant to purify the newly arrived. None of the chambers worked, and every doorway was propped open or dismantled. Obviously someone had been here. But there were no instructions, not even a handwritten note fixed to the last door. Washen had covered eight or nine kilometers in this subearth gravity, which was a few steps more than halfway to the habitat's single circular wall.

She paused again and placed her hands flush against the ceiling, and twisting her head, she judged from where those voices were coming. The acoustics were that fine.

She broke into an easy jog.

The room's only furnishings were hard gray pillows. The air was warm and stale, smelling of odd dusts and durable pheromones. Colors seemed forbidden. Even Washen's gaudy touristy clothes seemed to turn grayer by the moment.

The voices gradually grew louder, turning familiar. They were human voices, she realized. And after a little while, she could even tell who they were. Not by their words, which were still a tangled mess. But by their tone. Their self-importance. These were voices meant to give orders and to be obeyed instantly, without question or regret.

She stopped. Squinted.

Against the grayness was something darker. A spot, a blemish. Very nearly nothing, at this distance.

She called out, 'Hello?'

Then she waited for what seemed to be long enough, deciding that no one had noticed her voice, and as Washen started to shout, 'Hello,' again, several voices reached her, telling her, 'Hello,' and, 'This way,' and, 'Welcome, you're nearly late . . . !'

Yes, she was.

The Master's orders had given her two weeks to slip down to this odd place. Washen had said her good-byes to Pamir with some time to spare. But afterward, waiting for a cap-car in a little waystation, she had run into security troops who examined her fake identity and her donated genetics, then finally let her go again. After that, just to be certain that no one was hiding in her shadow, she had wandered another full day before starting for *here*.

Washen began to run.

But when the dark spot became people standing in knots and little lines, she slowed to a walk again, aiming for decorum.

A quiet rain of applause began, then fell away.

Suddenly, Washen couldn't count all the captains spread out before her, and putting on her most captainly smile, she joined them, almost laughing as she asked, 'So why, why, why are we here?'

No one seemed to know this had happened. But the captains had obviously spent the last few days talking about little else. Each had a pet theory to offer, and none had the bad taste to defend their words too far. Then that ritual was finished, at least for the moment, and colleagues asked Washen for stories about her travels. Where had she wandered, what marvels had she accomplished, and did she have two or twenty interesting ideas about this whole crazy business?

Washen mentioned a few touristy haunts but avoided any word that could, even by accident, remind anyone of Pamir.

Then with a shrug of her shoulders, she admitted, 'I

don't have guesses. I'm presuming this is a necessary business, and gloriously important, but until I have the facts, that's all that I can assume.'

'Bravo,' said one gray-eyed captain.

Washen was eating. And drinking. The first arrival had followed a steady drip-drip-dripping sound, coming to this place and discovering stacks of sealed rations and a dozen kegs of the ship's best wine, brought from the Alpha Sea district, raised by the hands and feet of tailored apes. Judging by the size of the drops and the small red puddle, the keg had opened itself the moment that first captain had stepped from the elevator.

Delicious wine, thought Washen.

Again, the captain said, 'Bravo.'

She looked at him now.

'Diu,' he said, offering a hand and a wide smile.

She balanced her mug on her plate, then shook his with her free hand, saying, 'We met at the Master's banquet. Twenty years ago, was it?'

'Twenty-five.'

Like most captains, Diu was tall for his species. He had craggy features and an easy charm that instilled trust in the human passengers. Even dressed in a simple gown, he looked like someone of consequence.

'It's kind of you to remember me,' he said. 'Thank you.'

'You're quite welcome.'

Even when he stood still, Diu was moving. His flesh seemed to vibrate, as if the water inside were ready to boil. 'What do you think of the Master's taste?' he inquired, gray eyes brightening. 'Isn't this a bizarre place to meet?'

'Bizarre,' Washen echoed. 'That's the word.'

For the moment, they looked at their surroundings. The ceiling and floor ended with a plain gray wall punctuated with a very rare window.

Bracing herself, Washen asked, 'Whatever happened to the leech? Does anyone remember?'

'They leaped into the sea below,' said Diu.

'No,' she muttered.

'Or we got them to their destination.'

'Which was it?'

'Both,' he reported. 'Or something else entirely. They're such a strange species. Apparently, they can't take any course without pretending to go a hundred other places at the same time.'

To confuse their imaginary enemies, no doubt.

'Wherever they are,' Diu assured her, 'I'm sure they're doing well.'

'I'm sure you're right,' Washen replied, knowing what was polite. In the face of ignorance, a captain should make positive sounds.

Diu hovered beside her, smiling as his flesh shivered with nervous energy.

Twenty-five years since they met . . . and what, if anything, did Washen remember about the man . . . ?

Her thoughts were interrupted.

A sudden voice, familiar and close, told her, 'You were nearly late, darling. Not that anyone noticed.'

Miocene.

Turning with a respectful haste, Washen found a face that she knew better than most. The Submaster's face was as narrow as an axe blade and less warm, and every bone beneath the taut flesh had its own enduring sharpness. Amused, the dark eyes had a chilly brightness. The short brown hair was streaked with snow. Taller than anyone else, Miocene's head brushed against the ceiling. Yet she refused to dip her head, even for the sake of simple comfort.

'Not that you know any more than the rest of us,' said the tall woman. 'But what do you believe the Master wants?'

Others grew quiet. Captains held their breath, secretly delighted that someone else had to endure the woman's scrutiny.

'I don't know anything,' said Washen, with conviction.

'I know you,' Miocene reminded her. 'You have a guess, or ten.'

'Perhaps . . .'

'Everyone's waiting, darling.'

Washen sighed, and gestured. 'I count several hundred clues here.'

'And they are?'

'Us.'

Their group stood near one of the rare windows – a wide slit of thick, distorting plastic. Nothing was outside but blackness and vacuum. The ocean of liquid hydrogen, vast and calm and unforgivably cold, lay fifty kilometers below their toes. Nothing was visible in the window but their own murky reflections. Washen glanced at herself, at her handsome, ageless face, her raven-and-snow hair pulled back in a sensible bun, her wide chocolate eyes betraying confidence as well as a much-deserved pleasure.

'The Master selected us,' she offered. 'Which means that we are the clues.'

Miocene glanced at her own reflection. 'What do you see, darling?'

'The elite of the elite.' Washen began singing off names, listing bonuses and promotions earned over the last millenia. 'Manka is a new second-grade. Aasleen was in charge of the last engine upgrade, which came in below budget and five years early. Saluki and Westfall have won the Master's Award more times than I can recall—'

'I bet they remember,' someone called out.

The captains laughed until they ran out of breath.

Washen continued. 'Portion is the youngest Submaster.

Johnson Smith jumped three grades with his last promotion. And then there's Diu.' She gestured at the figure beside her. 'Already an eleventh-grade, which is astonishing. You boarded the ship – correct me if I'm wrong – as a passenger. An ordinary tourist. Is that right?'

The energized man winked, saying, 'True, madam. And bless you for remembering.'

She shrugged, then turned.

'And there's you, Madam Miocene. One of the Master's oldest, most loyal and cherished assistants. When I was a little girl living in By-the-sea, I'd see you and the Master Captain sitting on the rocks together, planning our glorious future.'

'I'm an old hag, in other words.'

'Ancient,' Washen concurred. 'Not to mention one of only three Submasters with first-chair status at the Master's table.'

The tall woman nodded, drinking in the flattery.

'Whatever the reason,' said Washen, 'the Master wants her very best captains. That much is obvious.'

With an amused tone, the Submaster said, 'But darling. Let's not forget your own accomplishments. Shall we?'

'I never do,' Washen replied, earning a healthy laugh from everyone. And because nothing was more unseemly in a captain than false modesty, she admitted, 'I've heard the rumors. I'm slated to become the next Submaster.'

Miocene grinned, but she didn't comment on rumors. Which was only right.

Instead she took an enormous breath, and with a strong, happy voice, she asked everyone, 'Can you smell yourselves?'

The captains sniffed, in reflex.

'That's the smell of ambition, my dears. Pure ambition.' The tall woman inhaled again, and again, then with a booming voice admitted, 'No other stink is so tenacious, or in my mind, even half as sweet . . . !'

Five

ANOTHER TWO CAPTAINS arrived to applause and good-natured abuse. No one else was coming, though there was no way to know it at the time. Some hours later one of the last-comers was using the leech latrine – little more than a dilating hole in a random, suitably remote part of the room – and peering off in an empty direction, he noticed motion. With eyes sharper than any old-styled hawk's, he squinted, finally resolving a distinct *something* that seemed to be growing larger, moving toward him from a new, unexpected direction.

With both decorum and haste, the captain ordered his trousers back on and jogged back to the others, telling the ranking officer what he had seen.

Miocene nodded. Smiled. Then said, 'Fine. Thank you.'

'But what should we do, madam?' the young captain blurted.

'Wait,' the Submaster replied. 'That's what the Master would want.'

Washen stared into the distance, ceiling and floor meeting in a perfect line. After a long while, the perfection acquired a bump. A swollen bright bit of nothing was moving toward them, covering distance with a glacial patience. Everyone stood together, waiting. Then the bump split into several unequal lumps. The largest was bright as a diamond. The others spread out on either side, and that's when the captains began to whisper, 'It is. Her.'

Saying, 'Finally,' under their breaths.

An hour later, the undisputed ruler of the ship arrived.

Accompanied by a melody of Vestan horns and angel-voiced humans, the Master crossed the final hundred meters. While her officers still wore civilian disguises, she had the mirrored cap and sturdy uniform that her office demanded. Her chosen body was broad and extraordinarily deep. Partly, that body was a measure of status. But the Master also needed room to house a thoroughly augmented brain. Thousands of ship functions had to be monitored and adjusted, without delays, using a galaxy of buried nexuses. As another person might walk and breathe, the Master Captain unconsciously ruled the ship from wherever she stood, or sat, or found a spacious bed where her needy parts could sleep.

A vast hand skated along the oyster-gray ceiling, keeping the Master's head safe from being unceremiously bumped.

She had soft bright golden skin – a shade popular with many nonterran species – and fine white hair woven into a Gordian bun, and her pretty face was so round and smooth that it could have belonged to a toddler. But the radiant brown-black eyes and the wide grinning mouth conveyed enormous age and a flexible wisdom.

Every captain bowed.

As was custom, the Submasters dropped farthest.

Then a dozen low-grade captains began dragging the hard leech cushions toward her. Diu was among the supplicants, on his knees and smiling, even after the great woman had strolled past.

'Thank you for coming,' said a voice that always took Washen by surprise. It was a very quiet voice, and unhurried, perpetually amused by whatever those wide eyes were seeing. 'I know you're perplexed,' she assured, 'and I trust that you're concerned. A good sensible terror, perhaps.'

Washen smiled to herself.

'So let me begin,' said the Master. Then the child's face broke into its own smile, and she said, 'First let me tell you my reasons for this great game. And then, if you haven't been struck dead by surprise, I'll explain exactly what I intend for you.'

ACCOMPANYING THE MASTER were four guards.

Two humans; two robots. But you never knew which were the machines dressed as humans, or the humans with a machine's sense of purpose – an intentional ruse making it more difficult for enemies to exploit any weakness.

One guard released a little float-globe that took its position beside the Master.

The gray glow of the ceiling diminished, plunging the room into a late-dusk gloom. Then the amused voice said, 'The ship. Please.'

A real-time projection swallowed the float-globe. Built from data channeled through the Master's internal systems, the ship reached from the floor to the ceiling. Its forward face looked at the audience. The hull was slick and gray, cloaked in a colorful aurora of dust shields, a thousand lasers firing every second, evaporating the largest hazards. On the horizon, a tiny flare meant that another starship was arriving. New passengers, perhaps. Washen thought of the machine intelligences, wondering who'd meet them in her absence.

'Now,' said the Master, 'I'm going to peel my onion.'

In an instant, the ship's armor evaporated. Washen could make out the largest caverns and chambers and the deep cylindrical ports, plus the hyperfiber bones that gave the structure its great strength.

Then the next few hundred kilometers were removed. Rock and water, air and deeper hyperfiber were exposed.

'The perfect architecture,' the Master declared. She stepped closer to the shrinking projection, its glow illuminating a grinning face. Resembling an enormous young girl with her favorite plaything, she confessed, 'In my mind, there's no greater epic in history. Human history, or anyone else's.'

Washen knew this speech, word for word.

'I'm not talking about this voyage of ours,' the Master continued. 'Circumnavigating the galaxy is an accomplishment, of course. But the greater adventure was in finding this ship before anyone else, then leaving our galaxy to reach it first. Imagine the honor: to be the first living organism to step inside these vast rooms, the first sentient mind in billions of years to experience their majesty, their compelling mystery. It was a magnificent time. Ask any of us who were there. To the soul, we consider ourselves nothing but blessed.'

An ancient, honorable boast, and her prerogative.

'We did an exemplary job,' she assured. 'I won't accept any other verdict. In that first century – despite limited resources, the shadow of war, and the sheer enormity of the job – we mapped more than ninety-nine percent of the ship's interior. And as I could point out, I led the first team to find their way through the plumbing above us, and I was the first to see the sublime beauty of the hydrogen sea below us . . .'

Washen hid a smile, thinking, A fuel tank is a fuel tank is a fuel tank.

'Here we are,' the Master announced.

The projection had shrunk by nearly half. The ship's main fuel tanks were emerging from the frozen mantle, appearing as six tiny bumps evenly spaced along the ship's waist – each tank set directly beneath one of the main ports. The leech habitat was beneath the Master's straightened finger, and on this scale, it was no larger than a fat protozoan.

'And now, we vanish.'

Without sound or fuss, another layer of stone was removed. Then, another. And deeper slices of the fuel tanks revealed great spheres filled with hydrogen that changed from a peaceful liquid into a blackish solid, and deeper still, an eerily transparent metal.

'These hydrogen seas have always been the deepest features,' she commented. 'Below them is nothing but iron and a stew of other metals squashed under fantastic pressures.'

The ship had been reduced to a smooth black ball – the essential ingredient in a multitude of parlor games.

'Until now, we knew everything about the core.' The Master paused, allowing herself a knowing grin. 'Clear, consistent evidence proved that when the ship was built, its crust and mantle and core were stripped of radionuclides. The goal, we presumed, was to help cool the interior. To make the rock and metal still and predictable. We didn't know how the builders managed their trick, but there was a network of narrow tunnels leading down, branching as they dropped deeper, all reinforced with hyperfiber and energy buttresses.'

Washen was breathing faster now. Nodding.

'By design or the force of time, those little tunnels collapsed.' The Master paused, sighed, and shook her golden face. 'Not enough room for a microchine to pass. Or so we've always believed.'

Washen felt her heart beating, a suffused and persistent and delicious joy building.

'There was never, ever, the feeblest hint of any hidden chamber,' the Master proclaimed. 'I won't allow criticism on this matter. Every possible test was carried out. Seismic. Neutrino imaging. Even palm-of-the-hand calculations of mass and volume. Until some fifty-three years ago, there wasn't one sane reason to think that our maps were in any sense incomplete.'

A silence had engulfed the audience.

Quietly, smoothly, the Master said, 'The full ship. Please.'

Again, the iron ball was dressed in cold rock and hyper-fiber.

'We pivot ninety,' she said.

As if suddenly bashful, the ship's leading face turned away from her. Rocket nozzles swung into view, each large enough to cradle a moon. None were firing, and according to the schedule, none would fire for another three decades.

'The impact, please.'

Washen stepped closer, anticipating what she would see. Fifty-three years ago, passing through the Black Nebula, the ship collided with a swarm of comets. Nobody was surprised by the event. Brigades of captains and their staff had spent decades making preparations, mapping and remapping the space before them, searching for hazards as well as paying customers. But avoiding those comets would have cost too much fuel. And why bother? The swarm wasn't harmless, but it was believed to be as close to harmless as possible.

Gobs of antimatter were thrown at the largest hazards.

Lasers evaporated the tumbling fragments.

The captains watched the drama play out again, in rigorous detail: off in distant portions of the room, little suns flickered in and out of existence. Gradually the explosions moved closer, and finally, too close. Lasers fired without pause, evaporating trillions of tons of ice and rock. The shields brightened, moving from a dull blanket of red into a livid purple cloak, fighting to push gas and dust aside. But debris still peppered the hull, a thousand pinpricks dancing on its silver-gray face. And at the bombardment's peak, there was a blistering white flash that dwarfed the other explosions. The captains blinked and grimaced, remembering the instant, and their shared sense of utter embarrassment.

A mountain of nickel-iron had slipped through their vaunted defenses.

The impact rattled the ship. Gelatin dinners wiggled on their plates, and quiet seas rippled, and the most alert or sensitive passengers said, 'Goodness,' and perhaps grabbed hold of something more solid than themselves. Then for months, Remoras had worked to fill the new crater with fresh hyperfiber, and the nervous and bored passengers talked endlessly about that single scary moment.

The ship was never in danger.

In response, the captains had publicly paraded their careful schematics and rigorous calculations, proving that the hull could absorb a thousand times that much energy, and there would still be no reason to be nervous, much less terrified. But just the same, certain people and certain species had insisted on being afraid.

With a palpable relish, the Master said, 'Now the cross section. Please.'

The nearest hemisphere evaporated. In the new schematic, pressure waves appeared as subtle colors emerging from the blast site, spreading out and diluting, then pulling together again at the stern, shaking a lot of the ship's plumbing before the waves met and bounced, passing back the way they had come, back to the blast site where they met again, and again bounced. Even today, a thin vibration was detectable, whispering its way through the ship as well as the captains' own bones.

'AI analysis. Please.'

A map was laid over the cross section, everything expected and familiar. Except for the largest feature, that is.

'Madam,' said a sturdy voice. Miocene's voice. 'It's an anomaly, granted. But doesn't that feature . . . doesn't it seem . . . unlikely . . . ?'

'Which was why I thought it was nothing,' the Master concurred. 'And my most trustworthy AI – part of my own neural net – agreed with me. This region defines some change in composition. Or in density. Certainly nothing more.' She paused for a long moment, carefully watching her captains. Then with a gracious, oversized smile, she admitted, 'The possibility of a hollow core has to seem ludicrous.'

Submasters and captains nodded with a ragged hope-fulness.

But they hadn't come here because of anomalies. Washen knew it, and she stepped closer. How large was that hole? Estimates were easy, but the simple math created some staggering numbers.

'Ludicrous,' the Master repeated. 'But then I thought back to when I was a baby, barely a century old. Who would have guessed then that a jovian world could be made into a starship, and that I would inherit such a wonder for myself?'

Just the same, thought Washen, some ideas will always be insane.

'Madam,' Miocene said with a certain delicacy. 'I'm sure you realize that a chamber of these proportions would make our ship considerably less massive. Assuming we know the densities of the intervening iron, naturally . . .'

'But you're assuming that our hollow core is hollow.' The Master grinned at her favorite officer, then at everyone. Her golden face was serene, wringing pleasure out of her audience's confusion and ignorance. Calmly, she reminded them, 'This began as someone else's vessel. And we shouldn't forget that we still don't know why our home was built. For all we can say, this was someone's cargo ship, designed for moving things other than people, and here, finally, we've stumbled across the ship's cargo hold.'

Most of the captains shuddered.

'Imagine that something is hiding inside us,' the Master commanded. 'Cargo, particularly anything substantial, has to be restrained, protected. So imagine a series of buttressing fields that would keep our cargo from rattling around every time we adjusted our course. Then imagine that these buttresses are so powerful and so enduring that they can mask whatever it is that's down there—'

'Madam,' someone shouted.

After a pause, the Master said, 'Yes, Diu.'

'Just tell us, please . . . what in hell is down there . . . ?'

'A spherical object,' she replied. And with a slow wink, she added, 'It is the size of Mars, about. But considerably more massive.'

Washen's heart began to gallop.

The audience let out a low, wounded groan.

'Show them,' the Master said to her AI. 'Show them what we found.'

Again, the image changed. Nestled inside the great ship was another world, black as iron and distinctly smaller than the surrounding chamber. The simple possibility of such an enormous, unlikely discovery didn't strike Washen as one revelation, but as many, coming in waves, making her gasp and shake her head as she looked at her colleagues' faces, barely seeing any of them.

'This world – and it is a genuine world – has an atmosphere.' The Master was laughing quietly, and her quiet voice kept offering impossibilities. 'Despite the abundance of iron, the atmosphere has free oxygen. And there's enough water for small rivers and lakes. All of those delicious symptoms that come with living worlds are present here—'

'How do you know?' Washen called out. Then, in reflex, 'No disrespect intended, madam!'

'I haven't visited the world, if that's your question.' She giggled like a child, telling everyone, 'Yet fifty years of hard, secret work have paid dividends. Using self-replicating drones, I've been able to reopen one of those collapsed tunnels. And I've sent curious probes to the chamber for a first look. That's why I can stand here, assuring you that not only does this world exist, but that each of you are going to see it for yourselves.'

Washen glanced at Diu, wondering if her face was wearing the same wide smile.

'By the way, I named this world.' The Master winked and said, 'Marrow.' Then again, she said, 'Marrow.' Then by way of explanation, she said, 'It's a very old word. It means "where the blood is born."'

Washen felt her own blood coursing through her trembling body.

'Marrow is reserved for you,' the Master Captain promised.

The floor seemed to pitch and roll beneath Washen's legs, and she couldn't remember when she last took a meaningful breath.

'For you,' the giant woman proclaimed. 'My most talented, trustworthy friends . . . !'

Washen whispered, 'Thank you.'

Everyone said the words, in a ragged chorus.

Then Miocene called out, 'Applause for the Master! Applause!'

But Washen heard nothing, and said nothing, staring hard at the strange black face of that most unexpected world.

MARROW

THE SKY IS smooth as perfection and as timeless, round as perfection and supreme in every way that end of the universe should be.

A trillion faces ignore the sky.

Perfection is insignificant. Is boring.

What has consequences is sick and flawed and sad and angry, everything that you eat or wishes to eat you, and everything that is a potential fuck. Only imperfection can change its nature, or yours, and the sky never changes. Never. Which is why those trillion eyes look up only to watch for things flying or floating — everything nearer to them than that slick silvery roundness.

There is no perfection down here.

In this place nothing can be the same for long, and nothing succeeds that cannot adapt, swiftly, without hesitation or complaint, and without the tiniest remorse.

The ground beneath is not to be trusted.

The next deep breath is not a certainty.

Perhaps a thinking, reasonable, and self-aware mind would desire some taste of that glorious perfection.

To ingest the eternal.

To borrow its strength and grand endurance, if only for a little moment.

But that wish is too elaborate and much too spendthrift for these minds. They are weak and small and temporary. Focus on the instant. On eating and fucking, then resting only when there is no choice. Nothing else is so firmly etched into their hot genetic, swirling in the blood and riding tucked inside pollen and sperm.

Waste a moment, and perish.

This is a desperate and furious universe. Profoundly flawed, absolutely. But inside every tiny mind is what passes for a steely pride that says:

I am here.

I am alive.

On the backside of this leaf or perched on the crest of that hot iron pebble, I rule . . . and to those living things beneath my feet, too small to be seen by me. I am something that looks great and powerful . . .

Perfect in your pathetic little eyes . . . !

Six

SECRET WONDERS HAD been accomplished in mere decades.

Molelike drones had gnawed their way through thousands of kilometers of nickel and iron, reopening one of the ancient, collapsed tunnels. In their wake, industrial ants had slathered the walls with the highest available grade of hyperfiber. One of the fuel tank's reserve pumping stations had been taken off-line, then integrated with the project. Fleets of cap-cars, manufactured on-site and free of identification, waited outside the excavation, ready to carry the captains to the ship's distant center; while a brigade of construction drones had gone ahead, building a base of operations – an efficient and sterile little city of dormitories, machine shops, cozy galleys, and first-rate laboratories all tucked within a transparent blister of freshly minted diamond.

Washen was among the last to arrive at the base camp.

At the Master's insistence, she led the cleaning detail that carefully expunged every trace of the captains from inside the leech habitat.

It was a necessary precaution in an operation demanding seamless security, and it required hard, precise work.

Some of her cohorts considered the assignment an insult.

Scrubbing latrines and tracking down flakes of wayward skin was tedious and grueling. Certain captains grumbled, 'We're not janitors, are we?'

'We aren't,' Washen agreed. 'Professionals would have finished last week.'

Diu belonged to her detail, and unlike most, the novice captain worked without complaint, plainly trying to impress his superior. A charming selfishness was at work. She would soon wear a Submaster's epaulets, and if Diu could impress Washen with his zeal, she might become his benefactor. It was a calculation, yes. But she thought that it was a reasonable, even noble attitude. Washen believed there was nothing wrong with a captain making calculations, whether it involved the ship's course or the trajectory of his own important career. It was a philosophy that she'd often mentioned to Pamir, and that Pamir would never, ever accept in even the most polite ways.

It took two weeks and a day to finish their janitorial assignment.

Narrow, two-passenger cars waited to make the long fall to base camp. Washen decided that Diu would ride with her, and that their car would leave last, and Diu rewarded her with the charming and very trimmed story of his life.

'Mars-born, and born wealthy,' he confessed. 'I came to this ship for the usual touristy reasons. The promise of excitement. Or novelty. Adventure in safe, manageable doses. And of course, the unlikely possibility that someday, in some far and exotic part of the Milky Way, I'd actually become a better human being.'

'Passengers don't join the crew,' Washen stated.

Diu grinned, something about the face and bright expression perpetually boyish. 'Because it's so hard,' he admitted. 'Because we have to start at the bottom of the bottom. Our status, hard-won or stolen, has to be surrendered, and even if we were born wealthy, that doesn't make us fools. We understand. Talent comes in flavors, and our particular talents don't wear these clothes well.'

With no one here to see them, they again wore their mirrored uniforms.

Nodding, Washen touched the purple-black epaulets, asked, 'So why did you do it? Are you a fool?'

'Absolutely,' he sang out.

She couldn't help but laugh.

With the tone of a confession, he explained, 'I played the wealthy passenger for a few thousand years. Then I finally realized that despite all of my adventuring and all my of my determined smiles, I was bored and would always be bored.'

The car's windows were blackened. The only illumination inside the little cab came from a bank of controls, green smears of light promising that every system was working well. The green of a terran forest: A comforting color for humans; an evolutionary echo, Washen thought in passing.

'But captains never looked bored,' he told her. 'Pissed, yes. And harried, usually. But that's what attracted me to you. If only because people expect it, your souls are relentlessly and momentously busy.'

Diu had taken a unique journey into the ship's elite. He recited his postings and his steady climb through the hierarchy, first as a lowly mate, then as a low-ranking captain. But on the brink of sounding tedious, he held back. He stopped speaking, smiling until she noticed the smile. Then he quietly and respectfully asked Washen about her considerable life.

A hundred thousand years was described in eleven sentences.

'I was born inside the ship. By-the-sea was my childhood home. The Master needed captains, so I became one. I've done every job that captains do, plus a few others. For the last fifty millennia, I've welcomed and supervised our alien guests. According to my work record and my evaluations, I'm very good at my profession. I have no children.

My pets and apartment are self-sufficient. All things considered, I'm comfortable in the company of other captains. I can't imagine living anywhere but on this wondrous, mysterious ship. Where else in Creation can a person drink in so much diversity, every day of our lives . . . ?'

Diu's closed his gray eyes, then opened them. And as always, the eyes smiled along with the mobile wide mouth.

'Are your parents still on board?' he asked.

'No, they sold their shares once the ship entered the Milky Way, and they emigrated.' To a colony world, she didn't mention. A raw, wild place when they arrived, but now probably a crowded, frightfully ordinary place.

'I bet they'll feel an enormous pride,' Diu mentioned.

'Pride for what?'

'You,' he replied.

For an instant, Washen was confused, and perhaps her confusion showed on her usually unflustered face.

'Because they'll hear the news,' Diu continued. 'When the Master announces to the galaxy what we've found down here, and she tells about our roles in this great adventure . . . when that happens, I think everyone everywhere is going to know our story . . .'

In truth, she hadn't considered that very obvious prospect.

Not until this moment, that is.

'Our famous ship has something hidden inside it,' said Diu. 'Imagine what people will think.'

Washen nodded, agreeing . . . while a sliver of herself began to feel the softest gray chill . . . a sudden harbinger of what could be a strange little fear . . .

Seven

Newcomers weren't prepared for Marrow.

Washen hadn't seen images of their base camp or the world itself. Images, like whispers, had their own life and a talent for spreading farther than intended. Which was why she had nothing in mind but those schematics that the Master had shown to all of her captains, leaving her feeling like an innocent.

Their tiny car turned transparent as it pulled into a small garage. Hyperfiber lay in all directions, the silvery-gray material molded into a diamond framework that created berths and storage lockers and long, long staircases.

The car claimed the first available berth.

On foot, three stairs at a time, Diu and Washen conquered the last kilometer. They were inside a newly fabricated passageway, spartan and a little cool. Then the stairs ended, and without warning, they stepped out onto a wide viewing platform, and standing together, they peered out over the edge.

The diamond blister lay between them and several hundred kilometers of airless, animated space. Force fields swirled through that apparent vacuum, creating an array of stubborn buttresses. In themselves, the buttresses were a great discovery. How were they powered? How did they succeed for so long, without a moment's failure? Washen could actually see them: a brilliant blue-white light seemed to flow from everywhere, filling the gigantic chamber. The light never seemed to waver. Even with the blister's protection, the glare was intense. Relentless. Civilized eyes needed to adapt – a physiological task involving retinae and the tint of the lenses; an unconscious chore that might take an hour, at most – but even with their adaptable genetics,

Washen doubted that any person, given any reasonable time, could grow comfortable with this endless day.

The chamber wall was a great sphere of silver-gray hyperfiber marred only by the tiniest of crushed tunnels left behind from the time when it was created. The chamber enclosed a volume greater than Mars, and according to sensors and best guesses, its hyperfiber was as thick as the thickest armor on the ship's exceedingly remote hull, and judging by its purity and grade, probably stronger by a factor of two, or twenty. Or more, perhaps.

The silvery wall was the captains' ceiling, and it fell away smoothly on all sides, its silver face vanishing behind the rounded body of Marrow.

'Marrow,' Washen whispered, spellbound.

On just one little portion of the world, down where her squinting eyes happened to look first, perhaps a dozen active volcanoes were vomiting fire and black gases, ribbons of white-hot iron flowing into an iron lake that cooled grudgingly, a filthy dark slag forming against the shoreline. In colder, closer basins, hot-water streams ran into hot-water lakes that looked only slightly more inviting: mineral-stained bodies shot full of purples and swirling crimsons and blacks and thick muddy browns. Above those lakes, water, clouds gathered into towering thunderheads that were carried by muscular winds back over the land. Where the crust wasn't exploding, it was a scabrous shadowless black, and the blackness wasn't because of the iron-choked soils. What Washen saw was a vigorous, soot-colored vegetation that basked in the endless day. Forests. Jungles. Reeflike masses of photosynthetic life. A blessing, all. Watching from base camp, the captains could guess what was happening. The vegetation was acting like countless filters, removing toxins and yanking oxygen from the endless rust, creating an atmosphere that wasn't clean but seemed clean enough that humans, once properly conditioned, could breathe it, and perhaps comfortably.

'I want to get down there,' Washen confessed.

'Eventually,' Diu cautioned, pointing over her shoulder. 'Things that are impossible usually take time.'

The diamond blister enclosed more than a square kilometer of hyperfiber. Shops and dorms and labs hung down like stalactites, their roofs serving as foundations. On the blister's edge, scuttlebug drones were pouring fresh hyperfiber, creating a silvery-white cylinder slowly growing toward the rough black landscape below.

That cylinder would be their bridge to the new world.

Eventually, eventually.

There was no other route down. The buttressing fields had destroyed every sort of machine sent into them. For many reasons, some barely understood, those buttresses also eroded, then killed, every sort of mind that dared touch them. Captains with engineering experience had worked on the problem. The team leader was a wizard named Aasleen, and she had designed a hyperfiber shaft, its interior shielded with quasiceramics and superfluids. Good rugged theories claimed that the danger would end where the light ended, which was at the upper edges of Marrow's atmosphere. A brief, shielded exposure wouldn't kill anyone. But before the captains made history, there would be tests. Sitting in a nearby lab, inside clean spacious cages, were several hundred immortal pigs and baboons, uniformly spoiled and completely unaware of their coming heroism.

Washen was thinking about baboons and timetables.

A familiar voice broke her reverie.

'What are your impressions, darlings?'

Miocene stood behind them. In uniform, she was even more imposing, and more cold. Yet Washen summoned her best smile, greeting the mission leader with a crisp, 'Madam,' and a little bow. 'I'm surprised, madam,' she admitted. 'I didn't know that this world would be so beautiful.'

'Is it?' The knife-edged face offered a smile. Without looking down, she added, 'I wouldn't know. I don't have a feel for aesthetics.'

For one uncomfortable moment, no one spoke.

Then Diu offered, 'It's a spartan beauty, madam. But it's there.'

'I believe you.' The Submaster smiled off into the distance. 'But tell me. If this world proves as harmless as it is beautiful, what do you think our passengers will pay? To come here and have a look. Or perhaps go below and take a walk.'

'If it's a little dangerous,' Washen ventured, 'then they'll pay more.'

Diu nodded in agreement.

Miocene's smile came closer, growing harder. 'And if it's more than a little dangerous?'

'We'll leave it alone,' Washen replied.

'Dangerous to the ship?'

'Then we'll have to collapse our new tunnel,' Diu suggested.

'With us safely above,' Miocene added.

'Of course,' the captains said together, in a shared voice.

A wide grin filled Diu's face, and for a moment, it was as if he were grinning with his entire body.

Past the fledging bridge, clinging to the chamber's smooth face, were dozens of mirrors and arrays of complex antennae. Gesturing toward them, Diu asked, 'Have we seen any intelligent life, madam? Or perhaps a few artifacts?'

'No,' said Miocene, 'and no.'

It would be a strange place for sentience to evolve, thought Washen. And even if the ship's builders had left cities behind, they would have been destroyed long ago. Or at least swallowed up. The crust beneath them was probably not even a thousand years old. Marrow was an enormous forge constantly reworking not only its black face but also the hot bones beneath.

'This world has one big distinction,' Diu pointed out. 'It's the only part of the ship that comes with its own life-forms.'

True. When humans arrived, every passageway and giant room proved sterile. As life-free as the graceful clean hands of the finest autodoc, and then some.

'But that might just be coincidence,' Washen responded. 'Life usually requires an active geology to be born. The rest of the ship is cold rock and hyperfiber, and the enormous purification plants would have destroyed every ambitious organic compound, almost as it was formed.'

'Yet I can't help dream,' Diu confessed, staring at the two women. 'In my dreams, the builders are down there, waiting for us.'

'A delirious dream,' Miocene warned him.

But Washen felt much the same. Standing here, seeing this wondrous realm, she could imagine an ancient species of bipeds slathering the hyperfiber on the chamber's walls, then creating Marrow from the ship's own core. Why they would do it, she didn't know. She wouldn't even dare a secret guess. But imagining someone like herself, five or ten billion years removed from here . . . it was a compelling, frightening, and focusing insight . . . and something she wouldn't share with the others . . .

Who knew what they would find? This was a huge place, Washen reminded herself. They couldn't see more than a sliver of the world from this one tiny vantage point. And who could say what was beneath any of those iron-belching mountains, or beyond that rough horizon . . . ?

As she considered these weighty matters, Diu spoke. Buoyant words kept flowing from his tireless mouth. 'This is fantastic,' he exclaimed, staring down through the platform's diamond floor. 'And it's an enormous honor. I'm just thrilled that the Master, in her wisdom, included me in this project.'

The Submaster nodded, conspicuously saying nothing.

'Now that I'm here,' Diu blubbered, 'I can almost see it. The purpose of this place, and the entire ship.'

With a level glance, Washen tried to tell her companion: 'Be quiet.'

But Miocene had already tilted her head, eyeing her eleventh-grade colleague. 'I, for one, would love to hear all of your ideas, darling.'

Diu lifted his dark eyebrows.

An instant later, with a bleak amusement, he remarked, 'My apologies. But I think not, madam.' Then he glanced at his own hands, and with a captain's cool judgment, he added, 'Once spoken, the useful thought belongs to at least one other soul.'

Eight

EVEN INSIDE HER quarters, with the windows blackened and every lamp put to sleep, Miocene could sense the light outside. In her mind, she could see its harsh blueness even when her eyes were firmly closed, and she could feel its radiance slipping through the tiniest cracks, then piercing her flesh, wanting nothing more than to bother her old bones.

When did she last sleep well? She couldn't remember the night, which only made it worse. The pressure of this mission and its peculiar environment were ravaging her nerves, her confidence, and splitting her carefully crafted veneer.

Awake and knowing that she shouldn't be, the Submaster stared up into the darkness, imagining a different ceiling, and a different self. When Miocene was little more than a baby, her parents – people of extremely modest means – presented her with an unexpected, wondrous toy. It was an aerogel-and-diamond miniature of the deep-space probe that had recently discovered the Great Ship. At the girl's insistence, the toy was suspended over her bed. It resembled a bluish spiderweb that had somehow snared half a hundred tiny round mirrors. In its center was a fist-sized housing. Inside the housing was a simple AI holding the memories and personality of its historic predecessor. At night, while the girl lay still beneath the covers, the AI spoke with a deep, patient voice, describing the distant worlds that it had charted and how its brave trajectory had eventually carried it out of the Milky Way. The false mirrors projected images that showed thousands of worlds, then the cold black vacuum, and finally, the first dim glow of the ship. The glow brightened, swelling into the battered, ancient face, and then Miocene was past the ship, looking back at the mammoth engines that had helped throw that wonder toward her. Because the Great Ship was thrown toward her, she knew. At that age, and always.

Come morning, the toy always greeted her with envious words.

'I wish I had legs and could walk,' it claimed. 'And I so wish I had your mind and your freedom, and just half of your glorious future, too.'

She loved that toy. Sometimes it seemed to be her finest friend and staunchest ally.

'You don't need legs,' Miocene would tell it. 'Wherever I go, I'll take you.'

'People would laugh,' her friend warned.

Even as a child, Miocene hated being anyone's joke.

'I know you,' said her toy, laughing at her foolishness. 'When the time comes, you'll leave me. And sooner than you think.'

'I won't,' she blurted. 'Never.'

Naturally, she was wrong. Barely twenty years later, Miocene had an adult's body and the beginnings of an adult's intellect, and against brutal odds, she had won a full scholarship to the Belter Academy. Her illustrious career had begun in earnest, and of course she left her toys behind. Today her one-time friend was in storage, or lost, or most likely her parents – people not too bothered by sentimentality – had simply thrown it away.

And yet.

There were moments when she lay awake, alone or otherwise, and looking up, she would see her friend hanging over her again, and she would hear its deep heroic voice whispering just to her, telling her how it was to sail alone between the stars.

A DISEMBODIED VOICE said, 'Miocene.'

She was awake, alert. Had never been asleep, she was certain. But the bed lifted her until she was sitting upright, and a lamp came on, and only then did she notice the passage of time. Ninety-five minutes of uninterrupted dream sleep, claimed her internal clock.

Again, she heard, 'Miocene.'

The Master Captain was sitting on the far side of the room. Or rather, a simple projection of the Master sat in a hypothetical chair, looking massive even though she was composed of nothing but trained photons, that familiar voice telling her favorite and most loyal subordinate, 'You look well.'

Implying the exact opposite.

The Submaster gathered up all the poise at her disposal, then with the perfect little bow, she said, 'Thank you, madam. As always.'

A slight, lightspeed pause. Then, 'You're very welcome.'

The woman had a strange, quixotic sense of humor, which was why Miocene never tried to cultivate one of her own. The Master didn't need a laughing friend, but a sober assistant full of reason and devotion.

'Your request for additional equipment—'

'Yes, madam?'

'Is denied.' The Master smiled, then shrugged. 'You don't absolutely need any more resources. And frankly, some of your colleagues are asking questions.'

'I can imagine,' Miocene replied. Then with a second, lesser bow, she added, 'What equipment we have is adequate. We can reach our goal. But as I pointed out in my report, a second com-line and a new field reactor would give us added flexibility.'

'What resource wouldn't help you?' the Master asked. Then she laughed.

An eternity of practice kept Miocene from speaking or showing the simplest discomfort.

'They're asking questions,' the Master repeated.

The Submaster knew how to react, which was to say nothing.

'Your colleagues don't believe our cover story, I'm afraid.' The round face smiled, absorbing the lamplight, the golden skin shining brightly. 'And I went to such trouble, too. A fully fueled taxi. Robot facsimiles of you walking on board. Then the momentous launch. But everyone knows how easy it is to lie, which makes it hard to coax anyone into believing anything . . .'

Again, Miocene said nothing.

Their cover was a simple fiction: a delegation of captains had left for a high-technology world. They were to meet with a species of exophobes, the humans trying to coax them into friendship, or least to trade for their profitable skills. Such missions had happened in the past, and they typically were wrapped in secrecy. Which was why those other captains – the less qualified ones left behind – should know better than to spit gossip.

'If I sent you a reactor,' the Master explained, 'then someone might notice.'

Not likely, thought Miocene.

'And if we lay down a second com-line, then we double our risk that someone will send or hear something they shouldn't.'

A likely estimate, yes.

Quietly, the Submaster replied, 'Yes, madam. As you wish.'

'As I wish.' An amused nod. Then the Master asked the obvious question. 'Are you keeping up with your timetable?'

'Yes.'

'You'll reach the planet in six months?'

'Yes, madam.' As of yesterday, Aasleen's bridge was halfway to Marrow. 'We'll make every deadline, if nothing unexpected happens.'

'Which is the way it should be,' the Master pointed out.

A circumspect nod. Then Miocene volunteered, 'Our spirits are excellent, madam.'

'I have no doubt. They are in exceptional hands.'

Miocene felt the compliment warming her flesh, and

she couldn't help but nod and offer the tiniest of smiles before asking, 'Is that all, madam?'

'For the moment,' said the ship's leader.

'Then I shall leave you to more important duties,' Miocene offered.

'The important is finished,' she replied. 'The rest of my day is nothing but routine.'

'Have a good day, madam.'

'And to you. And to yours, darling.'

The image dissolved, followed by a pulse of thoughtful light that would search the comlink for leaks and weaknesses.

Miocene rose, standing at her room's only window.

'Open,' she coaxed.

The blackness evaporated. The relentless daylight poured over her, blue and harsh. And hot. Gazing out across her abrupt little city, watching drones and captains in the midst of their important motions, Miocene allowed her thoughts to wander. Yes, she was honored to be here, and endlessly pleased to be leading this vital mission. Yet when she was honest about her ambitions, she had to be honest about her own skills, not to mention the skills of her colleagues. Why had the Master chosen her? Others were more graceful leaders, more imaginative and with better experience in the field. But she obviously was the best candidate. And when she looked hard at herself, there was only one quality in which Miocene excelled above all others.

Devotion.

Aeons ago, she and the Master had attended the Academy together. They were much alike – ambitious students who absorbed their studies together, and who socialized as friends, and who occasionally confessed their deep feelings on matters they wouldn't admit to lovers, and sometimes wouldn't admit to themselves.

Both young women declared, 'I want to be first to that great ship.'

In the Master's dreams, she was leading the first mission. While in Miocene's dreams, she was merely an important organ in the mission's body.

A critical distinction, that.

Why, wondered Miocene, hadn't the Master herself come here?

Yes, there would have been problems. Logistical barriers and security nightmares, absolutely. But with holoprojections and robot facsimiles, she could rule the ship from anywhere. Which was why a bold, dynamic soul like hers must hate being so far removed from here. Perhaps in the end, at the last possible minute, the Master would swallow her good sense, then cram herself into one of the tiny capcars, coming here on the eve of their planetfall. Stealing Miocene's historic moment, in essence.

For the first time, the Submaster sensed how much she hated that prospect. A small anger began to practice inside her. It felt strangely delicious, and even better, it felt appropriate. A justified anger, and it would grow whenever it occurred to Miocene that maybe this was why she was here. The Master knew that she could take every advantage of her endless devotion. She could come here and steal the honor, and her Submaster would have no choice but to smile and nod, deflecting the credit and the fame that should have belonged to her.

Quietly, Miocene told the window to extend.

The transparent panel bowed outward, thinning like a bubble as it expanded.

Leaning forward, she looked down the side of the dormitory, through the diamond street, peering at the hot black face of that strange world . . . and to herself, with a quiet dry voice, she said, 'Please don't come here, madam.'

She said, 'Leave me the glory. Just this once, please.'

Nine

CAPTAINS ARE NOTHING without plans and without routines.

Planetfall occurred nine days and a year after the Master's briefing, and every historic event, small and otherwise, transpired exactly as the captains had anticipated. The touchdown site was selected for the maturity and apparent stability of its crust. The bridge was tweaked and teased into position, then lowered into the upper atmosphere, bellows taking a great breath, the stolen air subjected to every imaginable test. The bridge's final kilometers were added in a carefully orchestrated rush. At the last instant, sensors studied the rising land, mapping details to a microscopic level. Then a tip of razor-edged hyperfiber was shoved into the iron ground, and a specially designed car raced downward, protected by elaborate fields as well as its speed. The journey through the corrosive buttresses was swift and uneventful, and the first landing party arrived with a strict minimum of fuss.

There was a rumor that the Master herself was coming to take part. But like most rumors, it proved untrue, and afterward it seemed like a faintly ridiculous story. Why, after such careful security, would the woman take the obnoxious risk now?

It was Miocene who shouldered the privilege.

Accompanied by a swarm of cameras and security AIs, she stepped carefully onto Marrow's surface. Watching from base camp, Washen saw that too-calm face gazing at the alien landscape, and she noticed something in the wide, unblinking eyes. An amazement, perhaps. A genuine awe. Then the look, whatever it was, evaporated, and the narrow mouth opened, and with a forced sense of importance, Miocene declared, 'In service of the Master, we have arrived.'

The captains overhead cheered and broke into song.

The landing party took ceremonial samples of soil and foliage, then made the expected retreat back to base camp.

Dinner was late, and it was a feast. Bottomless glasses of authentic champagne washed down spiced meats and odd vegetables, and when the party was at its loudest, the distant Master sent her hearty congratulations.

In front of everyone, she called Miocene 'Your brave leader.' Then the projected body did a graceful turn, gesturing at the world beneath as she proclaimed, 'This is a momentous day in our ship's momentous history.'

No it wasn't, thought Washen.

A nagging disappointment only grew. Six teams, including Miocene's, journeyed to Marrow that next day, and studying the data harvests and live images, Washen found exactly what she expected to find. Captains were administrators, not explorers. Every historic moment was choreographed, routine. What Miocene wanted was for every bush and bug to have a name, and every rusty piece of soil to be memorized. Not even tiny surprises were allowed to ambush those hardworking, utterly earnest first teams.

That second day was thorough, and it was stifling. But Washen didn't mention her disappointment, or even put a name to her emotions.

Habit was habit, and she'd always been an exemplary captain. Besides, what sort of person hopes for injuries, or mistakes, or any kind of trouble? Which is what can come from the unexpected.

And yet.

On the third day, when her own team was set to embark, Washen forced herself to sound like a captain. 'We'll take our walk on the iron,' she told the others, 'and we'll exceed every objective. On schedule, if not before.'

It was a swift, decidedly strange journey. Diu rode beside Washen. He made that request, just as he'd requested being part of her team. Their shielded car began by retreating back up the access tunnel, into the garage, acquiring some distance before flinging itself downward. Then it streaked through the buttresses while a trillion electric fingers reached through the superfluid shields, then through their thin skulls, momentarily playing with everyone's sanity.

The car reached the upper atmosphere, and braked, the terrific gees bruising flesh and shattering minor bones. Emergency genes awoke, weaving protein analogs and knitting the most important aches in moments. The bridge was rooted in a hillside of cold rusting iron and black jungle. Despite a heavily overcast sky, the air was brilliant and furnace-hot, every breath tasting of metals and nervous sweat. The captains unloaded their supplies. As team leader, Washen gave orders that everyone already knew by heart. Their car was led from the bridge, then reconfigured. Their new vehicle was loaded and tested, and the captains were tested by their autodocs: newly implanted genes were already churning away, helping their flesh adapt to the heat and metal-rich environment. Then Miocene, sitting in a nearby encampment, gave her blessing, and Washen lifted off, steering toward their appointed study site.

The countryside was broken and twisted, split by fault lines and raw mountains and countless volcanic vents. The vents had been quiet, some for a century, some for a decade, or in some cases, for days. Yet the surrounding terrain was alive, adorned with pseudotrees reminiscent of enormous mushrooms, each pressed flush against its neighbors, their lacquered black faces feeding on the dazzling blue light.

Marrow was at least as durable as the captains flying above it. Growth rates were phenomenal, and for more reasons than the abundant light or a hyperefficient photosynthesis. Early findings supported an early hypothesis: the jungle was also feeding through its roots, the chisellike tips forcing their way through fissures, finding hot springs fat with thermophilic bacteria.

But were the aquatic ecosystems as productive? That was Washen's little question, and she had selected a small, metal-choked lake for study. They arrived on schedule, and after circling the lake twice, she set down on a slab of frozen black slag. The rest of the day was spent setting up their lab and quarters, and specimen traps, and as a precaution, installing a defense perimeter – three paranoid AIs that did nothing but think the worst of every passing bug and spore.

Night was mandatory.

Despite the perpetual light, Miocene insisted that each captain sleep four full hours, then invest another hour in food and ritual chores.

On schedule, Washen's team climbed into their six pop-up shelters, stripped out of their field uniforms, then lay awake, listening to the steady buzzing of the jungle, counting the seconds until it was time to rise again.

They sat in the open at breakfast, in a neat circle, and gazed up at the sky. A shifting wind had carried away the clouds, bringing hotter, drier air and even more light. The chamber's distant wall was silvery-white and smooth and remote. The captains' base camp was a dark blemish visible only because of the clear air. With the distance and the glare, the bridge had vanished. If Washen was careful, she could almost believe they were the only people on the world. If she was lucky, she forgot that elaborate telescopes were watching her sitting on her aerogel chair, eating her scheduled rations, and now, with her right hand, scratching the damp back of her very damp right ear.

Diu sat on her right, and when she glanced at him, he smiled wistfully, as if reading her thoughts.

'I know what we need,' Washen announced.

Diu asked, 'What do we need?'

'A ceremony. Some little ritual before we can start.' She rose and walked down to the lake, not sure why until she arrived. Blackish water lapped against rusting stones. Bending at the knees, she let one of her hands dip beneath the surface, feeling its easy heat, and between the fingers, the greasy presence of mud and life. A stand of dome-headed bog plants caught her gaze, and beside it was a specimen trap. Filled, as it happened. Washen rose and wiped her hand dry against her uniform, then carefully unfastened the trap and brought it back to camp.

On Marrow, pseudoinsects filled most animal riches.

In their trap was a six-winged dragonfly, moonstone blue and longer than a forearm. With the other captains watching, Washen gently eased her victim from the netting, folding back the wings and holding the body steady with her left hand as the right wielded a laser torch. The head was cut free, and the body kicked, then died. Then she stripped the carcass of its wings and its tail, the fat thorax set inside their tiny field kitchen. The broiling took seconds. With a dull boom, the carapace split open. Then she grabbed a lump of the hot blackish meat, and with a grimace, made herself bite and chew.

Diu laughed gently.

Another captain, Saluki, was first to say, 'We aren't supposed to.'

A twelfth-grade named Broq added, 'Miocene's orders. Unless there's an emergency, we stick to our rations.'

Washen forced herself to swallow.

Then with a wide smile, she told them, 'And you won't want to eat this again. Believe me.'

There weren't any native viruses to catch, or toxins that their reinforced genetics couldn't destroy or piss away. Miocene was playing the role of the cautious mother, and where was the harm?

Washen passed out the ceremonial meat.

Wanting to please her team leader, Saluki put the flesh to her tongue, then swallowed it whole.

Broq protested, then managed the same trick.

The next two, ship-born siblings named Promise and Dream, winked slyly at the sky and told Washen, 'Thank you.'

Last to accept his share was Diu, and his first bite was tiny. But he didn't grimace, and he took the rest of the carcass, his white teeth yanking out a fatrich chunk that he chewed before swallowing.

Then with an odd little laugh, he told everyone, 'It's not too horrible.'

He said, 'If my mouth just quit burning, I think I'd almost enjoy the taste.'

Ten

WEEKS OF RELENTLESS work made possibility look like hard fact.

Marrow had been carved from the ship's heart. Or more

properly, it was carved from the core of the young jupiter that would eventually become the Great Ship.

The world's composition and their own common sense told the captains as much. Whoever the builders were, they must have started by wrenching the uranium and thorium and other radionuclides from the rest of the jupiter, then injecting them into the core. With buttressing fields, the world was compressed, its iron packed closer and closer before the exposed chamber wall was braced with hyper-fiber. How that was accomplished, no one knew. Even Aasleen, with her engineering genius, just shook her head and said, 'Damned if I know.' Yet billions of years later, without apparent help from the builders or anyone else, this vast machine was still purring along quite nicely.

But why bother with such a marvel?

The obvious, popular reason was that the ship needed to be a rigid body. Tectonics fueled by any internal heat would have melted the chambers and shattered every stone ceiling, probably within the first few thousand years. But why go to so much trouble and expense to create Marrow? If you've got this kind of energy at your disposal, why not just lift the uranium out into space where you could put it to good use?

Unless it was used here, of course.

Some captains suggested that Marrow was the nearly molten remnant of an enormous fission reactor.

'Except there are easier, more productive ways to make energy,' others pointed out, their voices more polite than gentle.

But what if the world was designed to store energy?

It was Aasleen's suggestion: by tweaking the buttresses, the builders could have forced the world to rotate. With patience and power – two resources they must have had in abundance – the builders could have given it a tremendous velocity. Spinning inside a vacuum, held intact by the buttresses as well as a vanished blanket of hyperfiber, this massive iron ball would have served as a considerable flywheel.

Slowly, slowly, that energy was bled away by the empty ship.

Somewhere between the galaxies, the rotation fell to nothing, and that's when the ship's systems eased themselves into hibernation.

Aasleen went as far as creating an elaborate digital, as real to the eye as could be. In the early universe, heavy elements were scarce. The builders harvested the radionuclides from above and buried them here, and as Marrow grew hotter and hotter, its hyperfiber blanket began to decay. Degrade. And die.

Hyperfiber was rich in carbon and oxygen, hydrogen and nitrogen, every atom aligned just so and every bond strengthened with tiny predictable quantum pulses. Stressed past its limits, old hyperfiber would just fall apart, and the newly reactive elements would start dancing in celebration, giving life a reasonable chance to be born.

'It's absolutely obvious,' Aasleen declared. 'Once you see it, you can't believe anything else. You just can't!'

She made that dare at a weekly briefing.

Each of the team leaders was sitting in the illusion of a Master's conference room, each perched in an black aerogel chair, sweating in Marrow's heat. The surrounding room was sculpted from light and shadow, and sitting at the head of the long pearlwood table, between imposing gold busts of herself, was the Master's projection. She seemed alert but remarkably quiet. The expectation for these briefings was for crisp reports and upbeat attitudes. Grand theories were a surprise. But after Aasleen had finished, and after a contemplative pause, the Master smiled, telling her imaginative captain, 'That's an intriguing possibility. Thank you, darling. Very much.'

Then to the others, 'Considerations? Any?'

Her smile brought a wave of complimentary noise.

Washen doubted they were exploring someone's dead battery. But this wasn't the polite moment to list the problems with flywheels and life's origins. Besides, the bioteams were reporting next, and she had her own illuminations to share.

A tremor interrupted the compliments.

The image of one captain shook, followed by others. Knowing who sat where made it possible to guess the epicenter. When Washen felt the first jolt, then the rolling aftershocks, she realized it was a big quake, even for Marrow.

An alert silence took hold.

Washen was suddenly aware of her own sweat. A sweet oil, volatile and sweetly scented, rose up out of her nervous pores, then evaporated, leaving her flesh chilled despite the endless heat.

Then the Master, immune to the quake, lifted her wide hand, announcing in a smooth, abrupt way, 'We need to discuss your timetable.'

What about the bioteams?

'You're being missed up here. Which is what you hope to hear, I'm sure.' The woman laughed for a moment, alone. Then she added, 'Our delegation fiction isn't clever enough, or flexible enough, and the crew are getting suspicious.'

Miocene nodded knowingly.

Then the Master lowered her hand, explaining, 'Before I have a panic to fend off, I need to bring you home again.'

Smiles broke out.

Some of the captains were tired of the discomforts;

others simply thought about the honors and promotions waiting above.

Washen cleared her throat, then asked, 'Do you mean everyone, madam?'

'For the moment. Yes.'

She shouldn't have been surprised that the cover story was leaking. Hundreds of captains couldn't just vanish without comment. And Washen shouldn't have felt disappointment. Even during the last busy weeks, she found herself wishing that the fiction was real. She wanted her and her colleagues off visiting some high-technology exophobes, trying to coax them into a useful trust. That would a difficult, rewarding challenge. But now, hearing that their mission was finished, she suddenly thought of hundreds of projects worth doing with her little lake – enough work to float an entire century.

As mission leader, it was Miocene's place to ask:

'Do you want us cutting our work short, madam?'

The Master set one hand on one of the busts. For her, the room and its furnishings were genuine, and the captains were illusions.

'Mission plans can always be rewritten,' she reminded them. 'What's vital is that you finish your surveys of both hemispheres. Be sure there aren't any big surprises. And I'd like your most critical studies wrapped up. Ten ship-days should be adequate. More than. Then you'll come home again, leaving drones to carry on the work, and we can take our time deciding on our next important step.'

Smiles wavered, but none crumbled.

Miocene whispered, 'Ten days,' with a tentative respect. 'Is there a problem?'

'Madam,' the Submaster began, 'I would feel a little more at ease if we could be sure. That Marrow isn't a threat. Madam.'

There was a pause, and not just because the Master was thousands of kilometers removed from them. It was a lengthy, unnerving silence. Then the captain's captain looked off into the illusionary distance, asking, 'Considerations? Any?'

It would be a disruption.

The other Submasters agreed with Miocene. To accomplish that work in ten days, with confidence, would require every captain's help. That included those with the support teams. The base camp might have to be abandoned, or nearly so. Which was an acceptable risk, perhaps. But those mild, conciliatory words were obscured by clenched hands and distant, unsettled gazes.

The Master absorbed the criticisms without comment. Then she turned to her future Submaster, saying, 'Washen,' with a certain razored tone. 'Do you have any considerations to add here, darling?'

Washen hesitated as long as she dared.

'Perhaps Marrow was a flywheel,' she finally allowed. Ignoring every puzzled face, she nodded and said, 'Madam.'

'Is this a joke?' the Master responded, her voice devoid of amusement. 'Aren't we discussing your timetable?'

'But if this was a flywheel,' Washen continued, 'and if these magical buttresses ever weakened, even for an instant, Marrow would have thrown itself to pieces. A catastrophic failure. The hyperfiber blanket wouldn't have absorbed the angular momentum, and it would have shattered, and the molten iron would have struck the chamber wall, and the shock waves would have passed up through the ship.' She offered a series of simple, coarse calculations. Then avoiding Aasleen's glare, she added, 'Maybe this was an elaborate flywheel. But it also might have made an effective self-destruct mechanism. We just don't know, madam. We don't know the builders' intentions. We can't even guess if they had enemies, real or imagined. But if there are answers, I can't think of a better place to look.'

The Master's face was unreadable, impenetrable. Giant brown eyes closed, and finally, slowly, she shook her head, smiling in a pained fashion. 'Since my first moment on board this glorious vessel,' she proclaimed, 'I have nourished one guiding principle: the builders, the architects, whoever they were, would never have endangered their marvelous creation.'

Washen wished for the same confidence.

Then that apparition of light and sound rose to her feet, leaning across the golden busts and the bright pearl-wood, and she said, 'You need a change of duty, Washen. You and your team will take the lead. Help us explore the far hemisphere. If it's there, find your telltale clue. Then once your surveys are finished, everyone comes home.

'Agreed?'

'As you wish, madam,' said Washen.

Said everyone.

Then Washen noticed Miocene's surreptitious glance, something in her narrowed eyes saying, 'Nice try, darling.'

And with that look came the faintest hint of respect.

Eleven

ON THREE DISTINCT occasions, flocks of pterosaur drones had intensively mapped this region. Yet as Washen retraced the machines' path, she realized that even the most recent survey, completed eight days ago, was too old to be useful.

Battered by quakes, a once-flat landscape had been

heaved skyward, then split open. Torrents of molten iron ran down the new slopes. Over the hushed murmur of the engine, she could hear the iron's voice, deep and steady, and massive, and fantastically angry. Washen flew parallel to the fierce river, and where three maps showed a great oxbow lake, the iron pooled, consuming the last of the water and the mud. Columns of filthy steam and hydrogen gas rose skyward, then twisted to the east. As an experiment, Washen flew into the steam. Samples were ingested by the car's airscoops, then passed through filters and a hundred sensors and even a simple microscope, and peering into the scope, Diu started to giggle, saying, 'Wouldn't you know? Life.'

Riding inside the steam were spores and eggs and half-born insects, encased in tough bioceramics and indifferent to the blistering heat. Inside the tip of one needle flask, too small to be seen with the naked eye, were enough pond weeds and finned beetles to conquer a dozen new lakes.

Catastrophe was the driving force on Marrow.

That insight struck Washen every day, every hour, and it always arrived with a larger principle in tow:

In one form or another, disaster had always ruled the universe.

The steam could disperse abruptly, giving way to the sky's blue light, the chamber wall hanging far overhead, and beneath, stretching as far as Washen could see, lay the stark black bones of a jungle.

Fumes and fire had incinerated every tree.

Every scrambling bug.

The carnage must have been horrific. Yet the blaze had passed days ago, and new growth was already pushing up from the gnarled trunks and fresh crevices, thousands of glossy black umbrellalike leaves shining in the super-heated air.

Diu said something in passing. Broq leaned over Washen's shoulder, repeating the question. 'Should we stop? And have a look, maybe?'

In another fifty kilometers, they would be as far from the bridge as possible. The proverbial end of the world. Chilled champagne and some stronger pleasures waited for that symbolic moment. They would have to wait patiently, Washen decided, and through an implanted subsystem, she asked the car to find a level cool piece of ground where six captains could enjoy a little stroll.

The car hovered for a thoughtful instant, then dropped and settled.

The outside air was cool enough to breathe, if only in quick little sips. Following the mission's protocol, everyone took samples of the burnt soil and likely rocks, and they cut away pieces of things alive and dead. But mostly this was an excuse to experience this hard landscape, once strange and now, after weeks of work, utterly familiar.

Promise and Dream were examining a broad white tree stump.

'Asbestos,' Promise observed, fingers rubbing against the powdery bark. 'Pulled from the ground or out of the air, or maybe just cooked up fresh. Then laid around the roots, see? Like a blanket.'

'The trunk and branches were probably lipid rich,' her brother added. 'A living candle, practically.'

'Meant to burn.'

'Happy to burn.'

'Born to burn.'

'Out of love.'

Then they giggled to themselves, enjoying their little song.

Washen didn't ask what the words meant. These ditties

were ancient and impenetrable; even the siblings didn't seem sure where they came from.

Kneeling beside Dream, she saw dozens of flat-faced shoots erupting from the ravaged trunk. On Marrow, blessed with so much energy and so little peace, vegetation didn't store energy as sugars. Fats and oils and potent, highly compressed waxes were the norm. Some species had re-invented batteries, stockpiling electrical energies inside their intricate tissues. How much time would it take for chance and caprice to do this elaborate work? Five billion years? At the very least, she guessed. There weren't any fossils to ask, but the genetic surveys showed a fantastic diversity, implying a truly ancient beginning. They were in a garden that could be, perhaps, ten or fifteen billions years old. With that latter estimate verging on the preposterous.

Whatever was true, leaving Marrow was wrong.

Washen couldn't stop thinking it, in secret.

To the siblings, she said, 'I'm curious. Judging by their genes, what two species are the two most dissimilar?'

Promise and Dream grew serious, unwinding their deep, efficient memories. But before either could offer a guess, there was a hard jolt followed by a string of deep shudders, and Washen found herself unceremoniously thrown back on her rear end.

She had to laugh, for a moment.

Then somewhere nearby, two great masses of iron dragged themselves against each other, and piercing squealing roars split the air, sounding like monsters in the throes of some terrific fight.

When the quake passed, Washen stood and casually adjusted her uniform. Then she announced, 'Time to leave.'

But most of her team was already making for the car. Only Diu waited, looking at her and not quite smiling when he said, 'Too bad.'

She knew what he meant, nodding and adding, 'It is.'

THEIR EIGHT-DAY-OLD map was a fossil, and not a particularly useful fossil, at that.

Washen blanked her screen, flying on instinct now. In another ten minutes, maybe less, they would reach their destination. No other team would travel this far. Drawing a sturdy little satisfaction from the thought, she started to turn, ready to ask whoever was closest to check on their champagne.

Her mouth opened, but a distorted, almost inaudible voice interrupted her.

'Report . . . all teams . . . !'

'Who's that?' asked Broq.

Miocene. But her words were strained through some kind of piercing electronic wail.

'What do . . . see . . . ?' the Submaster called out.

Then, again, 'Teams . . . report . . . !'

Washen tried for more than an audio link, and failed.

A dozen other team leaders were chattering in a ragged chorus.

Zale boasted, 'We're on schedule here.'

Kyzkee observed, 'Odd com interference . . . otherwise, systems nominal . . .'

Then with more curiosity than worry, Aasleen inquired, 'Why, madam? Do you see something wrong?'

There was a long, jangled hum.

Washen linked her nexuses to the car's sensor array, finding Diu already there. With a tight little voice, he said, 'Shit.'

'What—' Washen cried out.

Then a shrill roar swept away every voice, every thought. And the day brightened and brightened, fat ribbons of lightning flowing across the sky, then turning, moving with a liquid purpose, aiming straight for them.

From the far side of the world came a twisted voice:

'The bridge . . . is it . . . do you see it . . . where . . . ?'

The car lurched as if panicking, losing thrust and lift, then altitude, every one of its AIs failing. Washen deployed the manual controls, and centuries of routine drills made her concentrate, nothing existing now but their tumbling craft, her syrupy reflexes, and a wide expanse of cracked earth and burnt forest.

The next barrage of lightning was purple-white, and brighter, nothing visible but its wild seething glare.

Washen flew blind, flew by memory.

Their car was designed to endure heroic abuse. But every system was dead and its hyperfiber must have been degraded somehow, and when it struck the iron ground, the hull was twisted until its weakest point gave way, and it shattered. Restraining fields grabbed helpless bodies. Then their perfect mechanisms failed. Nothing but padded belts and gas bags held the captains in their seats. Flesh was jerked and ripped, and shredded. Bones were shattered and wrenched from their sockets, slicing through soft pink organs, then slammed together again. Then the seats were torn free of the floor, tumbling wildly across several hectares of iron and cooked stumps.

Washen never lost consciousness.

With a numbed curiosity, she watched her own legs and arms break and break again, and a thousand bruises spread into a single purple tapestry, every rib crushed to dust and her reinforced spine splintering until she was left without pain or a shred of mobility. Lying on her back, still lashed to her twisted chair, she couldn't move her crushed head, and her words were slow and watery, the sloppy mouth filled with teeth and dying blood.

'Abandon,' she muttered.

Then, 'Ship.'

She was laughing. Feebly, desperately.

A gray sensation rippled through her body.

Emergency genes were already awake, finding their home in a shambles. They immediately protected the brain, flooding what was living with oxygen and antiinflammatories, plus a blanket of comforting narcotics. Trusted, pleasant memories bubbled into her consciousness. For a little moment, Washen was a girl again, riding on the back of her pet whale. Then doctoring genes began rebuilding organs and the spine, cannibalizing meat for raw materals and energy, the captain's body wracked with fever, sweating perfumed oils and black dead blood.

Within minutes, Washen felt herself growing smaller.

An hour after the crash, a wrenching pain swept through her. It was a favorable, almost comforting misery. She squirmed and wailed, and wept, and with weak, rebuilt hands, she freed herself from her ruined chair. Then on sloppy, unequal legs, she forced herself into a tilted stance.

Washen was twenty centimeters shorter, and frail. But she managed to limp to the nearest body, kneeling and wiping the carnage out of his face. Diu's face, she realized. He was injured even worse than she. He had shriveled like old fruit, and his face had been driven into a craggy fist of iron. But his features were half-healed. Mixed with his misery was a clear defiance, and he managed a mutilated grin and a wink, his surviving gray eye focusing on Washen, the battered mouth spitting teeth as he lisped, 'Wonderful, you look. Madam. As always . . .'

SALUKI WAS IMPALED on a spar of browned hyperfiber.

Broq's legs were severed, and in a numbed anguish, he had dragged himself to the legs and pressed them against the wrong sockets.

But the siblings were the worst. Dream had slammed

into an iron slipfault, and her brother then impacted against her. Flesh and bone were mixed together. Slowly, slowly, their carnage was separating itself, their healing barely begun.

Washen repositioned Broq's legs. Then with Diu's help, she eased Saluki off the spar and set her in its shade to mend. And with Diu keeping watch over the siblings, she searched the wreckage for anything useful. There were field rations and field uniforms, but the machines wouldn't operate. She tried to coax them awake, but none of them was well enough to declare, 'I am broken.'

If there was luck, it was that the crust seemed stable for the moment. They could afford to do nothing but heal and rest, eating triple shares of their rations. Later, Saluki even managed to find two pop-up shelters and their survival packs, plus a full diamond flask of champagne. Hot as the ground, by now. But delicious.

Sitting in the shadow of a pop-up, the six captains drank the flask dry.

Pretending it was night, they huddled and discussed tomorrow, options named and weighed, and most of them discarded.

Wait, and watch; that was their collective decision.

'We'll give Miocene three days to find us,' said Washen. Then she caught herself trying to access her implanted timepiece, out of pure habit. But every one of her implants, every minuscule nexus, had been fried by the same electric fire that had ripped them out of the sky.

In a world without night, how long was three days?

They made their best guess, then waited an extra day, in case. But there wasn't any trace of Miocene or any other captain. Whatever had crippled their car must have left everyone else powerless. Seeing no choice in the matter, Washen looked at each of her companions, and she smiled as if embarrassed, and she admitted to them,

'If we want to get home, it looks as if we're just going to have to walk.'

Twelve

DO SOMETHING NEW, and do nothing else, and do that one thing relentlessly – particularly if it is painful and dangerous and utterly unplanned – and your memory begins to play one of its oldest, sneakiest tricks.

Washen couldn't remember being anywhere else.

She would find herself standing at the base of a tall newborn mountain, or deep within some trackless black-bellied jungle, and it was as if everything she remembered about her former life was nothing but an elaborate, impossible dream, more forgotten than remembered, and those memories, at their heart, utterly ridiculous.

This hike was a deadly business. Covering any distance was slow and treacherous work, even when the captains learned little tricks and big ones to keep themselves moving in what they prayed was the right direction.

Marrow despised them. It wanted them dead, and it didn't care how it achieved their murder. And the hatred was obvious to everyone. Washen felt its mood every waking moment, yet she refused to admit it, at least in front of the others. Except for cursing, which didn't count. 'Fucking mountain, fucking wind, fucking shit-eating fucking weeds . . . !' Everyone had their favorite insults, saving the most savage words for the worst challenges. 'Stupid shit iron, I hate you! Hear me? I hate you, the same as you hate me!'

Each day was a hard march punctuated with the constant search for food. What they had eaten before as a ceremony became their standard fare: they caught giant insects, ripped loose their wings, and broiled them over hot fatty fires. The strong meat held enough calories and nutrients to put the captains back to full size again, and very nearly their old health. Washen slowly learned which insects tasted the least awful. A desperate descendant of hunting apes, she taught herself the bugs' haunts and the best ways to catch them, and after what might have been the first year – or a little less, or maybe a little more – Washen didn't fall asleep hungry anymore. No one had to live famished. Promise and Dream sampled the lush vegetation, vomiting what was bitter beyond words, but mastering the slow careful cooking of everything else.

Where the tongue adapts, the soul follows.

Early in that second year, there was a good day. Genuinely, truly good. Simple wakefulness began it for Washen and the others. The captains' first meal was filling. Then the six of them began to jog toward the horizon, their few possessions carried on their hips and their wide wet backs. They were retracing their flight path. Without digital maps, they had to rely on shared memories of odd volcanic peaks and twisted black gorges and the occasional mineral-stained sea. Marrow enjoyed draining its seas and detonating its mountains, and that brought confusion, doubts, and delays. Where new barriers had been heaved skyward, they had to make long detours. At the first sign of being lost, the captains had to stop and reconnoiter. Without stars or a sun, there was always the risk of becoming profoundly and embarrassingly lost. But on that very good day, they held their course throughout. Diu found a knifelike ridge where field boots found easy running, and the sky was pleasantly overcast with a thin cooling drizzle falling over them, keeping them nearly cool. Pressing until comfortably exhausted, they ran to the next landmark – a vast black escarpment that loomed over them by day's end.

Camp was made in the deepest shadows of a likely valley. A rainwater stream danced down a jerky narrow bed probably not fifty years old. Rainwater was always better than springwater. True, they could taste the iron in every swallow. And there was usually a sulfurous residue. But it wasn't the mineral-choked, bacteria-choked stew that came from underground. In fact, it was cool enough for bathing, which was a genuine luxury. Washen scrubbed herself raw, then dressed – except for her battered boots – and she stretched out beneath an enormous umbrella tree, studying her long bare feet and the busy water and noticing an unexpected emotion that was inside her. It was an emotion that seemed, against all odds, to resemble contentment. Even happiness, in a diluted fashion.

Diu appeared. One moment, Washen was utterly alone, and then Diu came from no particular direction, the top of his uniform removed, dangling behind him like the spent carapace of a growing insect. Under one arm, he carried his dinner – a beetlelike apparition, black as band iron and longer than a forearm – and he turned and smiled at Washen in a way that implied that he already knew where she was. He smiled, and his dinner moved its eight legs in a steady, complaining fashion. He ignored the legs. Stepping closer, he offered a nebulous laugh, then asked, 'Would you like to share?'

For a captain, he was pretty. Diu had a pretty chest, hairless and sculpted by the last hard year. And his gray eyes had a sparkle that only grew brighter when he stepped into the shadow of the umbrella tree.

Washen said, 'Fine. Thank you.'

Diu just kept smiling.

For an instant, Washen felt uncomfortable, ill at ease. But when she searched for reasons, she discovered only that here was another one of those odd moments that she couldn't have predicted. A thousand centuries old, yet she had never imagined that she would be sitting in a place like this, under these hard circumstances, staring at a man named Diu, her mouth genuinely growing wet from the anticipation.

For a well-cooked beetle, or for something else?

Washen surprised herself, admitting to both of them, 'I can't remember the last time I was this happy.'

Diu giggled for a moment.

'It's been a good, good day,' she confessed.

He said, 'Yes,' in a certain way.

Then Washen heard herself saying, 'Tie your friend down. For now, would you?' Then she threw him her best handmade rope, adding, 'Only if you want. If you don't mind. I want to see you out of those clothes, Mr Beetleman.'

THE BRIDGE WAS their final landmark.

In the brilliant light, looking out from high on a windy ridge, the landmark resembled a rigid thread, dark and insubstantial against the silver-white chamber wall. Sheered off in the stratosphere, it was hundreds of kilometers too short. There was no escape route for them. But it was their destination. More than three years had been invested in reaching this place, and that was enough reason to keep marching past the usual fatigue. Yet this was exceptionally rough country, even for Marrow. And worse, the captains were traveling across the grain of every local fault and stream, and the little stretches of flat ground were choked with old jungles and elaborate deadfalls.

Reaching the last high ridge, they found more ridges waiting in ambush, and the bridge was a fatter thread, but still agonizingly distant.

They collapsed under the next ridge.

It wasn't a true camp. They were lying where they fell in a rust-cushioned bowl surrounded by raw nickel, and when a mist turned into a hard rain, they ignored it. Thousands of zigzagging kilometers and three years had made Washen and her team indifferent to this little dose of weather. They lay on their backs, breathing when they needed, and quietly, with soft exhausted voices, they made themselves mutter hopeful words.

Imagine the other captains' surprise, they told each other.

Imagine, they said, when we come out of the jungle tomorrow . . . ! Won't all this be worth it, just to see the surprise on their noble faces . . . ?

Except no one was waiting to be caught off guard. Late that next day, they arrived at the bridge and found a long-abandoned encampment, overgrown and forgotten. The solid, trusted hilltop where the bridge was rooted had been split open by quakes, and the hyperfiber was a sickly, degraded black. The structure itself was tilting precariously away from them. Dead doors were propped open with a simple iron post. A makeshift ladder reached up the dark inner shaft, but judging by the frosting of soft rust, no one had used the ladder for months. If not for several years.

Circling through the jungle, Broq found a sketchy path. They picked a random direction and followed the path until it was swallowed by the black vegetation. Then they turned and retraced their course until the path was wide enough that a person could jog, then run, relaxing because someone had been down this way. Someone was here. And suddenly Washen was in the lead, streaking ahead at a full sprint.

But the time they reached the river bottom, everyone was breathless.

The path bled into a wider, well-worn trail, but they had to slow again, panting as they jogged, coming around every bend with a jittery sense of anticipation.

In the end, they were the ones with surprised faces.

The six captains were trotting in the bright shadows. Some trick of the light hid the woman standing before them. The light and her mirrored uniform kept Washen from seeing her until the familiar face seemed to pop into existence. Miocene's face, unchanged at first glance. She looked regal and well chilled. 'It took you long enough,' the Submaster deadpanned. And only then was there a smile and an odd tilt to the face, and she added, 'It's good to see you. All of you. Honestly, I'd given up all hope.'

WASHEN SWALLOWED HER anger along with her questions.

Her companions asked the obvious question for her. Who else was here? they wondered. How were they making do? Did any machinery work? Had the Master been in contact with them? Then before any answers could be offered, Diu inquired, 'What sort of relief mission is coming for us?'

'It's a cautious mission,' Miocene replied. 'So cautious that it fools you. It makes you believe that it doesn't even exist.'

Her own anger was rich and strong, and well practiced.

The Submaster beckoned them to follow, and as they walked in the bright shade, she explained the essentials. Aasleen and others had cobbled together several telescopes, and at least one captain was always watching the base camp overhead. From what they could see, the diamond blister was intact. Every building was intact. But the drones and beacons were dead, and the reactor was off-line. A three-kilometer stub of the bridge was next to the blister, and it would make the perfect foundation for a new structure. But Miocene shook her head, quietly admitting that there wasn't any trace of captains, or anyone else, trying to mount any sort of rescue attempt.

'Maybe they think we're dead,' said Diu, desperate to be charitable.

'I don't think we're dead,' Miocene countered. 'And even if we were, someone should be a little more interested in our bones, and in answers.'

Washen didn't say one word. After three years of hard work, lousy food, and forced hopefulness, she suddenly felt sick and desperately sad.

The Submaster slowed her pace, working her way back through the questions.

'Every machine was ruined by the Event,' she explained. 'That's our little name for that very big phenomenon. The Event. From what we've pieced together, the buttresses merged. Those beneath us, and those above us. And when it happened, our cars and drones, sensors and AIs, were left as so much fancy trash.'

'Can't you fix them?' asked Promise.

'We can't even be sure how they were broken,' Miocene replied.

People nodded, and waited.

She offered a distracted smile, admitting, 'We are surviving, however. Wooden shelters. Some iron tools. Pendulum clocks. Steam power when we go to the trouble. And enough homemade equipment, like the telescopes, that lets us do some toddler-type science.'

The trail made a slow turn.

The jungle's understory had been cut down and beaten

back, leaving the mature trees to give precious shade. The new encampment stretched out on all sides. Like anything built by determined captains, the community was orderly. Each house was square and strong, built from the gray trunks of the same kind of tree, iron axes squaring them up and notching them and the little gaps patched with a ruddy mortar. The paths were lined with smaller logs, and someone had given each path its own name. Center. Main. Left-behind. Rightbehind. Golden. And every captain was in uniform, and smiling, standing together in careful lines, trying to hide the weariness in their eyes and their sudden voices.

More than two hundred captains shouted, 'Hello!'

In a practiced chorus, they shouted, 'Welcome back!'

Washen could smell their sweet perspiration as well as an assortment of home-brewed perfumes. Then the wind gusted, bringing her the rich, very familiar odor of bug flesh broiling over a low fire.

A feast was being prepared, in their honor.

She spoke, finally. 'How did you know we were coming?'

'Your bootprints were noticed,' Miocene reported. 'Up by the bridge.'

'I saw them,' said Aasleen. She stepped forward, glad to take credit. 'Counted them, measured them. Knew it was you, and came home to report.'

'There's a quicker route than the one you found,' Miocene cautioned.

'Quicker than three years?' Diu joked.

Am embarrassed laughter blossomed, then fell away. Then Aasleen felt like telling them, 'It's been closer to four.'

She had a clever quick face, skin black as band iron, and among her peers, she seemed the only happy soul – this one-time engineer who had gradually become a captain, and who now had the responsibility of reinventing everything that humans had ever accomplished. Starting from scratch, with minimal resources . . . and she couldn't have looked more contented . . .

'You didn't have clocks,' she warned them. 'You were living by how you felt, and humans, left without markers, fall into thirty- or thirty-two-hours days.'

Which wasn't a surprise to anyone, of course.

Yet Saluki exclaimed, 'Four years,' and marched into the brightest patch of light, glancing up through a gap in the canopy, perhaps trying to find the abandoned base camp. 'Four long years . . . !'

If only a single captain had stayed behind at the base camp. One warm body could have called for help, or at least made the long climb to the fuel tank and leech habitat, then to the Master's quarters . . . assuming, of course, that there was someone up there to find . . .

Thinking the worst, Washen recoiled. And finally, with her most careful voice, she forced herself to ask, 'Who isn't here?'

Miocene recited a dozen names.

Eleven of them had been Washen's friends and associates. The last name was Hazz – a Submaster and a voyage-long colleague of Miocene's. 'He was the last to die,' she explained. 'Two months ago, a fissure opened, and the molten iron caught him.'

A silence fell over the little village.

'I watched him die,' Miocene admitted, her eyes distant, and damp. And furious.

'I've got one goal now,' the Submaster warned. Speaking in a grim, hateful voice, she said, 'I want the means to return to the world above. Then I will go to the Master myself and I'll ask her why she sent us here. Was it to explore this place? Or was this just the best awful way to be rid of us . . . ?'

Thirteen

BITTERNESS SERVED THE woman well.

Miocene despised her fate, and with a searing rage, she blamed those unconscionable acts that had abandoned her on this horrible, horrible world. Every disaster, and there were many of them, helped feed her emotions and fierce energies. Every death was a tragedy erasing an ocean of life and experience. And each rare success was each a minuscule step toward making right what was plainly and enormously wrong.

The Submaster rarely slept, and when her eyes dipped shut, she would descend into vivid, confused nightmares that eventually shook her awake, then lingered, left in the mind like some sophisticated neurological toxin.

Her immortal's constitution kept her alive.

Ancestral humans would have perished here. Exhaustion or burst vessels or even madness would have been the natural outcome of so little sleep and so much undiluted anger. But no natural incarnation of humanity could have lived a single day in this environment, subsisting on harsh foods and ingesting every sort of heavy metal with each breath and sip and bite. Once it was obvious that the Master wasn't pulling her fat carcass down the tunnel to rescue them, it also become plain that if Miocene were to escape, it would take time. Deep reaches of time. And persistence. And genius. And luck, naturally. Plus everyone else's immortal constitution, too.

Hazz's death had driven home every hard lesson. Two years later, she still couldn't stop seeing him. A gregarious, Earthborn man who loved to talk about bravery, he was nothing but brave at the end. Miocene had watched helplessly as a river of slag-covered iron trapped him on a little island of old metal. Hazz had stood up tall, looking at the fierce slow current, breathing despite the charring of his lungs, putting on a grimacing sort of smile that seemed, like everything else in this awful place, utterly useless.

They tried desperately to save him.

Aasleen and her crew of engineer-minded souls had started three separate bridges, each melting before they could finish. And all that time, the iron river got deeper, and swifter, shrinking the island down to a knob on which the doomed man managed to balance, using one foot until it was too badly burned, then using the other.

He was like a heron bird, in the end.

Then the current surged, and the thin black slag burst open, a red-hot tongue of iron dissolving Hazz's boots, then boiling away both of his feet and setting fire to his flesh. But the engines of his metabolism found ways to keep him alive. Engulfed in flames, he actually managed to stand motionless for a long moment, the grimacing smile getting brighter and sadder, and very tired. Then with every captain watching, he said something, the words too soft to be audible, and Miocene screamed, 'No!,' loudly enough that Hazz must have heard her voice, because suddenly, on boiling legs, he made an heroic attempt to walk himself across the slag and molten metal.

His tough, adaptable body reached its limits. Quietly and slowly, Hazz slumped forward, his mirrored uniform and his smiling face and a thick tangle of blondwhite hair bursting into dirty flames. The water inside him exploded into steam and rust and hydrogen. Then there was nothing left but his shockingly white bones, and a wave of hotter, swifter iron pulled the skeleton apart and took the bones downstream, while a rising cloud of blistering fumes drove the other captains away.

Miocene wished that she could have retrieved the skull.

Bioceramics were tough, and the tough mind could have survived that heat for a little while longer. And weren't there stories of miracles being accomplished by autodocs and patient surgeons?

But even if he was past every resurrection, Miocene wished she had Hazz's skull now. In her dreams she saw herself setting it beside one of the Master's golden busts, and with a deceptively calm voice, she would tell the Master who this had been and how he had died, and then with a truer, angrier voice, she would explain to the captains' captain why she was a disgusting piece of filth, first for every awful thing that she had done, then for every good thing that she had failed to do.

Bitterness brought with it an incredible, fearless strength.

More and more, Miocene trusted that strength and her resolve, and more than at any time in her spectacularly long life, she found herself with a focus, a pure, unalloyed direction to her life.

Miocene relished her bitterness.

There were moments, and there were sleepless nights, when she wondered how she had ever succeeded in life. How could anyone accomplish anything without this rancorous and vengeful heart that would never, no matter what the abuse, stop beating inside its blazing, fierce chest?

WASHEN'S RETURN HAD been an unexpected success. And like most successes, it was followed by disaster. The nearby crust rippled and tore apart, a barrage of quakes shattering the river bottom as well as the nearby hillside. The old remnant of the bridge pitched sideways, and with a creaking roar, its sick hyperfiber shattered, the debris field reaching across fifty kilometers of newborn mountains.

The fall of the bridge was momentous, and unseen.

The captains' encampment had already been obliterated

by a mammoth geyser of white-hot metal. The neat houses were vaporized. Two more captains died, and the survivors fled with a bare minimum of tools and provisions. Lungs were cooked during the retreat. Hands and feet were blistered. Tongues swelled and split wide, and eyes were boiled away. The strongest dragged the weakest on crude litters, and finally, after days of stumbling, they wandered into a distant valley, into a grove of stately blue-black trees that lined a deep pool of sweet rainwater, and there, finally, the captains collapsed, too spent to curse.

As if to bless them, the trees began discharging tiny balloons made from gold. The shady, halfway cool air was filled with the balloons' glint and the dry music made when they brushed against one another.

'The virtue tree,' Diu called them, snagging one of the golden orbs with both hands, squeezing until he squeezed too hard and it split, hydrogen escaping with a soft hiss, the skin collapsing into a whiff of soft gold leaf.

Miocene set her people to work. New homes and new streets needed to be built, and this seemed an ideal location. With iron axes and their enduring flesh, they managed to hack down half a dozen of the virtue trees. The golden fat inside the wood was nourishing, and the wood itself was easily split along its grain. The beginnings of twenty fine houses were laid out before the hard ground ripped open with an anguished roar.

Wearily, the captains fled again.

Again, they scrambled over ridges sharper than their axes, and the country behind them burned, then melted, consumed by a lake of iron and slag.

Nomadic blood had taken hold.

When they settled again, no one expected to linger. Miocene asked for simple houses that could be rebuilt anywhere in a ship's day. She ordered Aasleen and her people to build lighter tools, and everyone else stockpiled food for the next migration. Only when those necessities were assured could she risk the next step: they needed to study their world, and if possible, learn to read its fickle moods.

Miocene put Washen in charge of the biological teams.

The first-grade captain picked twenty helpers, including the five from her first team, and with few tools but keen senses and their good memories, they fanned out across the nearby countryside.

Three months and a day later, every team brought home their reports.

'Breeding cycles are the key,' Washen reported. 'Maybe there are other keys. But certain cycles are pretty close to infallible, it seems.'

The captains were packed into the long narrow building that served as a cafeteria and meeting hall. The central table was a block of iron dressed with gray wooden planks. Chairs and stools were crowded around the table. Bowls were filled with grilled flame ants and sugarhearts, then ignored. Cold tea was the drink of choice, and it smelled acidic and familiar, mixing with the tired oily sweat of women and men who had been in the field too long.

Miocene nodded, at Washen and at everyone. 'Go on, darling. Explain.'

'Our virtue trees,' said the first-grade. 'Those gold balloons are their eggs, just as we assumed. But they typically make only one or two in a day. Unless they feel the crust becoming unstable, which is when they use all of their stockpiled gold. In a rush. Since the adults are about to be torched, and the land will be remade—'

'If we see another show,' Diu interrupted, 'we're being warned. We've got a day, or less, to get out of here.'

In a grim fashion, the other captains laughed.

Miocene disapproved with a look and a cold silence, but nothing more. Normally, she demanded staff meetings that were disciplined and efficient. But this was a special day, and more special than anyone else had guessed.

Washen's team spoke about the species worth watching and each warning sign of impending eruptions.

During stable times, certain winged insects transformed themselves into fat caterpillars, some longer than any arm. If they grew new wings, the stability was finished.

At the first sign of trouble, crab-sized, highly social beetles launched themselves in fantastic migrations, thousands and millions scrambling overland. Though, as Dream noted, the herds often went charging off in the very worst direction.

At least three predatory species, hammerwings included, would suddenly arrive in areas soon to be abandoned. Perhaps it was an adaption to the good hunting that would come when locals rushed out of their burrows and nests.

In dangerous times, certain caterpillars sprouted wings and took up the predatory life.

And slight changes in water temperature and chemistry caused aquatic communities to panic or grow complacent. Just what those changes were, no one was certain. It would take delicate instruments and years more experience to read the signs as easily as the simplest black scum seemed to manage it.

Everything said was duly recorded. A low-grade captain sat at the far end of the table, taking copious notes on the huge bleached wings of copperflies.

Once finished, it was Miocene's place to invite questions.

'How about our virtue trees?' asked Aasleen. 'Are they behaving themselves?'

'As if they'll live forever,' Washen replied. 'They're still early in their growth cycles, which means nothing. Eruptions can come anytime. But they're putting their energies into wood and fat, not into gold balloons. And since their roots are deep and sensitive, they know what we can't. I can guarantee that we can remain here for another two or three, or perhaps even four whole days.'

Again, the grim laughter.

Washen's confidence was contagious, and useful. Losing her would have been a small disaster. Yet years ago, the Master had sent this talented woman to the far side of Marrow, doing her accidental best to get rid of her.

Miocene nodded, then lifted a hand.

Quietly, almost too quietly to be heard, she said, 'Cycles.'

The closest captains turned, watching her.

'Thank you, Washen.' The Submaster looked past her, and shivered. Without warning, she felt her own private eruption. Thoughts, fractal as any quake, made her tremble. Just for the briefest moment, she was happy.

Diu asked, 'What was that, madam?'

Again, louder this time, Miocene said, 'Cycles.'

Everyone blinked, and waited.

Then she turned to the leader of the geologic team, and with a barely hidden delight, she asked, 'What about Marrow's tectonics? Are they more active, or less?'

The leader was named Twist. He was a Second Chair Submaster, and if anything, he was more serious-minded than Miocene. With a circumspect nod, Twist announced, 'Our local faults are more active. We have nothing but crude seismographs, of course. But the quakes are twice as busy as when we arrived on Marrow.'

'How about worldwide?'

'Really, madam . . . at this point, there's no competent, comprehensive way for me to address that question . . .'

'What is it, madam?' asked Diu.

Honestly, she wasn't absolutely certain.

But Miocene looked at each of the faces, wondering what it was about her face that was causing so much puzzlement and concern. Then quietly, in the tone of an apology, she said, 'This may be premature. Rash. Perhaps even insane.' She swallowed and nodded, and more to herself than to them, she said, 'There is another cycle at work here. A much larger, much more important cycle.'

There came the distant droning of a lone hammerwing, then silence.

'My self-appointed task,' Miocene continued, 'is to keep watch on our former base camp. It's a hopeless chore, frankly, and that's why I don't ask for anyone's help. The camp is still empty. And until we can find the means, I think it will remain abandoned.'

A few of the captains nodded agreeably. One or two sipped at their pungent tea.

'We have only one small telescope, and a crude tripod.' Miocene was unfolding a copperfly wing, her long hands gently trembling as she told everyone, 'I leave the telescope set on the east ridge, on flat ground inside a sheltered bowl, and all I use it for is to watch the camp. Five times every day, without exception.'

Someone said, 'Yes, madam.'

Patiently, but not too patiently.

Miocene rose to her feet, spreading out the reddish wings covered with numbers and small neat words. 'When we lived beneath the camp, we rarely adjusted our telescopes. Usually after a tremor or a big wind. But now that we've moved here, fifty-three kilometers east of original position . . . well, I'll tell you . . . in these last weeks, I've twice had to adjust my telescope's alignment. I did it again just this morning. Always nudging it down toward the horizon.'

Silence.

Miocene looked up from the numbers, seeing no one. She asked herself, 'How can that be?'

With a quiet, respectful voice, Aasleen suggested, 'Tremors are throwing the telescope out of alignment. As you said.'

'No,' the Submaster replied. 'The ground is flat. It's always been flat. I've tested for that exact error.'

It was a steadily growing error; she saw it in the careful numbers.

Quietly, Miocene read her data. When she felt absolutely sure that she understood the answer, she asked, 'What does this mean?'

Someone offered, 'Marrow has started to rotate again.'

The flywheel hypothesis, again.

Aasleen said, 'It could be the buttresses. With a fraction of their apparent energies, they could act on the iron, causing it, and us, to move a few kilometers . . .'

A few kilometers. Yes.

One of Miocene's long hands lifted high, silencing the others. 'Perhaps,' she said with a little smile. 'But there's still another option. Involving the buttresses, but in a rather different fashion.'

No one spoke, or blinked.

'Imagine that the Event, whatever it was . . . imagine it was part of some grand cycle. And after it happened, the buttresses under our feet started to weaken. To loosen their grip on Marrow, if only just a little bit.'

'The planet expands,' said someone.

Said Washen.

'Of course,' Aasleen trumpeted. 'The interior iron is under fantastic pressures, and if you took off the lid, even a little bit—'

Perhaps unconsciously, half a dozen captains inflated their cheeks.

Miocene grinned, if only for a moment. This very strange idea had taken hold of her gradually, and in the excitement of the moment, she summoned up old instincts, telling everyone. 'This is premature. We'll need measurements and many different studies, and even then we won't be certain about anything. Not for a very long while.'

Washen glanced at the ceiling, perhaps imagining the faraway base camp.

Diu, that low-grade charmer, laughed softly. Happily. And he took his lover's hand and squeezed until she noticed and smiled back at him.

'If the buttresses below us are weakening,' Aasleen pointed out, 'then maybe the ones in the sky are getting dimmer, too.'

Twist said, 'We can test that. Easily.'

Nothing was easy here, Miocene nearly warned them.

But instead of discouraging anyone, she took back those copperfly wings and her precious numbers, and with the simplest trigonometry, she interpolated a rugged little estimate. Only in the dimmest back reaches of her mind did she hear Washen and the engineers spinning new hypotheses. If the expansion was real, perhaps it would give away clues about how the buttresses worked. Clues about what powered them, and why. Aasleen suggested that a cycle of expansion and compression was the obvious means through which excess heat, from nuclear decay or other sources, was bled away from Marrow. It might even explain how the bright buttresses overhead were refueled. The whole ad hoc hypothesis sounded perfectly reasonable. And perhaps it was even a little bit true. But its truth was inconsequential. All that mattered were the dry little answers appearing beneath Miocene's stylus.

She lifted her head.

The motion was so abrupt that the room suddenly fell

silent. A flock of jade-crickets broke into song, then, as if sensing a breach in etiquette, stopped.

'Assuming some kind of expansion,' Miocene told her captains, 'this world of ours has grown a little less than a kilometer since the Event. And at this rate, assuming that Marrow can maintain this modest pace for another five thousand years . . . in another five millenia, the world will fill this entire chamber, and we'll be able to walk back to our base camp.'

In her own grim, determined way, Miocene laughed.

'And after that,' she whispered, 'if need be . . . we'll be able to walk all the way home . . .'

Fourteen

IT WAS SLEEPTIME for the children.

Washen intended to visit the nursery. But as she approached she heard the gentle murmurs of a voice, and she hesitated, then eased closer, an adult caution and her own curiosity making a game out of this routine chore.

The community nursery was built from iron blocks and iron bricks, black umbra wood making the steeply pitched roof. Next to the cafeteria, this was the largest structure in the world, and easily the most durable. Washen leaned against the wall, an ear to one of the little shuttered windows, listening carefully, realizing that it was the oldest boy who was speaking, telling everyone a story.

'We call them the Builders,' he was explaining. 'That's our name for them because they built the ship and everything within it.'

'The ship,' whispered the other children, in one voice.

'The ship is too large to measure,' he assured them, 'and it is nothing but beautiful. Yet when it was new, there was no one to share it with. There were only the Builders, and they were proud, and that's why they called out into the darkness, inviting others to come fill its vastness. To come see what they had done and sing about their lovely creation.'

Washen leaned against the wall, smelling the shutter's sweet wood.

'Who came from the darkness?' asked that oldest boy.

'The Bleak,' dozens of voices answered instantly.

'Was there anyone else?'

'No one.'

'Because the universe was so young,' the boy explained. With utter confidence, he picked his own odd course through what the captains had taught him. 'Everything was new, and there were only the Bleak and the Builders.'

'The Bleak,' one little girl repeated, with feeling.

'They were a cruel, selfish species,' the boy maintained. 'But they always wore smiles and said careful words. They came and sang praises to our lovely ship. But what did they want? Even from the earliest moment?'

'To steal our ship,' the others answered.

'In the night, as the Builders slept unaware,' he said with a practiced foreboding, 'the Bleak attacked, slaughtering most of them while they lay helpless in their beds.'

Every child whispered, 'Slaughtered.'

Washen eased her way closer to the nursery door. Each child had his own little bed positioned according to some personal logic. Some of the beds were close together, in twos and threes and fives, while others preferred distance and a comparative solitude. Peering through the shuttered door, she found the storyteller. He was apart from the others, sitting up in his little bed, his face catching one of the bright slivers of light that managed to slip through the heavy ceiling. His name was Till. He looked very much like his mother, tall with a tall, thin face. Then he moved his head slightly, and he resembled no one but himself.

'Where did the surviving Builders go?' he asked.

'Here.'

'And from here, what did they do?'

'They purified the ship.'

'They purified the ship,' he repeated, with emphasis. 'Everything above us had to be killed. The Builders had no choice whatsoever.'

There was a long, reflective pause.

'What happened to the Builders?' he asked.

'They were trapped here,' said the others, on cue.

'And?'

'They died here. One after another.'

'What died?'

'Their flesh.'

'But is flesh all that there is?'

'No!'

'What else is there?'

'Their spirits.'

'What isn't flesh cannot die,' said that very peculiar boy.

Hands against the warm iron frame of the door, Washen waited, trying to recall when she had last taken a meaningful breath.

In a songful whisper, Till asked, 'Do you know where the Builders' spirits live?'

'Inside us,' the children replied with a palpable delight.

'We are the Builders now,' Till's voice assured them. 'After the long, lonely wait, we have finally been reborn . . . !'

AFTER EIGHT DECADES, life on Marrow had become glancingly comfortable and halfway predictable. Twist's tectonics team had mapped the local plumes and vents and every major fault, and as a consequence, they knew where the iron crust was thickest and where to build homes that would linger. Food was abundant and was only going to be more so. Washen's biologists were cultivating wild plants, and in the last few years, they had begun raising the most palatable bugs in cages and special huts. Various attempts at science, no matter how clumsy, were making gains. Miocene had been right: Marrow was expanding at a steady, almost stately pace as the buttressing fields grew weaker, and the sky's brilliant light had already faded by more than a percentage point. Aasleen's people, fueled by genius and sanguinity, had invented at least ten difficult schemes that would allow everyone to escape from Marrow.

It would only require another forty-nine centuries, give or take.

Children were inevitable, and essential. They brought new hands and new possibilities, and they would replace the losses inflicted by this awful place. Then once they had their own children, a slow-motion demographic onslaught would have begun.

Every female captain owed the world at least one healthy boy or girl; that was Miocene's pronouncement.

But her words slammed up against modern physiologies. There wasn't one viable egg or a motile sperm inside any captain. In modern society, complex medicines and delicate autodocs were used to tease long-lived people into fertility. They had neither. That's why it took twenty years of determined research before Promise and Dream, working in their own laboratory, discovered that the black spit of a hammerwing, poisonous to most native life-forms, could induce a temporary fecundity in human beings.

There were dangers, however. A woman required very

high, even toxic dosages, and the effects on a developing embryo were far from clear.

Miocene volunteered to be first.

It was an heroic act, and if successful, it would be a selfish act, her child destined to be the oldest. She ordered the two captains to collect sperm from every donor, and alone, the Submaster impregnated herself. As far as Washen could tell, no one but Miocene could be certain who Till's father was.

Miocene carried the boy for the full eleven-month term. The birth itself was uneventful, and for those first few months, Till seemed perfectly normal. He was happy and engaged, ready to smile up at any face that smiled at him. Later, as they tried to piece together events, it wasn't apparent when the baby had changed. It must have happened slowly, and only later were the effects obvious. Till was a happy, giggling boy riding gracefully on his mother's hard hip, and then it was a different day, and people began to notice that he was much more quiet, still riding that hip without complaint, but his gaze distant, and always, in some odd, undefinable fashion, distracted.

HAMMERWING SPIT WASN'T to blame.

Maybe the boy would have grown up the same way on the ship. Or Earth. Or anywhere else, too. Children are never predictable, and they are never easy. In the following years, the encampment began to fill up with strangers. They were small and fierce, and they were endlessly entertaining. And more than anyone anticipated, the children were challenges to the captains' seamless authority.

No, they didn't want to eat that bug dinner.

Or poop in the neat new latrines.

And thank you, no, they wouldn't play nice, or sleep during the arbitrary night, or listen to every important word when their parents explained what Marrow was and what the ship was and why it was so very important to eventually escape from their birthplace.

But these were little problems. Over the last decades, Washen had tried every state of mind, and optimism, far and away, was the most pleasant. She worked hard to remain positive about everything difficult and gray.

Good, sane reasons were keeping them from being rescued. The most likely explanation was the simplest: the Event was a regular phenomenon, and it had reached beyond Marrow, collapsing the access tunnel so completely that digging it out again was grueling, achingly slow work. That's what must have happened to the original tunnels, too. Earlier Events had destroyed them. And the Master could only act with caution, balancing the good of a few captains against the unknown dangers, the well-being of billions of innocent and trusting passengers taking easy precedence.

Other captains were optimistic in public, but in private, in their lovers' beds, they confessed to darker moods.

'What if the Master's written us off?'

Diu posed the question, then immediately offered an even worse scenario.

'Or maybe something happened to her,' he grunted. 'This was an utterly secret mission. If she died unexpectedly, and if the First Chair Submasters don't even know that we're down here . . .'

'Do you believe that?' asked Washen.

Diu shrugged his shoulders as if to say, 'Sometimes.'

Through the heavy walls and sealed shutters came the drumming of a hammerwing. Then, silence.

For a moment, it felt as if Marrow were listening to them.

Playing Diu's own game, Washen reminded him, 'There's another possibility.'

'There's many. Which one?'

'The Event was bigger than we realize. And everyone else is dead.'

For a moment, Diu didn't react.

It was the unmentionable taboo. Yet Washen kept pressing, reminding him, 'Maybe we weren't the first ones to find this derelict ship. Others came before. But the builders had left behind some kind of booby trap, primed and ready.'

'Perhaps,' he allowed. Then he sat up in bed, iron springs squeaking as his smooth strong legs dropped over the edge, toes kissing the cool dark floorboards. Again, softer this time, he said, 'Perhaps.'

'Maybe the ship cleanses itself every million years. The Event destroys everything foreign and organic.'

A tiny grin emerged. 'And we survived . . . ?'

'Marrow survived,' she replied. 'Otherwise, this would be barren iron.'

Diu pulled one of his hands across his face, then with his fingers, he combed the long coffee-colored hair. Even in the bedroom's enforced darkness, Washen could see his face. After so many years, she knew it better than she knew her own features, and in the vastness that was her remembered life, she couldn't think of any man to whom she had felt this close.

'I'm just talking,' she told him. 'I don't believe what I'm saying.'

'I know.'

Placing a hand on his sweaty back, she realized that Diu was watching the crib. Their infant son, Locke, was hard asleep, blissfully unaware of their grim discussion. In another three years, he would live in the nursery. He would live with Till, she kept thinking. A month had passed since Washen had overheard that story about the Builders and the Bleak. But she hadn't told anyone. Not even Diu.

'There are more explanations than we have people,' she admitted.

Again, he wiped the sweat from his face.

Then she said, 'Darling,' with an important tone. 'Have you ever listened to the other children?'

He glanced over his shoulder. 'Why?'

She explained, in brief.

Since they built this house, the same sliver of light had slipped its way through the shutters. Changing the tilt of his head, the light hit his gray eye and the high strong cheek. 'You know Till,' was Diu's response. 'You know how odd he can seem.'

'That's why I didn't mention it.'

'Have you heard him tell that story again?'

'No,' she admitted.

'But you've been eavesdropping, I'd guess.'

She said nothing.

Her lover nodded wisely and came close to a smile. Then with a little wink, he stood up, bare feet carrying him to the crib.

But Diu wasn't looking at their son. Instead, he was fingering the mobile hung over the crib on a thick, trustworthy cord. Painted pieces of wood bounced gently on nearly invisible wire, showing Locke all those wonders that he couldn't see for himself. The ship was in the center, largest by a long way, and surrounding it were tinier starships and several generic birds as well as a Phoenix that his mother had carved for her own reasons, then hung there without explanation.

After a moment, Washen joined Diu at the crib.

Locke was a quiet baby. Patient, uncomplaining. From his parents he had acquired a stew of immortal genes and an easy strength, and from this world, his birthplace, came . . . well, what about him was Marrow? Not for the first time, Washen wondered if it was wrong to allow children on a world barely understood. A world that could probably kill all of them. And kill them tonight, if the urge struck it.

'I wouldn't worry about Till,' said Diu.

'I don't,' she promised, speaking more to herself than him.

But the man still explained himself. 'Children are imagination machines,' he said. 'You never know what they're going to think about anything.'

Washen was remembering the Child, that part-human, part-Gaian creature that she raised for Pamir, and with a bittersweet grin, she replied, 'But that's the fun in having them. Or so I've always been told . . .'

THE BOY WALKED alone, crossing the public round with his eyes watching his own bare feet, watching them shuffle across the hot, sky-baked iron.

'Hello, Till.'

He seemed incapable of surprise. Pausing, he lifted his gaze slowly, a smile waiting to shine at the captain. 'Hello, Madam Washen. You're well, I trust.'

Under the sky's blue glare, he was a polite, scrupulously ordinary eleven-year-old boy. He had a thin face joined to a small, narrow body, and like most of his peers, he wore as little as the adults let him wear. Modern genetics were such a tangle; Washen had given up guessing who was his father. Sometimes she wondered if Miocene even knew. She obviously wanted to be his only parent, openly grooming him to stand beside her someday. Whenever Washen looked at the half-feral boy wearing nothing but a breechcloth, she felt a nagging resentment, petty as can be, and since it was directed at an eleven-year-old, simply foolish.

'I have a confession to make,' she said, using her own

smile. 'A little while back, while you were in the nursery, I overheard you talking to the other children. You were telling them a very elaborate story.'

The eyes were wide and brown with darts of black inside them, and they didn't so much as blink.

'It was an interesting story,' Washen conceded.

Till looked like any boy who didn't know what to make of a bothersome adult. Sighing wearily, he shifted his weight from one brown foot to the other. Then he sighed again, the portrait of pure boredom.

'How did you think up that story?'

A shrug of the shoulders.

'I know we like to talk about the ship. Probably too much.' Her explanation felt sensible and practical. Her biggest fear was that she would come across as patronizing. 'Everyone likes to speculate. About the ship's past, and its builders, and the rest of it. All our chatter has to be confusing. And since we are going to be rebuilding the bridge, with your help . . . it does rather make you into a species of Builder, doesn't it . . . ?'

Till shrugged again, his eyes looking past her.

On the far side of the round, in front of their machine shop, a team of sweating captains fired up their latest turbine – a primitive wonder built from rough steel and vague memories, plus considerable trial and error. Homebrewed alcohols combined with oxygen, creating a delicious roar. While it was working, the engine was powerful enough to do any job they could offer it, at least for today. But it was dirty and noisy, and it was inefficient, and the sound of it almost obscured the boy's strong voice.

'I'm not speculating,' he announced. 'Not about anything.'

Washen said, 'Excuse me?' as if she hadn't heard him.

'I won't tell you that. That I'm making it up.'

The turbine sputtered, then fell silent.

Washen nodded, smiling in a defeated way. Then she noticed an approaching figure. From the shop, wearing her old epaulets on a simple robe of handwoven fabric, Miocene looked weary as always, and angry in a thousand ways.

'I don't make up anything,' the boy protested.

His mother asked, 'What don't you do?'

Till didn't say.

For a moment, he and Washen exchanged looks, as if making a pact. Then he turned to Miocene, complaining, 'That machine . . . it sounds awful.'

'It does. You're right.'

'Is that how the ship is? Big engines screaming all the time?'

'No, we use fusion reactors. Very efficient and quiet, and extremely safe, too.' She glanced at Washen, asking, 'Don't we, darling?'

'Fusion, yes,' Washen offered, her hands trying to straighten the stiff fabric of her own handmade uniform. 'The best reactors in the galaxy, I would think.'

Then like a trillion mothers, Miocene said, 'I haven't seen you for too long. Where have you been, Till?'

'Out there,' said Till. He waved in a distant, imprecise fashion, three of his fingers smaller than the rest. And paler. Regenerating after a little accident, no doubt.

'Were you exploring again?'

'But not far from here,' he told her. 'Always in the valley.'

He was lying, thought Washen. She heard the lie between the words.

Yet Miocene nodded with conviction, saying, 'I know you were. I know.' It was a self-imposed delusion, or it was an act meant for public eyes.

There was an uncomfortable moment of silence. Then, the turbine fired up again and rattled along with a healthy vigor. The sound of it drew Miocene's attention, leading her back toward the machine shop.

Washen smiled at the boy, then knelt beside him.

'You like to make up things,' she observed. 'Don't you?'

'No, madam.'

'Don't be modest,' she warned.

But Till shook his head stubbornly, staring down at his toes and the black iron. 'Madam Washen,' he said with a boy's fragile patience. 'What is, is. It's the only thing that can never be made up.'

Fifteen

LOCKE WAITED IN the shadows – a grown man with a boy's guilty expression and the wide, restless eyes of someone expecting disaster to lash out from every direction.

His first words were, 'I shouldn't be doing this.'

But a moment later, responding to the anticipated response, he said, 'I know, Mother. Promises given are promises always.'

Washen hadn't made a sound.

It was his father who offered second thoughts. 'If this is going to create troubles,' Diu muttered, 'maybe we should slip back home again.'

'Maybe you should,' their son allowed. Then he turned and abruptly walked off, never inviting them to follow, knowing they wouldn't be able to help themselves.

Washen hurried up the path, feeling Diu in her

footsteps. A young jungle of black umbra trees and elegant lambda bushes dissolved into a sudden landscape of bare iron: black pillars and arches created an indiscriminate, infuriating maze. Every step was a challenge, an act of conscious grace. Razored edges sliced exposed flesh, criss-crossing fingers and calves with thin pink wounds. Bottomless crevices beckoned to passersby, wind and drip-ping rainwater echoing out of the metal ground. Worst of all, Washen's body was accustomed to sleep at this hour. Fatigue slowed her senses and her common sense. When she saw Locke standing on the rusty lip of a cliff, waiting for them, she noticed nothing but his wide back and the long golden hair tied into an elaborate set of braids. She stared at the simple black shirt woven in the village loom, from mock cotton, the shirt that his mother had patched more than once, and always badly.

Until she stood beside him, Washen was oblivious to the deep valley spread out below them, long and rather narrow, its flat floor covered with a mature stand of black-as-night virtue trees.

'Black as night,' Washen whispered.

Her son rose to the bait. Shaking his head, he said, 'Mother. There's no such thing.'

As night, he meant.

In his world, he meant.

This was lucky ground. When the world's fiery guts began to pour out on all sides, this thick and durable slab of crust had fallen into the great fissure. The virtue jungle had burned but it hadn't died. Its roots could be a century old, or older. As old as the human tenure on Marrow, perhaps. There was a rich, eternal feel to the ground, and perhaps that's why the children had chosen it.

The children.

Washen knew better, but despite her careful intentions,

she couldn't think of them as anything but young, and in some profound sense, vulnerable.

'Quiet,' Locke whispered, not bothering to look back at them.

Who was talking here? she wondered. But she didn't ask.

Then with nothing but his own deeply callused flesh between himself and the iron, Locke jumped from perch to perch, grunting softly with each impact, then pausing just long enough to glance up from below, blinking against the bright skylight as he added with an almost parental concern, 'And keep close to me. Please.'

His parents' field boots had fallen apart decades ago. They wore clumsy sandals made from mock cork and rubber, and they had to work to stay with him. On the valley floor, in the living shadows, the air turned slightly cooler and uncomfortably damp. Blankets of rotting vegetation had fallen from the canopy, leaving the ground watery-soft, a rotting organic stink still smelling utterly alien to Washen. A giant daggerwing roared past, intent on some vital business. Washen watched the animal vanish into the gloom, then reappear, tiny with the distance, its cobalt-blue carapace shining in a patch of sudden skylight.

Locke turned abruptly, silently.

A single finger lay against his lips. Just for a moment, in that light, he looked like his father. But what Washen noticed most was his expression, his gray eyes showing a pain and worry so intense that she had to try and reasure him with a touch.

Diu had wormed the secret out of their son. The children were meeting in the jungle, and these meetings had been going on for more than twenty years. At irregular intervals, Till would call them to a secluded location, and it was Till who controlled everything that was said and done.

'What's said?' Washen had asked. 'What's done?'

Locke wouldn't explain. First he shook his head with defiance and shame. Then with a quiet disappointment, he admitted to them, 'I'm breaking my oldest promise by repeating any of this.'

'Then why tell?' she had pressed.

'Because.' Locke's expression was complicated, his soft gray eyes changing with each blink. Finally a compassionate, halfway fearful look settled on him, and he explained, 'You have every right to hear. So you can decide for yourselves.'

He cared for his parents. That's why he broke his promise, and that's why he had no choice but to bring them here.

Washen wouldn't think of it any other way now.

A few more quiet steps, and she found herself staring at the largest virtue tree that she had ever seen. Age must have killed it, and rot had brought it down, splitting the canopy as it crumbled. Adult children and their little brothers and sisters had assembled in that pool of brilliant bluewhite sky-light, standing in clumps and pairs, some wearing hammerwing tails shoved into their hair. Soft quick voices merged into a senseless buzz. Till was there, pacing back and forth on the wide black trunk. He looked fully adult, ageless and unexceptional, wearing a simple breechcloth and two bracelets, one of steel and the other gold. His dark braids resembled a long rope. His young, almost pretty face showed a timid, self-conscious expression that gave Washen the strangest little moment of hope. Maybe this was nothing but the old game swollen up into some kind of social gathering. Till would perform for the children, telling his elaborate stories that no sensible mind could believe but that everyone, in one fashion or another, would take pleasure from.

Locke didn't look back or say a word. He simply pressed ahead, through a low wall of lambdas and out into the bright busy clearing.

'Hello, Locke,' said twenty voices.

He said, 'Hello,' once, loudly, then joined the oldest children in front.

Obeying their promise, his parents knelt in the jungle, ignoring the hiss and sputter of a thousand little bugs.

Nothing happened.

A few more children filtered into view, and there was quiet conversation, and Till, oblivious to it all, continued to pace. Maybe this was all that would happen. It was certainly easy to hope so.

Till stopped.

In an instant, the worshipers fell silent.

With a quiet voice, Till asked, 'What do we want?'

'What is best for the ship,' the children answered, each with his own quiet voice. Then together, in one voice, they said, 'Always.'

'How long is always?'

'Longer than we can count.'

'How far is always?'

'To the endless ends.'

'Yet we live—'

'For a moment!' they cried. 'If that long!'

The words were absurd, and chilling. What should have sounded ludicrous to Washen wasn't, the prayer acquiring a muscular credibility when hundreds were speaking in a smooth chorus, every syllable endowed with a practiced surety.

'What is best for the ship,' Till repeated.

But the words were a question. His narrow and very

appealing face was filled with a curiosity, a genuine longing.

Quietly, he asked his audience, 'Do you know the answer?'

In a muddled shout, the children said, 'No.'

'Do I know the answer?'

Quietly, respectfully, they told him, 'No.'

'True, and true,' their leader professed. 'But when I'm awake, I am searching for what is best. Best for our great ship, and for always. And when I sleep, my dream self does the same.'

'And so do we,' his followers chanted.

Then Washen thought, No, it wasn't a chant. It was too disheveled and honest-sounding, each one of them making the solemn vow to himself.

There was a brief, unnerving pause.

Then Till asked, 'Do we have business today?'

'We have newcomers!' someone cried out.

For a slippery instant, Washen thought they meant her and Diu. She glanced over her shoulder, looking at Diu for the first time: he appeared calm in that electric, perpetually busy way of his, and he seemed thankful for the look. One hand took her by the arm as Till's voice shouted, 'Bring them up here.'

The newcomers were genuine children. Seven-year-old twins, as it happened. Brother and sister climbed the rotting trunk slowly, as if terrified, trembling hands clinging to the fluted velvet-black bark. But Till offered his hands, and with a crisp surety, he suggested deep breaths. 'We're your brothers and sisters,' he reminded them, more than once. Then when they finally smiled, he asked, 'Do you know about the ship?'

The little boy glanced at the sky, saying, 'It's very old.'

'Nothing is older,' Till confided.

'And it's huge.'

'Nothing can be larger. Yes.'

His sister fingered her navel, waiting to feel brave. When Till looked at her, she lifted her gaze and told everyone, 'It's where we came from. The ship is.'

The audience laughed at her.

Till lifted a hand, bringing silence.

Her brother corrected her. Quietly and fiercely, he said, 'The captains came from there. Not us.'

Till nodded, waiting.

'But we're going to help them,' the boy added, infinitely pleased with that destiny. 'We'll help them get back up to the ship. Soon.'

There was a prolonged and very cold silence.

Till allowed himself a patient smile, patting both of their heads. Then he looked out at his followers, asking, 'Is he right?'

'No,' they roared.

The siblings winced and tried to vanish.

Till knelt between them, and with a steady, untroubled voice said, 'The captains are just the captains. But you and I and all of us here . . . we are built from the stuff of this world, from its flesh and water and air . . . and from the old souls of the Builders, too . . .'

Washen hadn't heard that nonsense in a quarter of a century, and hearing it now, she couldn't decide whether to laugh or explode.

'We are the Builders reborn,' Till assured everyone. Then he stood, and with his hands fondly draped over the children's slumping shoulders, he hinted at the true scope of this rebellion. 'Whatever our purpose is, it is not to help the captains. That is the one truth about which I am certain.'

Staring off into the shadowy jungle, he exclaimed, 'The captains only think they have a tight hold on the ship. But friends, if you will . . . think of all the wonders that can happen in a single day . . . !'

MIOCENE REFUSED TO believe any of it.

'First of all,' she told Washen, and herself, 'I know my own son. What you've described is ridiculous. Ludicrous. And frankly, stupid. Second of all, according to your count, this rally involved more than half of our children—'

Diu interrupted. 'Most of them are adults. With their own homes.' Then he added, 'Madam,' and framed the word with quick nods.

An angry silence descended.

Then Washen admitted, 'I checked. Several dozen children slipped out of the nurseries last night—'

'And I'm not claiming they didn't. And I'm very sure they slipped off somewhere.' Then with a haughty expression, Miocene asked, 'Will the two of you listen to me? Will you give me that much consideration, please?'

'Of course, madam,' said Diu.

'I know what's possible. I know exactly how my child was raised, and I know his character, and unless you can offer me some credible motivation for this fable . . . this shit . . . then I think we'll just pretend that nothing has been said here . . .'

'What about my motivation?' asked Washen. 'Why would I tell such a story?'

With a chill delight, Miocene said, 'Greed.'

'Toward who?'

'Believe me, I understand.' The sullen eyes narrowed, silver glints in their corners. 'If Till is insane, your son stands to gain. Status among his peers, at the very least. And eventually, genuine power.'

Washen glanced at Diu.

They hadn't mentioned Locke's role as informant, and

they'd keep it secret as long as possible – for a tangle of reasons, most of them selfish.

They were inside the Submaster's one-room house. The place felt small and crowded, its nervous air nearly too hot to breathe. There was a shabbiness here, despite the fact that Miocene kept every surface as clean as possible. A shabbiness, and a deep weariness, and in the darkest corners, there was a cold, living fear. Washen could almost see the fear staring out at her with its dim red eyes.

She couldn't help herself. 'Ask Till about the Builders,' she insisted. 'Ask what he believes.'

'I won't.'

'Why not?'

The woman took a moment, vainly picking at the barbed spores and winged seeds that were trying to root in her sweat-dampened uniform. Then with a cutting logic, she said, 'If your story is a lie, he will say it's a lie. And if it's true and he lies, then he'll just say that I shouldn't believe you.'

'But what if he admits to it?'

'Then Till wants me to know.' She stared at Washen as if she were the worst kind of fool. Her hands had stopped picking at the seeds, and her voice was angry and sturdy and perfectly cold. 'If he confesses, then he wants me to find out, Washen. Darling. And you're just serving as his messenger.'

Washen took a breath and held it tight.

Then Miocene looked through her open door, out into the public round, adding, 'And that isn't a revelation that I want delivered at his convenience.'

THERE HAD BEEN warnings.

A rising chorus of tremors were noted. Little spore storms reminded the captains of blizzards on cold worlds.

The discharge from half a dozen hot springs changed color, a vivid and toxic blueness spreading into the local streams. And a single Hazz tree had wilted, pulling its well-earned fat and water deep underground.

But as warnings went, they were small, and the highest-ranking captains were too distracted to pay attention.

Three ship-days later, while the encampment slept, a great hand lifted the land several meters, then grew bored and flung it down again. Captains and children stumbled into the public rounds. Within moments, the sky was choked with golden balloons and billions of flying insects. Experience said that in another twelve hours, perhaps less, the land would blister and explode, and die. Moving like a drunken woman, Washen began running through the aftershocks, moving from one round to its neighbor, finally reaching a certain tidy home and shouting, 'Locke,' into its empty rooms.

Where was he?

She moved along the edge of the round, finding nothing but empty houses. A tall figure stepped from Till's tiny house and asked, 'Have you seen mine?'

Washen shook her head. 'Mine?'

Miocene said, 'No,' and sighed. Then she strode past Washen, shouting, 'Do you know where he is?'

Diu was standing in the center of the round.

'Help me,' the Submaster promised, 'and you'll help your son, too.'

With a nod and quick bow, Diu agreed.

A dozen captains rushed off into the jungle. Left behind, Washen forced herself to pack their household's essentials and help other worried parents. New quakes came in threes and fours. Hours passed in a well-rehearsed chaos. The crust beneath them had been shattered, fissures breaking up the rounds and a worrisome heat percolating to the surface. The gold balloons had vanished, replaced with clouds of iron dust and the fat-blackened stink of burning jungle. The captains and youngest children stood in the main round, waiting nervously. Sleds and balloon carts had been loaded, but the ranking Submaster, giddy old Daen, wouldn't give the order to leave. 'Another minute,' he kept telling them. Then he would carefully hide his crude clock inside his largest pocket, fighting the urge to watch the relentless turning of its tiny mechanical hands.

When Till stepped into the open, he was grinning.

Washen felt a giddy, incoherent relief.

Relief collapsed into shock, and terror. The young man's chest cavity had been wrenched open with a knife, the first wound healing but a second wound deeper, lying perpendicular to the first. Ripped, desiccated flesh fought to knit itself. Shockingly white ribs lay in plain view. Till wasn't in mortal danger, but he wore his agony well. With an artful moan, he stumbled, then managed to right himself for an instant before collapsing, slamming against the bare iron just as his mother emerged from the black jungle.

Miocene was unhurt, and she was thoroughly, hopelessly trapped.

Numbed and sickened, Washen watched as the Submaster knelt beside her boy, gripping his thick brown hair with one hand while the other hand carefully slipped her blood-drenched knife back into its steel hilt.

What had Till said to her in the jungle?

How had he steered his mother into this murderous rage?

Because that's what he must have done. As each event happened in turn, Washen realized this was no accident. There was an elaborate plan reaching back to the instant when Locke told her about the secret meetings. Her son had promised to take her and Diu to one of the meetings.

But whom had he promised? Till, obviously. Till had conscripted Locke into joining this game, ensuring that Miocene would eventually learn of the meetings, her authority suddenly in question. And it was Till who lay in his mother's arms, knowing exactly what would happen next.

Miocene stared at her son, searching for some trace of apology, some faltering of courage. Or perhaps she was simply giving him a moment to contemplate her own gaze, relentless and cold.

Then she let go of him, and she picked up a fat wedge of dirty black iron – the quakes had left the round littered with them – and with a calm fury, she rolled Till onto his stomach and shattered the vertebrae in his neck, then swung harder, blood and shredded flesh flying, his head nearly chopped free of his paralyzed body.

Washen grabbed an arm, and yanked.

Captains leaped on Miocene, dragging her away from her son.

'Let me go,' she demanded.

A few backed away, but not Washen.

Then Miocene dropped the lump of bloody iron and raised both arms, shouting, 'If you want to help him, help him. But if you do, you don't belong with us. That's my decree. According to the powers of rank, my office, and my mood . . . !'

Locke had just emerged from the jungle.

He was first to reach Till, but barely. Children were pouring out from the shadows, already in a helpful spring, and even a few of those who hadn't vanished in the first place now joined ranks with them. In a blink, more than two thirds of the captains' offspring had gathered around the limp, helpless figure. Sober faces were full of concern and resolve. A stretcher was found, and their leader was made comfortable. Someone asked which direction the captains would move. Daen stared at the sky, watching a dirty cloud of smoke drifting in from the west. 'South,' he barked. 'We'll go south.' Then with few possessions and no food, the wayward children began to file away, conspicuously marching toward the north.

Diu was standing next to Washen.

'We can't just let them get away,' he whispered. 'Someone needs to stay with them. To talk to them, and listen. And help them, somehow . . .'

She glanced at her lover, her mouth open.

'I'll go,' she meant to say.

But Diu said, 'You shouldn't, no,' before she could make any sound. 'You'd help them more by staying close to Miocene.' He had obviously thought hard on the subject, arguing, 'You have rank. You have authority here. And besides, Miocene listens to you.'

When it suited her, perhaps.

'I'll keep whispering in your ear,' Diu promised. 'Somehow.'

Washen nodded, a stubborn piece of her reminding her that all this pain and rage would pass. In a few years or decades, or maybe in a quick century, she would begin to forget how awful this day had been.

Diu kissed her, and they hugged. But Washen found herself looking over his shoulder. Locke was a familiar silhouette standing at the jungle's margins. At this distance, through the interlocking shadows, she couldn't tell if her son was facing her or if she was looking at his back. Either way, she smiled and mouthed the words, 'Be good.' Then she took a deep breath and told Diu, 'Be careful.' And she turned away, refusing to watch either man vanish into the gloom and the gathering smoke.

Miocene stood alone, almost forgotten.

While the captains and the loyal children hurried south

together, making for the nearest safe ground, the Submaster remained rooted in the center of the round, speaking with a thin, dry, weepy voice.

'We're getting closer,' she declared.

'What do you mean?' Washen asked.

'Closer,' she said again. Then she looked up into the brilliant sky, arms lifting high and the hands reaching for nothing.

With a gentle touch, Washen tried to coax her.

'We have to hurry,' she cautioned. 'We should already be gone, madam.'

But Miocene picked herself up on her toes, reaching even higher, fingers straightening, eyes squinting, as she leaked a low, pained laugh.

'But not close enough,' she whimpered. 'No, not quite. Not yet. Not yet.'

Sixteen

ONE OF THE sweet problems about an exceedingly long life was what to do with your head. How do you manage, after many thousands of years, that chaotic mass of remembered facts and superfluous memories?

Just among human animals, different cultures settled on a wide range of solutions. Some believed in carefully removing the redundant and the embarrassing – a medical procedure often dressed up in considerable ceremony. Others believed in sweeping purges, more radical in nature, embracing the notion that a good pruning can free any soul. And there were even a few harsh societies where the mind was damaged intentionally and profoundly, and when it would heal again, a subtly new person would be born.

Captains believed in none of those solutions.

What was best, for their careers and for the well-being of their passengers, was a skilled, consistent mind filled with minute details. 'Forget nothing,' was their impossible ideal. Ruling any ship required mastery over detail and circumstance, and nobody could predict when her trusted mind would have to yank some vital but obscure fact out of its recesses, the captain – if she was any sort of captain – accomplishing her job with the predictable competence that everyone rightly demanded of her.

Miocene was forgetting how to be a captain.

Not in a serious or unexpected way. Time and the intensity of her new life naturally shoved aside old memories. But after more than a century on Marrow, she could feel the erosions of small, cherished talents, and she found herself worrying about her eventual return to duty, wondering if she could easily fill her old seat.

Which captains last earned the Master's award, and for what?

Past the most recent fifty winners, she wasn't certain.

What was that jellyfish species that lived in the cold ammonia-water Alpha Sea? And that robotic species that lived in special furnaces, and that at room temperature would freeze rigid? And that software species, dubbed Poltergeists for its juvenile sense of humor . . . where did it come from originally?

Little details, but to millions of souls, utterly vital.

There was a human population in the Smoke Canyons . . . antitechnologest who went by the name of . . . what . . . ? And they were founded by whom . . . ? And how did they accept living entirely dependent upon the greatest machine ever built . . . ?

Five course adjustments should have been made in the last hundred-plus years – all previously scheduled, all minor. But even though the ship's course was laid out with a delicate precision, stretching ahead for twenty millennia, Miocene could bring to mind only the largest of the burns.

Little more than an informed passenger, she was.

Of course plenty will have changed before she returned. Ranks and faces, and honors, and perhaps even the ship's exact course . . . all were subject to contingencies and hard practicalities, and every important decision, as well as the trivial ones, were being made without Miocene's smallest touch . . .

Or perhaps, no decisions were being made.

She had heard the whispered speculations. The Event had purged the ship of all life, leaving it as a derelict again. That explained the lack of any rescue mission. The Master and crew and that myriad of ill-matched passengers had evaporated in a terrible instant, every apartment and great hallway left sterile and pure. And if there was a local species that was brave enough or foolish enough to board the ship today, it would probably take aeons for them to find their way down to this horrible wasteland.

Why was that such an appealing image?

Because it did appeal to Miocene, particularly in her blackest moments.

After Till and the other Waywards abandoned her, she found the possibility comforting: total carnage. Billions dead. And what was her own tragedy but a small thing? A sad detail in the ship's great history. And since it was only a detail, there was the credible, intoxicating hope that she could forget the horrible things that her son had said to her, and how he had forced her to banish him, and she would eventually stop having these poisonous moments when her busy, cluttered mind was suddenly thinking of him.

MIOCENE'S DIARY BEGAN as an experiment, an exercise that she gave little hope. At the arbitrary end of each day, sitting alone in the shuttered darkness of her present house, she would fill the long stiff tail of a tasserbug with fresh ink, then using her smallest legible print, she would record the day's important events.

It was an ancient, largely discredited trick.

As a means of enhancing memory and recording history, the written word had been supplanted by digitals and memochips. But like everything else in her immediate life, this technology had been resurrected, if only for this little while.

'I hate this place.'

Those were her first words and among her most honest.

Then to underscore her consuming hatred, she had listed the captains who were killed by Marrow, and the horrible causes of death, filling the rough bone-colored paper with livid details, then folding each sheet and slipping it inside an asbestos pouch that she would carry with her when this house and settlement were abandoned.

The experiment gradually became a discipline.

Discipline bled into a sense of duty, and after ten years of fulfilling her duty, without fail, Miocene realized that she truly enjoyed this writing business. She could tell the page whatever she wished, and the page never complained or showed doubt. Even the slow, meticulous chore of drawing each letter had a charm and a certain pleasure. Each evening, she began with the day's births and deaths. The former outnumbered the latter by a fat margin. Many of her captains were having new children, and their oldest offspring – the rare ones who had proved loving and loyal

– were throwing themselves into their own brave spawning. Marrow was a hard world, but productive, and its humans had become determined and prolific. Births outnumbered deaths by twentyfold, and the gap was only growing. It was the rare captain who didn't offer eggs or sperm to the effort. Of course if there was a shortfall, Miocene would have commanded total compliance. Even quotas. But that wasn't a necessary sacrifice, thankfully. And more to the point, that freedom allowed Miocene to be one of the captains who chose not to offer up another son or daughter to this demographic tidal wave.

Once was ample; more than ample, frankly.

Another captain scarred by her experience was Washen. At least that was Miocene's assumption. Both had sons running with the Waywards. Both knew the dangers inherent in giving birth to another soul. This was why humans so often embraced immortality, Miocene had decided. They wanted to keep responsibility for the future where it belonged, with finished souls who were proven and trustworthy.

'That's not my excuse,' Washen had replied, anger framed with a careful half-smile.

Quietly, firmly, Miocene had repeated that inappropriate word. 'Excuse?' she said. 'Excuse?' Then she shook her head and took a sip of scalding tea, asking, 'What exactly do you mean by "excuse"?'

It had been an unusual evening. Washen happened by, and on a whim, the Submaster asked the woman to join her. Sitting on low stools outside Miocene's house, they watched the nearly naked children, full grown and otherwise, moving about the public round. A low canopy of fabric and interwoven sticks supplied shade. But there were holes and gashes left by gnawing insects, little places where the skylight fell through. That light had barely diminished in the last one hundred and eighty years. It was still bright and fiercely hot, and on occasions, useful. The Submaster had set a parabolic steel bowl beneath one hole, focusing the raw energies on a battered, much-traveled teapot. The rainwater was coming to a fresh boil, and for her guest, Miocene used a rag, preparing a big mug of tea. Washen accepted the gift with a nod, remarking, 'I already have a son.'

Miocene didn't say what she thought first. Or what she thought next. Instead, she simply replied, 'You do. Yes.'

'If I find a good father, I'll have another one or two.'

Washen had difficulty picking lovers. Diu was a traitor. How else to describe him? But he was a useful traitor, finding ways to feed them information on the Waywards activities' and whereabouts.

Washen said, 'Mass-producing offspring . . . I just don't believe that's best . . .'

Miocene nodded, telling her, 'I agree.'

'And I find myself . . .' She hesitated, a smooth political sensibility causing her to shape her next words with care.

'What?' the Submaster prodded.

'The morality of it. Having children, and so many of them, too.'

'What do you mean, darling?'

The gift tea was sipped, swallowed. Then Washen seemed to decide that she didn't care what Miocene thought of her. 'It's a cynical calculation, making these kids. They aren't here because of love—'

'We don't love them?' Miocene's heart quickened, for just a moment.

'We do, of course. Absolutely. But their parents were motivated by simple pragmatic logics. First, and always. Children offer hands and minds that we can shape, we hope, and those same hands and minds are going to build the next bridge.'

'According to Aasleen's plans,' Miocene added.

'Naturally, madam.'

'And aren't those very important reasons?'

'We tell ourselves they are.' Marrow had changed Washen's face. The flesh was still smooth and healthy, but her diet and the constant UV-enriched light had changed her complexion, her skin now a brownish-gray. Like smoke, really. And more than her flesh, her eyes were different. Always smart, they looked stronger now. More certain. And the mind behind them seemed more willing than ever to put a voice to its private thoughts.

'Shouldn't we try to escape?' Miocene pressed.

'But what happens afterward?' the captain countered. 'We need so many bodies in the next forty-eight hundred years. If we're going to have the industrial capacity that Aasleen envisions, and assuming that Marrow continues to expand, of course. Assuming. Then we're back home again, and let's imagine that we're heroes, and so on . . . but what happens to this raw little nation-state that we've spawned . . . ?'

'Not everything needs to be decided now,' Miocene replied.

'Which is the worst problem, I think.'

'Excuse me?'

'Madam,' said the captain. 'In the end, it's not our place to decide. It's our childrens' and grandchildrens' future.'

Suddenly, Miocene wished it was time for bed. Then she could excuse herself without losing face, and in her private darkness, she could replicate the day in her diary. A few lines of tiny script were enough. The paper was as thin as technically possible today, but as the years mounted, it was becoming increasingly difficult to carry the burgeoning history.

'Our ship,' said the Submaster, 'has embraced every sort of passenger. An odd alien is more demanding than our children can ever be.'

Silence.

Miocene smoothed her uniform. It was a cool white fabric, porous to their fragrant, endless sweat, and sewn through it were threads of pure silver meant to symbolize the mirrored uniforms of the past. Out on the public round and everywhere else, the children wore nothing but breech-cloths and brief skirts and tiny vests. Miocene long ago accepted their near nudity, if only because it allowed the ancient captains, dressed in their noble garb, to stand apart.

Bored with waiting, she asked her companion, 'What bothers you, darling?'

'These children,' said Washen.

'Yes?'

'As if they're the only ones.'

'You mean the Waywards.' Miocene nodded and laughed, and she made a show of finishing her own tea. Then she told the first-grade, 'I just assumed they'd want to remain here, where they're happiest. On Marrow, and we could lock them in here. Nice and tight.'

A NEW CATAGORY had eased its way into the Submaster's scrupuously accurate tally of gains and losses. There were the born, of course, and the dead. And now, in small but swelling numbers, there were the missing.

It was presumed, with reason, that these new casualties were slinking away, taking nothing but the provisions and light tools suitable for a good march. If rumor and physical evidence could be believed, the nearest Waywards were a thousand kilometers past the horizon. It was a daunting journey to any reasonable soul, but Miocene could almost believe that children – the most susceptible to go missing – might convince themselves that here was a worthy challenge, an undertaking sure to answer some vague need or a trivial absence in their very brief lives. She could even picture their reasons. Boredom. Curiosity. Political ideas, sloppy or muscular. Or perhaps they didn't see advancement for themselves here, inside the Loyalist camp. They were slow, lazy, or difficult people, and maybe the Waywards would be less demanding. Unlikely, but that's what the missing must have told themselves. And off they marched, singly and in little groups, blissfully counting on youth and good fortune to bring them to their just rewards.

Some died en route.

Alone, in nameless and temporary valleys, they were swallowed by the flowing iron, or flash-baked in a burst of fiery gases.

Miocene's first instinct had been to dispatch search parties, then punish the children for their treachery. But more charitable voices, including her own, cautioned against rough measures. Who mattered were those who remained behind, the willing and the genuinely far-sighted ones.

Each night, placing her daily entry into its asbestos envelope, then into the asbestos trunk, Miocene rewarded herself with small congratulations. Another day accomplished; another centimeter closer to their ultimate goal. Then she would sit on her little bed, typically alone, and because she often forgot to eat during the arbitrary heart of the day, she would force down a slice of heavily spiced fat. She made herself feed a body that rarely felt hunger anymore, but that needed calories and rest, and at least she was able to give it the former. Then Miocene would lie in the imperfect night, typically on her back, and sometimes she would sleep, and dream, and sometimes she just stared up into the contrived darkness, forcing herself to remain motionless for a full three hours, her mind working with a dreamy vagueness, planning the next day, and the next week, and the five thousand years to come.

THE FIVE HUNDREDTH was a ripe moment for grand gestures.

A year-long observance of their lives on Marrow culminated in a week-long celebration, and the celebration peaked with a lavish parade around the Grand Round of Hazz City. Half of the world's Loyalists were in attendance. Painted bodies marched, friends and family locking arms, or they stood in the Round's tent-shrouded center, or they watched the parade from one of the fifty wood and plastic buildings that rimmed the neat outside edge of the public area. Fifty thousand happy, well-fed souls were present, and each one of them looked up as Miocene stepped to the podium, glancing at the clock in one hand as the other hand lifted, a long thin finger dropping as a signal, her strong voice announcing:

'Five hundred years.'

Magnified and projected from cumbersome speakers, her voice seemed to boom across the city and the world.

There was a great cheer, sloppy and full throated, and honest.

'Five centuries,' she repeated, her voice louder than the crowd's. Then Miocene asked the nation, 'Where are we now?'

A few jokes were muttered.

'Where we always are!' someone called out.

A thin trickle of laughter diminished into a respectful, impatient silence.

'We are climbing,' the Submaster declared. 'Constantly, endlessly climbing. At this moment, we are being lifted skyward at the graceful, glorious rate of a quarter of a meter to the year. We are building new machines and new citizens, and despite the hardships that the world throws at us daily, we are prospering. But what is more important, by a thousandfold, is that you remember what we are climbing toward. This world of ours is only a small place. It is like a hammerwing larva nestled inside its large and infinitely more impressive cocoon.

'We are in the center of a starship. A great vessel, complex and vast. This starship is racing through a universe that you have never seen. About which you know next to nothing. A universe of such scope and beauty that when you see it, I promise, all of you won't be able to hold back your tears.'

She paused, just for an instant.

'I promise. All of you will see this great universe.

'For the willing and the loyal, your rewards will be vast and glorious, and you will have no fear or want for the rest of your endless lives.'

A small cheer rose, then collapsed on itself.

'I know how hard it can be,' she told them. 'To believe in places and wonders that none of you have witnessed for yourselves. It takes a certain type of thinking. A grand, dreaming mind. It takes courage and trust, and I am so pleased with each and every one of you. For your work. Your patience. And your boundless love.'

A larger, self-congratulatory cheer blossomed, hands clapping each other and flat wet bellies before the crowd slowly let itself grow quiet again.

'We old captains thank you. Thank you!'

That was a prearranged signal. The surviving captains were sitting behind Miocene according to rank. As a body, they rose to their feet, their silvered uniforms catching the light, and after a communal bow, they sat again, staring purposefully at the back of her head.

'Your lives here have only become richer with time,' she remarked. 'We old captains brought knowledge with us, a small taste of what is possible. You see the impact of that knowledge every day, everywhere. We can now predict eruptions months in advance, and we farm the local jungles with great efficiency, and who is our equal at building new and fantastic machines? But those aren't our greatest gifts to you, our children. Our grandchildren. All of our beautiful, loving descendants.

'Our greatest gifts are charity and honor.

'Charity,' she repeated, 'and honor.'

Miocene's voice ran off into the distance, bouncing off the High Spines and returning again. Softer now, and kinder.

She smiled grandly, then said, 'This is what charity is. On my authority, today and for the next complete year, there is a full pardon in effect. A full pardon intended for any person belonging to the Wayward camps. We want to include you in our dream. Yes, the Waywards! If you are listening to me now, come forward. Come out of the wild forests! Come join us, and help us build for this great day coming!'

Again, the echoes bounced off the nearby mountains.

Surely the Waywards were hiding on those slopes, watching the great celebration. Or closer, perhaps. Rumor had it that spies crept in and out of the Loyalist cities every day. But even when she heard the thunder of her own voice, Miocene didn't believe that any Wayward would ever willingly accept her charity.

Yet only one year later, typing into the bulky and very stupid machine that passed for an AI, the Submaster could write, 'Three souls have returned to us.'

Two were Loyal-born, desperately unhappy with the hard Wayward existence. While the third convert was one of Till's grandchildren, which meant that she was one of Miocene's great-grandchildren.

Of course the Submaster had welcomed each of them. But she also made certain that the three newcomers were shadowed by special friends, and their conversations were recorded and transcribed, and nothing of technical merit, no matter how trivial, was put in easy reach.

Every night, just before her sleepless sleep, Miocene typed into the machine's simple magnetic mind, 'I hate this world.

'But,' she added with a grim satisfaction, 'I will have it by its heart, and I'll squeeze that heart until it can never beat again.'

Seventeen

A DECADE LATER, the High Spines were about to die.

Seismic evidence showed an ocean of liquid metal rising beneath them, and the local virtue trees were equally convinced. A string of hard, sharp tremors caused a panic in the jungles and up on the raw black iron, and inside Hazz City people were knocking their most cherished buildings off their foundations, preparing to carry them away, abandoning the region according to precise, exacting plans.

What the grandchildren were doing was wrong. They knew it was foolish and dangerous, and they expected to pay a stiff penalty. Yet the promise of wildfires and utter devastation – more carnage than they had ever witnessed in their little lives – was too much temptation to resist.

A dozen youngsters, the absolute best of friends, borrowed asbestos suits and boots and bright blue-painted titanium oxygen tanks, carrying those treasures to the foothills in a series of secret sleeptime marches. Then as their home city was being wrestled to safer ground, they assembled near the main round, and in order to swear eternal secrecy for what they were about to do, each cut off one of his or her little toes, the twelve bloody pieces buried in a tiny, unmarked grave.

They weren't true grandchildren. Not to the captains, at least. But they were called 'grandchildren' because that was the tradition. Girls and boys anywhere from tenth- to twentieth-generation Loyalists marched together toward the High Spines, in a neat double row, and pushing through the first traces of smoke and caustic vapor, they told some of the traditional jokes about the ancient ones.

'How many captains does it take to get off Marrow?' one boy asked.

'None,' his girlfriend chimed. 'We do all the work for them!'

'How big is this ship we ride inside?'

'It gets bigger every day,' another girl offered. 'At least in the captains' minds!'

Everyone had a good little laugh.

Then another boy asked, 'What is happier than our leader?'

'A daggerwing on a dinner spit!' several of his friends shouted, on cue.

'Why is that?' he inquired.

'Because the bug is going to die soon, while our leader just keeps turning on her spit, feeling the flames!'

Miocene's dark moods were famous. Indeed, they were a source of great fondness among the average grandchild. Looking at that very tall woman, you actually saw the gloom in those dark ageless eyes, and it was easy to believe her desperate need to leave Marrow, returning to that wondrous and most peculiar place called 'the ship.'

On Marrow, a cheery, optimistic leader would never inspire. No one else could deserve the kind of support and ceaseless work that the Loyalists gave freely and almost without question.

At least in this little group, that was everyone's definite opinion.

As their march continued, the laughter grew louder and more nervous. These were city children, after all. They knew the jungle well enough, but this district had been tectonically quiet for most of their lives. The snapping fires and swirling black ash were new to them. In secret, each girl and boy realized that they'd never imagined such a persistent, withering heat. Sometimes they'd burn a hand intentionally, taking what comfort they could from the quick healing of their wounds. Passing too near a little fumarole, half of them scorched the insides of their mouths and cooked their lungs, and coughing hard, they had to huddle beneath a massive baybay tree, slashing its bark to let the cool sap seep out and soothe their aches.

In secret, it occurred to each of them that they would die today. But none could find the simple courage to admit what they were thinking, and each heard herself or himself coaxing the others to hurry, squinting into the black clouds, lying when they claimed, 'I can see the mountains.'

Saying, 'It isn't far now, I think.'

I hope.

Using a homing beacon, they found their firesuits and air tanks. Without that simple precaution, they would have stumbled past the cache, the landscape already transformed by the wildfires.

Everyone dressed, not one of the suits fitting properly.

But who cared if there were gaps in the seams, and the brutal heat was leaking inside too quickly? They were brave, and they were hopelessly together in this undertaking, and as if Marrow were trying to entertain them, a sudden vent opened up nearby, letting a deep plume of molten red-hot metal slip a finger out into the open air, under pressure, hot enough to make unshielded eyes blink, running like a river down the floor of the doomed valley.

'Closer,' the children screamed at each other. 'Get closer.'

They didn't bother with safety lines or lifeguards. What mattered was to get near the shoreline, watching the blazing iron push downhill, feeling its enormous, irresistible weight through your sweating toes.

Like a living monster, it was.

And like all good monsters, it possessed a surprising, intriguing beauty.

With a massive grace, the river melted the ground beneath it. Ancient tree trunks evaporated in its presence. Chunks of cold iron were tossed into the river, sinking where it was deep. Larger knobs and boulders of iron resisted the flow for an instant or two, then were shoved downstream with a plaintive screeching scream.

One boy crept up behind a spellbound girl – the subject of a little crush – and with both hands, he gave her a hard little shove.

Then he grabbed her.

She howled and jabbed him with both elbows, then tried to turn around. But she was clumsy in that heavy misfitting suit, one boot slipping and her body yanked free of the fond grip, tumbling back toward the molten metal until she grabbed the boy's belt, yanking him hard toward her.

For an instant, they hung in the incandescent air.

Then they fell slowly and clumsily onto the cooler

ground, laughing in each other's arms, the simple raw danger of the moment leaving them in love.

While the other children played by the river, they slipped away.

On a burnt hillside, wearing nothing but the thick-soled boots, they made love. He was behind her, holding her against him by her hips, then her hard little breasts. They didn't dare sit; the ground was far too hot. There were moments when the fumes rose and found them, and they would suck at the bottled air, or they would hold their breath, feeling a quick dizzyness that became a warm electric buzz as their physiologies coped with the lack of oxygen.

Eventually, the game lost its intoxicating charm.

The urgency had left them. Little regrets started to nag. To obscure their feelings, they talked about the grandest imaginable things. The girl pulled up her insulated trousers, asking, 'Where are you going to live afterward?'

When we reach the ship, she meant.

'By that big sea,' the boy replied. 'The one where the captains first lived.'

It was a common response. Everyone knew about the great bodies of water, the illusion of an endless blue sky suspended overhead. The most artistic captains had done paintings, and without exception, the grandchildren were in awe of the idea that there could be so much water, and it would be so clean, and that living inside it would be great creatures like those mythical whales and squid and tuna.

Running a hand across her lover's Gordian bun, the girl confessed, 'I'm going to live outside the ship.'

'On another world?'

She shook her head. 'No. I mean on the ship's hull.'

'But why?'

She wasn't entirely serious. These were words, and fun. Yet she felt a surprising conviction in her voice, explaining, 'There are people who live out there. Remoras, I think they're called.'

'I've never heard of them,' the boy admitted.

So she explained the culture. She told how the Remoras lived inside elaborate suits, eating and drinking nothing but what their suits and bodies produced. Worlds unto themselves, they were. And wherever they were on the ship's hull, half of the universe was overhead. Near enough to reach, beautiful beyond words.

She was a strange girl, the boy concluded. In important little ways, he suddenly didn't like her very much. He heard himself say, 'I see,' without a shred of comprehension. Then with a forced sincerity, he promised, 'I'll come visit you there. Sometime. Okay?'

She knew that he was lying, and somehow that was a relief.

They stared off into the distance, in different directions, struggling with the shared problem of extracting themselves from this awkward place.

After a few moments, the boy gave a little cough and said, 'I see something.'

'What?'

'In the iron river. There.'

In horror, she asked, 'Is it one of us?'

'No,' he remarked. 'At least, I don't think so.'

The girl started to dress again, forgetting two seams as she struggled to get ready for a rescue attempt. When had she ever been a bigger fool, coming here like this? Unprepared, and doing *this* with this extremely ordinary boy?

'Where is it?' she called out.

With a marksman's care, he pointed upstream, and she

laid her head against his long arm, squinting now, peering through the clouds of rising fumes to find herself watching a round silvery lump, something that looked odd as can be, immune to the heat and calmly bobbing its way down the iron river.

'That's not one of us,' she said.

'I told you it wasn't,' he snapped.

Then he said something else, but she didn't hear him. She had pushed her helmet over her head and scrambled out of their hiding place, and in her heavy, ill-fitting firesuit, she was racing down the hillside, shouting and waving, begging for anyone's attention.

THEY HAD JUST enough time to unwrap a pair of new safety lines, making loops at the ends and running down to where the iron river was narrowest, flinging the loops out at the strange silvery object.

One line fell short, tangled in newborn slag and melted. But the second line fell on the silvery surface, its loop tightening around some kind of thumb-like projection. Eleven grandchildren grabbed the line, and tugged, and screamed hard in one voice, and tugged. The second line was melting in that open blast furnace, but the object was close to shore, its invisible belly rubbing against half-molten ground. Three more expensive, nearly irreplaceable lines were destroyed before they could drag their prize out of the river, and if not for a favorable eddy and the river's cutting a new channel on its north, they wouldn't have retrieved the object at all.

But they had it now, and that was something.

The prize proved to be a little larger than a big person tucked into a tight ball, and it was stubbornly massive. Moving that much mass proved to be hard work, particularly while it was still radiating the iron's heat. But later, after several kilometers of practice and the crushing of two makeshift sleds, the grandchildren learned that simply rolling their prize was easiest. Whatever the object was – and it could have been just about anything – the cold metal ground didn't seem to dent it or even smudge its mirrored face.

They were halfway home when they were discovered. A lone figure appeared on the main trail, jogging up into the shadow of a virtue tree, then standing motionless, watching as they worked their way closer.

At a distance, it was obvious that this was a captain. A woman, wasn't she? She wore a captain's clothes and a captain's disapproving face, but when everyone saw whose face it was, they gave a collective sigh of relief.

'Hello, Madam Washen!' a dozen voices called out.

With another captain, there would have been immediate miseries. But not with smart old Washen. She had a reputation for understanding what was perfectly obvious to any happy grandchild, and for knowing how to punish without killing the happiness, too.

'Having fun?' she inquired.

Of course they were. Didn't it look as if they were having fun?

'Not entirely,' the ancient woman admitted. She looked at each of their faces, saying, 'I count twelve,' with an ominous tone. Then she sighed and shook her head, asking, 'Where's Blessing Gable? Was she with you?'

'No,' they said together, with a mixture of surprise and relief. Then one of the boys explained, 'She's way too old to float with us.'

The girl who liked Remoras realized what had happened. 'Blessing has gone missing, hasn't she?'

The captain nodded.

'To the Waywards, maybe?' Blessing was a quiet girl, and

if she was too old for them, she was the perfect age for that nonsense.

'Maybe she's left us,' Washen admitted with a sad, resigned tone. Then without another word, she stepped past the grandchildren.

Their prize sat in the middle of the trail, bright despite the tree's shadows.

Someone asked, 'See what we found?'

'No,' said Washen. As a joke. Then her long fingers played across the still-warm surface, the dark old eyes staring at her own distorted reflection.

'Do you know what it is?' asked the boy who wanted to live by the sea.

Washen fingered the knobs, and instead of answering, she asked, 'What do you think it is?'

'A piece of the old bridge. The one you came down on.' The boy had given the matter some thought, and he was proud of his careful reasoning. 'After it tumbled down, the iron swallowed this piece and kept it until now. I think.'

Several others voiced their agreement. Wasn't it obvious?

The captain didn't seem to think so. She looked at the Remora girl, then with her calm and smooth and happy voice asked, 'Any other guesses?'

Someone asked, 'Is it hyperfiber?'

'I don't know what else it would be,' Washen admitted.

'But the bridge was ruined by the Event,' the Remora girl offered. 'In our history books, it says it was made brown and weak, somehow, and all its little bonds kept breaking apart. Somehow.'

Washen winked, making the girl feel important, and smart.

'And it isn't just hyperfiber,' the girl added, talking too quickly now. 'Because it's so heavy, and hyperfiber isn't. Is it?'

Washen shrugged, then said, 'Tell me how you found it. And where.'

The girl tried. And she meant to be perfectly honest, though she never mentioned sex, and the story came charging out of her mouth as if she were taking credit for everything.

Her one-time lover protested. 'I saw the stupid thing first,' he complained. 'Not you.'

'Good eyes,' Washen offered. 'Whoever was using them.'

The girl bit her own stupid, careless tongue.

'What does this look like?' asked Washen.

'A piece of the sky,' said the boy. 'Sort of, it does.'

'Except it's brighter,' another boy offered.

'And bumpy,' another girl offered.

With the salty taste of blood in her mouth, the Remora girl observed, 'It's sort of like a tiny, tiny version of the Great Ship. Those knobs are the rocket nozzles, see? Except they aren't really big enough. Not like the nozzles in the paintings.'

'But there is a resemblance,' Washen conceded. Then she stood and wiped her hand on the leg of her uniform, and looking off toward the doomed High Spines, she said, 'Honestly.' Her voice was gentle. 'I don't know what this is.'

Eighteen

FOR THE NEXT one hundred and eight years, the artifact lay in storage, wrapped within a clean purple woolbark blanket and tucked inside a steel vault designed to hold nothing else. Aasleen and her engineers had been given the fun of divining its secrets. But at least one Submaster had to be present whenever studies were undertaken, and if the artifact was to be moved, as it was during two eruption cycles, a Submaster as well as a platoon of picked and utterly trustworthy guards accompanied the relic, weapons politely kept out of sight but a palpable air of suspicion obvious to all.

For many reasons, that century was dubbed The Flowering.

There were finally enough grandchildren, mature and educated and inspired, that something resembling an industrialized nation was possible. A lacework of good smooth roads was built between the cities and largest villages, then rebuilt after each eruption. More important were the crude smear-signal transmitters, hung high on mountain peaks and steel poles, that network allowing anyone to speak with anyone within a thousand-kilometer zone. Clumsy carbide drills gnawed through the crust, reaching the molten iron, then simple-as-can-be geothermal plants were erected, supplying what seemed to be a wealth of power to the labs and factories and increasingly luxurious homes. Life on Marrow remained a hard, crude business. But that wasn't what the captains said in public. In front of the grandchildren, they mustered up every imaginable praise for the new biogas toilets and the cultured bug-based meats and the frail, fixed-wing aircraft that could, if blessed with good weather, crawl all up into the cold upper reaches of the atmosphere. They weren't trying to mislead so much as encourage. And really, they were the ones who needed most of the encouragement. Life here might not match the serene pleasures found inside the ship, but to a youngster barely five centuries old, it was obvious that his world had grown more comfortable in his lifetime, and more predictable, and if he could have known about the captains' real disappointments, he would have felt nothing but a pitying, even fearful puzzlement.

The Flowering culminated with a clumsy but muscular laser, designed from Aasleen's recollections and adapted to local resources, then helped along with her staff's countless inspirations and other making-dos.

Hundreds attended the first full-strength firing of the laser.

The artifact was its target. The hyperfiber shell was presumably ancient, but it had to be a premium grade. To slice a hair-wide hole through the shell meant an enforced blackout, the power from some fifty-odd geothermal plants fed directly into Aasleen's newest laboratory, into a long cramped room built for this precise moment, a series of microsecond pulses delivered in what sounded like a monster's roar, lending drama to the moment as well as jarring quite a few nerves.

Miocene sat in the control room, hands tied together in a tense lump.

'Stop!' she heard Aasleen bark. Finally.

The laser was put to bed. Then an optical cable was inserted into the fresh hole, and the engineer peered inside, saying nothing, forgetting about her audience until Miocene asked, 'Is there anything?'

'Vault,' Aasleen reported.

Did she want the artifact set back into its vault?

But before anyone could ask, she added, 'It looks a lot like a memory vault. Not human-made, but not all that strange, either.'

With an impatient nod, Miocene said, 'What else?'

'A standard bioceramic matrix, with some kind of holoprojector. And a dense ballast at the center.' Aasleen looked in the general direction of her audience, blind to everything but her own quick thoughts. 'No power cells, from what I can tell. But what good would they be after a few billion years? Even the Builders couldn't make a battery that would ignore this kind of long-term heat . . .'

'But does this vault still work?' Miocene growled.

'Too soon to tell,' Aasleen replied. 'I've got to peel back the shell and feed power to the systems . . . which will mean . . . hey, what's the date . . . ?'

Twenty voices told her. Counting from the first day of the mission, up in the leech habitat, the date was 619.23.

'Working at night, making one cut at a time . . . and of course I'll have to refurbish the laser once every week or so . . . so maybe by 621 or 621.5. Maybe . . . ?'

The Submasters were openly disappointed.

Miocene spoke for them, asking, 'Is there any way to speed up this process?'

'Absolutely,' Aasleen responded. 'Take me back upstairs, and I can do everything in three minutes. At the most.'

'Upstairs' was the latest term for the ship. Informal, and by implication, a place that was relatively close by.

Miocene was disgusted, and happy to show her feelings. She shook her head and rose to her feet. Half a hundred of the captains' children and grandchildren were in attendance. After all, this was their mystery, too. Facing them, she asked the engineer, 'What are the odds that this memory vault remembers anything at all?'

'After being immersed in liquid iron for several billion years . . . ?'

'Yes.'

Aasleen chewed on her lower lip for a thoughtful moment, then said, 'Next to none. Madam.'

Disappointment hung in the air, thick and bitter.

'But that's assuming that the bioceramics are the same as the grades seen before, of course. Which might be unlikely, since the Builders always seemed to know just how good their machines needed to be.'

Disappointment wrestled with a sudden hope.

'Whoever they were,' Aasleen reported, 'the Builders were great engineers.'

'Undoubtedly,' Miocene purred.

'Begging to differ,' someone muttered. Who? Washen?

Miocene gave her a quick glance and a crisp, 'And why not, darling?'

'I've never known an engineer, great or lousy, who didn't leave behind at least one plaque with her name on it.'

When Aasleen laughed, almost everyone began to laugh with her.

Giggling, nodding her happy face, the engineer admitted, 'That's the truth. That's exactly how we are!'

MAYBE THE BUILDERS were clever and rich with foresight, but the artifact — the ancient memory vault — was found empty of anything other than a few shredded, incoherent images. Shades of gray laid over a wealth of blackness.

The sorry news was delivered by one of Aasleen's genuine grandsons.

It was five days before the year 621 began. The speaker, named Pepsin, was a stocky, vivacious man with an easy smile and blue-black skin and a habit of talking too quickly to be understood. As evidence mounted that nothing of consequence waited in the vault, Pepsin had inherited the project from his famous grandmother. And like the good descendant of any good captain, he had taken this dead-end project and made it his own, carefully and thoroughly wringing from it everything that was important.

A small group of disappointed captains and Submasters were in attendance. No one else. Miocene herself sat in the back, reviewing administrative papers, barely noticing when that fast, fast voice announced, 'But information comes in many delicate flavors.'

What was that?

Pepsin grinned and said, 'The hyperfiber shell degraded over time. Which gives us clues about its entombment.'

Washen was sitting in the front. She noticed that Miocene wasn't paying attention, which was why she took it upon herself to ask, 'What do you mean?'

'Madam,' he replied, 'I mean what I say.'

Sarcasm caused the Submaster to lift her head. 'But I didn't hear you,' she growled. 'And this time, darling, talk slowly and look only at me.'

The young engineer blinked and licked his lips, then explained. 'Even the best hyperfiber ages, if stressed. As I'm sure you know, madam. By examining cross sections of the vault's shell, at the microscopic level, we can read a crude history not only of the vault, but of the world that embraced it, too.'

'Marrow,' the old woman growled.

Again, he blinked. Then with a graceless cleverness, added, 'Presumably, madam. Presumably.'

With her quietest voice, Miocene advised, 'Maybe you should proceed.'

Pepsin nodded, obeyed.

'The hyperfiber has spent the last several billion years bobbing inside liquid iron. As expected. But if there were no breaks in that routine, the degradation should be worse than observed. Fifty to ninety percent worse, according to my honorable grandmother.' A glance at Aasleen; no more. 'Hyperfiber has a great capacity to heal itself. But the bonds don't knit themselves quite as effectively at several thousand degrees Kelvin. No, what's best is chilly weather under a thousand degrees. Deep space is the very best. Otherwise, the hyperfiber scars, and it scars in distinct patterns. And what I see in the microscope, and what everyone else here sees . . . measuring the scars, we have evidence of approximately five to fifteen hundred thousand distinct periods of high heat. Presumably, each of those periods marks time spent in Marrow's deep interior—'

'Five to fifteen billion years,' Miocene interrupted. 'Is that your estimate?'

'Basically. Yes, madam.' He licked his lips, and blinked, and conjured up a wide contented smile. 'Of course we can't assume that the vault was always thrown to the surface, and there surely have been periods when it was submerged several times during a single cycle.' Again, the lips needed moisture. 'In different words, this is a lousy clock. But being a clock whose hands have moved, it points to what we have always assumed. For my entire little life, and this last brief chapter in your great lives . . .'

'Just say it,' Aasleen snarled at her grandson.

'Marrow expands and contracts. Again, we have evidence.' He grinned at everyone, at no one. Then he added, 'Why this should be, I don't know. And how it does this trick is difficult for me to conceive.'

Miocene couldn't leave those mysterious words floating free.

With a quiet certainty, she said, 'Our standard model is that the buttressing fields squeeze Marrow down, then relax. And when they relax, the world expands.'

'Until when?' asked Pepsin. 'Until it fills the chamber?'

'We shall see,' the Submaster conceded.

'And what about the buttresses?' he persisted. Foolish, or brave, or simply intrigued, he had to ask the great woman, 'What powers them?'

It was an old, always baffling question. But Miocene employed the oldest, easiest answer. 'Hidden reactors of some unknown type. In the chamber walls, or beneath our feet. Or perhaps in both places.'

'And why go through these elaborate cycles, madam? I mean, if I was the chief engineer, and I needed to keep Marrow firmly in place, I don't think I'd ever allow my fancy buttresses to fall halfway asleep. Would you, madam? Would you let them fall partway asleep every ten thousand years?'

'You don't understand the buttresses,' Miocene replied. 'You admitted it just a few breaths ago. Nobody knows how they refuel themselves, or regenerate, or whatever is happening. These mysteries have worked hard to remain mysteries, and we should give them our well-deserved respect.'

Pepsin hugged himself, nodding as if the words carried a genuine weight. But the eyes betrayed distance, then a revelation. Suddenly they grew wide, and darker somehow, and with an embarrassed grin, he said, 'You've already had this debate with my grandmother. Haven't you?'

'A few times,' the Submaster conceded.

'And does Aasleen ever win?' the young man inquired.

Miocene waited an instant, then told Pepsin, and everyone, 'She always wins. In the end, I always admit that we haven't any answers, and her questions are smart and valid and vast. And sadly, they are also quite useless to us here.

'A waste of breath, even.'

Then Miocene pulled a new piece of paper to the top of the pile, and dipping her head, she added, 'Get us home, darling. That's all that matters. Then I will personally give you the keys to a first-class laboratory, and you can ask all these great questions that seem to be keeping you awake nights.'

A QUIET LITTLE party followed Pepsin's announcement. Talk centered more on new gossip than grand speculations:

who was sleeping with whom, and who was pregnant, and which youngsters had slipped away to the Waywards. Washen quickly lost interest. Claiming fatigue, she escaped, walking past the security stations, and alone, walking home to the newest Hazz City.

A rugged metropolis of eighteen thousand, the Loyalist capital lay in the bottom of a wide, flat, and well-watered rift valley. Every home was sturdy but ready to be abandoned. Every government building was just large enough to impress, bolted to its temporary foundation of bright stainless steel. With the late hour, the streets were nearly empty. Thunderheads were piled high in the western sky, stealing heat from a dying lava flow; but the winds seemed to be shoving the storms elsewhere, making the city feel like a quiet, half-abandoned place being bypassed by the world's great events.

Washen's house looked out over a secondary round. It was smaller than its neighbors, and in the details, was a duplicate of her last five houses. Blowing fans kept the air fresh and halfway cool. With shutters closed, a nightlike gloom took hold, and Washen allowed herself the wasteful pleasure of a small electric lamp burning above her favorite chair.

She was in the middle of a report projecting coming demands for laboratory-grade glassware. The utterly routine work made her fatigue real. Suddenly it seemed ridiculous to look three centuries into the future, or even three minutes, and Washen responded by yawning, closing her eyes, then dipping into a hard, dreamless sleep.

Then she was awake again.

Awake and confused, she reached for the mechanical clock dangling from her belt on a titanium chain. The clock was a gift from various grandchildren. They had assembled it themselves, using resurrected technologies and patient hands. The overhead lamp still burned, and the wasted energy flowed over the delicately embossed casing, its bright silver mixed with enough gunk to lend it strength. She opened the round case and stared at the numbers. At the slowly turning hands. This was the middle of the night, and she sleepily realized that what had awakened her was a slow, strong pounding against her front door.

Washen turned off the lamp, rose and opened the door. The harsh glare of the sky flowed over her. She blinked, aware of two figures waiting for her, wearing nothing but the light. Then her eyes adapted, weakening enough for her to see two welcome faces.

In the middle of the night, apparently unnoticed, Washen's son and his father had strolled into the heart of the city.

DIU OFFERED A wry grin.

He looked the same as always . . . except for the breechcloth and a leanness that ended with his strong thick legs. And his skin had the smoky tint that Marrow gave everyone. His scalp was shaved free of every hair. And after years of hard wandering, his feet had been pounded into wider, flatter versions of their old selves.

Locke spoke first. He said, 'Mother,' as if the word had been thoroughly practiced. Then he added, 'We've brought meat. Several tons, dried and sweetened. We'll give it to you, if you'll give us the vault.'

The Waywards knew everything, it was said. And with good reason.

Instantly, without blinking, Washen told them, 'The vault's empty. And pretty much useless, too.' Then she saw the other Waywards, several dozen of them, and the crude wooden sleds each of them had pulled, pack-animal fashion, each sled loaded high with bales of blackish and reddish carcasses.

Diu smiled with his mouth and his quick eyes, conceding, 'We know it's empty.'

'We.' In the past, on those rare occasions when they had spoken, Diu had always referred to the Waywards as 'they' or 'them.'

Washen jumped to her next rebuttal.

'It's not my decision to give the vault to you. Or anyone else, for that matter.'

'Of course not,' he agreed. 'But you're the one who can wake up those who'll make that decision.'

Which was what she did. The four surviving Submasters were roused out of their three beds, and with Miocene presiding, the meats were inspected and the Wayward offer was debated in whispers. There had been a shortfall of good protein lately. For all of its stampeding success, the Flowering meant machines and energy. Not new farms or fresh efficiencies in cultivation. Which the Waywards must have known, too.

Standing on the hot black round, Washen wondered when her son and Diu had started this trek. The nearest Wayward camp was at least six hundred kilometers from here, and they couldn't have used the local roads without being noticed and intercepted. Pulling sleds over sharp ridges and through the jungles . . . they were obviously determined, and fantastically patient, and cocksure about how things would end . . .

Miocene approached Washen, and with the other Submasters, they rejoined their guests.

'Agreed,' said Miocene grudgingly.

Locke grinned for a moment. Then with an easy politeness, he said, 'Thank you, madam.'

Unlike his father, Locke hadn't shaved his scalp; his

golden hair was long and simply braided. In a world without cattle or horses, Waywards used their own bodies as resources, for work and for raw materials. Her son's belt was a tightly braided length of old hair. His breechcloth was a thin soft leather stained white by sweat salts. A knife and a flintlock pistol rode on his hips, and both handles had the whiteness of cherished bone, carefully carved from leg bones lost — she prayed — in violent accidents.

Again Locke said, 'Thank you, madam.'

The Submaster let her mouth drop open, a question waiting to be asked. But then she changed her mind and closed her mouth. She had decided not to mention her own son, even in passing.

Washen knew her that well.

Centuries of living close to this woman had left her easy to read. And as always, Washen felt a mixture of pity for the mother and scorn for the power-mad leader. Or was it scorn for the mother, and pity for the poor leader?

Miocene offered to press Locke's hand, signaling the end of negotiations. But something lay in his hand. It was disc-shaped and wrapped tight inside a folded green hammerwing.

He handed it to Miocene, then said, 'As a gift. Look.'

The Submaster warily unfolded the wing and stared at the gift. A disc of pure yellow sulfur lay in her palm. Like so many light elements on Marrow, sulfur was in short supply. The sight of it was enough to make Miocene blink and look up in surprise.

'What would you give us for a ton of this?' asked Locke.

Then before she could answer, he added, 'We want a laser like yours. That powerful, and with enough spare parts.'

'There isn't another one,' she replied instantly.

'But you're building three more.' He nodded with an

unimpeachable authority, then added, 'We want the first of the three. Which should be next year, if we're not mistaken.'

Because it was pointless to lie, Washen told them, 'You're not mistaken.'

Miocene just stared at the sulfur cake, probably counting the industries that would be begging for the smallest taste.

Another Submaster – nervous, worried Daen – had his face screwed up in disgust, asking their guests, 'But what do you need that kind of laser for?'

Diu laughed, a quick hand wiping the oily sweat from his scalp. Then he asked the obvious question: 'If your little group sitting on this tiny patch of planet can find one vault, by accident . . . how many more do you think *we* might be sitting on . . . ?'

Nineteen

THE CAPTAINS AND their favorite children began searching for the vaults. Every local vent and fissure was watched, first by volunteers, then by automated cameras. Inside their territory, and sometimes beyond, picked teams would inspect stretches of cold iron with the latest generation of seismographs, sonic probes, and eventually, neutron beams, each device making the crust a little more transparent, and knowable, and predictable – a mostly fruitless search for vaults, but yielding a fat wealth of information about ore deposits and quake predictions.

Occasionally, one of those search teams was sent deep

into the Wayward lands. The volunteers were armed, but typically in secret ways. They usually stumbled across a village filled with adults and young children who spoke a broken dialect of the ship-terran, and who claimed to have never seen Loyalists. The villages were spartan, haphazard in their layout, but basically clean. Their inhabitants were fit and happy, and as a rule, they acted utterly incurious about life in the burgeoning cities.

The Loyalists happily chattered about their latest technological marvels and all the comforts being added to their daily lives. The Waywards seemed to listen, but they rarely asked even simple questions or offered the smallest, most glancing praise.

The evictions were inevitable, though they were usually polite.

A local chief or president or priest – his exact station was nebulous – would shove aside a plate of half-eaten mite cake or a bowl of raw steel-worms. Then he, or she, would rise with a certain majesty, reminding their guests, 'You are very much our guests here.'

The Loyalists would nod, push aside their harsh food, and wait.

'Our guests here.' The pattern was repeated again and again, sometimes with the same words. '"Here,"' the chief would tell them, 'means the center of the universe. Which is Marrow. "Our" implies the discretion always given to rightful owners. "Guests" are always temporary. Impermanent. And when the Builders wish, we will have no choice but to exclude you from the center of the universe.'

The words were always delivered with a smile.

Then, with an easy gravity, the chief would add, 'When you sit with us, you make the Builders unhappy. We can hear their anger. In our dreams and behind our eyes, we hear it. And for your sake, we think that you should return to your guest quarters. Now.'

They were talking about the Loyalist cities.

If the guests refused to leave, there would be a string of petty thefts. Then expensive sensors and field generators would evaporate mysteriously, and if that didn't change their minds, then their munitions boxes would vanish from their hiding places, each one jammed full of the newest guns and grenades.

Just once, Miocene ordered a team not to retreat. She called for volunteers, then asked, 'What are the Waywards capable of?' She was talking to herself, and to them. 'Let them steal everything,' she ordered. 'Everything short of your lives. That's what I want.'

The team was flown to an eruption site two thousand kilometers from the capital, and after a few coded transmissions relayed from high-altitude drones, nothing more was heard of them. Then it was six years later, and Diu led a group of Waywards into a settlement on the border. He brought the missing team with him. Standing barefoot and virtually naked on a street paved with new steel, he said, 'This shouldn't have happened. It needn't have. Tell that bitch Miocene if she wants to play, let her play with her own important life.'

A dozen bodies lay on a dozen sleds, unbound and on their backs, and alive only by the tiniest of degrees. Eyelids had been pinned back, letting the skylight blind them. Barbed hooks kept the mouths pulled open, allowing the light to bake tongues and gums. Famine and a total lack of water had shriveled their bodies to a third of their original size. But worst of all was the way each prisoner had his neck broken. Three times a day, without exception, one of the strong young Waywards would smash the vertebrae and the spinal cord, keeping ahead of the sluggish healing mechanisms, leaving their guests helpless, limp and cut free of their dignity in precisely the same way that Miocene had once treated her son.

USUALLY ONCE EVERY century, and sometimes twice, the Loyalists came across one of the ancient vaults.

They were always empty, and after a thorough examination, each vault was declared useless and available for sale to the Waywards, in exchange for sulfur and silicon and rare earths. Deals were typically made in the same little city where Diu had brought the prisoners. Happens River was named for a feature obliterated centuries ago, and the city had moved several times since. A Submaster always handled the prolonged, increasingly difficult negotiations, and Locke always represented the Waywards. Washen and Diu served as observers, present because they had always been, but unnecessary to any of the tedious, long-winded business.

Like any old lovers, they took a slightly uncomfortable pleasure in each other's company.

Washen was under strict orders to speak with Diu, though she didn't need prodding. Standing next to Diu, she looked tall and elegant, dressed in her newest uniform, ancient epaulets shining in the skylight as she strolled along a new river's shoreline. Diu, by contrast, seemed small, his body a little shrunken by the hard Wayward existence, fatless muscle wearing nothing but the only breechcloth that he owned. A mock wool breechcloth, she noted. Not leather. He still was too much of a captain to skin himself alive.

Still and always, Diu was a jittery man. Nervous, quick. And relentlessly, effortlessly charming.

Not thinking of her orders but curious for herself, Washen mentioned the Waywards. 'Our best guess is that you've got twice our population. Or four times. Or eight.'

'Your best guess?' he laughed.

'Stinks,' she allowed.

Then he nodded, and grinned, and after a dramatic pause, he admitted, 'Eight times is too little. Sixteen times is closer to the mark.'

That gave the Waywards better than twenty-five million citizens. A huge mass of bodies and minds. She let herself wonder what so many modern minds, designed for endless and interesting lives, would think about. Without literature and digitals and sciences and history to embrace, and an ascetic's endless denial of pleasure . . . what kinds of ideas could keep such a mind engaged . . . ?

She was trying to frame the question. But when she spoke, something else entirely came out of her mouth.

'Do you remember ice cream?'

Diu giggled.

'That little shop.' She pointed, then said, 'It sells the next best thing.'

In that perpetual heat, anything cold tasted fine. In a sugar-poor world, everything sweet was a treasure, even if the treasure was the product of dead chew-chews and biochemical magic. The shop owner conspicuously ignored the Wayward man. Washen paid for both treats as well the rental of the steel bowls and steel spoons. They sat by the river, on a little gold-embossed table set on a patio of iron bricks doctored with cyanides, giving them a blue cast. The river was a mixture of native springs and the runoff from local industries, creating a chemical stew to which Marrow had quickly adapted. The bacterial smell wasn't pleasant, but it had a strength and an honesty. That's what Washen was thinking as she watched Diu take a careful bite of the ice cream. Then his eyes grew wide, and he asked, 'Is that how chocolate tastes?'

'We aren't sure,' she admitted. 'When you've got nothing to go on but your thousand-year-old memories . . .'

Both of them laughed quietly.

People sauntered past on the nearby walkway: lovers holding one another. Friends chattering. Business associates planning for a prosperous future. A couple had their toddler strapped into a wheeled cart. Like everyone else, they never quite looked at the Wayward sitting in plain view, eating ice cream. Only their child stared in amazement. Washen found herself thinking about the prisoners that Diu had brought back to Happens River. He had had no role in their torture. She had never asked, but he had volunteered his innocence just the same. Decades ago, now. Why even think about it? Then she looked at him, and smiled, trying to change the flow of her ancient mind.

Perhaps Diu guessed her thoughts.

Whatever the reason, he suddenly asked, 'How are those people, by the way? The poor souls that we brought back to you?'

'They healed,' she allowed. 'In most ways.'

He shook his head sadly, then said, 'Good. Good.'

Together, they watched a pair of children – probably brothers – running hard on the blue-bricked walkway. There was no railing or wall between them and the river. So when the older brother decided to shove the younger, the smaller boy stumbled and fell over the brink, his screaming face leading the way into the toxic waters.

Washen rose immediately.

But then their parents appeared, and while the mother reprimanded, the father scrambled down the face of the steel retaining wall, balancing on rocks as he fished his battered son out of a rancid goo, both of them filthy and angry, the father handing him up to his brother's hands, then shouting, 'Showers cost! Good water's never cheap!'

Emotional equations suddenly changed. A potential disaster had turned petty. Washen made herself sit again, telling her companion, 'I used to drown.'

'Did you?'

'A few times,' she allowed. 'I was little. I had a pet whale. I would ride him across the Alpha Sea—'

'I remember the story, Washen.'

'Did I tell you? How I used to make him dive deep, down where the great squids lived, and the pressure would crush me until I was unconscious and in a coma that lasted for hours. Sometimes for a full day.'

He stared as if seeing a stranger. A worrisome, possibly insane stranger.

'My parents were pissed. As you can imagine.' She narrowed her eyes, wondering where to take this story. 'My argument was that I couldn't die, really die, just from being underwater. But carelessness bred carelessness, they said, and what if I was swept off my whale, too? What if nobody found my body?'

Something in those words made Diu laugh quietly, privately.

Washen shook her head, adding, 'I just had this other memory. All of a sudden. And it's a strange one.'

'Oh,' he said. 'A strange one.'

She ignored the tone, looking off toward the new buildings across the river and seeing none of them. Instead, she saw the city where she was born, and the Master Captain was sitting with the original Submasters. For some reason, Washen was brought to them. But she was just a tiny girl. For some unimaginable reason, the Master spoke to her, asking some question. Washen couldn't recall the question, much less her reply. But she clearly remembered sitting in the Master's chair. And when she climbed out of it, a gust of wind had come out of nowhere, knocking the chair off its feet.

She reported that recollection, then asked, 'What does it mean?'

'It didn't happen,' Diu replied. Instantly, without doubts.

'No?'

'And even if it happened,' he added, 'it means nothing.'

For a moment, she heard something in his voice. Then Washen blinked and looked back at the rugged face, hairless save for the thick dark eyebrows, and she found a smile waiting – a broad smile in the mouth if not in those bright steel-gray eyes.

WITHIN EACH OF the ancient vaults, buried inside its uranium ballast, was an elegant little device, apparently useless and mostly ignored. One day, an empty vault was being fed test data while a piece of nearby machinery, purely by coincidence, emitted a low-frequency sound. The sound triggered an echo, a powerful and instantaneous throb noticeable for kilometers in every direction. A homing signal, perhaps? If so, it would only work with an operational vault, and there was no such creature. But to be thorough, the Loyalists sent the appropriate pulses into the crust, then listened for the hypothetical 'Here I am' returns.

Because their equipment was crude, the first positive returns went unnoticed. But then a soft, imprecise echo was identified, and debated, and most observers denied the data, arguing on technical grounds while emotional reasons went unmentioned.

Newer, more sensitive microphones were designed, and built, and found wanting.

But the third generation of sensors produced not only a definite return, they also confidently supplied a location.

The echo came from a point a little more than nine kilometers deep, from inside a quiet eddy of molten iron.

A small, hopefully secret project was born. Under the camouflage of a new mantle-based geothermal works, lasers began boring a series of deep holes. The local crust was a fat three kilometers thick. Beneath the crust, ceramic pipes and pumps were employed. The red-hot iron had to be lifted to the surface, and cooled, and set out of the way. Since the mantle was far from rigid, their target had a nagging habit of wandering. The grandchildren likened the adventure to putting an arm into lake muck, trying to grab one of those hot black winklewarts that just had to be down there.

A full eight years were invested in the drilling.

When success was imminent, a coded message was sent to Miocene. But before she arrived, something solid was ingested, and the pumps mindlessly pulled and pulled, bringing the vault to the surface. It looked the same as the other vaults – a simple replica of the Great Ship. Yet it was nothing like the others. Everyone sensed it. Even the captain in attendance – an unimaginative, hardworking man named Koll – felt a surge of anticipation, watching as his crew and a squad of robots yanked the treasure out of that wet iron, then immersed it in a deep basin of ice water.

Blinking against the steam, Koll ordered the treasure moved indoors.

Who knew who was watching?

The pump station was a suitable hiding place. A large, rambling building without the tiniest window, it held the rarest thing on Marrow. Darkness. Koll walked beside the mechanical walker that was carrying the vault, the false rocket nozzles pointed upward. A young granddaughter was at the helm. As soon as they were inside, Koll ordered the door closed behind them, and locked. He intended to call for the lights. 'A soft setting,' he would have told the main computer. But after sixteen hundred years in endless daylight, Koll had learned to cherish anything that resembled night. Standing with his eyes open and blind, he noticed that glow. Soft, and colored. Not coming from the vault, no. The light seemed to be spilling from everywhere else.

Ancient systems had been triggered.

The uranium ballast served as a kind of battery. There was just enough power remaining to make a weak, ghostly projection. And Koll, a stolid, hard-to-impress man, stared at the images, a full minute passing before he remembered to breathe again.

'Do you see this?' he asked the woman.

'I do,' she replied weakly. 'Yes.'

She was sitting on the walker, silhouetted against flashes of light, her face wearing a look of stunned awe.

After another minute, she asked Koll, 'What does this mean?'

There was no point in lying. He told her simply, 'I don't know what it means.' In circumstances like this, who could know?

The woman said, 'Goodness.'

She laughed nervously, then said, 'You don't suppose—?'

'Maybe it's nothing,' the captain interrupted. Then he said, 'Nothing,' once again, with a genuine hopefulness. But because he was a rigorously honest man, he added, 'Yet it could be very important. Which, I suppose, makes this a very important day.'

Twenty

STRIPPED OF ITS hyperfiber shell, the device seemed elegant but not particularly impressive. Various ceramics were knitted into a white buckeyball sphere, rather like an oversized child's kick ball. The vault rode on the floor in front of Miocene, and she touched it lightly, and with a flat, matter-of-fact voice, she reported, 'I feel confident. About how things will go from here, I mean. Basically, essentially confident.'

Washen nodded, then faced forward again. With both hands on the controls, she repeated the word, 'Confident.'

'I am,' the Submaster promised. 'With luck and some care, this should help heal the old rifts.'

'With luck,' Washen echoed, knowing it would take a lot of that mecurial substance.

She was steering a large walker. Behind them, the latest incarnation of Happens River was dropping over the horizon. What passed for a road would soon become a starved trail, then nothing but jungle and raw mountains. They were already approaching Wayward lands, yet it would be another two hundred kilometers before the rendezvous. Nobody with an official invitation had ever moved this deep into their territory, and it had been at least three centuries since the uninvited had last passed here.

As the day progressed, Washen kept tabs on the walker's progress. The latest AI pilots still weren't particularly smart or adaptable, and it wouldn't impress anyone to have their machine – the culmination of sixteen centuries of technical wizardry – trip over a piece of mountain, ending up on its back like a clumsy crap bug.

The jungle path lifted up onto a wide, newborn plateau,

then vanished. A hard hot rain was falling on the open ground, collecting in little basins and pools where black algae grew in silky blankets. In another year, all of this would be a vigorous young jungle. But which species would dominate? Sixteen hundred years of research gave Washen the expertise to admit that she didn't know how the succession would progress. Not on this ground, or any other. Chemical makeups varied from vent to vent, and even within a single flow. Rains were common but no longer reliable. Little droughts and hard floods could change initial conditions. Plus there was the pure creative randomness of the spores and seeds and eggs that would come here. A chance wind could bring a flotilla of gold balloons that might, or might not, lead to a lofty forest of pure virtue trees. Or the fickle wind would steer the balloons somewhere else. To an established jungle and their deaths, most likely, where hungry mouths waited in abundance. At least a hundred native species loved to chew on the gold foil, incorporating the metal into their own elaborate carapaces, showing the world and their prospective mates both a beauty and a gaudy strength.

Initial conditions were critical. That was essential in jungle ecologies, and in human ecologies, too.

What if Miocene were a better parent? More patient, and nurturing, and just a little more forgiving? If she and Till had been closer, resolving their differences in private, civilized ways, the history of Marrow would certainly have been much quieter. And if she had been a worse mother, she would have murdered her son. Then driven by the other captains' outrage, Miocene would have been ousted, another Submaster named their leader. Daen, perhaps. Or more likely Twist. Which would have radically changed the evolution of their ad hoc civilization . . .

The burden of intelligence: you can always imagine all

those wonderful places where you can never belong.

The young plateau gave way to a younger volcanic cone, now sleeping. Dirty iron and nickel had frozen into a rough-faced slag. As the machine scrambled up the naked slope, the rains slackened, and the clouds were shoved far ahead, allowing Washen to glance over her shoulder, looking back across the swollen face of the world.

The sky was dimmer than ever.

As the buttresses weakened, the ambient light fell away proportionally. Still brilliant, but not the same cutting-to-the-bone brilliance. Temperatures were following the same smooth curve downward. Gravity weakened as the world expanded, subtly changing the architecture of plants and mountains and the largest, most important buildings. The atmosphere was growing cooler and quieter but not deeper, since it was spreading across more and more surface area. Likewise, there was only a finite amount of water. The metallic lavas were parched, bringing up nothing but rare earths and heavy metals. Less rain was falling and rivers were smaller, and if these various trends continued apace, there was the promise of long, hard droughts.

Near the horizon, far too small to be seen by the naked eye, was the sky's only flaw. The original base camp still clung to the silvery hyperfiber, its modern buildings and diamond walkways still empty and alone. And in another thirty-four centuries, the camp would remain just as empty, but it would gaze down on a radically different world. The buttresses' light would have fallen away to nothing, revealing a lovely starlike sparkle marking cities and well-lighted lanes.

That was the instant when a person could escape. And thinking that, Washen glanced at the vault again, feeling a cold, unnerving pain.

'We don't know if it's true,' she muttered to herself.

Miocene glanced at her, nearly asking, 'What did you say?'

But the Submaster thought better of it, placing both hands on that ball of smooth gray-white ceramics, the gesture protective, hands and her tilting body conveying a strange fondness for the terrible artifact.

AN UNMAPPED RIVER of iron meant a prolonged detour.

They were an hour behind schedule when they arrived at the appointed clearing. Three in the morning, ship time, according to Washen's silver clock.

The clearing began as a lava plain, but when its molten heart retreated underground, the flat countryside collapsed into a natural amphitheatre. A great flat slab was the stage, and the black iron rose up on all sides, in oversized stairsteps. The shadowless play of the light and the angle of the slopes made everything appear closer than it was. As instructed, Washen parked in the middle of the stage, both captains climbing into plain view, and with two of its jointed limbs, the walker carefully lowered the vault to the iron. Then the first Waywards appeared, mere dots against the blackness. Even trotting at a respectable pace, it took them forever to work their way down the long slope. Besides breechcloths, each wore an ornamental mask made from soft leather stretched over a framework of carved bone. Leather made from their flesh; bone torn from their own enduring bodies. Every mask was painted with blood and with urine. Each showed the same wild, almost fluid face. Like electricity with eyes but no mouth. A Builder's face, Washen recalled. How they had arrived at that imagery, she didn't know. Diu claimed that Till was preyed upon by visions. The Wayward's leader was convinced that the Builders were visiting him, and in some ways, they were his only true friends.

As the first Waywards approached, they slowed to a dignified walk and lifted their masks back up on top of their heads.

Nearly fifteen centuries had passed since Washen last saw Till. Yet she knew him immediately. She knew him from the drawings and from a captain's crisp memories. But she also recognized his mother in his face and in his measured, imperious stride.

He was a smaller, prettier version of Miocene.

The rest of the party – the finest priests and diplomats and cabinet members – followed at a respectful distance. They were staring at the prize. Washen had plugged an umbilical into the vault, and the walker's generator was feeding it. A smooth living hum came from within, infusing the air with a palpable hint of possibilities.

Only Till wasn't staring at the prize. He watched Miocene. Wariness was mixed with other, less legible emotions. For an instant, his mouth opened. Then he took a quick breath and turned to Washen, asking, 'May I examine the device?'

'Please,' she told him; she told all of them.

Locke was standing closest to Till. It was a sign of rank, perhaps, and as always, that brought Washen an unexpected pride.

'How have you been, Mother?' he inquired. Always polite; never warm.

'Well enough,' she allowed. 'And how are you?'

His answer was an odd wincing smile, and silence.

Where was Diu? More of the Waywards were climbing up on the stage, and she looked at each man as he lifted his mask, watching their faces, assuming that Diu was somewhere close, hidden by the growing crush of bodies.

Till was kneeling, caressing the vault's slick surface.

Miocene studied him, but her eyes seemed empty. Blind.

A few thousand honored Waywards had gathered around the stage. All were nursing women, each with at least one infant sucking on their swollen breasts. A thick, oddly pleasant scent lay on the breeze. Tens of thousands more streamed out of the jungle, from every direction, moving purposefully and quietly, footfalls and breathing making a sound, soft and vast, like the beating of a distant surf that grew closer. Something about the sound was irresistible, and beautiful, and at the heart of things, frightening.

Among them were Locke's children and grandchildren.

In principle, Washen could have a hundred thousand descendants among these people. Which wasn't a small accomplishment for one old woman who could claim only one child of her own.

The vault's hum grew louder, increased in pitch, then stopped altogether. It was Locke who lifted an arm, shouting, 'Now,' to the multitude.

Everyone else repeated the gesture, the word. A great shared voice rippled its way to the top of the amphitheatre, and then a sudden smear of gold appeared along one edge, expanding rapidly, bright in the skylight as hundreds of strong bodies dragged it forward. Countless golden balloons helped hold the fabric aloft. It was a foil of gold, hectares in size and pounded thin and strengthened . . . how . . . ? Whatever the trick, it was strong enough and light enough to be pulled across the entire amphitheatre, enclosing everyone, creating a temporary, impermeable roof.

The sky fell dark.

Sensing the perfect darkness, the vault opened itself, revealing a new sky and a younger world. Marrow was suddenly barren and smooth, and it was covered with a worldwide ocean of bubbling, irradiated iron.

The audience found itself standing on that ocean,

unwarmed, watching an ancient drama play itself out.

The Builders' enemies appeared.

Without warning, the hated Bleak squirmed their way through the chamber's walls, emerging from the countless access tunnels – insectlike cyborgs, each one enormous and cold and frighteningly swift. Like angry jackwasps, they dove at Marrow, spitting out gobs of antimatter that slammed into the molten surface. Scorching white-hot explosions rose up and up. Liquid iron swirled and lifted, then collapsed again. In the harsh shifting light, Washen glanced at her son, trying to measure his face, his mood. Locke was spellbound, eyes wide and his mouth ajar, his muscular body drenched with a glossy, almost radiant perspiration. Almost every face and body was the same. Even Miocene was enthralled. But she was staring at Till, not at the spectacle overhead, and if anything, her rapture was worse than the others'. While her son, in stark contrast, seemed oddly unmoved by these glorious, holy images.

A hyperfiber dome burst from the iron.

Lasers fired, consuming a dozen of the Bleak. Then the dome dove under the iron again, whale-fashion.

The Bleak brought reinforcements, then struck again. Missiles carried antimatter deep into the iron, seeking targets. Marrow shook and twisted, then belched fire and searing plasmas. Maybe the Bleak had won, killing the last of the Builders. Maybe the Great Ship was theirs. But the Builders' revenge was in place. Was assured. The Bleaks' forces pressed on, filling the narrow sky with their furious shapes. Then the buttresses ignited, bringing their blue-white glare. Suddenly the monsters seemed tiny and frail. Before they could flee, the lightning storm – the Event – swept across the sky, bright enough to make every eye blink, dissolving every wisp of matter into a plasma that hung overhead as a superheated mist that would persist for millions of years, cooling as Marrow contracted and enlarged again, the world beating like a great slow heart, cooling itself gradually, a temporary crust covering the blistering iron.

A billion years passed in a moment.

The Bleaks' own carbon and hydrogen and oxygen became Marrow's atmosphere and its rivers, and those same precious elements slowly gathered themselves into butter bugs and virtue trees, then became the wide-eyed children standing in the present, in that natural depression, weeping in the deep, perfect darkness.

On a signal, the canopy was torn open, the gold foil splitting and falling in great long sheets that shimmered in the skylight.

Washen opened her watch, measuring the minutes.

Into that wide-eyed present, Miocene called out, 'There is more. Much more.' Her voice was urgent. Motherly. She stared only at Till, explaining, 'Other recordings show how the ship was attacked. How the Builders retreated into Marrow. This lump of iron . . . this is where they made their final stand . . . whoever they were . . . !'

A hundred thousand bodies stirred, making a softly massive sound.

Till wasn't awestruck. If anything, he seemed merely pleased, grinning as if amused by this vindication of a vision that needed no vindication.

For a slim moment, their eyes met. Then obeying some unspoken pact, mother and son looked away again. Indifference in one face; in the other, a wrenching pain.

The pained face glared at the sky. 'We never see the Builders themselves,' Miocene announced. 'But this thing, this gift that Washen and I have brought to you . . . it's given us a better, fuller understanding of the species . . .'

Till contemplated the same sky, saying nothing.

'Listen to me,' Miocene cried out, unable to contain her frustrations. 'Don't you understand? The Event that trapped us here, in this awful place . . . the Event was an ancient weapon. An apocalyptic booby trap that we probably triggered ourselves by sending our teams across Marrow . . . and that might have . . . probably did . . . kill and consume everyone above us, leaving the ship empty, and us trapped here . . . !'

Washen imagined a hundred billion vacant apartments and the long ghostly avenues and seas turned to a lifeless steam; once again, the ship was a derelict, plying its way blindly among the stars.

If true, it was a horrible tragedy.

Yet Till's reaction was different, singular. 'Who is trapped?' he called out, his voice carrying farther than his mother's, buoyed up with a smooth, unnerving calm. 'I'm not trapped. No believer is. This is exactly where we belong.'

Miocene's eyes betrayed her anger.

Till conspicuously ignored her, shouting to the audience, 'We are here because the Builders called to the captains. They lured the captains to this great place, then made them stay, giving them the honor to give birth to us!'

'That's insane,' the Submaster growled.

Washen scanned the crowd, searching for Diu. Again and again, she would recognize his features in a Wayward's face, or eyes, or his nervous energy. But not the man himself. And they needed Diu. An intermediary with an intimate knowledge of both cultures, he could help everyone . . . and why hadn't Diu been invited to this meeting . . . ?

A cold dread took Washen by the throat.

'I know where you got this nonsense.' Miocene said the words, then took a long step toward Till, empty hands lifting into the air. 'It's obvious. You were a boy, and you stumbled across a working vault. Didn't you? The vault showed you the Bleak, and you hammered together a ridiculous story . . . this crazy noise about the Builders being reborn . . . and you conveniently at the center of everything . . .'

In a mocking, almost pitying fashion, Till grinned at his mother.

Miocene raised her hands still higher, and she spun in a slow circle, a majestic rage helping her scream, 'Understand me! All of this is a lie!'

Silence.

Then Till shook his head, assuring everyone, 'I didn't find any vault or artifact.' He made his own turn, proclaiming, 'I was alone in the jungle. Alone, and a Builder's spirit came to me. He told me about the ship and the Bleak. He showed me everything that this vault contains, and more. Then he made me a promise: when this long day ends, as it must, I will learn my destiny, and your destinies as well . . . !'

His voice trailed off into the enraptured silence.

Locke unfastened the umbilical from the vault, and glancing at Washen, his flat, matter-of-fact voice told her, 'We'll bring the usual payment to Happens River.'

Miocene roared.

'What do you mean? The usual payment . . . ? But this is the best artifact yet!'

The Waywards gazed at her with a barely restrained contempt.

'This one functions. It remembers.' The Submaster was stabbing at the air, reminding everyone, 'The other vaults were just empty curiosities!'

Till said, 'Exactly.'

Then, as if it were beneath their leader to explain the

obvious, Locke stepped forward, telling them, 'Vaults are usually crypts. They hold the Builders' souls. And the ones you sold us were empty because their souls have found better places to reside.'

Till pulled his blood-and-piss mask back over his face again, hiding everything but his bright eyes.

Every Wayward repeated the motion, a great rippling reaching to the top of the amphitheatre. And Washen had to wonder if this elaborate meeting, with all of its pagentry and rich emotion, was intended not for a hundred thousand devoted souls, but for two old and very stubborn captains.

With his face obscured, Locke approached his mother.

A premonition made her mouth dry.

'Where is he?' she inquired.

Her son's eyes changed. Softened, sweetened.

'His soul is elsewhere now,' he replied, as a Wayward should. Then he gestured at the hard iron ground.

'Elsewhere?'

'Eight years ago.' There was a sadness in his body and his voice. 'There was a powerful eruption, and he was taken.'

Washen couldn't speak, or move.

A warm hand gripped her by the elbow, and a caring voice asked, 'Are you all right, Mother?'

She took a breath, then told the truth.

'No, I'm not all right. My son's a stranger, my lover's dead, and how should I damn well feel . . . ?'

She pulled free of his hand, then turned away.

Miocene – the cold, untouchable Submaster – dropped to her knees on the hard iron, hands clasped before her weeping face. Their promising mission was ending with this. With Miocene pleading.

She said, 'Till,' with genuine anguish. 'I'm so very, very

sorry, darling. I was wrong, hitting you that way . . . and I wish you would try to forgive me . . . please . . . !'

Her son nodded for a moment, saying nothing.

Then as he turned, preparing to leave, Miocene used her final plea.

'But I do love the ship,' she told him. And everyone. 'You were wrong then, and you're still wrong. I love and cherish the ship more than you ever could! And I'll always love it more than I love you, ungrateful little bastard . . . !'

Twenty-one

A CARDE OF captains and gifted architects had designed the Grand Temple, and for a thousand years the best artisans had labored over it, while every adult Loyalist gave time and willing hands to its construction. Even half-finished, the Temple was a beautiful structure. Six gold-faced domes were arranged in a perfect circle. Graceful parabolic arches of tinted steels straddled the domes, riding higher and higher on each other's backs. The central tower was the tallest structure on Marrow, and the deepest. Its foundation already reached a full kilometer into the cold iron, and in its basement was a reservoir of pure water where the occasional neutrino would collide with a willing nucleus, the resulting explosion producing a lovely cone of light that proved to priests and to children what every Loyalist needed to accept without question: Marrow was a small part of a much greater Creation, a Creation invisible to the eye but not to the believing mind.

The Wayward defector had asked to be brought to the temple, which was a perfectly ordinary request.

But the Submaster had reviewed the field reports as well as the transcripts of both official interrogations, and the only certainty was that nothing else about this defection was ordinary, much less simple.

The temple administrator was a nervous woman made more so by events. Wearing the soft gray robes of her office and a tortured expression, she greeted Miocene with a crisp, 'Madam,' and a cursory bow, then blurted out, 'It is an honor,' even as she prepared to complain what a great disruption this business was.

Miocene didn't give her the opportunity. Firmly and not too gently, she said, 'You've done a marvelous job, so far.'

'Yes, madam.'

'So far,' she repeated, reminding her subordinate that failure was always just one misstep away. Then with a softer voice, she asked, 'Where's our guest?'

'In the library.'

Of course.

'He wants to see you,' the administrator warned. 'He practically demands that I bring you to him.'

They were standing at one of the minor entranceways, the heavy door carved from a single virtue tree, ancient and gigantic. Because she refused to be rushed by anyone, Miocene paused, letting one hand caress the old wood, dark as clotted blood and perforated with spongelike holes where nodules of battery fats had been. Her guards – a pair of trunklike men with quick, suspicious eyes – stood nearby, watching the quiet side street. For an instant, Miocene's mind was elsewhere. She found herself thinking about the ship, and in particular, her wood-lined apartment not five hundred meters from the Master's quarters.

Then she blinked and gave a sigh, feeling a familiar little sadness, and a knot of secret fears . . .

'Well, then,' she muttered, straightening her back, then the creases of her uniform. 'Take me to our new friend.'

Public services were being held in each of the six main chambers. Citizens elected their priests, and as a result, each had his own style and perspective. Some spoke endlessly about the Great Ship. Its beauty, its grace; its unfathomable age, and its endless mystery. Others readied parishioners for the glorious day they would meet their first aliens. And an ecletic few dwelled on more abstract and far-reaching topics: the stars and living worlds and the Milky Way, and the vast universe that dwarfed everything that humankind could see and touch or even pretend to comprehend.

One service was wrestling with such cosmic wonders. A satin-voiced gentleman was singing praises of G-class suns. 'Warm enough to bring life to more than many worlds at a time,' he called out, 'and long enough lived to feed a creative evolution. Our home world, the great Earth, was born beside such a golden sun. Like the seed of a virtue tree, it was. It is. And our universe is full of billions of seeds. Life in its myriad forms is everywhere. Life thick and life lovely, and life forever.'

'Forever,' chanted the small audience, in careless unison.

Ceramic arches and potted flycatchers separated the hallway from the chamber. A few faces happened to glance to one side, noticing the Submaster striding past. Murmurs rose, spread. But the priest standing up front, leaning hard against the diamond podium, ignored the noise, pressing on with his speech.

'We must prepare, sisters and brothers. The day is waning, gradually but inexorably, and we will see the time when each of us is needed. Our hearts and hands, and our minds, will be thrown into the construction of the bridge.'

'The bridge,' some repeated. While others, distracted by the concrete and the present, watched Miocene and her guards pass behind the altar, followed closely by the flustered administrator. The altar was built from native diamonds mounted in a tube no wider than a human arm. At its base was an intricate mock-up of the city and the finished temple. The tube rose up to the domed ceiling that was painted to resemble a darker sky, and where the ragged stump of the first bridge clung tight, the diamond bridge joined seamlessly, flecks of bright light forever streaking upward, showing the migration of the loyal multitudes – their glorious reward for so much sacrifice and enthusiastic hope.

Miocene barely glanced at the parishioners.

It was perfectly acceptable for her to visit the temple, and she didn't want them noticing anything remarkable in her manner or her eyes.

'When the time is right,' the priest shouted, 'we shall climb. Climb!'

Then he whirled, his gray robe fluttering and one arm beginning an overly dramatic gesture at the diamond spire, and when he noticed the Submaster and her tiny entourage, his surprise collapsed into instant ritual.

Bowing, he cried out, 'Madam.'

The audience behind him shouted, 'Madam,' and fell forward in their iron seats.

Thankfully, she had reached the library stairs. After a hurried wave and the briefest look, Miocene turned and began to climb, leading her guards and them worrying because of it. The senior guard told her, 'No, madam,' and unceremoniously slowed her with a strong hand to the shoulder.

Fine.

She eased her gait, perhaps more than necessary. The guard passed her as the staircase spiraled its way up through the heart of the great building. If memory served, the stair's architect was a difficult grandchild with a narrow genius. She had used the shape of DNA as her inspiration. The fact that only a sliver of modern genetics were encoded in that delicate compound made no difference. It had struck the architect as a suitable symbol. Rising through the oldest language to reach the newest . . . or some equally forced symbolism, wasn't it . . . ?

To Miocene, symbols were crutches for the lame. It was a very old opinion for her, and the last three millenia had only reinforced it.

Like the temple, this quasireligion was thick with symbols. G-class suns were equated with virtue seeds. What nonsense! There were only so many colors in the universe, at least to human eyes. And Miocene had seen many, many Sol-like suns. If she wished, she could warn the parishioners that under no circumstances would a sun and a seed be confused. Not in brightness, or in color. Gold was a simple thing, and sunlight never was. Ever.

And yet.

This temple and its cobbled-together faith were as much her idea as anyone's. And the Submaster hadn't ordered the temple's construction for easy cynical reasons. No, the temple would serve as the foundation for the coming bridge. Physically, and otherwise. It was imperative that the Loyalists understood what was going to happen. If they didn't comprehend and embrace these goals, and keep themselves unswayed by the Waywards' bizarre faith, there was no point in escaping from Marrow. This temple, and dozens of smaller temples scattered across the land, were meant to be places of education and focus. If people required symbols and sloppy metaphors to build a consensus, then so be it. Miocene just wished that the grandchildren would stop being so inventive, and so earnest, particularly with things about which they knew almost nothing.

The lead guard slowed, then muttered something to someone around the bend. A full squad waited in the library, all armed with heavy-caliber weapons, all watching with a decidedly unscholarly interest as a boyish man, dressed in common clothes and a Gordian wig, paged his way through a dense technical synopsis of the ship.

According to his interrogators, he was named for the tree.

He went by Virtue.

Miocene said the name, just once and not loudly. The man didn't seem to hear, eyes focused on a diagram of an antimatter-spiked fusion reactor. Instead of repeating his name, she stood on the far side of the table, and she waited, watching as the gray eyes absorbed the meaningful words and the elegant lines, these intricate plans drawn from memory by one of her colleagues.

Slowly, slowly, the defector grew aware of the newcomers.

He lifted his gaze, and as if emerging from some private fog, he blinked a few times, then said, 'Yes.'

He said, 'This is wrong.'

'Excuse me?' Miocene inquired.

'It won't work. I'm certain.' He touched the black corner of the page, and the book moved to the next page. The same reactor was pictured, conjured from the same memory but a different vantage point. 'The containment vessel isn't strong enough. Not by half.'

Like so many grandchildren, he was a difficult genius.

With a look and a slashing gesture, Miocene told the guards and soldiers to leave the two of them alone.

The temple administrator had to ask, 'How long will you need the library?' Then to explain her boldness, she added, 'Researchers are coming from Promise-and-Dream's biolabs. They've got some priority project—'

'Make them wait,' she growled.

'Yes, madam.'

Then Virtue told everyone, 'I don't know if I'd trust a word in this place.' He spoke loudly and without a hint of charm. 'I thought I'd be drinking from some fucking fountain of wisdom, or something. But I just keep finding mistakes. Everywhere I look, mistakes.'

Mildly, the Submaster told him, 'Well. Then it's a good thing that you happened by.'

The defector closed his current volume, in disgust.

To her personal guards, Miocene said, 'Out of earshot. Wait.' Then to the administrator, she said, 'Go downstairs. Go down and tell all those worshipers that the Submaster would appreciate a long and very loud song.'

'Which song?' the woman sputtered.

'Oh, that's their choice,' Miocene replied. 'It's always theirs.'

THE DEFECTOR WAS an emotional alloy: two parts arrogance, one part fear.

It was a useful combination.

Sitting at the table with Miocene, Virtue seemed to recall that smiles were a helpful gesture. But he wasn't particularly skilled with the expression, his smile looking more like a pained wince, his light gray eyes growing larger by the moment.

'I told them that I absolutely had to see you,' he reported. 'Only you, and as soon as possible.'

'Madam Miocene.'

His genius wavered. A stupid voice said, 'Pardon?'

'I am your single hope,' she replied, leaning back in the tall chair as if disgusted by the creature before her. 'You live out the day if I let you. Otherwise, you die. And I think that I'm entitled to hear my name used in the proper fashion, at the proper times.'

He looked at his own hands.

Then, quietly, 'Madam Miocene.'

'Thank you.' She showed him a narrow grin, then with a slow, almost indifferent set of motions, she opened the bright chromium case of her electronic file box, pretending to read what she already knew by heart. 'To my associates, you claimed that you had something to tell me. News fit only for my ears.'

'Yes . . . Madam Miocene . . .' He swallowed hard, then said, 'It has to do with this world of ours—'

'This isn't my world,' she interrupted.

Virtue nodded, and waited. His eyes couldn't have been larger.

Miocene pretended to concentrate on the screen. 'It says here . . . that you're a second-generation descendant of Diu—'

'He was my grandfather, yes. Madam.'

'And your father . . . ?'

'Is Till.'

She looked up, staring as if she had never noticed the familial resemblance. After a lengthy pause, she mentioned, 'Many Waywards are Till's children. As I understand these things.'

'Yes, Madam.'

'No real honor to it, since there's so awfully many of you.'

'Well, I don't know if I would . . .' He hesitated, then said, 'No, madam, I suppose there isn't a specific honor, no.'

She touched a key, then another, scrolling through the transcripts and the written accounts of each interrogator. Every entry gave clues to this man's character, or lack of it. And none could be trusted as the final word on anything concerning him.

'So our texts are inaccurate. You're claiming.'

Virtue blinked, and he held his breath.

Souls were a fluid alloy. The arrogance hid deep inside him, replaced on the surface by a growing, strengthening sense of fear.

'Are they inaccurate, or aren't they?'

'In places, I think so. Yes.'

'Have you built a fusion reactor like the one in those diagrams?'

'No, madam.'

'Are there any reactors like it in the Wayward nation?'

'No.'

'You're certain?'

'I can't be absolutely certain,' he admitted.

'And we haven't built them, either,' she confessed. 'Our geothermal plants are quite sufficient for our very modest demands.'

The defector nodded, then attempted a compliment. 'This is an amazing city, madam. They let me see pieces of it on my way here.'

'That was their mistake,' she replied.

He hunkered, a little bit.

Then she gave him a smile, inquiring, 'Do you Waywards have cities this large? With almost a million people in one place?'

'No. No, madam.'

'We've mastered some marvelous tricks,' she continued. 'The crust beneath us is thick and solid, and we keep it that way. Quakes are diffused or bled away. The fluid iron is steered into managed zones. Artificial vents, in essence.'

Sensing her wishes, he allowed, 'The Waywards don't have that technology.'

'You're still nomads, aren't you? Basically.'

He started to answer, then hesitated. 'I'm not a Wayward anymore,' he finally offered. Then with a tight little voice, he added, 'Madam.'

'But you could tell me much about them. I would imagine.'

A cursory nod.

'You know about their lives,' she continued. 'About their technologies. Perhaps even their ultimate goals.'

'Yes,' he said. 'And yes. And no, madam.'

'Oh? You don't know what Till wants?'

'Not in any clear way, no.' He swallowed as if in pain. 'My father . . . well, Till doesn't exactly confide in me . . .'

Again, Miocene touched the keys. 'Maybe that's why you lost the Wayward faith. Is that a possibility?'

'I'm not sure that I ever believed.'

'All that noise about Builders and Bleaks and ancient souls entombed inside those hyperfiber coffins . . . ?'

'The truth is that I don't know what's real. Madam.'

She looked up, suspicion mixed with fascination. 'So you might believe. If circumstances were changed in some way, that is.'

The arrogance resurfaced. Quietly, angrily, he asked, 'Wouldn't you change your mind? If you suddenly realized that your mind was wrong, I mean.'

'As I recall, you demanded to be brought here. To this temple specifically. I can only assume that you're eager to see the Great Ship for yourself, and to that noble end, you want to help our holy mission . . .'

'No, madam.'

Miocene feigned surprise, then disgust. With her own

quiet anger, she asked the defector, 'In what do you believe?'

'Nothing.' He sounded defiant, but like a child too full of himself, too impressed with the keen edge of his own exceptional mind. 'I don't know why Marrow is here,' he complained, 'much less who built it. Or why. And I'm absolutely convinced that no one else has answers for those questions, either.'

'The artifacts—?'

'There's another obvious explanation for them.'

But she didn't want to hear any groundless speculations. What was important here – what was vital and even urgent – was to ascertain the real talents of this taciturn young man. A contemptuous snarl preceded her firm declaration: 'I don't have use for Wayward scientists. We've had a few of you defect, once a century or so, and as a rule, you're badly educated. Unimaginative. And you trade on the names of your insane fathers.'

'I am well educated,' Virtue replied, in a sudden fever. 'And I'm extremely imaginative. And I don't use your son's name to my advantage!'

She stared at him, the picture of skepticism.

'Don't you appreciate the risks that I've taken? For your sake, and everyone's?' He barked the words, then with a wince and grunt restrained himself. A nervous hand threw open the book, as if one of its intricate, flawed pages would lend support for his cause. Then with a soft, furious tone, Virtue explained, 'I was Chief of Delving at the main research facility at the Grand Caldera. In secret, I taught myself how to fly. Alone, I stole one of our fastest pterosaurs, and I flew to within a hundred kilometers of the border. Inside a rainstorm, I jumped. I left the pterosaur to be shot down, and without armor or a parachute, I dropped through the canopy. When my shattered legs healed, I ran. I ran all the way to that shithole checkpoint of yours. That's how badly I wanted to be here, Grandmother. Madam Miocene. Whatever the fuck you want to be called . . . !'

'It's a grand epic,' Miocene offered. 'All that's missing is the motivation.'

Glowering silence.

'Chief of Delving,' she repeated. 'What were you delving into at the Grand Caldera?'

'Energy.'

'Geothermal energy?'

'Hardly.' He glanced at his own hands, reporting. 'There has always been a problem, and both nations know it. There's too much energy running through this place. Energy to light the sky, and power enough to compress an entire world and hold it in one place. That's power beyond what fission can supply. Or normal fusion. Even the great captains are at a loss to explain such a thing.'

'Hidden matter-antimatter reactors,' Miocene offered.

'Something's hidden,' he agreed. One hand pulled a braid into his mouth, and he sucked on the wig's dark hair for a moment. Then he spat it out again, and he told the Submaster, 'I was delving into the deepest regions.'

'Of Marrow?'

A cursory nod. 'Looking for your hidden reactors, I suppose.'

'Don't you know what you were hunting?' she countered.

His hot gray eyes lifted, glaring at his accuser. 'I know. You think I'm difficult, and you're not the first to think it. Believe me.'

Miocene said nothing.

'But between us, who's more difficult? You've lived on Marrow for thirty centuries, ruling a tiny piece of what you claim is a tiny world. You claim that only you and the other captains understand the beauty and enormity of the great universe, while your son and the other Waywards are idiots because they tell simple stories that halfway explain everything, making us into the reborn kings of the universe . . .

'We aren't kings,' he proclaimed. 'And I don't believe that an arrogant old woman like you really understands the universe. Great and glorious and nearly boundless, it is, and what tiny fraction of it have you seen in your own little life . . . ?'

Miocene watched the eyes, saying nothing.

'I was peering inside Marrow,' the youngster reported. 'The Waywards have a larger, more sensitive array of seismic ears than yours. Since most of the world is theirs, after all. And since they believe in living with quakes, not in defusing them.'

'I know about your seismic array,' said Miocene.

'Using three thousand years of data, I built a thorough, detailed picture of the interior.' As he spoke, a rapture took hold of his gray eyes, his narrow face, then his small body. 'Arrogance,' he said again, with a harsh disgust. 'By your own admission, you piloted the Great Ship for a hundred millenia before you realized that Marrow was here. And now you've lived here for another three millenia, and hasn't it ever occurred to you, just once, that the mysteries don't stop? That there's *something* hiding deep inside Marrow, too?'

Suddenly Miocene heard the distant singing, muted by walls and the spiraling staircase, the voices ragged and earnest and in their own way beautiful.

She heard herself ask, 'What is this . . . this something . . . ?'

'I don't have any idea.'

'Is it large?'

'Fifty kilometers across. Approximately.' The young man sucked on another braid, then said, 'I want to find out what it is. Give me the staff and the resources, and I'll determine if the buttresses are being fed from down there.'

The Submaster took a breath, then another. Then she quietly, honestly, told the defector, 'That can't be our priority. Interesting as it is, the question has to wait.'

Gray eyes stared, then pulled shut.

A bilious voice reported, 'That's exactly what Till told me. Word for fucking word.'

When the eyes opened, they saw a laser cradled in the Submaster's right hand.

'Hey, now,' he whined.

Miocene aimed for the throat, then panned downward. Then she rose and came around the table, completing the chore with delicacy and thoroughness. Only the face and the mind behind it remained unconsumed, a voiceless scream having pulled the mouth wide open. The stink of cooked flesh and a burned wig made the air close, distasteful. Working quickly, Miocene opened a satchel and dumped the head inside. Then she walked between the stacks of books, her guard waiting as ordered, out of earshot.

He took the satchel without comment.

'As always,' was all she needed to say.

With a nod, the loyal guard left, using the emergency exit. The defector's interrogations had only just begun; and if he could prove his worth, he would be reborn into a new, infinitely more productive life.

Miocene took her time repacking the electronic filebox and adding a vial of ash to the ash pile – exactly what would be left by a man's head. Then she picked up the book that had so bothered her grandson, and on a whim, she opened it to the reactor. Virtue had been correct, she realized. And she made a footnote to future scholars before she carefully returned the volume to its proper shelf.

The temple administrator was waiting in the stairwell.

With her hands wrapped in front of her, half-hidden by her lumpy robe, she looked up at the Submaster, winced and began to ask, 'Where is he—?'

Then she smelled death, or she saw it walking the stairs with Miocene.

'What . . . ?' the woman sputtered, never more nervous.

'The defector,' Miocene replied, 'was a spy. A transparent attempt to plant an agent in our midst.'

'But to kill him . . . here, in the temple . . . !'

'To my mind, there's no more appropriate location.' The Submaster pushed past her, then remarked, 'You may clean up. I would be most thankful if you would do me this favor, and that you never mention any of this to anyone.'

'Yes, madam,' a tiny voice squeaked.

Then Miocene was in the open hallway again, the rattling, ill-disciplined voices singing about the bridge soon to be built and the rewards to be won, and for no precise reason, it seemed important for her to step out into the expansive chamber, facing the ranks of devoted worshipers.

It was chilling and enchanting to realize how easily, almost effortlessly, children embraced the words and dreams of another. Miocene looked at the startled, smiling faces, seeing nothing but the purest belief. Yet these people knew nothing about the worlds beyond their own. None had walked the ship's smallest hallway, much less witnessed the beauty and majesty of the Milky Way. They sang of this great quest to return to the world above, ready to make any sacrifice to move past their simple silver sky. A sky unblemished, save for that lone patch of darkness directly above – the base camp, still and always abandoned.

Abandoned like the ship itself?

Billions might have died, and Miocene didn't care. Perhaps she once hated the idea that her people, following her reasonable instructions, had triggered an elaborate, ancient booby trap, causing every organism above them to be murdered. But what had horrified once was now history, past and murky as only history can be, and how could Miocene accept any blame for what was surely unavoidable?

The ship might be dead, but she most definitely was alive.

To the pleasure of several thousand parishioners, this living embodiment of everything great about themselves joined in with their singing, Miocene's voice strong and and relentless and untroubled by its melodic failures.

How easily they believe, she thought with a fond contempt.

Then as she sang about the sweet light of G-class stars, Miocene asked herself, in her most secret voice, 'But what if it's the same for the great souls?'

She wondered:

'What do I believe too willingly and too well . . . ?'

Twenty-two

THE COLD IRON would occasionally shift on its own, giving no warning. The old faults never moved quickly or particularly far, and they rarely caused damage of consequence. The tremor-abatement facilities absorbed the event's energies, and where feasible, what was harvested was piped into the main power grid. In that sense, quakes were a blessing. But the unscheduled events had a nagging habit of interrupting a certain captain's deepest sleep, causing her to awaken suddenly, her dreams swirling out of reach in those delicious few moments before she found herself lucid again.

That morning's quake lingered. Awake in her bed, lying on her right side, Washen felt the shudder falling away slowly, turning into the quiet, steady, and purposeful drumming of her own heart.

The calendar on the wall displayed the date.

4611.277.

Sheer curtains cut to resemble the unfolded wings of a lusciousfly let in the anemic skylight, illuminating the bedroom in which she had slept for the last six centuries. Steel walls covered with polished umbra wood gave the structure a palpable, reassuring strength. The high steel ceiling bristled with hooks and potted plants and little wooden houses, drab as dirt, where domesticated lusciousflies roosted and made love. A rare species in the bright, hot days after the Event, the lovely creatures had been growing more abundant as the overhead buttresses diminished – a cycle presumably aeons old. At Promise-and-Dream's Genetic Works, the siblings had tinkered with their colors and size, producing giant butterflylike organisms with elaborate, every-colored wings. Every Loyalist seemed to have his own flock. And since there were twenty million homes in the nation, the sibling captains had made themselves a tidy, even enviable profit.

As Washen sat up in bed, her lusciousflies came out to greet her. With the softness of shadows, they perched on her bare shoulders and in her hair, licking at the salt of her skin and leaving their subtle perfumes as payment.

She shooed them away with a gentle hand.

Her old clock lay open on the tabletop. According to

the slow metal hands, she could sleep for another hour. But her body said otherwise. While the mirrored uniform dressed her, Washen remembered dreaming, and the tremor. For a few wasted moments, she tried to resurrect her last dream. But it had slipped away already, leaving nothing but a vague, ill-fed disquiet.

Not for the first time, it occurred to Washen that she could build a universe from her lost dreams.

'Maybe that's their real purpose,' she whispered to her pets. 'When my universe is finished, so am I.'

Laughing quietly, she set her mirrored cap on her head. *There.*

Breakfast was peppered bacon over a toasted sweetcake, everything washed down with hot tea and more hot tea. The Genetics Works were responsible for the bacon, too. A few centuries ago, responding to the captains' complaints, Promise and Dream had cultured several familiar foods in lab vats; respectable steaks and cured meats were the result. But it was a minor project, finished quickly and cheaply. Instead of trying to resurrect the genetics of cattle and boars, from memory, the siblings used the only available meat-bearer – humans – tweaking the genetics enough to make a fleshy product that wasn't human. Not in texture, or in flavor. Or hopefully, in spirit.

Just which captains were used as a model was a secret. But persistent rumors claimed it was Miocene – a possibility that perhaps accounted for the popularity of the foods, among both captains as well as certain grandchildren.

With an extra hour in her day, Washen took her time. She ate slowly. She read both competing news services; neither offered anything of real interest. Then she stepped from her house out into her very long yard, strolling on a path of native iron blocks rusted into a pleasant shade of drab red, little tufts of grayhair and sadscent growing in the gaps.

Gardening was a recent hobby. Her one-time lover, long-time friend Pamir used to be an accomplished gardener. What were his flowers of choice? The Ilano-vibra, yes. Maybe he was gardening today, if he was alive. And if he was, wouldn't that old criminal be astonished, seeing Washen's ambitious soul bending at the knees, plucking at the blackish weeds with her bare fingers?

As the buttresses weakened, as the skylight fell away into a twilightlike glow, the Marrow ecosystem continued to transform itself. Obscure species that lived only in caves and the deepest jungles weren't simply abundant, they were huge. Like the elfhearts in the middle of her garden. A species that was mature when it was hip-high inside the deepest shade had transformed itself into stout trees with trunks nearly a meter thick and a richly scented purple-black foliage, giant leaves and flowers mixed into a single elaborate structure that was fertilized by the lusciousflies, then curled into a black ball that matured into a fatty fruit, only a little toxic and with a lovely, if somewhat strong taste.

Washen kept the trees for their scent and her flies, and for their almost-terran limbs.

She kept them because some decades ago, a boyish lover had allowed himself to be taken in this orchard, and taken again.

Past the orchard were wide iron steps leading down to Idle Lake. No body of water on the world was older. Born fifteen hundred years ago, this patch of crust could lay claim to being the most ancient slab of iron ever to exist on Marrow: a testament to the captains' ingenuity and persistence. Or was it their obsessive need for order?

The old lake was still and stained red with rust and

ruddy planktons. Above, stretching like some great steel ceiling, the chamber's wall looked near enough to touch. This was a pure illusion, of course. Marrow's atmosphere ended fifty kilometers short of the wall. The radiant buttresses still ruled above the swelling world. They remained dangerously strong, if considerably thinner. And for the next three hundred-plus years, they would continue to thin, and Marrow would expand, and according to every forecast and every carefully plotted graph, the buttresses would reach their minimum when Marrow's atmosphere began to lick against the chamber wall.

Finally, the captains would be able to climb to the base camp, and the access tunnel, and if the tunnel hadn't crumbled, they could move up into the vastness of the ship itself. Which was a derelict now, probably. Assuredly. Millennia of debate hadn't produced any other reasonable explanation for their long, perfect solitude, and three more centuries probably wouldn't change that grim assessment.

Washen opened the silver lid of her old, much-cherished timepiece, deciding that in this great march of centuries, she still had a few moments to waste.

Old, light-starved virtue trees had made the planks that were fixed to the stainless steel pontoons that held up Washen's dock. She strolled out to the end, listening to the pleasant sound of her dress boots striking wood. A tiny school of hammerwing larvae swam away, then turned and came back again, perhaps wanting handouts. Fins sloshed. Big many-faceted eyes saw a human figure against the hyperfiber sky. Then Washen closed the lid of her little clock, and the sudden click caused the school to dive deep in a single smooth panic, only swirls of red water betraying their presence.

Idle was an ancient lake, and by Marrow standards, it was impoverished, senile. An ecosystem built on frequent, radical change didn't appreciate stability and a thousand years of eutrophication.

Washen slipped the clock and its titanium chain into a trusted pocket, and her dream suddenly came back to her. Without warning, she remembered being somewhere else. Somewhere high, wasn't it? Perhaps on top of the bridge, which was only reasonable; she worked here every day. Only somehow that possibility didn't feel right, either.

Someone else was in her dream.

Whom, she couldn't say. But she had heard a voice, clear and strong, telling her with such sadness, 'This is not the way it is supposed to be.'

'What's wrong?' she had asked.

'Everything,' the voice declared. 'Everything.'

Then she looked down at Marrow. It seemed even larger than it was today, bright with fire and with molten, white-hot lakes of iron. Or was that iron? It occurred to Washen that the glow looked wrong . . . although she couldn't seem to piece together an answer from the sparse, ill-remembered clues . . .

'What is "everything"?' She had asked the voice.

'Don't you see?' the voice replied.

'What should I see?'

But no answer was offered, and Washen turned, trying to look at her companion. She turned and saw . . . what . . . ?

Nothing came to mind, save for the odd and thrilling sensation of falling from a very great height.

HER PUTTERCAR NEEDED surgery.

Time and the hard steel roads had dismantled is suspension, and the simple turbine engine had developed an odd, nagging whine. But Washen hadn't gotten around to seeing it fixed. The vehicle still ran, and there was the salient fact that every machine shop in the capital had priorities. Personal transportation held a low priority. On Miocene's orders, every device that directly served the growing bridge held sway over personal concerns. And while Washen could have claimed privilege – wasn't she a vital part of this heroic effort? – she felt uncomfortable demanding favors.

For six hundred years, with rare exceptions, she had driven this route into the metropolis. Her local road merged with a highway that took her straight through older, more densely settled neighborhoods. Fifty-story apartment buildings stood in the mandatory parks, the black foliage mixed with playground equipment and the scrambling, energetic bodies of screaming children. Single houses and row houses and houses perched on aging, enfeebled virtue trees testified to the wild diversity of people left to their own logic. No two structures were the same, including the tallest buildings. And no two neighborhood temples could be confused for one another, sharing nothing but the dome-hearted architecture and a certain comfortable majesty.

Washen's feelings about this faith were complex, and fickle. There were moments and years when she believed Miocene was a cynical leader, and this religion was as contrived as almost every other faith that Washen had met, and much less beautiful, too. But there were also unexpected, if fleeting moments when the hymns and the pageantry and everything else about it made sudden and perfect sense.

There was an ethereal charm to this bizarre mishmash.

The ship was real, she reminded herself. The object of their devotion was a miraculous, amazing machine, and empty or otherwise, it was plying its way through a wondrous universe. And even after her long isolation, the captain inside her felt a powerful duty toward that ball of hyperfiber and cold rock.

The puttercar highway grew wide, then evaporated into the central district.

Three hundred-story skyscrapers rose from the trustworthy ground. Steel skeletons were cloaked in acrylic windows and set on frictionless, sway-resistant foundations. A different logic had created the administrative headquarters. Fashioned from titanium and tough ceramics, it resembled a giant puffball – no windows showing to the outside world, its base reinforced in a hundred ways, walls armored and bristling with hidden weapons. The enemy was never mentioned, but it wasn't much of a secret. A Wayward assault was Miocene's most paranoid fear, offered without the slightest evidence. Yet it was a fear that Washen shared, if only on certain days. No, she didn't look at those impregnable walls with pride, exactly. But they didn't make her bristle, either.

Past the puffball were the six domes of the Great Temple. And standing at its center, directly beneath the abandoned base camp, was the only object that truly mattered to the Loyalist nation.

The bridge.

No wider than a large skyscraper and pale gray against the silver sky, the structure seemed lost at first glance. By ship standards, its hyperfiber shell was of a poor grade. But each gram of the stuff had come at great cost, grown inside sprawling, muscular factories built for no other purpose. True, most of the hyperfiber was thrown away, inadequate even for simple structural duties. But just to reach this modest point was a marvel. Aasleen and her teams had done miracles. Despite shortages of key elements, tons of hyperfiber had been created, one little droplet at a time, and then teams under Washen's gaze had slowly and carefully poured those gray droplets into molds that pushed the bridge higher every day. On the very best days, the bridge rose a full fat meter.

'I know that I'm asking too much,' Miocene had admitted on many occasions. 'A slower pace would be fast enough, and there wouldn't be as many hardships on our grandchildren. But these are only hardships. Not lives. And I want our people to see their energies going toward something genuine. Something they can touch, and climb – with our permission – and something that is visibly progressing.'

What the eye found unimpressive at first glance was quite tall, and even to an old woman who had seen plenty of marvels, the bridge had a magnificence that always made her blink and shiver. It was far taller than any neighboring skyscraper. Taller than all of them set on top of each other, in fact. It reached up into the cold stratosphere. If they didn't add another centimeter, Marrow's own expansion could lift it up until it nearly kissed the surviving nub of the old bridge, and their escape would be complete.

But that led to a problem.

Washen had always doubted Miocene's rationale. Maybe their people needed something tangible. Although hadn't they always been wonderfully motivated by the abstract charms of the mythlike ship? And maybe this was a project that should be completed as quickly as possible, regardless of costs and deprivations. But the fledging bridge stood on an island of iron, and the iron was drifting on a slow, ancient ocean. Plumes of white-hot metal were rising beneath them, each plume wrestling with its neighbors. Heat and momentum played a slow, relentless game. True, the abatement teams had managed to steer the plumes, forcing them to cancel each other's effects. Drifting ten meters north or sixty east were workable issues. But they still had three centuries of tectonic tampering ahead of them, and what was difficult today would only become more so. With the crust acting as a blanket, the trapped heat could only grow, the molten iron would rise faster and faster, and like any liquid that needs to move, the iron would show persistence and a low cunning.

'This is too soon,' she had told the Submaster. The ancient woman had become a recluse over these last centuries. She had her own elaborate compound between the factories and the bridge. She ruled by dispatches and digitals. Walls of scrap hyperfiber hid whatever passed for a life, and sometimes an entire year would pass without the two women meeting face-to-face. Miocene only emerged for the annual Submaster feast, which was where Washen asked her bluntly, 'What if Marrow pushes the bridge completely out of alignment?'

But Miocene possessed her own form of persistence. 'First of all,' she replied, 'that will not happen. Hasn't the situation been well in hand for the last thousand years?'

With the buried heat escalating all the time, yes.

'And second of all, is any of this your responsibility? No, it is not. In fact, you have no role in any key decision.' Miocene seemed cold and troubled, shaking her head as she explained, 'I gave you a role in the bridge's construction, Washen, because you motivate the grandchildren better than most. And because you're willing to make your own decisions without troubling the Submasters every day.'

Miocene didn't like to be troubled anymore.

There were whispers about her hermitage. Sad rumors, typically. Some claimed that Miocene wasn't at all alone. She kept a secret cadre of young grandchildren whose only function was to entertain her, sexually and otherwise. It was a ludicrous story, but centuries old just the same. And what was that old warning? If you tell a lie often and if you tell it well, then the truth has no choice but to change Her face . . .

With a hard thump of tires, Washen pulled into the main garage.

The Great Temple was always open to the public. From the basement garage to the old library, she was surrounded by crowds of worshipers from across the city and from every end of the Loyalist nation. Happens River had sent a dozen grinning pilgrims bearing a special gift – a giant, hugely massive nickel bust of Miocene – and the temple administrator wore a pained, confused expression, telling them thank you in the same breath that she warned them that all gifts needed to be registered beforehand. 'Do you see my point? And thank you so much, again. But how else can I keep this place from being a cluttered mess? With so much devotion, don't we need a system?'

There were many ways into the bridge.

Most of the routes were subterranean, and armored, and typically locked. Washen preferred to enter through a small door at the back of the library. The important security measures were thorough but subtle. But to convince visitors of the facility's impregnability, armed guards stood in plain view, eyeing everyone; even high-ranking captains deserved a look of cold suspicion.

Twice in twenty meters, Washen was scanned and registered.

Reaching a secondary elevator, she signed her name into the register, then allowed an autodoc to take a snip of tissue, a sip of blood.

With confidence, the nearest guard said, 'Good morning, Madam Washen.'

'Hello, Golden,' she replied.

For the last twenty years, without fail, the man had sat at his station, never complaining, observing the comings and goings of thousands of talented, determined workers. Besides a square face and a name, he seemed to have no identity of his own. If Washen asked about his life, he deflected the question. It was their game. At least it was her game. But she didn't feel like playing it today. Watching her hand scrawl her name on the thinking plastic, she found herself recalling her dream again, wondering why it was bothering her so much.

'Have a good day, madam.'

'You, too, Golden. You, too.'

Alone, Washen sat in the car and rode to the top of the bridge. Another square-faced guard welcomed her by name, saluted briefly, then reported the most important news of the day. 'Rain is coming, madam.'

'Good.'

The only windows on the bridge were here. A series of tall diamond panes looked out on the near vacuum of the stratosphere. The sky was hyperfiber and a tired blue glow came from nowhere, from everywhere. And fifty kilometers below was the city and its surrounding ring of farms, dormant volcanoes, and aging red lakes reaching out to a horizon that looked as if it were about to press up against the chamber's wall.

Only from here did Marrow resemble a faraway place.

This was a view that any captain could appreciate.

As promised, a line of thunderstorms were drifting toward the city. The tallest clouds were intricate and clean and white, beautifully shaped and constantly twisted by winds into even more beautiful shapes. But the clouds were little more than bumps above the remote terrain. As the buttresses weakened, storms grew less frequent, and less angry. Without light and an abundance of water to feed them, they tended to fade and fall apart as swiftly as they formed.

Another three-plus centuries, and Marrow would be immersed in darkness.

And for how long?

Maybe a ship-day. Or maybe twenty years. Either was a viable estimate, and nobody knew enough to feel certain. But each of the native species had a reservoir of unexpressed genes, and in laboratory conditions, bathed in night, the genes awakened, allowing the vegetation and blind insects to fall into a durable hibernation.

The buttresses would vanish, it was assumed. Or at least fade to negligible levels. And the Loyalists would climb up this wondrous makeshift bridge, reaching the base camp, then the ship beyond.

In polite company, nobody even discussed the possibilities that lay beyond that point. After forty-six centuries, the same theories ruled. And every other bizarre explanation had been offered, then debated in depth, and finally, mercifully, buried in a very deep, unmarked grave.

Whatever was, was.

That's what Washen told herself as she entered her small, spartan office, taking her seat before a bank of controls and monitors and simple-minded AIs.

'Whatever is, is.'

Then like every other morning, she let herself gaze out the diamond window. Maybe the bridge was too much and too soon. But even still, it was a marvel of engineering and ad hoc inventiveness, and sometimes, in a secret part of herself, Washen wished there was some way to carry it along with the grandchildren.

To show the universe both treasures in which she felt such pride.

'MADAM WASHEN?'

She blinked, turned.

Her newest assistant stood in the office doorway. An intense, self-assured man of no particular age, he was

obviously puzzled — a rare expression for him — and with
a mixture of curiosity and confusion, he announced, 'Our
shift is over.'

'In another fifty minutes,' she replied, pushing aside her
daily report. Washen knew the time, but the habit of her
hands was to open her silver watch, eyes glancing at the
slow hands. 'Forty-nine minutes, and a few seconds.'

'No, madam.' Nervous fingers tugged at the dangling
Gordian braids, then attempted to smooth the crisp blue
fabric of his uniform. 'I was just told, madam. Everyone is
to leave the bridge immediately, using every tube but the
Primary.'

Washen looked at her displays. 'I don't see orders.'

'I know—'

'Is this a drill?' Drills happened from time to time. If
the crust beneath them subsided, they might have only
moments to evacuate. 'Because if it's an exercise, we need
a better system than having you wandering about, tapping
people on their shoulders.'

'No, madam. It's not that.'

'Then what—?'

'Miocene,' he blurted. 'She contacted me personally. On
a secure line. Following her instructions, I've dismissed our
construction crews, and I've placed our robots into their
sleep mode.'

Washen said nothing, thinking hard.

With a barely restrained frustration, he added, 'This is
very mysterious. Everyone agrees. But the Submaster is
fond of her secrets, so I'm assuming—'

'Why didn't she talk to me?' asked Washen.

The assistant gave a big lost shrug.

'Is she coming here?' she asked. 'Is she using the
Primary?'

A quick nod.

'Who's with her?'

'I don't know if there's anyone else, madam.'

The Primary tube was the largest. Fifty captains could ascend inside one of its cars, never brushing elbows with each other.

'I already looked,' he confessed. 'It's not a normal car.'

Washen found the rising car on her monitors, then tried to wake a platoon of cameras. But none of them would respond to her commands.

'The Submaster asked me to take the cameras off-line, madam. But I happened to get a glimpse of the car first, by accident.' The assistant grimaced as he made his confession. 'It's a massive object, judging by the energy demands. With an extra-thick hull, I would surmise. And there are some embellishments that I can't quite decipher.'

'Embellishments?'

He glanced at his own clock, pretending that he was anxious to leave. But he was also proud of his courage, smiling when he explained, 'The car is dressed up inside pipelike devices. They make it look like someone's ball of rope.'

'Rope?'

With a dose of humility, he admitted, 'I don't quite understand that apparatus.'

In plain words, 'Please explain it to me, madam.'

But Washen explained nothing. Looking at her assistant – one of the most loyal of the captains' loyal offspring; a man who had proved himself on every occasion – she shrugged her shoulders, took a secret breath, then lied.

She said, 'I don't understand it, either.'

Then, as an afterthought, she inquired, 'Was my name mentioned, by any chance? While you and Miocene were chatting, I mean.'

'Yes, madam. She wanted me to tell you to stay here, and wait.'

Washen took a little breath, saying nothing.

'I'm supposed to leave you here,' he whined.

'Well, then, do what our Submaster wants,' was Washen's advice. 'Leave right now. If she finds you here, I guarantee she'll throw you down the shaft herself.'

Twenty-three

FOR CENTURIES, VIRTUE had proved himself with his genius and his passion for the work. On all occasions, contrived or genuine, he had acted with as much loyalty as anyone born into the Loyalist nation. Yet even now – particularly now – Miocene couldn't make herself completely trust the little man.

'It might not work,' he warned her, again.

She said, 'It will,' and looked past him, watching the sealed and simple mechanical door, imagining it opening and her stepping that much closer to the end. Another barrier crossed, if only a small one. Then she reminded Virtue, 'In your simulations, success is a ninety percent event. And we both appreciate how difficult you make your simulations.'

The Wayward scalp had grown hair. A Gordian bun and implanted gemstones made him look like any Loyalist, while the busy gray eyes had acquired a fondness for the Submaster, deeply felt and surprising to both of them.

Quietly, angrily, Virtue told her, 'This is too soon.'

She said nothing.

'Another two years, and I can improve the odds—'

'One or two percent,' she quoted. Then staring at the

fond eyes, Miocene wondered why she didn't trust him. Was she that suspicious, or that gifted? Either way, she would feel better if she could find a fair reason to send him home again.

'Miocene.'

He said her name tenderly, hopefully. Fondness dissolved into a stew of deeper emotions, and where the voice stopped, a small tidy hand reached out, reached up, grabbing hold of her right breast.

After so long, a Wayward gesture.

She said, 'No,' to him, or to herself.

Again, he said, 'Miocene.'

The Submaster removed his hand with one of hers, bending back two of his fingers until his face filled with a pained surprise.

'That little quake helped the alignment,' she reminded him. '"By nearly half a meter," you said. "But the next quake or two could steal our advantage."'

'I said it,' he agreed. 'I remember.'

'Besides,' she whispered. 'If we wait, we'll likely lose the gift of surprise.'

'But we've kept our work secret for this long.' When determined, Virtue could look like his father. Like Till. The narrow face was full of emotions, and you were never sure which emotion would bubble out next. 'What would it injure? Give me another full day, and I'll recheck every system and recalibrate the guidance system, plus both back-ups—'

'But,' Miocene interrupted, 'this is the day. This is.'

He had no choice but to sigh and shake his empty hands, and surrender. And just like that, he suddenly looked nothing at all like Till.

'Don't you believe in destinies?' she asked. 'You're a Wayward, after all.'

'Not now,' he grumbled, hurt by the insult. 'If I ever was.'

'Destinies,' she repeated. 'I woke this morning knowing that this was the morning. I understood that fully, and I have no idea why.' She felt herself smiling, looking through him as she explained, 'I'm not superstitious. You know that much about my character. And that's why I know that this is the right, perfect moment. Intuition is instructing me. Every day that I make ready is another opportunity to be found out, and why would I want that? My Loyalists. Your Waywards. Let's allow both our peoples as much ignorance as they can possibly cherish. Isn't that what we agreed?'

Virtue nodded helplessly.

As a lover, he reached for the comforting curve of her breast, and Miocene intercepted the hand, lowering it and holding tight to the fingers, gazing into the warm and caring steel-gray eyes.

From the charred remains of his mind, she had resurrected him – never letting him forget on whose charity his existence was perched. But even with that intimacy, and after living for centuries in her private compound, surrounded by luxuries and every research toy that Marrow could provide – not to mention her own compliant body – the little man insisted on surprising her. That's why she could only trust him to a point. She didn't know him perfectly, and now, at this point, she never would.

Tenderly, he said, 'Darling.'

He confessed, 'I don't want to lose you, darling.'

Quietly and fiercely, Miocene promised, 'If you don't do this one thing for me, you'll most assuredly lose me. I won't see you to shit on you. And you know I mean it.'

He shrank.

He started to say, 'Darling,' once again.

But the car was deaccelerating, and the massive door

was preparing to unseal itself. To her lover and to herself, Miocene said, 'This is the moment.'

At long last.

AS ORDERED, WASHEN was waiting.

As the door opened outward, the first-grade peered into the tiny cabin, eyes the color of band iron staring at the stranger – at Virtue – even as her steady, mocking voice asked, 'Madam, are you insane? Do you really think this can work?'

Then she answered her own questions.

'No, you aren't insane,' she said. 'And yes, you've got to think it can.'

'Washen,' Miocene replied. 'I'd recognize your wit anywhere, darling.'

She stepped out of the car. The Submaster had never visited the control room, but it was exactly like its holo-plans, complete to the banks of glowing instruments and the absence of human bodies. Most of its systems had barely been tested. Why bother when it would be another three centuries before they were meant to be used?

'You'll need me to oversee,' Washen assumed. Then she stared at Virtue, remarking, 'I don't know you.'

'She doesn't need you, and you don't know me,' the man replied. Bristling now.

Miocene faced her captain, and exactly as she had imagined the moment, she said, 'No, my associate will oversee the launch. He's fully versed in this equipment.'

Washen nearly blinked.

Then to her credit, she focused on the larger issue. 'You've got to have accuracy to do this. Because what we're talking about here is shooting a fat cannonball between two cannons. Am I right?'

A nod. 'Always, darling.'

'And if you can hit the old bridge true, you'll still have enough time and distance to brake your momentum. True?'

'A rough, abrupt stop. It has to be.'

'But even as thin and weak as the buttresses are . . . this ugly little ship has got to do an impressive job of protecting you.'

'It will,' Miocene replied.

Virtue took a deep, skeptical breath.

Washen examined the car in person, touching the outside of the hatch, fondling the odd, ugly pipes. 'Aasleen suggested something along these lines,' she allowed. 'I can't remember when, it was that long ago. But after she was done explaining herself, you said no. You said it would be too clumsy and too limited, not to mention the technical hurdles, and you ordered us to put our efforts into richer ground.'

'I said those things. Yes.'

For lack of anything better, Washen smiled, and she said, 'Well, then. The best of luck to you.'

Miocene let herself show a grin. 'Good luck to both of us, you mean. The interior, as you see, seats two.'

The woman was brave, but she wasn't fearless or a fool. She had to flinch and think hard about her next breath, eyeing the Submaster for a long moment before asking, 'Why? Me?'

'Because I respect you,' Miocene replied, honestly and without qualms.

The dark eyes grew larger.

'And because if I order you to accompany me, you will. Now.'

Washen took a careful breath, and another. Then she admitted, 'I suppose all of that's true.'

'And truthfully, I need you.'

That declaration seemed to embarrass everyone.

To kill the silence, Miocene turned to Virtue, telling

him, 'Start the procedures.' She paused. Then quietly, she added, 'As soon as we're on board.'

The man looked ready to cry.

She didn't leave him the opportunity. With a crisp wave and a defiant stride, Miocene reentered the car. Not for the first time, she thought how it resembled the Great Ship – a thick body with a hidden hollow sphere at its center.

To Washen, she said, 'Now, darling.'

The first-grade was obviously considering her next step, and everything else, too. Long, strong hands wiped themselves dry against her uniform, and with a mixture of stiffness and grace, she bent over and climbed through the hatchway, then examined the twin seats, padded and set on greased titanium rails. The seats would always keep their backs to the accelerations. As if to appreciate the technology, she touched the simple control panel, then the inner wall. The hand pulled away abruptly, and she said, 'Cold,' with a quiet little voice.

'Crude, chilly superconductors,' Miocene admitted.

Then the Submaster touched the panel, and as the hatch pulled itself shut, she said, 'Virtue.' She looked out at him and said, 'I trust you.'

The man was crying. Nothing but.

The hatch closed and sealed itself, and as the two women sat together, back to back, Washen said, 'You trust him, and you respect me, too.' She was securing her protective straps, and laughing. 'Trust and respect. From you, on the same day.'

Miocene refused to look over her shoulder. She busied herself making last-instant checks, saying to the controls, 'You're more gifted than I am when it comes to other people. You can speak to the grandchildren, and the other captains . . . and that's a sweet skill that could prove an enormous advantage . . .'

Washen had to ask, 'Why is that an advantage?'

'I could explore the ship alone,' Miocene allowed. 'But if the worst has happened – if everything above us is dead and empty – then you, I think, Washen . . . you are the better person to bring home that terrible news . . .'

Twenty-four

HERE WAS THE culmination of more than four thousand years of single-minded labor – two captains ready to throw themselves off Marrow. Washen found herself strapped into the primitive crash chair, part of her demanding some task, some worthwhile duty, even when she knew full well that there was nothing to do now but sit and wait and wish for the best.

With a crisp, dry voice, Miocene worked her way down a precise checklist.

Her mysterious companion might resemble Till, or Diu, but his voice was far too slow and uncertain to belong to either man. He spoke across an intercom, alternating, 'Good,' and 'Yes,' and, 'Nominal,' with little pained silences.

The captains sat back to back. Unable to see the Submaster's face, Washen found herself thinking about little else. It was the same cold, confident face that it had always been, and it wasn't. Washen always marveled at how Marrow had changed that rigid woman. A metamorphosis showed in the wasted, haunted eyes, in the taut corners of the pained mouth. And when she spoke, as she did now, even a simple word felt infinitely sad, and a little profound.

'Initiate,' that sad voice commanded.

There was a pause.

Then the little man said softly, with resignation, 'Yes, madam.'

They were falling, accelerating down a dark, airless shaft. This wasn't a bridge, and it was never supposed to be. It was a vast piece of munitions, and everything depended on its accuracy. Descending to the starting point, to the electromagnetic breech, Miocene whispered technical details. Terminal velocity. Exposure to the buttresses. The transit time. 'Eighteen point three seconds.' Which was nearly as long as they spent inside the buttresses on their way down. But without the same levels of protection, or backup systems, or even a single field test beyond the laboratory.

The ugly cannonball stopped abruptly, then its thick walls began to hum. To crackle, and sputter, and seemingly ripple as the protective fields were woven tightly around them.

Again, Miocene said, 'Initiate.'

There was no response this time. Would the man obey? But as she thought those words, Washen was slammed back into her seat, bone pressed against dense padding, gee forces mounting, tearing flesh and bursting blood vessels.

Then came the sensation of drifting.

A pleasant, teasing peace.

After leaving the shaft, there was perhaps a half second of streaking up through the last breaths of the atmosphere, a cluster of little rockets firing on the hull, correcting for the very thin winds. In her mind's eye, Washen saw everything: Marrow's storm clouds and cities and tired volcanoes falling behind while the slick sliver of the chamber wall descended on them. Then they struck the buttresses, and her eyes filled with random colors and senseless shapes, while a thousand incoherent, terrified voices screamed inside her dying mind.

Madness.

Eighteen point three seconds of nothing else.

Time dragged. That's what she promised herself when she managed to concentrate, carving a sensible thought out of that screaming chaos. It was a symptom of the buttresses, this compression of the seconds. Because if more than eighteen seconds had passed, they had simply missed their target, falling short, and now they were tumbling in a close, fatal orbit around Marrow.

No, we can't be, Washen whimpered.

The frightened voices lent her their fear, and a ragged wild panic took her by the throat, by the colon. Nausea came in one savage thrust. Washen bent forward as far as the padded straps allowed, and with her left hand she managed to yank the silver clock from its pocket, then open it, that sequence of practiced motions requiring what seemed to be hours of relentless work.

She stared at the fastest hand.

A solid click meant that a full second had passed.

Then, another.

Then her seat, and Miocene's, unlocked and slipped on the titanium rails, meeting at the opposite end of the little cabin, locking again with a crisp determination.

Washen looked up.

Swallowing a burning mouthful of bile and vomit, she stared up at where she had just been, and she saw herself restrained in an identical chair, her own face twisted in misery, gazing down, hair hanging loose and long, unlike Washen's bunned hair, and the mouth opening as if this hallucination were ready to offer a few tortured words.

Washen watched herself, and in rapt attention, listened.

But then they had pierced the buttresses, and a string of angry rockets fired beneath Washen, braking the vehicle as it plunged, she hoped, into the battered remains of the original bridge.

Impact.

Washen felt the car scrape hard against hyperfiber. There was a sloppy shrieking on her right as pipes and boiling superconductors were stripped away. Then an instant of silence, followed by a second, deeper roar from her left, their car bouncing down the shaft.

Rockets barked again, killing momentum at all costs.

The final impact was abrupt and crushing, and it was over before her mind registered the barest pain.

The chair fell back into its original position.

A voice said, 'There.'

Miocene's voice. Then the Submaster fought her way out of her belts and made herself stand, holding her long sides as she sipped each breath, acting as if her ribs had been shattered.

Washen's ribs were on fire. She eased herself out of her chair, feeling the delicious warmth as the curved bones knitted themselves. Emergency genes synthesized machinery that turned masticated flesh into new bone and blood, giving her strength enough to stand. She sipped one breath, then another. The hatch began to open itself, creaking with each slow millimeter. If it jammed, they were trapped. Doomed. But that would be a ridiculous finish. Ludicrous. Which was why she dismissed the possibility, refusing to worry.

The hatch gave a squeal and jammed.

Then after a prolonged silence, it freed itself with a white-hot screech.

Darkness fell on them. Miocene stepped out into the silence, into the darkness. Her exhausted black eyes were huge. She was staring at the empty berths as Washen climbed and joined her, the two women standing close enough to touch each other, but avoiding that gesture, busily scouring their memories for the way out of the unlit assembly station.

At the same moment they pointed in the same direction, saying, 'That way.'

Base camp had been without power for forty-six centuries. The Event had crippled every machine. Reactors, drones, all of it. The magnetic latches on every sealed door had failed. Pushing the last door aside, they stepped out into the soft, muted light of the dying buttresses.

'Wander,' Miocene ordered. 'For half an hour. Then meet at the observation station, and we'll go on from there.'

'Yes, madam.'

Washen started for the dormitories, then thought better of it. Instead she crept into the biolabs, opening curtains for light and dislodging dust that fell softly over dust. Every system was ruined. Cages with tough mechanical locks remained sealed – an ancient precaution – and inside each cage lay mounds of colorless dust. Washen found keys left hanging above a captain's empty desk. Eventually she found the key that would fit and turn, and quietly, she crept into one of the cages, stepping over a child's doll, then kneeling to reach into the largest dust pile.

Without food or water, the abandoned lab animals had dropped into comas, and as their immortal flesh lost energy and moisture, they had quietly and thoroughly mummified themselves.

Washen picked up one of the mandrill baboons – an enormous male weighing little more than a breath – and she held it against her own body, looking into the desiccated eyes, feeling its leathery heart beat, just once, just to say, 'I waited for you.'

She set him down carefully, and left.

Miocene was standing on the viewing platform, impatient and concerned, gazing expectantly at the horizon. Even at this altitude, they could only see the captains' realm. The nearest Waywards were hundreds of kilometers removed from them. Which might as well have been hundreds of light-years, as much as the cultures interacted anymore.

'What are you looking for?' Washen asked.

The Submaster said nothing.

'They'll find out what what we've done,' Washen had to tell her. 'If Till doesn't know already, I'd be surprised.'

Miocene nodded absently, taking a deep, deep breath.

Then she turned, and never mentioning the Waywards, she said, 'We've wasted enough time. Let's find out what's upstairs.'

TINY CAP-CARS REMAINED in their berths, untouched by any hand and shielded by kilometers of hyperfiber. Their engines remained charged, but every system was locked into a diagnostic mode. The com-links refused to work. The ship was dead, said the silence. But then Washen remembered that the com-link was singular and tightly guarded, and after a century's wait, the security systems would have ripped out the only tongue, as a reasonable precaution.

Miocene offered a code that brought one car to life.

Occasionally Washen would glance at the Submaster, measuring the woman's stern profile, and her silence, wondering which of them was more terrified. The long access tunnel led straight upward, not a trace of damage or disruptions showing anywhere along the narrow shaft. Then the tunnel ended with a slab of hyperfiber. Touch codes caused the slab to detach and fall inward, revealing an abandoned fuel line – a vertical shaft better than five kilometers across.

Against that vastness, the doorway closed again, vanishing.

The car skimmed along the surface of the fuel line, always climbing, gradually turning onto its back as they slipped closer to the vast fuel tank. If the great ship's engines were firing, not so much as a shiver reached them. But those engines rarely ignited, Washen reminded herself. The stillness meant nothing.

Nothing.

Between the women, a pact had formed. Neither mentioned where they were going. After such an enormous wait, neither dared make the tiniest speculation. Possibilities had been exhausted. What was, was. Each said it with her eyes, her silence. It was implicit in the way their long hands lay in their laps, peacefully wrestling with one another.

The vast tunnel passed sleeping pumps larger than some moons.

Quietly, Washen asked, 'Where?'

The Submaster opened her mouth, then hesitated.

Finally, strangely, she asked, 'What do you think is best?'

'The leech habitat,' Washen allowed. 'Maybe someone lives there now. And if not, we could still borrow its com-lines.'

'Do that,' Miocene replied.

They entered through the fuel tank, flying high above the dark hydrogen sea. The leech habitat was exactly as Washen remembered it. Empty. Clean. Forgotten. A scan showed nothing alive and warm. She slipped into its docking berth, then they climbed into the gray hub. With a breath and a slack, numbed expression, Miocene touched the aliens' only com-panel, and nothing happened. In frustration, she said, 'Shit,' and stepped back, telling Washen, 'Do it for me. Please.'

But there wasn't anything to do.

'It's malfunctioned, or there's no com-system anymore.' Washen said the words, then felt her belly knot up and ache.

Miocene glared at the dead machinery.

After a long moment, they turned away, saying nothing as they climbed back into the waiting cap-car.

A narrow service tunnel angled upward, passing through a series of demon doors, an atmosphere building with each crisp crackle. And in a soft, whispering voice, Miocene asked, 'How many were on board? Do you remember?'

'One hundred billion.'

The Submaster closed her eyes and held them closed.

'Plus the machine intelligences. Another one hundred billion, at least.'

Miocene said, 'Dead. They all are.'

Washen couldn't see through her tears. With the back of a hand, she wiped her face, and she muttered, 'We don't know,' with a contrived hopefulness.

But Miocene said, 'Dead,' again. She was defiant about her pronouncement. Then she straightened the clumsy fabric of her uniform, staring at her hands and the reflections that seemed to float inside her chest, and she sighed and looked up, staring straight ahead and sighing once again before announcing, 'There is a higher purpose. To all of this. Since we're still alive, there must be.'

Washen didn't respond.

'A higher purpose,' the woman repeated. Smiling now. That wide strange smile said as much as her words.

The service tunnel ended inside one of the deepest passenger districts. Suddenly they were skimming along the obsidian floor of a broad, flattened tunnel – a minor passageway barely half a kilometer across – and it was plainly, horribly empty. No traffic. No important, busy lights. And to herself, in misery, Washen said, 'Maybe the crew and passengers . . . maybe we were able to evacuate everyone . . .'

'Doubtful,' was Miocene's response.

She turned to stare at Washen, ready to say something else honest, and harsh. But her expression changed abruptly. The eyes went distant, and wide, and Washen looked back over her shoulder in time to see a vast machine appear behind them, bearing down on them until a collision was imminent, then skipping sideways with a crisp, AI precision. And the machine passed them. A car, it was. A light-filled diamond hull held a lake of warm saltwater, and floating in the center of the lake was the sole passenger – a whalelike entity with a forest of strong-handed symbionts rooted on its long back – and as it passed them at a blurring, impolite speed, the entity winked. Three of its black eyes winked just as humans would wink, offering them nothing but a friendly, casual greeting.

It was a Yawkleen.

More than four millenia removed from her post, yet Washen immediately remembered the species' name.

With a flat, disbelieving voice, Miocene said, 'No.'

But it was true.

Suddenly another dozen cars caught up with them, then slipped past. Washen saw four harum-scarums, and what could have been a pair of humans, and then an insectish creature that reminded her, with its intricate jaws and long black back, of the crap-sculptor beetle from the Marrow jungles.

From back home, Washen was thinking.

Where, if the truth were told, she'd almost prefer to be.

Twenty-five

A SMALL, OBSCURE waystation lay on the tubeway's floor.

With a pained voice, Miocene ordered Washen to stop. Their car passed through a series of demon doors, an atmosphere spun around them. Then they did nothing. The Submaster sat erect, hands trembling and her face iron-taut and her mouth opened just enough to pull in a series of quick deep breaths, that private little wind whistling across her angry lips, a wild fury spreading from her eyes into her face, her body, then filling the car until Washen couldn't help but feel her own heart hammering against her new ribs.

Finally, with a soft choked voice, Miocene said, 'Go into the station.'

Washen climbed from the car.

'Do it,' Miocene commanded.

She was shouting at herself, staring at her folded legs and her trembling hands, then at the single hand that Washen offered, along with a quiet voice that reminded her, 'Whatever is, is. Madam.'

The Submaster sighed and stood without accepting help.

The station's lounge was small and tidy, flexible furnishings meant for almost any traveler, its floor and arching walls decorated with beds of false limestones, buttery-yellow and white and gray, each bed impregnated with a different stew of artificial fossils that looked terran at first glance. Which was the only glance that Washen allowed herself, stepping through the last demon door and finding no one present but the resident AI.

'The Master Captain!' Miocene barked. 'Is she alive and well?'

With a smooth cheeriness, the AI reported, 'The woman is in robust good health. And she thanks you for inquiring.'

'How long has she been healthy?' Washen pressed, in case there was a new Master.

'For the last one hundred and twelve millenia,' the machine replied. 'Bless her, and bless ourselves. How can we do otherwise?'

Miocene said nothing, her face red with blood, her rage thick and tireless.

One of the fossil walls was sprinkled with com-booths. Washen stepped inside the nearest booth, saying, 'Emergency status. Captains' channel. Please, we need to speak directly to the Master.'

Miocene stepped into the booth, then sealed its thick door.

The Master's station appeared, spun from light and sound. Three captains and the usual AIs stared at them. Three captains meant this was the nightwatch, the exact time and date floating in the air behind them. Washen opened her clock and stared at the turning hands, realizing that Marrow's clocks had been wrong by a little less than eleven minutes – a minor triumph, considering that the marooned captains had had to reinvent time.

Three human faces stared at them, dumbfounded, while their AIs, full of poise, simply asked, 'What is your business, please?'

'Let me see her!' Miocene thundered.

There was a delay brought by distance, and a longer delay brought by stupidity. Finally, one of the captains remarked, 'Maybe so. Who are you?'

'You know me,' the Submaster replied. 'And I know you. Your name is Fattan. And yours is Cass. And yours, Underwood.'

Cass whispered, 'Miocene . . . ?'

His voice was soft, full of astonishment and doubt.

'Submaster Miocene! First Chair to the Master Captain!' The tall woman bent over the nearest captain, shouting, 'You remember the name and rank, don't you? So act. Something's wicked here, and I need to speak to the Master!'

'But you can't be,' said the cowering man.

'You're dead,' said another captain. Underwood. Then she glanced at Washen, and with a strange pity, she confided, 'You're both dead. For a long time now . . .'

'They're just holos,' the third captain announced. With an obstinate certainty, Fattan said, 'Holos. Projections. Someone's little joke.'

But the AIs had checked their reality by a thousand lightspeed means, and following some secret, long-buried protocol, it was the machines that acted. The image swirled and stabilized again. The Master apeared, sitting up in her great bed. Dressed in a nightgown made from shaped light and airborne pearls, she looked exactly as Washen remembered, her skin golden and her hair a snowy white. But the hair was longer, and instead of being worn in a bun, it lay loose over the broad meaty shoulders. Preoccupied in ways that only a Ship's Master can be, she had to pull her attentions out of a hundred tangled nexuses, then focus on her abrupt guests. Suddenly her bright brown eyes grew huge. In reflex, she touched her own nightgown, probably wondering about their crude, almost laughable imitations of the standard ship uniform. A look of wonder and amazement swept over the broad face, and just as a smile appeared, it collapsed into an instant and piercing fury.

'Where are you?' she snapped. 'Where have you been?'

'Where you sent us.' The Submaster refused to say,

'Madam.' Approaching the bed, her hands pulled into fists, she said, 'We've been on that shit-world . . . on Marrow . . . !'

'Where?' the woman spat.

'Marrow,' the Submaster repeated. Then in exasperation, 'What sort of ridiculous game are you playing with us?'

'I didn't send you anywhere, Miocene . . . !'

In a dim, half-born way, Washen understood.

Miocene shook her head, asking, 'Why keep our mission secret for this long?' Then in the next breath, she answered her own question. 'You meant to imprison us. That's what this was. The best of your captains, and you wanted to push us aside!'

Washen took Miocene by the arm.

'Wait,' she whispered. 'No.'

'The best of my captains? You?' The giant woman gave a wild, cackling laugh. 'My best captains just don't vanish without warning. They don't stay hidden for thousands of years, doing who-knows-what, in secret!' She gasped, the gold of her face brightening. 'Thousands of years,' she said, 'and without so much as a whisper. And it took all of my genius and experience, and every last power at my disposal, to explain your disappearance and steer this ship away from panic!'

Miocene glanced at Washen, her expression astonished. Devastated. In a low, muttering voice, she said, 'But if the Master didn't—'

'Someone else did,' Washen replied.

'Security!' the giant woman cried out. 'Two ghosts are talking to me! Track them! Catch them! Bring them to me!'

Washen killed the link, buying them a moment.

The two ghosts found themselves standing inside the darkened booth, stunned and alone, trying to make sense out of the pure insanity.

'Who could have fooled us?'

Asked Washen.

Then in her next breath, she knew how it could have been: someone with resources and access, and enormous ingenuity, would have sent orders in the Master's name, bringing the captains together in the leech habitat. Then the same ingenious soul deceived them with a replica of the Master, sending them rushing down into the ship's core.

'I could have done this,' Miocene confessed, thinking along the same seductive, paranoid lines. 'Gathered the machinery and fooled all of you. If I'd wished. Assuming that I had known about Marrow, and if I had time, and some compelling reason.'

'But you didn't, and you didn't, and you didn't,' Washen whispered.

'Who did?' Miocene wondered aloud.

They couldn't answer that brutally simple question.

Washen asked the booth for the roster of Submasters and high-ranking captains. She was hunting for suspects, and maybe for a friendly name on which she could place her frail trust.

In a bitter, low voice, Miocene said, 'My seat. Has been filled.'

But the name that leaped out at Washen – what made her legs weak and breath quicken – was the captain occupying her former office.

Pamir.

'Who?' Miocene rumbled.

But in the next instant, she remembered the name. The crime. And with a weak exasperation, the Submaster said, 'This just isn't our ship. It can't be.'

Washen ordered the booth to contact Pamir. On an audio-only line, she warned who was calling. There was a

pause, just long enough for Miocene to say, 'Try another.'
But then Pamir's original face emerged from the darkness.
Strong and homely, the face smiled with a wild amazement. The reborn captain was standing inside his old quarters, surrounded by a meadow of singing llano-vibra plants.

'Quiet,' he told his plants.

Washen and Miocene were standing in the same meadow. The man facing them was bare-chested, tall and powerful through the shoulders, and he was breathing like a sprinter, gasping when he spoke.

'You're dead,' he managed. 'A tragic mishap, they say.'

'What about you?' Washen had to ask.

Pamir shrugged his shoulders as if embarrassed, then said, 'What with the shortfall of talent, there was a general pardon—'

'I don't want your story,' Miocene interrupted. 'Listen. We have to explain . . . we need to tell you what happened . . . !'

But the meadow suddenly turned quiet, and the vegetation grew thin and pale, and Washen could see her own feet through the fading Ilano-vibra, Pamir's fine face vanishing along with the rest of the scene.

Miocene asked, 'What's happening, booth?'

Again the booth was dark; it had nothing to say.

Washen eyed the Submaster, feeling a chill in her hard, hungry belly. The booth's door was sealed, and dead. But the mechanical safeties operated, and with their shoulders they managed to shove the door open. Then together, in a shared motion, they stepped out into the waystation's lounge.

A familiar figure stood in plain view, calmly and efficiently melting the resident AI with a soldier's laser.

It was a machine, Washen realized. The machine was wearing a drab bone-white robe and nothing else. But if it were clothed in a mirrored uniform, with the proper epaulets on its shoulders and the proper voice and vocabulary and manners, then that mechanical device would have been indistinguishable from the Master Captain.

The AI's mind lay in a puddle on the floor, boiling and dead, while an acrid steam rose up and made Washen cough.

Miocene coughed.

Then a third person cleared his throat in a quiet, amused fashion. The captains turned in the same motion and saw a dead man staring at them. He was wearing a tourist's clothes and a simple disguise, and Washen hadn't seen the man for centuries. But the way he stood there with his flesh quivering on his bones, and the way his gray eyes smiled straight at her heart . . . there was absolutely no doubt about his name.

'Diu,' Washen whispered.

Her lover and the father of her child lifted a small kinetic stunner.

Too late and much too slowly, Washen ran.

Then she was somewhere else, and her neck had been broken, and Diu's face was hovering against the gray sky, eyes and the smiling mouth all laughing as he spoke, every word utterly incomprehensible.

Twenty-six

WASHEN CLOSED HER eyes, and her hearing returned.

Another voice descended. 'How did you find Marrow?'

Miocene's voice.

'Remember your mission briefing,' Diu replied. 'But the telltale impact occurred in the early stages of the galactic voyage. Some curious data were gathered. But there were easier explanations, and your dear Master dismissed the idea of a hollow core. The data waited for me to find it. As you recall, I began as a wealthy passenger. With means and the time, I could afford to chase the unlikely and the insane.'

'How long ago was this?'

'When I found Marrow? Not too long after the voyage began, actually.'

'You opened the access tunnel?' asked Miocene.

'Not personally. But I had drones manufactured, and they dug on my behalf, and replicated themselves, and eventually their descendants reached the chamber. Which was when I followed them down.'

A soft laugh, a reflective pause.

'I named Marrow,' Diu announced. 'It was my world to study, and I watched it from above for twenty millennia. When I understood the world's cycles, I commissioned a ship that could cross the buttresses when they were thin and weak. And I touched down first and stepped out onto the iron. Long before you ever did, Madam Miocene.'

Washen opened her eyes again, fighting to make them focus.

'Madam,' Diu sang out, 'I've lived on that wondrous planet more than twice as long as you. And unlike you, I had all the skills and AI helpers that a wealthy man can afford to bring on his adventures.'

What looked like a gray sky became a low gray ceiling, bland and endless. Slowly, very slowly, Washen realized that she was back inside the leech habitat – inside its two-dimensional vastness; who knew where? – and looking the length of her body, she found Diu's face and body framed by the diffuse gray light, his kinetic weapon held in his strong right hand.

'Unlike you,' he reminded, 'I didn't have to reinvent civilization.'

Miocene was standing beside Washen, her face taut and tired but the eyes opened wide, missing nothing.

She glanced down, asking, 'How are you?'

'Awful,' Washen managed. But her voice was dry and clear, and the shattered vertebrae and spinal cord were healing. She was well enough that her hands and toes were waiting for her to notice them, and her body was strong enough that she managed a breath, then lifted herself, sitting upright.

One deep gulp of stale air let her ask, 'How long have we been here?'

'Moments,' Diu replied.

'Did you carry me?'

'My associate did that chore.'

The false Master stood nearby, its white hair brushing against the low ceiling as it turned and turned, watching everything, a dead expression centered on glassy eyes, the stubby emerald-and-teakwood laser bolted to one of its thick forearms.

For as far as Washen could see, twin planes of perfect gray reached into infinity – an assuring endlessness, if you were a leech.

She turned her healing neck. The habitat's wall and a long window were behind her, and aging pillows were strewn about the gray floor. Knowing the answer, she asked Diu, 'Why here?'

'I want to explain myself,' he replied. 'And we have privacy here, as well as a certain symbolism.'

An old memory surfaced. Washen saw herself standing before a leech window, looking at the captains' reflections while Miocene spoke fondly about ambition and its sweet, intoxicating stink.

In an angry low voice, Miocene asked, 'Who knows that you're alive?'

'Except for you, nobody.'

Washen stared at the man, trying to recall why she ever loved him.

'The Waywards saw you die,' said the Submaster.

'They watched my body being consumed by the molten iron. Or at least seemed to be.' He shook his head, boasting, 'When I first came to Marrow, I brought huge stockpiles of raw materials and machinery. I stowed everything in hyperfiber vaults that float inside the liquid iron. When I need them, they surface. When I need to vanish, I can live inside the vaults. Underground.'

Miocene seemed to stare at him. But while Washen glanced at her — just for a slippery instant — the walnut eyes focused on the infinite, their gaze intense and unreadable, a subtle hope lurking somewhere inside them.

Washen said, 'Ambition.'

'Pardon?' asked Diu.

'That's what all of this is about,' she offered. 'Am I right?'

He regarded them with an easy contempt. Then he shook his head, remarking, 'Captains don't understand ambition. I mean real ambition. Rank and tiny honors are nothing compared to what is possible.'

'What is possible?' Miocene barked.

'The ship,' said Washen. Quietly, with certainty.

Diu said nothing.

On clumsy legs, Washen tried to stand, pausing with her knees still bent and breathing with deep gasps. Then Miocene offered her hand, yanking her upright, and the two women embraced like clumsy dancers fighting to keep their balance.

'Diu wants the ship,' Washen muttered. 'He gathered up the most talented captains, then made certain that we were trapped on Marrow when the Event came. He knew we would be marooned. He guessed that we'd have to build a civilization in order to escape. And everything since has been orchestrated by him . . .'

'The Waywards,' Miocene barked. 'Did you create them, Diu?'

'Naturally,' he replied with a wide, smug grin.

'A nation of fanatics being readied for a holy war.' Washen looked at the Submaster, adding, 'With your son as their nominal leader.'

Miocene stiffened, releasing her grip on Washen's arm.

'You fed him those ridiculous visions,' she remarked, eyes peering at the infinite. 'It's always been you, hasn't it?'

'But really,' the grinning man replied. 'If you honestly think about it, aren't you mostly to blame for driving him away?'

A cold, suffocating silence descended.

Washen found the strength to take a step, and with both hands, she massaged the new bone and flesh inside her neck.

Miocene said nothing.

'The Builders,' said Washen.

Diu winked and asked, 'What about them?'

'Were they real? And did they fight the Bleak?'

Diu drank in the suspense, smiling at both of them before admitting, 'How the fuck should I know?'

'The artifacts—' Miocene began.

'Six thousand years old,' Diu boasted. 'Designed and constructed by one of our alien passengers . . . a creative soul who believed that he was making a puzzle intended for the ship's entertainment industry . . .'

'Everything's a lie,' said Washen.

Diu glanced over his shoulder at the false Master. Then he looked back at them, his smile darkening as he explained, 'That elaborate holo you saw? With the Bleak fighting the Builders? It began as a dream. I was the only person on Marrow, and I saw the battle in my sleep. There's always the chance that it was a genuine vision, although, honestly, it felt like nothing but a good vivid dream. Evil pitted against Good. Why not? I thought. A simple faith could be intoxicating for the children to come . . . !'

'But why pretend to die?' Washen asked.

'Death offers freedom.' A boy was lurking behind the smile. 'Being a disembodied soul, I see more. Being deceased, I can disguise myself and walk wherever I want. And sleep where I wish. And I can make babies with a thousand women, including quite a few in the Loyalist camp.'

Silence.

Then a slight whisper, as if a breath of wind were coming.

Miocene took a half-step, then admitted, 'We spoke to the Master.'

'She knows everything,' Washen added. 'We told her—'

'Nothing,' Diu snapped. 'That's exactly what you told her. I know.'

'You're certain?' Washen asked.

'Absolutely.'

'But by now she knows we were at the waystation,' Miocene threatened, 'and she'll hunt for us. With all of her energies.'

'She's been on that same hunt for better than four thousand years.' Diu kept smiling. He almost danced. Then with a hint of confession, he admitted, 'You did surprise me in one way, Miocene. Darling. I knew you were building that little cannonball vehicle, but I didn't think you'd try this soon. If I'd known today was the day, I would have arranged some little accident to keep you on Marrow.' Then he shrugged, adding, 'I didn't want to come chasing after you. But I did. And in a much superior version of your cannonball, I should add.'

Silence.

Then Washen admitted, 'The Master hasn't found us. Not yet. But this time she has a starting point. Someone will eventually come here, and who knows what they'll find . . . ?'

'A silent, obvious point. Thank you.' He passed his weapon from hand to hand, explaining, 'Because of you, I will close the access tunnel from below. And keep it closed forever, perhaps. A series of antimatter charges will obliterate every trace of its existence. And even if the Master guesses right, which is doubtful, it would take centuries to dig to Marrow again.'

'With you trapped down there,' Washen offered.

Diu shrugged again. 'How does that old story play? It's better to rule in one realm than serve in another—?'

There was an abrupt, soft squeal.

The false Master had stopping moving, eyes staring back toward the center of the habitat, something seen and the machine repeating the squeal again. Louder this time, and more focused.

If there was an echo, Washen couldn't hear it.

Irritated, Diu asked, 'What is it?'

Then he turned and stepped toward the robot, asking, 'Is something wrong?'

With the Master's voice, it said, 'Motion.'

'From the entranceway?'

'Along the line, yes.'

'What about now?'

'Nothing.'

'Watch,' was Diu's advice. Then he faced his prisoners, and with an odd little smile, focused on Miocene. 'You've done something else surprising,' he decided. 'Am I right? You've fooled me in another way. Haven't you, darling?'

'I didn't build one escape pod,' Miocene confessed. 'There are two pods. Both serviceable.'

The man took a breath, then held it. Then he said, 'So,' with a low, contemptuous voice. 'Two more captains have followed you up here. So what?'

He turned to the false Master.

'Shoot—' he began to order.

'No,' Miocene interrupted, taking a step and lifting both hands. 'I didn't invite any captains. And believe me, you don't want to open fire on them.'

The false Master was aiming at a target too distant for human eyes.

Diu growled, 'Wait.'

He turned back to the women, his expression merely surprised. He seemed to be just a little angry. Then he lifted his kinetic weapon, fingers to the trigger as he said, 'Who, then? Tell me.'

'My son,' said Miocene.

The false Master was still as a statue, waiting for the correct word.

'Till,' Miocene whispered. 'I hoped he'd be curious enough. Through his spies, I sent a message. Virtue was under orders to launch Till to the bridge. I gave him the codes to awaken a second cap-car. I just wanted him to have this chance to see the Great Ship for himself.'

'Well,' Diu said softly, defiantly. Then he looked off into the distance, contemplating that narrow infinity, and after a few moments of hard thought, he told his machine, 'Kill them. I don't care who they are. Kill them.'

The laser gave a sharp, sudden crack.

Miocene ran, screaming now, hands reaching as Diu turned and calmly shot her in the chest, a fat explosive charge burrowing through bone and the wildly beating heart, then detonating with a wet pop.

She collapsed into a shockingly red pool of blood.

Following protocols, the robot turned, ready to defend its master. For that simple instant, Washen knew she was doomed. She ducked down, by instinct, and watched the laser's barrel swing for her, charged again and ready to turn her water and flesh into an amorphous, lifeless gas. But when the next crack shattered the silence, the beam missed. She felt the heat pass overhead and watched in amazement as the false Master panned up and up, aiming at nothing, the golden face turning bright as it absorbed blistering, unrelenting energies.

Quietly, with an eerie grace, the face collapsed into a molten goo.

The barrel of the laser dropped and pulled sideways, then fired again, punching a hole in the wall behind Washen, holding steady until that vast body and its weapon turned to a thick liquid, the robes burning as a Marrow-like pond melted its way into the gray floor.

Diu was screaming and backing up as he fired twice.

Washen tackled him from behind.

They wrestled, and she threw a forearm into his exposed throat, and for a delicious moment she thought she could win. But her body wasn't perfectly healed. A thousand weaknesses found her, and Diu bent her back, hard, then gave her a smooth strong shove, and when she tumbled, he aimed his weapon at her heaving chest.

'Till heard you,' she sputtered. 'With these leech acoustics—'

'So,' he replied.

She said, 'He knows everything—!'

Diu hit her with one explosive round, pushing her back against the window.

'What's changed? Nothing's changed!' he roared. Then he shot again, and again. As if from a great distance, Washen heard him shout, 'I have a million sons!', and the next round punched through one of the gaping holes in her body, cutting deep into the insulated window before detonating with a dull, almost inaudible thud.

Quietly, with the blood filling her mouth, Washen said, 'Shit.'

Diu was aiming again. Aiming at her head.

Washen blinked and fell to the floor, watching with a thin interest and a genuine impatience, thinking this wasn't how it was meant to be.

This was wrong.

Behind Diu, a running figure appeared. Legs and arms and a familiar, welcome face came sprinting out of the grayness, a laser drill clasped in one hand.

He wasn't whom she expected. Instead of Till, she saw her son.

Locke called out, 'Father.'

Startled, Diu turned to face him.

And Locke shot him with the drill, emptying its energies into that jittery body, that old metaphor of the flesh ready to boil coming true.

In a moment, Diu evaporated.

Vanished.

Then Locke stepped toward Washen, his face torn with compassion and a wild fear. He dropped the drill and blurted, 'Mother.' But she couldn't hear his voice. Something louder, and nearer, interrupted him. Then came the sensation of motion, sudden and irresistible, and Washen felt herself being sucked through a small hole, her ravaged

body spinning and freezing, and falling, the blackness everywhere, and a tiny voice inside her whispering:

'Not like this.

Not now.

No.'

Twenty-seven

THERE WAS A screaming wind and the harsher, nearer wail-
ing of a lone man.

Miocene pried open her eyes and found herself mirac-
ulously sitting upright, her chest ripped open and her
uniform splattered with dying blood and bone and the
shredded and blackened muscle of her dead heart. Diu and
the false Master had vanished. But the newcomer was
running straight for her, sprinting with the roaring wind
. . . a Wayward man, half-naked and barefoot, shorn of his
hair and every dignity, his miserable voice screaming,
'Mother, no . . . !'

Was this her child?

Miocene couldn't place his face. But just the same, she
tried to grab him, aiming for one of his legs and losing
her balance as a consequence, dropping to her side and
the man leaping over her helpless body, again screaming,
'No . . . !', with a voice as pitiful and lost as she was feeling
now.

For a moment, or a year, the ancient woman shut her
eyes.

The wind fell away to a whistling murmur. The leech
habitat was repairing its damage, and she realized that her

miserable carcass was trapped here. The screaming man was near the wall, sobbing now. Slobbering. 'I should have . . . done it faster . . . fired at him sooner . . . !' he was complaining to someone. Then with a massive disgust, he confessed, 'But he's my father, and my hand froze—!'

'But Locke,' a second voice remarked, 'don't you realize? He was probably my father, too.'

Miocene recognized that voice.

Plainly stunned, Locke asked, 'Was he? How do you know?'

The Submaster inhaled, and again she forced her eyes to open. Her son was kneeling before her, eyes focused on her eyes, that charming, pretty face breaking into a knowing smile. 'Am I right, Mother? Was Diu my father?'

One of her most cherished secrets. All those vials of semen, and she selected a donor with gifts but minimal status. A father who wouldn't be in any position to contest her role as the child's sole parent . . .

Miocene nodded.

The whistling had stopped now. With blood on her tongue, she softly asked, 'How long . . . have you known . . . ?'

Till laughed for a moment. Then he said, 'Always.'

Locke stumbled into view, at least as shocked as Miocene. 'We're brothers, and you always knew it,' he muttered, wrestling with the possibilities. Then he quietly and fearfully asked, 'What else did you know?'

Miocene spat out the blood, then said, 'It was always Diu. Always.'

Her son had deep cold eyes.

Locke stepped nearer, whispering, 'But you knew that, too.' He was staring at Till, saying, 'I saw you. While Diu was confessing, I saw it in your face. You already knew all about his deceptions!'

Till winked fondly at his mother.

Then he looked at his half brother, and with a smooth, untroubled voice, said, 'Our father was an agent. A means. A great tool of the Builders. But Diu's work was finished, and you did exactly what was necessary, and nothing has changed. Do you hear me, Locke? You had to kill that man, or he would have murdered someone in whom the Builders have all their great, glorious hopes . . .'

Locke glanced at new gray wall, his face slick with tears.

Till looked down and said, 'Mother,' with a firm, low voice.

'I've been wrong,' said the shattered woman. 'Wrong, and stupid.'

'You have been,' he allowed.

'I'm sorry,' she said. 'You don't know how sorry.'

Till said nothing.

Then she whimpered, 'Forgive me. Can you, please?'

His expression gave his answer. He smiled warmly, if only for an instant. Then he stood and remarked to Locke, 'We need to hide our presence. As best as we can, then better. Then we'll use Diu's fancy machine to return to Marrow, and we'll shut the tunnel as our father planned.'

Carefully, Locke asked, 'What about my mother?'

Till sighed and said, 'Let her sleep. For now, that's all that we can do.'

Locke wiped at his tears, but he moved like a man who knew his duty, who understood what was expected of him.

Waywards could make wonderful followers, thought Miocene. Then she coughed, and with a stronger voice, she suggested, 'You could go above . . . and look at the ship for yourself. Just once.'

Till regarded her with pity and with amusement. 'What did you find up there, Mother?'

Miocene's old anger fused with a new rage. Emotion

helped her sit up again, her trembling hand grasping a piece of dead heart muscle, crushing it as she said, 'The Master's an idiot, unfit for her office . . . obviously, obviously . . .'

Till nodded knowingly.

'For my forgiveness,' he asked, 'what are you willing to give?'

'Anything,' Miocene muttered. 'Tell me what you want . . . !'

But her son merely shook his head, and with a sad, sturdy voice, he said to Locke, 'Your laser.' Then with the weapon in both hands, he said to his mother, 'You're wrong. Don't you see? I have never wanted *you* to follow me.'

'No?' she squeaked.

'That's not my destiny,' he promised. 'Or yours.'

Then she understood – suddenly; perfectly – and her eyes grew wide.

Till aimed the laser at her broken body, and with a flash of blue-white light, he destroyed everything but her tough old mind, plus enough skull and unburnt hair to serve as a trustworthy handle.

THE MASTER'S
CHAIR

THIS WAS WHAT it was: a trillion voices assembled into the least disciplined of choirs, every singer screaming its own passionate melody, each using some cumbersome, intensely personal language, and inside that mayhem and majesty, only one entity was capable of hearing the plaintive squeak of the softest, shyest voice.

Such was the Master Captain's burden, and her consuming, exhilarating joy.

With perfect ears, she listened to the wind profiles over the enormous Alpha Sea. The Blue Sea. Lawson's Sea. Blood-as-Blessing Sea. And those other five hundred and ninety-one major bodies of standing water. She heard the ship's shield strengths. The health of its laser arrays. The repair status on its forward face: fair, good, excellent. (Never poor, and mostly excellent.) Plus the hydrogen harvests from the extrasolar environment, in metric tons per microsecond. She knew the oxygen profiles of every chamber, hallway, and inhabited closet. (Two tenths of a percent too high in the Quagmire, endangering its minimally aerobic passengers.) Carbon dioxide levels to the same warm precision. Biologically inactive gases, less so. And there were the ambient light levels. And voices that spoke of temperature. Humidity. Toxin checks. Photosynthetic rates, measured by direct means and by implication. Decay rates and decay agents. Biological; chemical; unknown. Census figures, updated with precision every seven seconds. Immigrants; emigrants; births; asexual divisions; and the occasional wail of Death. Comprehensive lists of passengers were complied and recompiled. By species. By home world. By audible name, or structured touch, or the distinct and enriching scent of an individual fart. And according to their payment, too. Ship currency, or barter, or through gifts of knowledge. Profit was as critical as hydrogen harvests and oxygen counts, and it was calculated on twenty-three separate and elaborate scales, none of which was perfectly *accurate. But linked together, they built a comprehensive estimate that wasn't too much of a shambles, and it was that heavy-shouldered estimate that was beamed toward the now distant Earth, once every six hours, along with a comprehensive sketch of the ship's last quarter of a day: in essence, reminding whoever might be listening thirty thousand years from today that here they were and and their voyage was progressing according to schedule and the going was going quite well, thank you.*

Said the Master's own voice.

The one-time derelict had evolved into a vibrant ship, rich and fundamentally happy – at least so far as a Master's many nexuses could measure qualities as ethereal and private as happiness.

But one matter kept worrying both nexuses and the woman, and that was the nagging, impossible mystery about Miocene and the other missing captains.

When her captains first vanished, the Master's response was a purposeful, magnificent panic. She dispatched security troops, uniformed and otherwise, who combed the vast ship, hunting for a few hundred women and men. At first the troops used subtle means, then after a barren week, random sweeps were implemented. And after another month of conspicuous failure, the troops gathered up known troublemakers and unlikable souls and held an assortment of surgical interrogations.

Yet the missing captains – the best of the best – still would not be found.

Colleagues soon realized the scope of things, and as whispered words let the news slip, first to the low-ranking crew members, then to the passengers themselves, explanations became mandatory. Which was why the Master fabricated the story about a secret mission to a distant world, leaving the purpose and exact destination undefined, allowing her audiences' imagination and paranoia to fill in the unknowns. All that mattered was that she repeated the story often enough, forcing others to believe it, and after a century without any word from the missing captains, or even one plausible sighting, the Master put on a sorrowful face, then made a very public announcement.

'The captains' ship is missing,' she reported.

It was her annual banquet; thousands of lesser captains blinked at the news, putting on their own sorrowful faces as the words sank deep.

'Their ship is missing and presumed destroyed,' she continued. 'I wish I could explain their mission. But I cannot. Suffice to say that our colleagues and good friends are heroes, and we are forever in their debt, as is the Great Ship.'

New security measures were in charge. Devised by the Master and implemented by her elite guard, these paranoias were intended to keep watch over the remaining captains. Old escape routes, wise in an earlier age, were forbidden and ordered dismantled. New nexuses incorporated into her vast body did nothing but report on the captains' whereabouts and activities, failures and successes, and without being too intrusive, passed along certain thoughts, too.

By then, the shortfall of captains was a real and pernicious issue. Only a few percent of the roster were missing. Yet efficiencies had dropped by a full quarter, and innovation had collapsed by nearly sixty percent. The Master found herself studying the talents of every crew member, then the human passengers, too. Who among these warm immortal bodies would make a passable captain? Whom could she trust with some little part of the ship, if only to dress them in the proper uniform and march them up and down the public avenues, lending confidence to those who needed it most?

Talent — genuine instinctive lead-us-around-the-galaxy talent — was in short supply.

Even with training, time, and genetic tinkering, few souls had the deep ambition and the need for duty that captains required. The Master found herself automating more and more nexuses, making her days and nights even busier. Plainly, a few willing

*and talented souls would be a blessing. But how to find them?
Her ship was so far from the Terran colonies, and her needs were
so terribly, unbearably urgent . . .*

'What about a general amnesty . . . ?' suggested her new First
Chair.

His name was Earwig, and he was thrilled with Miocene's
disappearance. Which was exactly as it should be. But Earwig
lacked his predecessor's better qualities, including Miocene's good
sense to publicly admit her ambitions. Not to mention her notorious inability to forgive and forget.

'An amnesty?' said the Master, her voice doubtful. But not
decided.

'At last count, madam, eighty-nine captains have left the ranks.
Some are imprisoned for minor crimes, while others long ago
vanished into the general population, assuming new names and
faces, and lives without responsibility.'

'We need such people?' asked the Master.

'If they willingly start at a low rank,' he argued. 'And if their
crimes are small enough that you, in your magnificence, can forgive
them. I should think yes, we might make good use of them. Yes.'

She summoned the list herself.

In a fraction of a second, AI functionaries digested those eighty-
nine lives and service records, and her conscious soul looked at
the names, remembering most, surprised by the talent listed there.
A smooth strong finger pointed at the highest-ranking name while
her voice rumbled. 'What do you think happened to your predecessor?'

'Madam?'

'To Miocene. I want your best guess.' She held her giant hand
steady, repeating the obvious. 'Several hundred colleagues vanished
on the same day, and we haven't found so much as a lost finger,
and where do you think they must be?'

'Far away,' was his verdict.

Then sensing her mood as any good First Chair should, he

added. 'It was an alien influence.' Several species were named, all local and all suspicious. 'They could have bribed our captains, or kidnapped them. Then smuggled them off the ship.'

'Why those captains?'

Ego made him say, 'I don't know why. Madam.'

It wasn't a matter of talent, he seemed to be claiming. Even though both of them knew otherwise.

'You should trust your new security measures.' Earwig was dragging the conversation back toward the amnesty issue. 'We can watch each of these forgiven captains. If they disappoint, we act appropriately. You can act, madam. There is absolutely no chance of a repetition of these events, madam.'

'Am I worried about a repetition?'

'Maybe I am,' he replied. Then he remembered to smile, looking at the list of fallen captains, at the name that the Master had firmly under her finger.

Quietly, he said, 'Pamir,' aloud.

She watched her First Chair, then asked. 'Do you really believe that a general amnesty would work? That a man like Pamir would give up his freedom for this uniform?'

'Give up his freedom?' Earwig sputtered, not understanding those words.

Then, struggling to please the Master, he added, 'I remember Pamir. He was a talented, natural captain. Sometimes abrasive, yes. But whatever else is said about him, madam . . . Pamir was adept at wearing our uniform . . .'

THE AMNESTY WAS well advertised in the more discreet venues, and it was given a life span of exactly one century.

During its first two minutes, half of the imprisoned and AWOL captains accepted its terms, begging forgiveness for their various crimes. Quietly but openly, each was returned to service, given a modest rank and obscure responsibilities, and after five decades of reliable service, they were awarded small promotions of pay and station.

Pamir hadn't appeared.

The Master was disappointed but not surprised. She had known that man forever, it seemed. In a passing sense, she even understood him. It wouldn't be like Pamir to join that first wave of supplicants. A laudable mistrust was part of his makeup, true. But more importantly, he was a creature of tremendous, almost crippling pride. In the amnesty's final years, as more lost souls came forward, Pamir's absence grew more notable. Even the Master decided that if he was still alive and still living on the ship — two enormous suppositions — then it would take a gift sweeter than forgiveness to bring him home to her.

Twenty minutes before the amnesty ended, a large man wearing a contemplator's robe and sandals and loosely fitting Pamir's description strolled into the security office at Port Beta, sat with a casual calm, and told everyone in earshot, 'I've gotten bored out there, I want my job back, or something halfway close to it.'

Deep scans matched him to the missing captain.

'You need to beg for the Master's forgiveness,' he was told. With twenty tough purple and black clad police officers sitting and standing on all sides of the big unhandsome man, the resident general explained. 'It's a basic term of the amnesty. In fact, it's the only term. She can see you and hear you. Beg now. Go on.'

Pamir wouldn't.

Several thousand kilometers removed, the Master watched the man shake his head, telling his audience. 'I won't apologize for any of it. And you might as well not tire your mouth by asking.'

Stunned, the general blinked and said, 'You don't have any choice, Pamir.'

'What was my crime?' he replied.

'You allowed a dangerous entity on board. And you were implicated in the destruction of one of our finest waste-treatment plants.'

'And yet,' Pamir shrugged his shoulders, then admitted, 'I

don't feel particularly guilty. Or even a little bit sorry.'

Thousands of kilometers away, the Master watched. Listened. And behind the great flat of her hand, she smiled.

'I did what was right,' he added. Then he looked past his accusers, guessing where the security eye was hiding. Speaking only to the Master, he pointed out, 'I can't ask for forgiveness, real forgiveness, if I don't feel guilt.'

'True enough,' she whispered to herself.

The officers were less appreciative. One after another, they shook their heads in disgust, and the angriest man — a long-armed fellow laced with ape genes and a graceless temper — made a stupid threat.

'We'll arrest you, then. A trial, a quick conviction. And you spend the rest of this long long voyage sitting in the tiniest, darkest cell.'

Pamir regarded the angry man, nothing showing on his face.

Then he rose to his feet, pointing out, 'The amnesty has another eight minutes. I can still leave. But I suppose you could forget the time and wrestle me down. If that's what you've got your hearts and stomachs set on, that is.'

Half of the officers were thinking about tackling him.

As if to tease, Pamir took a long step toward the office door. Then he pretended second thoughts. He halfway laughed, halfway turned. Looking back at the security eye again, at the Master, he said, 'Remember all those vanished captains? The ones who, according to that ridiculous story of yours, left us on that secret mission . . . ?'

No one spoke, or moved, or remembered to breathe.

'A week after she'd dropped out of sight . . . I saw one of your captains . . .'

The ship's trillion voices went silent.

Suddenly the Master heard nothing but Pamir, and she saw no one else. From her quarters just beneath Port Alpha, she shouted, 'Whom did you see?'

At lightspeed, it seemed to take forever for her voice to reach its audience. But it boomed nonetheless, causing every head but one to jerk in surprise.

'Leave the room,' she roared. 'Everyone but Captain Pamir leaves!'

For an instant, Pamir let the police see his smile. They bristled, made hard fists, and filed away. Then it was just the two of them, and the Master severed every input and output save one, and she appeared before him as shaped light and a panicky voice, demanding from the man, 'Which of my captains did you see?'

Quietly, and appearing almost amused, he said, 'Washen.'

Pamir and Washen had been close friends, if memory served.

For that wide instant, she wasn't the Master any longer. The trillion voices were forgotten, the Great Ship left to drift through space without her direction, and the effect, if anything, was pleasant. Bracing, buoyant. Welcome.

'Where did you see Washen?'

In crisp, certain detail, Pamir told enough to be believed.

Then with a wise grin, he added, 'I want my old rank back. You don't have to pay me or trust me. But I'd be bored and useless if I were a millionth-grade captain.'

She was almost startled. With her own forced grin, she asked, 'Why do you deserve any consideration?'

'Because you need talent and experience,' *he replied with a cold certainty.* 'And because you don't know what Washen was doing, or where she's gone. And since I know more than a little bit about vanishing, maybe I can help you find her. Somehow, someday. Maybe.'

It was the rarest of moments:

The Master Captain, ear to every voice, didn't know what to say.

Then Pamir shook his head, and with an unwelcome prescience, he said, 'Madam.' *He bowed and said,* 'No disrespect intended, *madam. But the ship is a very big place, and frankly, you don't know it half as well as you think you do.*

'*And it doesn't know you a quarter as well as you think it should . . .*'

Twenty-eight

PAMIR WAS BORN on a shabby little colony world. His father was barely thirty years old, a near child in these immortal times; while his mother, a self-proclaimed priestess and seer, was thousands of years their senior. Mother had a mercurial beauty and an almost incalculable wealth, and with those blessings she could have taken almost any local man, plus a fair fraction of the local women, too. But she was a singularly odd woman, and for some compelling reason, she decided to court and marry an innocent boy. And in their own peculiar ways, those two badly mismatched people became a stable, even happy couple.

Mother had a fondness for alien faiths and alien gods. The universe was built from three great souls, she believed: Death, and Woman, and Man. As a boy, Pamir was taught that he was an embodiment of Man, and Woman was his partner and natural ally. That's why Death was rarely seen anymore. Working together, the two gods had temporarily suppressed the third, leaving it weakened and ineffectual. But stability was an illusion in a triad. Death was plotting its return, Mother assured him. Someday, in some deeply clever fashion, Death would seduce Man or Woman, and the balances would shift again. Which was natural, and right. She said that each god was just as beautiful as the others, and each deserved its time to reign . . . or the universe would collapse under the weight of the grand imbalance . . .

For months and years, Pamir lay awake every night, wondering if Death would come to his bed after he fell asleep, whispering to him in his dreams, and if he would find the strength to resist Death's horrible charms.

Finally, in despair, Pamir confessed his fears to his father.

The boyish man laughed and took his son under an arm, warning him, 'You can't believe everything your mother says. She's sick in the mind. We all are, of course. But she's got it worse.'

'I don't believe you,' the boy growled. He tried to shake off his father's arm, and failed. Then he asked, 'How can anyone be anything but healthy?'

'You mean, because she's got a modem brain?' Father was a large, ugly man, Caucasian and Aztec heritages bolstered with a stew of cheap, quantum-tiny genetics. 'The sweet truth is that Mom is so old that she lived most of a normal life before being updated. Before they knew how to make flesh and bone halfway immortal. She was living on Earth. She was already a hundred years old and worn out when the autodocs finally started to work on her. She was one of the very first. Which was why they didn't have the technologies quite right. When her old brain was turned into bioceramics and the like, some of her oldness remained with it. Memories were lost, and a bunch of little errors crept in. With a few big errors, too. Although I didn't tell you that, and if you repeat it to anyone, I'll tell the world that you're sick with imagination and can't be trusted.'

Physically, Pamir was his father's child. But in temperament and emotions, he was very much like his mother.

Bracing himself, the boy asked, 'Am I crazy like her?'

'No.' The man shook his head. 'You've got her temper and some of that knife-wit. And things that nobody's found a name for. But those voices she hears belong to her. Alone. And those foolish ideas come straight out of her sickness.'

'Can she be helped?' the boy asked.

'Probably not. Assuming she'd want to be helped, that is . . .'

'But maybe someday . . . ?'

'The sad, simple truth,' his father continued, 'is that these tricks keeping us young also stop us from changing. Almost without exception. A sick mind, like any good healthy one, has key patterns locked into its ultracortex. Once there, nothing gets them out.'

Pamir nodded. Without fuss and remarkable little pain, he came to terms with his mother's condition, accepting it as another one of life's burdens. What bothered him more – what eventually kept the young man awake at night – was that persistent and toxic idea that a human being could live for so long and see so much, yet despite standing on all that experience, he still couldn't change his simplest nature.

If that's true, the boy realized, then we're all doomed.

Forever.

PAMIR'S WORLD WAS desert and high desiccated mountains, oxygen-impoverished air and little seas laced with toxic lithium salts. Twenty million years ago, life was abundant, but an asteroid had murdered everything larger than a microbe. Given time, new multicellular life-forms would have evolved, just as they once managed to do on the ancient, pulverized Earth. But humans didn't give the world that opportunity. In a few decades, the colonists had spread widely, immigrants and their children creating instant cities where there was nothing but salt and rock; every sea was scrubbed clean of its toxins, then stocked with slightly tweaked but otherwise ordinary examples of earthly life; and great blue aerogel clouds sucked up the potable water, then rainboys shepherded the clouds inland and squeezed them dry, bringing soft rains to new farms and the young green forests.

By the time he was thirty, Pamir had decided that his home was a dull place being made duller by the day.

Sometimes he would lie on a high ridge, the dusty pink sky darkening as night spread, revealing an even dustier mass of cold and distant stars. And he would lift his young hand, holding it up to the sky, dwarfing all those fierce little specks of light.

That's where I want to be, he thought to himself.

There.

As soon as escape was possible, Pamir visited his mother, hungry to tell her that he was emigrating and would never see her again.

Mother's house was beautiful in odd ways, like its owner. She lived inside an isolated, long-dead volcanic peak. The underground mansion had a contrived, utterly crazy majesty made even more chaotic because it was perpetually under construction. Robots and tailored apes kept the atmosphere full of dusts and curses. Every room was carved from soft rock, according to Mother's volatile plans, and most of the hallways were empty volcanic tubes aligned according to a magmatic logic.

Mother distrusted sunlight. Windows and atriums were scarce. Instead, she decorated with thick carpets of perfumed compost and manure, synthesized at great cost and leavened with the spores of tailored fungi. Mushrooms became huge in that closed, damp air, leaking a weak light, ruddy and diffuse, from beneath their broad caps. Smaller fungi and puffballs and furlike species produced gold and bluish glows. To keep the forest in check, giant beetles wandered about like cattle. And to keep the beetles under control, dragonlike lizards slithered about in the damp darkness.

It took Pamir three full days to find his mother.

She wasn't hiding. Not from him, or from anyone. But it had been nearly five years since his last visit, and the construction crews, following her explicit directions, had closed every hallway leading to her. There was no way in but a single narrow crevice that didn't appear on anyone's map.

'You look upset,' were Mother's first words.

Pamir heard her before he saw her. Trudging through the glowing forest, he came around the massive stalk of a century-old death's-mistress mushroom, finding himself staring at a two-headed dragon. A conjoined twin, and his mother's favorite.

Mother sat on a tall wooden chair, pretending to hold a gold-chained leash. The dragon hissed with one mouth, while the other – on the head that Pamir had never trusted – tasted the air with a flame-colored tongue.

Tasting him.

Mother was ancient, and insane, yet she always managed to look more beautiful than mad. Pamir always assumed that's how she could lure young men to become her husbands. She was small and paler than her fungi, except for a long thick mass of black hair that only made her paleness more obvious. The sharply pretty face smiled, but in a disapproving way. She reminded her son, 'You don't visit me often enough to be a real son. So you must be an apparition.'

He carefully said nothing.

The dragon took a sliding step forward, pulling the chain out of its mistress's hands. Both mouths gave low, menacing hisses.

'They don't remember you,' Mother warned.

Pamir said, 'Listen to me.'

His rough voice gave away everything. The woman winced and said, 'Oh, no. I don't need any sour news today, thank you.'

'I'm going to leave.'

'But you just arrived!'

'On the next starship, Mother.'

'You're cruel, saying that.'

'Wait till I do it. That should really hurt.'

Her chair was rotting, creaking beneath her, as she lifted herself up on her sticklike arms, not quite standing, breathing in deep regular gulps.

Finally, in pain, she asked, 'Where are you going?'

'I don't care.'

'That next ship is an old bomb-wagon. The *Elassia*.' For someone who lived as a recluse, Mother seemed in touch with everything that happened on their world. 'Wait ten years,' she suggested. 'A Belter liner is coming, and it's a nice new one.'

'No, Mother.'

The woman winced again, and moaned. Then she told her private voices, 'Quiet,' before she closed her eyes and began to chant, managing a ragged version of a Whistleforth prayer.

Whistleforths were a neighboring species. Tiny creatures, rather dimwitted and superstitious. A few weakwilled humans believed that the Whistleforths could see into the future as well as the remote past. Using the proper rituals coupled with a pure spirit, any species could accomplish their magic. How many times had Pamir argued the subject with this crazy woman? She didn't understand the alien's logic. What those little beasts believed, more than anything, was that the past was as murky as the future, their chants working in both directions, and never particularly well.

Regardless, the woman muttered the potent phrases.

Then she stepped onto the bare black ground, and lifting her long skirt, she pissed between her feet, reading the pattern of the splatters.

Finally, with a forced drama and a strange, unexpected smile, she announced, 'It's a good thing.'

She told him, 'Yes, you need to leave. Right away.'

Pamir was startled, but he fought to keep his mood hidden. Stepping forward, he opened his long arms, ready to offer the old woman a kiss and a long hug. He would never again come to the place, never again see the most important person in his life; the enormity of the moment made him deeply and astonishingly sad, and a real part of him wanted to do nothing but cry.

'It's your destiny, that ship is.'

She said those words so earnestly, with such unalloyed conviction, that a part of Pamir couldn't help but believe her.

'You must do this,' she proclaimed. The smile only grew brighter, and everything about that pale little face became crazier. 'Promise me that you'll leave now.'

It was a trap. She was setting a clumsy, stupid trick to grab his emotions.

But Pamir heard himself grunt, 'I promise.'

Mother pretended pleasure, something in her big pale eyes conveying, of all things, an absurd, overwelling awe.

'Thank you,' she told him, kneeling before him, sinking into her own pee.

Her conjoined dragons hissed and took a step toward Pamir. And because he had always wanted to do it, he made a fist and swung at the head that he didn't trust, snapping it back with a clean sharp thunk, then feeling the dull steady pain as a broken finger began to heal.

Again, softer this time, Mother chanted in that alien tongue.

'Why can't you be normal?' was the last thing he ever said to the woman.

Then he turned and walked away, following his own footprints through the sickly-sweet, black-as-night manure.

★ ★ ★

THERE WASN'T SUCH a creature as Immortality.

But modern life, infused with its technical wonders and medical prosperity, had a strength, a genuine stubbornness, that carried its citizens through disasters as well as simple indifference.

On three occasions in the next two thousands years, Pamir stepped as near to Death as possible, just enough of his soul coming out of the mayhem for his body to be recultured, his memories awakened, and his belligerent nature kept pure.

As the bomb-wagon dropped into orbit, a gift was delivered from his mother. A tidy sum was accompanied by an odd note claiming, 'I chanted; I saw. This is precisely how much you will need. Of money.'

It wasn't a fortune, which was why Pamir became an engineer's apprentice. There wasn't any salary with the post, but it meant a free-passage; what's more, if one of the genuine engineers quit or died, an apprentice would be ready to step into the gap, already trained by the starship's library and drilled numb by his superiors.

The lowest-ranking engineer was a harum-scarum – the human name for a humanoid species famous for its ugly moods.

Pamir decided that he wanted the alien's job.

Knowing the dangers, he visited the creature's large cabin, sat without asking permission and made his pitch. 'First of all,' he remarked, 'I'm a better engineer than you. Agreed?'

Silence. Meaning 'agreed.'

'Second, the crew likes me. They prefer me to you in about every way. Am I right?'

Another agreeable silence.

'And finally, I'll pay you to resign.' He named a carefully calculated sum, then added, 'You'll be making enough.

And at our next port, you'll find a new crew that doesn't care what a shitty pain you are.'

From his eating hole, the harum-scarum made a low, slightly wet sound.

From the other facial hole – the one that breathed and spoke – came a harsh squeal containing its blunt reply.

'Fuck your ape self,' said the translator.

'You are an idiot,' Pamir assured him.

The alien rose to his feet, towering over the large human.

'All right, fine,' Pamir conceded. 'Give yourself a year to think, then I'll make the same offer. With less money in the pot, next time.'

Insulting a harum-scarum brought revenge, without exception. But the suddenness and the scope of the attack took the young Pamir by surprise.

'A scuttlebug's gone missing,' the Master Engineer reported. It was twelve hours later, and with a mischievous wink, she added, 'Sounds like a good chore for you. Last we heard, it was down near the push-plate, somewhere near the navel.'

On better ships, scuttlebugs hunted for their own kind. But they could be expensive machines, and on an old bomb-wagon, they were normally in short supply. Squeezing into a lifesuit meant for a smaller man, then donning a second suit of hyperfiber and a satchel of second-hand tools, Pamir was ready for the chore. It was a three-kilometer drop to the stem, the last half kilometer accomplished on foot. The push-plate was a vast dish originally built from metal-ceramic alloys, but patched with diamond armors, then cheap-grade hyperfibers, as gaps and fractures developed over the centuries. Minimal, shock-resistant passageways allowed access. The plate itself shuddered beneath him – a blurring tremor caused by the constant detonation of small nukes. In that realm, a weak, unreliable man became claustrophobic, and his bored mind invented faces and voices to fill the drudgery. As much as anything, this duty was a test of character, and Pamir accepted the test without complaint, reminding himself that sooner or later he would have the power to send an apprentice down this same awful corridor.

The navel wasn't set precisely at the plate's center. A fat fraction of a kilometer across and perfectly round, it served no function whatsoever. A premature detonation had boiled away a great volume of armor, and since the navel was in the thickest portion of the plate, its repair could wait until the next overhaul.

A sputtering blue-white light greeted Pamir.

Pausing, he called up to the Master Engineer, who in turn contacted the Master Captain, requesting an engine shutdown while promising a minimal disruption. Passengers and crew were warned that the sluggish gee-forces were about to vanish. Command programs were unleashed. Then the nukes quit firing, and the quick blue-white light vanished, and in an instant, the plate grew perfectly still.

Pamir made his head and feet exchange places, then he moved to where the passageway's roof had been blasted away, his boots holding fast to the scarred and blackened floor.

The scuttlebug was in the center of the blast crater, which was a strange place to be. Why would the machine wander out there?

It was dead. And worse than that, it was probably useless, too, and he might as well leave it there. But Pamir felt an obligation to be thorough, which was why he lifted his boots and used his squirt-pack, rocketing his way down the shallow crater while clumsy hands reached for the necessary tools that would pop off the machine's head, letting him see if anything inside was salvageable.

Why he looked up, he was never sure.

Later, struggling to replay events, Pamir wondered if he had meant to look at their destination. The bomb-wagon was falling toward a K-class sun and its two young planets, both of which were being terraformed by human colonists. He must have tilted his head because he wanted a naked-eye look. He was a young man admiring his first new sun, and in turn, admiring a life sure to be long and filled with many exotic places . . . and that's why he saw a flash of light, an unexpected nuke ascending . . . and that's why he had just enough time to turn his massive self and aim for the passageway, dropping the tools in both hands as he ordered his squirt-pack to burn every gram of fuel in a fraction of an instant . . .

Pamir was flung back the way he had come.

Too soon, he thought he would escape unscathed, and wouldn't he enjoy seeing the harum-scarum's face now?

But his aim was wrong by half a meter, his left arm and shoulder clipping the blackened armor, his spinning body ricocheting against the opposite wall, precious momentum lost . . . and the nuke detonated with a fantastic light that chased after him, catching him too soon and obliterating very nearly everything . . .

WHAT SURVIVED WAS the heavily armored helmet and a well-cooked, vaguely human skull. But the ship surgeon and onboard autodocs were relatively skilled – a consequence of the ship's questionable safety record – and within three months, Pamir's soul had been decanted into a new mind and a freshly grown body that was recognizable as his own.

As the starship pulled into a berth above the first new world, the Master Engineer slipped into the therapy chamber, watching Pamir finish a two-hour cycle of isomet-rics. Then quietly, with a mixture of scorn and curiosity, she told him, 'Harum-scarums don't appreciate bribes. Ever.'

Pamir nodded, vacuuming the oily sweat from his face and chest.

'You gave him no choice,' said the older, more cautious engineer. 'According to his nature, the poor fellow had to seek vengeance.'

'I knew all that,' he replied. 'I just didn't expect a nuke up my ass.'

'What did you expect?'

'A simple fight.'

'And you thought you'd win?'

'No. I figured that I'd lose.' Then he laughed in a calm, grim fashion. 'But I also figured that I'd survive. And the creature would have to give me his job.'

'But that's my decision to make,' warned the Master.

Pamir didn't blink.

His commander sighed heavily, gazing off in a random direction. 'Your opponent's gone,' she admitted. 'Along with half of my staff. These terraformers are paying bonuses for good engineers, and bad ones, trying to make their lumps of rock livable.'

Pamir waited a moment, then asked, 'So did I earn my post?'

The old woman had to nod. 'But you could have done nothing,' she told him. 'Nothing, and you would have gotten what you wanted anyway.'

'That's two different things,' was his response.

'What do you mean?'

'Either you pay for something, or it's charity,' he explained. 'And I don't care how long I live. Everything I get, I pay for. Or my hands won't hold it.'

★ ★ ★

BUOYED BY TALENT and discipline and a disinterest in better work, Pamir eventually rose to the position of Master Engineer.

In the next sixteen hundred years, the old ship underwent two rehabilitations. The final rehab stripped away its outdated bomb drive, a fusion drive installed in its place, complete with merry-go-round nozzles and antimatter spiking. They were running ten thousand colonists out to an Earth-class world. Ahead of them were the thick fringes of another sun's Oort cloud. Oorts were lousy places for starships. Obstacles were too scarce to map, too common to ignore. But the risks were usually slight, and because of time and a fat debt riding with them, the Master Captain decided to cut through the fringes.

When the ship was rehabilitated, the old push-plate was stripped of its extra mass and bolstered with new grades of hyperfiber, and the whole clumsy apparatus was fastened to the nose. The plate absorbed dust impacts. Railguns obliterated pebbles and little snowballs, while the old bomb drive launched nukes at the largest obstacles, vaporizing them at what was hopefully a safe distance.

An engineer was necessary to oversee sudden, unexpected repairs of key systems. On most starships, the Master Engineer delegated the job. As a young man, Pamir might have had the stomach for that kind of bullying. But he had lived most of his life on this cranky ship, and he knew it better than anyone else. That's why he dressed in a lifesuit and armor, then walked up into the push-plate's familiar passageways, living inside his suit for twenty-five full days, half a dozen malfunctions cured because of his quick, timely work.

Pamir never saw the incoming comet.

His only warning was the rapid, almost panicked firing of railguns and nukes. Then the nukes quit launching when the target was too close, and with a mathematical clarity, Pamir realized that the impact was coming, and for no useful reason, he pulled himself into a ball, hands over his knees and a deep last breath filling his lungs—

Then, blackness.

More empty than any space, and infinitely colder.

EVERYONE HOVERING AROUND him was a stranger, and none wanted to tell him about the passengers, the crew, or the fate of his ship.

Finally, a well-intentioned Eternitist minister let out the news. 'You're a fortunate, fortunate man,' he proclaimed, his smiling face matching his smiling, almost giddy voice. 'Not only did you survive, dear man. But a ship of kind Belters found your remains inside that old push-plate.'

Again, Pamir's body was being decanted from almost nothing. Still unfinished and desperately weak, he was lying in a white hospital bed, inside a zero-gee habitat, a soft webbing strung over his naked body, bristling with sensors that tirelessly marked his steady progress.

Despite his weakness, he reached for the minister.

Thinking it was a gesture of need, the man tried to take the hand with his hands. But no, the hand slipped past and closed on the nearest shoulder, then yanked at the heavy black fabric of his robe. And with a voice too new to sound human, Pamir grunted, 'What about . . . about the rest of them . . . ?'

With a blissful surety, the minister said, 'Long, happy lives received their deserved rest. Which is precisely as it should be.'

Pamir clamped his hand around the exposed neck.

The minister tried removing the hand, and failed. 'All of them died in a painless instant,' he croaked. 'Without worry. Without the slightest suffering. Isn't that the way you, in your time, would wish to die?'

The hand tightened, then let up again. And with that new voice, Pamir said, 'No,' as the newborn eyes gazed off into the distance, losing their focus. 'I want suffering. I want worry. When you see Death – soon, I hope – I want you to tell It. I want the worst It has. The shittiest worst. I want it all the way till the miserable end . . .'

CENTURIES HAD PASSED while Pamir's body drifted between the stars. He found himself living in a thinly colonized region of human space, among scattered settlements reaching to the brink of the Milky Way. Only one event of consequence had occurred in his absence, and it was enormous. Pamir learned that an alien starship had been discovered between the galaxies. No one knew where it came from or why it was here. But every important world and species were marshaling resources to reach it and claim it for themselves.

By simple luck, humans had seen it first. They had the jump. The Belter guild, vast in its reach and rich with experience, had opted to build a fleet of swift ships. And to get a lead on the other groups, the guild would launch its first ships before they were finished – small asteroids chosen for the proper mix of metals and carbonaceous goo and water ice, minimal tunnels cut through them, durable habitats built deep and safe, then engines and vast fuel tanks strapped to the raw exterior.

Every engineer in the region had been put under contract by the Belters: for their know-how and their hands, and oftentimes, just to keep the talent pool dry, making life hard for their competitors.

His deep-space experience meant that Pamir was included on the lead team.

Rumors promised that some fraction of the team would be included on the great mission. At first, Pamir assumed that he would be invited to join the Belters, and that he would refuse. The alien ship was interesting enough, but this district was a virtual wilderness. A man with wealth and his own starship could visit dozens of alien worlds, none of which had ever seen a human face before. As adventures went, he believed that was the bigger one. And with that decided, Pamir believed his future was set.

One early morning, he found himself floating inside a grimy, dust-choked tunnel, ignoring a heated discussion between architects and bolidologists. The precise angle of this very minor tunnel was the subject, and Pamir couldn't have been more bored. Prayers for a distraction, any distraction, were answered suddenly. A hundred captains appeared, drifting along in a loose chain, each having just arrived from places deep inside the Milky Way and all wearing the new mirrorlike uniforms that had been invented specifically for this one great mission.

Leading the group were a pair of Belter women – one tall and the other taller, the latter rumored to be the frontrunner for the Master Captain's chair.

Her companion, knife-faced and magisterial, noticed Pamir drifting by himself.

She nodded in his direction, then said, 'This one, madam. He's the gentleman who survived the *Elassia*'s disaster.'

Centuries had passed, yet they still remembered.

Pamir returned the nod, saying nothing. And the debate about the tunnel's angle came to an abrupt, embarrassing halt.

The future Master smiled, then decided that this moment required a graceless touch.

'I'd like to have this one with us,' she proclaimed. 'He'd bring us luck!'

But the knife-faced captain had to disagree. 'The luck was his, madam. He didn't share it with his ship.'

Pamir felt an easy hatred for the woman. Peering through the black dust, he read her nameplate. *Miocene*, he read. What did he know about her?

She was young, said the rumors. And ambitious like no one else.

The future Master winked at her lowly engineer. 'Are you interested, darling? Would you like to leave the galaxy behind?'

He thought, Thank you, no.

But there was something about the circumstances, about the drifting dust and the two captains and this talk about luck . . . all of those factors, and more, combined inside him, making him say, 'Yes, I want to go. Absolutely.'

'Good,' the giant woman replied. 'We can use all the luck we can put on board. Even if you hoard it for yourself.'

It was a joke, and a bad one. Pamir couldn't make himself laugh, even though the other captains and architects and rock experts were giggling themselves sick.

The only other person unmoved was Miocene.

'Who goes,' she reminded everyone, 'are the people who deserve to go. Nobody else. Since our ship is going to be built on the way, without anyone's help, we haven't space or the patience for those who aren't the very best.'

In that instant, Pamir realized that he had made the right choice; he wanted nothing but to be part of this grand mission. For the next year, he worked without complaint, never fighting with commanders, and leading his little teams with a quiet competence. But as the deadline approached, an uneasiness took hold. Disquiet evolved into a massive black dread. Pamir knew exactly what he was. He was a good engineer, and nothing more. The men and women around him cared more for machinery than people. They told jokes about fusion engines and gossiped about each other's designs, and their best friends were machines. A few engineers openly and happily lived with robots of their own design, their physical forms doctored only to a point, their machineness obvious under the warm rubber glands and those worshipful, doll-like faces.

When the final roster was released, dread turned to resignation.

But Pamir went through the ritual of hunting for his name, and despite knowing better, he felt a numbing surprise not to see 'Pamir' on that list.

Surprise descended into a low-grade anger made worse by two days and nights of strong drink and the ingestion of several potent drugs. In his altered haze, revenge seemed like a sweet possibility. With a harum-scarum's logic, Pamir fashioned a weapon from a laser drill, cutting off the safeties and retuning its frequencies. Then with the laser dismantled and hidden, Pamir drifted past the security troops, entering the half-born starship, thinking of Miocene when he muttered to himself, 'I'll show her some luck.'

The captains already lived on board. Maybe Pamir meant to injure them, or worse. But once the possibility of revenge became the reality, his anger dissolved into a pure, unalloyed self-loathing.

He had never felt this way.

It was the drugs in his system; he wanted to believe nothing else. But if anything, those chemicals were only flattening his emotions, distorting all reason, forcing him to keep searching for his pain's watershed.

Luckier, more talented engineers were working in the main habitats.

Pamir crept up a long dead-end shaft.

At the end of its voyage, this starship would be among

the finest ever built by human hands and human minds. But not his hands, he knew. Inside that dark, choking hole, he discovered that he didn't care about this ship. All that mattered was the ship. That dead relic that was plummeting from nowhere, heading straight for him . . . !

Maybe it was the drugs, or the despair. Or maybe it was exactly as it seemed to him just then. But the motions of his life – leaving home when he did; traveling with the *Elassia*, then as a corpse; and the remarkable good luck that caused him to be found – these unlikely events suddenly looked like Fate and Grand Design. Every important event in his life, and the tiny ones, had occurred in order to put him here, hunkering down in this unseemly place, and in that drunken, drugged, and self-possessed state, nothing seemed more obvious to Pamir than his personal destiny.

He had to find some means of staying on board.

But a stowaway couldn't stay hidden for long. Not for a century, much less for thousands of years.

The only solution was obvious; it was inevitable.

Few other men could have done what Pamir did next. To a human given thousands and perhaps millions of years of uninterrupted life, the idea of placing such a treasure in mortal danger was unthinkable.

But Pamir had died before.

Twice.

Not only did he power up the laser, but his hands were steady as stone. He found himself growing happier by the moment, by the breath. He carefully positioned his body at the back of the cramped tunnel, taking time to judge how the tarlike carbonaceous crap would melt and flow around his incinerated corpse, and how its blackness would merge and conceal his own.

In the end, for a slender instant, he felt afraid.

He wasn't a singing man. But waiting for the laser to charge, then fire, he heard his own rough voice pushing its way through an old Whistleforth melody that, if memory served, his mother used to sing to him, and to her dear two-headed dragon.

'All of the universe,' she would sing, 'and I am the only one.

'All of Creation, and there's only this one of me.

'All of Everything, and what I am now will never come again.

'With every step I change.

'With every step, I die.

'Always and forever, here, here, here, I be . . . !'

Twenty-nine

PAMIR HAD NEVER seen the Master's station in such turmoil.

Demon doors were at full strength, armored hatches sealed and locked. Brigades of security troops wore imposing weapons and bullying faces. An infectious, intoxicating paranoia hung in the bright damp air. Pamir was interrogated by two captains and a Submaster. How many searches of his body and uniform were carried out discreetly, he couldn't say. He was asked point-blank about Washen and Miocene. What had he seen? What had he heard? And what, if anything, had he said to their missing officers? He volunteered all of it, no detail too mundane. Then in a by-the-way tone, he confessed that a fat twenty seconds had passed before he contacted the Master, informing her that a pair of ghosts had appeared to him, and learning that those same apparitions had spoken to her first.

'They may be dead,' he offered, 'but they still respect the pecking order.'

Pamir was asked about his route to the ship's bridge, his mode of transportation, and whether he had seen anything even a little bit peculiar.

No journey through the ship, no matter how brief, lacked for oddities. Pamir described watching a pair of blue-necked ruffians copulating in plain view, and seeing a school of Hackaback squids that had gotten their rolling bubble caught in a shop's doorway, and mentioned that while his priority cap-car approached the ship's bridge, he had spotted a lone human male wearing nothing but a simple handwritten placard that declared:

The End Is Here!

Each interrogator recorded every oddity. Later, their staffs would rank these events by presumed importance, and where necessary, investigate.

It was a magnificent, spellbinding waste of minds and time.

The last hatch was opened, and Pamir stepped onto the station itself. And AI staffer glared at him through a rubber face, then with a jittery glee said, 'Finally.' It turned all of itself but its face and shouted, 'Follow me! At a run!'

Pamir sprinted the length of the station.

The ship's administrative center was three kilometers long and half as wide, great arches of green olivine overhead, a webwork dangling from the ceiling, captains and their assistants, human and otherwise, clinging to their work stations, chattering in the station's compressed dialect. They were talking about the missing captains. Pamir heard noise about this sweep and that sweep, all deep inside the ship. Security teams had just finished, and new sweeps were to commence, and when the humans paused to breathe, the AIs continued talking in their own chittering tongues, manipulating oceans of warm data to find anything that could be confused for a useful pattern.

Ghosts make a pair of holocalls, and look at the mayhem it brings.

The rubber face inflated as they covered the last hundred meters, and the AI warned, 'She wants honesty today. Nothing but.'

Normally, the Master didn't approve of too much truth-telling. But Pamir took a deep breath, then said, 'Don't worry.'

'But that's my job,' the AI replied, wounded now. 'Worry is.'

They pulled up in front of the Master's quarters. Pamir removed his cap and let his uniform straighten and clean itself of sweat and grime. Then after a calming gasp, he stepped up to the hyperfiber door, and it pulled open, exposing several dozen security generals – men and women cloaked in armored black uniforms, each of their profes-sionally fierce faces regarding the newcomer with a mixture of mistrust and practiced disgust.

In their minds, Pamir would always be the traitor: the treacherous captain who had forced their Master into granting him a full pardon, complete with his old, much dishonored rank.

Towering over her generals, the Master stared in Pamir's general direction, wide brown eyes seemingly lost. Then she closed her eyes and waved both arms, telling every-one else, 'For now, there's nothing. No one and nothing. But keep searching, and report everything immediately. Am I understood?'

'Yes, madam,' said thirty bowing faces.

In an instant, it was just the two of them, and a

thousand hidden AIs, and a multitude of simple instinct machines.

The Master's quarters were smaller than most. Even Pamir's apartment seemed spacious by comparison. She required only half a hectare divided into a multitude of little rooms, each decorated with the blandest of living rugs and wall hangings of no artistic worth and potted jungles composed of standard terran species and the jungle-colored furnishings intended for nothing but the uninspired comfort of her visitors.

The Master dominated every room, which was the way she wanted it. She loomed over Pamir now, and from all the possible expressions to show him, she decided on a wide warm smile ending just short of flirtatious.

The smile took him by surprise.

Then a warm voice said, 'Pamir,' with fondness.

But he hid his surprise, giving the customary bow and saying, 'Madam,' while staring at her long, long feet, bare and fleshy-gold, and the snowy marble floor in which those same feet had worn soft ruts over the course of their voyage.

'How may I help you?' he inquired.

Then again, 'Madam.'

'I've studied your account of events,' she told him. 'Excellent, thorough work. As usual. I'm sure you left nothing out.'

'Nothing.' He looked at her uniform, then at the reflection of his own puzzled face. 'Have you found either of them, madam?'

'No.'

Would she tell him if she had?

'No,' she repeated, 'and I'm beginning to believe that there's nobody to find. At least not among my missing captains.'

He blinked, considering those words.

'So it wasn't Washen who spoke to us . . .'

'It was, I suppose, someone's idea of a wicked joke.' She wasn't smiling at Pamir so much as she was smiling at that simple notion. It was a reassuring possibility, and in its contrived fashion, almost rational. 'Holoprojections. Synthetic personalities. We've traced the source to a certain waystation that was destroyed moments later. Obviously in order to give this fiction even greater credibility.'

Pamir waited for a moment, then said, 'You're wrong. Madam.'

She watched him, waiting.

'I saw Washen,' he assured. 'I recognized her, but she had definitely changed. The smokey-colored skin, and that crude uniform of hers—'

'I remember how about both of them looked. Yes, thank you.'

'Besides,' he continued, 'why would any person, or alien, or whoever—'

'Fake her and Miocene's reappearance?'

The Master was playing one of her games. What she believed was secondary to what she wanted from Pamir, and her wishes would be revealed only at her convenience. Or perhaps, never.

'An enemy could have managed this trick,' she offered, nodding with a sudden surety. 'Someone who's eager to make myself and my great office look like utter fools.'

Pamir said nothing.

'Authentic or not,' the Master continued, 'these ghosts contacted only the two of us. I can see why I would be singled out. And you, of course. You've always claimed to have seen Washen *after* her disappearance. Haven't you?'

He said, 'Yes.'

Nothing else.

'That shit-world. Marrow,' the Master quoted.

Pamir waited.

'Does that word have any significance to you?'

'Where blood is born. And that's all it means to me.'

She gestured at a bank of AIs. 'They've listed every known world with that name or some permutation. In alien tongues, typically. But none of our suspects are near us. Not now, and rarely in the past.'

'It's an odd detail,' Pamir observed. 'If you're making a joke, that is.'

Now the Master decided to remain quiet; it was her turn to wait.

Pamir knew what she wanted. 'I don't know anything, madam. Seeing Washen and Miocene . . . it was a complete and total shock . . .'

'I believe you,' she replied, without conviction.

Then with a hard glare, she asked, 'What do you believe? Based on your total ignorance, naturally.'

With his heart pounding and an invisible hand to his throat, Pamir told her, 'They were genuine, these ghosts were. And I think they're still on the ship. Washen. Submaster Miocene. And presumably the other missing captains, too.'

'Each is free to his opinion.'

He bristled, secretly.

'Twice,' she said. 'Once, and again. Twice.'

'Pardon me, madam?'

'I have taken my chances with you. Do you remember, Pamir?' The smile was wide and malevolent. 'I nearly forgot the first time. But you remember it, don't you? In the beginning, when the engineers uncovered your ruined carcass . . . they wanted to leave you in that state until you could be delivered to an appropriate prison facility . . .'

'Yes, madam.'

'But I saved you.' She said it with a mixture of bitterness and sublime pleasure. 'I decided that a soul who wanted to be with us that badly had to be valuable, regardless of his talents. Which was why I ordered you reborn. And when your fellow engineers refused to accept you, wasn't I the wise one who invited you to become a captain . . . ?'

Not precisely. Joining the captains' ranks was his idea and his initiative. But he knew better than to debate the point, nodding without kowtowing, saying to her big bare feet, 'I have tried to serve you and the ship.'

'With a lapse or two thrown in.'

'One lapse,' he replied, refusing to fall into simple traps.

'You honestly know nothing about these prank calls. Do you?'

'Or even if they are pranks, no. I don't, Madam.'

'Which puts us where, Pamir? I want to hear this from you.'

With a quiet, firm voice, he told the Master, 'If you wish. If I might. I could hunt the ship for Washen. For all those missing captains. In an official capacity, or otherwise.'

Eyes lifted. 'You'd be willing to do that?'

'Gladly,' he said, meaning it.

'I suppose you're qualified,' she remarked. Then taking delight in old wounds, she pointed out, 'You did manage to evade my security teams for a long, long while. And apparently without much effort.'

He could do nothing but glance at her face, holding tight to his breath.

'And since you mentioned it,' she continued, 'I could use a little more reassurance. About your loyalty, if nothing else.' She paused for a half-moment, then added, 'If you find Washen, perhaps I can stop watching every step you take. Understood?'

It was easy to forget why he had rejoined the captains' ranks.

Showing the Master a thin, cool smile, Pamir said, 'Madam.'

Then he bowed slightly, pointing out, 'If I find these lost captains, and they're alive, then you'll be too busy worrying about them to bother with me . . .

'Madam . . . !'

Thirty

PAMIR SAT IN the darkened garden room, on the fragrant stump of a dusk pinkwood. The garden was at the heart of a luxury apartment set inside one of the oldest and finest of the human districts. A peculiar couple shared its spacious rooms and hallways – a man and woman married back in the early millennia of the voyage – and throughout Pamir's visit, the lovers would hold hands and whisper into each other's ears, causing their gruff visitor to suffer the sour beginnings of envy.

Quee Lee was a wealthy and extraordinarily ancient woman. Born on the Earth, she had inherited her fortune from a Chinese grandfather who made his money through shipping and legal drugs. On other occasions, she would talk about their home world with both fondness and horror. She was nearly as old as Pamir's mother would be today, though he never mentioned that crazy woman. Quee Lee was old enough to remember when spaceflight was anything but routine and people counted themselves fortunate, or cursed, to live for a single century. Then came the day when the first alien broadcasts fell from the sky, washing away the Earth's isolation. By the time she was middle-aged, everything had changed. Twenty technologically adept species were known, and their knowledge, coupled with a home-brewed intellectual explosion, brought things like star drives and eternal genetics, and the probes that would leave the Milky Way, and eventually, this great and ancient and undeniably wondrous ship in which they rode in luxurious splendor.

Her young husband was born on the ship. Perri had been a Remora, one of those strange souls who lived on the ship's hull. But he decided to leave that bizarre culture, preferring the greater strangeness of the ship's interior. When Pamir was a captain on the rise, the two men were enemies. But after Pamir had abandoned his post, taking on new faces and identities, Perri had slowly evolved into an ally and an occasional friend.

Only certain specialist AIs knew the ship better than Perri.

A masculine face, more pretty than handsome, was studying a series of holomaps. The occasional glowbat was gently waved out of the way, then the same hand adjusted the maps' controls, changing the perspective, or the district being examined, or the scale of everything that he was examining with a perfect concentration.

'Another drink?' asked Quee Lee.

Pamir looked at his empty glass. 'Thank you. No.'

She was a beautiful woman in any light. An ageless face was wrapped around ancient, warm eyes. She had a fondness for one-color sarongs and ornate, exceedingly alien jewelry. Clinging to one of her husband's hands, she looked at the map, and with a gentle sigh, she confessed, 'I always forget.'

'How big the ship is,' said Perri, completing her thought.

'It is,' she echoed, looking up at their guest. 'It's wonderfully huge.'

Perri marked a likely cavern, then moved to the next district. He didn't volunteer why that place was worth a look. Instead, he asked the obvious question.

'Who are you hunting?'

Then with a smile that couldn't have been more charming, he gave the answer. 'It's those missing captains, I bet. I bet.'

Familiarity was a powerful tool.

Pamir didn't need to reply. He simply held his mouth closed and gave his head a slight, somewhat suggestive tilt.

Reading his posture, Perri nodded and grinned with a private satisfaction. Then again, he marked a location. 'There's a little river running through a practically bottomless canyon. Honestly, there might be a million square kilometers down there. All of it vertical. Black basalt and epiphyte forests. I know two settlements. Neither human. Between them, there's room for a few hundred thousand people. If they were careful, and a little lucky, nobody would ever know they were there.'

Quee Lee regarded her husband with fond eyes.

'That canyon was searched last month,' Pamir replied. 'By security robots, and thoroughly.'

'Captains would know tricks,' said Perri. 'Shit, you've used those same tricks. It would be easy enough to make the machines see nothing but rock and clingweed.'

'You think I should look there?'

'Maybe.'

In other words: 'I don't see why they would be there.'

Pamir said nothing.

Again, the map changed districts. Suddenly Perri was staring at a deeply buried city, nothing about its selection random. A wealth of colors and complicated shapes showed the presence of alien species. With a knowing touch, he moved past the catacombs and main arteries, following an obscure capillary to a waystation that appeared as a strong golden light, open for operation, welcoming all visitors.

Perri marked the waystation, then giggled.

'What's funny?'

He smiled at the captain, saying, 'This. What I know is what the gossip says. That someone destroyed this nowhere place. It was a random, meaningless act. Isn't that the official verdict? Yet within minutes, the Master ordered a thorough sweep of a hundred districts centered on that single station.'

Again, Pamir used silence. And with it, a hard look.

Perri doctored the map's scale, pulling back and back. Suddenly they were looking at nearly a tenth of one percent of the ship – a vast region, complicated and oftentimes empty, with a hundred thousand kilometers of major passageways blurring into a geometric puzzle too irregular to appear planned, much less attractive, and to any mind large enough to appreciate the distances, this was obviously a puzzle without any worthwhile solution.

Not for the first time, Pamir felt utterly helpless.

'This is how big the sweeps got,' said Perri. 'And people are still talking about them. A couple species living down here have strong feelings about authoritative presences. One hates them, while the other loves them. Those sweeps made them feel important, and they're still singing about them today.'

'I can imagine.'

Inside that vast region, Perri's six dozen markers appeared as purple dots of light. With his free hand, he gestured, remarking, 'This is a waste. All of it.'

'Excuse me?'

'You're bright enough, I mean. But really, you and the

rest of the uniforms are attacking this problem in all the obvious ways.'

Pamir grimaced.

Knowing the captain's temper, Quee Lee leaned forward and smiled as if everything depended on it. 'Are you sure you don't want a fresh drink?'

Pamir shook his head, then echoed the words, '"The obvious ways."'

'It's about your missing captains. And that's not just a reasonable guess on my part. One of your Master's AIs leaked that news to its psychiatrist, who dribbled it to a lover, who mentioned it in public once . . . at least that's the way I heard it happened . . .'

Pamir waited.

'You've been busy since. I know that, too. You've been interviewing all your old contacts . . . for how long now . . . ?'

'Six weeks.'

'So how does my list compare? With the others, I mean.'

'It's thorough. It's reasonable. I'll find what I want in one of those places.'

'Well, I don't think so.'

Quee Lee pulled her hand away from her husband's, and with her short and smooth index finger, she touched the lowest, most isolated of the violet lights.

'What's this place?' she inquired.

Perri said, 'An alien habitat.'

'For the leech,' the captain added. 'It's been abandoned for a long while now.'

'Did the Master search it?' asked Perri.

He nodded. Then he added, 'By proxy, and with some security people, too.'

'What I think,' Perri offered, 'is that you have to accept a difficult fact first. Are you listening to me?'

'Always.'

'You know absolutely nothing about this ship.' Suddenly it was as if Perri were angry. This perpetually charming man, who lubricated every social circumstance with a glib shallowness, leaned close enough that his liquored breath mingled with the night odors of the ancient garden. 'Absolutely nothing,' he repeated. 'The same as everyone else.'

'I know enough,' Pamir countered, meaning it.

Perri shook his head, shook his empty hands. 'The fuck you do! You don't know who built this ship, or when, or even where it happened!'

The captain wanted that drink suddenly, but he decided to sit quietly and say nothing, letting his posture and his glare do their worst.

'And worst of all,' said Perri, 'you don't even know why this machine was built. Do you? Without compelling evidence, you can't even pretend to have a workable theory. Just some half-broiled guesses that haven't been changed in a hundred millennia. All of this is someone's galaxy-hopping ship. You hope. Launched too late, or too soon. Although does anyone have any real evidence to say this is so?'

Pamir said, 'No.'

Perri leaned back and grinned like a man who knew that he had just won an important fight, his hands knitted together and stuck behind his head.

Quietly, the captain said, 'Marrow.'

'Excuse me?'

It was the first time that he had said the word since seeing the Master, and the only reason he used it now was to deflect the conversation.

'Do you know anyplace with that name?'

'Marrow?'

'That's what I said. Do you know it?'

Perri closed his eyes, considering the single word until finally, with a grudging conviction, he could admit, 'Nothing comes to mind. Why? Where did you hear about it?'

'Make a half-broiled guess,' Pamir advised.

The man had to laugh. At himself and his companion, and at everything else, too. 'Is that where the missing captains are?'

'If I only knew . . .'

Then Quee Lee said 'Marrow' in a different way, using an extinct dialect. Straightening her finger, she said, 'Long ago, before human beings were reengineered to live forever . . . back when we were simple and frail, marrow was in the middle of our bones. Not like today. Not laced through our muscles and livers, too.'

Both men turned and stared at her.

'You're too young to remember,' she offered, as if giving them an excuse. Then she turned her finger, pointing down past the deepest purplish lights. 'Marrow sometimes meant the center of things. Their heart. Their deepest core.'

Then she glanced up, smiling now, her very round, very old-fashioned face lit up by the map's glow.

Again, Pamir thought that she was a beautiful woman.

'Look at the ship's core,' she advised.

Quietly and almost politely, the two men enjoyed a good long laugh at poor Quee Lee's expense.

Thirty-one

PAMIR CONSTRUCTED A list of promising sites, then made foot-and-eye searches of each, always in disguise, always taking the sort of time and obsessive care that comes naturally to an immortal working alone. Over the next few years, he uncovered an ocean of sharp rumor, slippery lies, and dreamy half-sightings. As far as he could determine, the only certainty was that every sentient organism had seen the missing captains at least once, and judging by the sightings, the captains were everywhere. Even Pamir was infected with the hysteria. Missing colleagues appeared without warning. Old lovers, usually. Washen, more than not. Without warning, he would see a tall human woman casually strolling down a busy avenue, her gait and color and the bun of her gray and brown hair recognizable from half a kilometer away. Pamir would break into a sprint, and as he drew closer, a dead run. But by the time he reached Washen, she had turned into another handsome woman, flustered and perhaps a little flattered to have a strange man tugging on her arm. On a different occasion, he spotted Washen sitting cross-legged in the middle of an otherwise empty chamber, nude and elegantly beautiful. But in the time it took Pamir to approach, she turned into a statue twenty meters tall, and just when he convinced himself that this was his first genuine clue, her statue became nothing but a suggestive pile of badly lit rubble. Then it was a year later, and Washen was kneeling on a ledge among the purple epiphytes growing above the grave bar where Pamir had made camp. Glancing up, he saw her familiar face smiling at him, watching as he baked a fresh-killed chinook salmon. Then the wind gusted, and he heard Washen's voice asking, 'Enough for two?' But by then Pamir knew his mind, and he didn't allow himself excitement. A gust of wind lifted, and Washen's face turned to a knot of dead leaves. And Pamir shook his head, smiled at his own foolishness, then set the fish closer to the sputtering fire.

Passengers and the crew learned about his hunt, and for every conceivable reason, they led him astray.

Some wanted money for their lies.

Others begged for attention, for praise and love and fame.

While a few were so genuinely eager to please, they didn't know they were lying, inflating half-memories with wishful thoughts, building coherent epics that could withstand every battery of physiological testing.

The missing captains were living with radical luddites somewhere in the Bottoms.

They had formed their own luddite community hidden inside an unmapped chamber somewhere beneath the Gossamer Sea.

They had been abducted by the Kajjan-Quasans – a tiny part-organic, part-silicon species who kept them as slaves and rode them like livestock.

A gel flow in the Magna district had entombed them.

Or there was the common, almost plausible story of bitter, vengeful aliens. Phoenixes were the preferred villains, though there were many worthy candidates. Whoever they were, they had returned to the ship in secret, and in retribution for the Master's ancient crimes, they murdered her best captains.

One earnest human claimed that an unknown alien had carved away the captains' high mental functions, then left the brain-damaged survivors living inside a local sewage-treatment plant. Unlikely as it sounded, the witness remembered seeing a woman identical to Washen. 'I talked to her,' he swore. 'Poor lady. Dumb as can be now. Poor lady.'

With a worried hopefulness, Pamir slipped inside the vast chamber. The original recycling machinery was now augmented with a forest of tailored fungi – a scene that couldn't help but remind the captain of his mother's long-ago home. Mushrooms towered overhead, feasting on the waste of a thousand species. A village of low huts and smoky fires was exactly where he expected to find it – a human colony not on any map, official or otherwise. Slowly and carefully, he approached the nearest hut, and after a good deep breath, he stepped out and smiled at the woman standing in the open doorway.

He recognized the face. Without doubt, she resembled a one-time engineer who had helped build the Belters' starship, then later joined the captains' ranks.

'Aasleen?' he asked, stopping at a throw's distance.

The face was mostly unchanged, yes: a rich lustrous black over smooth, elegant features, with a radiant yellowy-white smile. Her smile was very much the same, too. The longer Pamir stared at the apparition, the more certain he felt.

She said, 'Hello,' quietly, almost too quietly to be heard.

'I'm Pamir,' he blurted. 'Remember me, Aasleen?'

'Always,' she replied, and the smile brightened.

Her voice was too soft and too slow. It wasn't the right voice, yet what if some creature had mutilated her in some elaborate fashion . . . ? With each word, the voice grew a little closer to what he remembered, to what he expected. Pamir found himself enjoying this illusion, stepping closer and watching as the face continued to change, evolving until it was very much the ex-lover's face.

He asked, 'What are you thinking, Aasleen?'

Her mouth opened, but no sound emerged.

'Do you know how you got here?' He stepped even closer, smiling as he repeated the question. 'Do you know how?'

'I do,' she lied. 'Yes.'

'Tell me.'

'By accident,' she replied. 'That's what it had to be.'

Pamir reached for her face, and when she tried to back away, he said, 'No. Let me.' Then his wide hand passed through a projection of light and ionized dust. The fungus hut and the fires were equally unreal. This wasn't a community, it was an entertainment. Someone had thrown away their empathic AI, probably in the morning shit, and somehow it had survived the fall and the sterilization procedures, eventually landing in the goo beneath his feet.

Pamir left the entertainment where he found it, unmapped.

He abandoned the search zone, traveling halfway around the ship to a place that would mean plenty to Washen and Aasleen. He climbed inside the antimatter tank where the Phoenixes once lived. As he expected, the facility was empty. Utterly clean and empty. Not even one of Washen's ghosts was waiting for him. Standing at the bottom, on a floor of slick, ageless hyperfiber, Pamir found himself staring up at the vastness, the tank making him feel tiny even as a knowing part of him warned that this was nothing, that the ship dwarfed this little cylinder, and the universe dwarfed the ship, and all these grand designs and silver wonders were nothing set against the endless reaches through which everything soared.

Eighteen years and three weeks had been invested in a careful, thorough search for the captains, and nothing had come of it.

Nothing.

Out of simple habit, Pamir referred to his original list of searchable sites, each site carefully deleted over the years, tired eyes tracking down to that final odd word:

'leech.'

This would be the last place he ever looked. Years of labor and hope had been wasted, nothing learned but that nothing wanted to be learned. Making the long fall to the alien habitat, Pamir decided that Washen and Aasleen, and Miocene, weren't waiting around any proverbial curve. He could suddenly believe those theories that the Master held close to her heart. Another species had hired away her best captains, or more likely, kidnapped them. Either way, they were off the ship, and lost. And Washen's mysterious re-appearance was someone's peculiar joke, and the Master was cunning-wise not to let herself be distracted by a sick, misguided humor.

The leech would be a suitable end, he decided.

As he stepped out of the hub, out into that planar gray-ness, Pamir nearly dismissed the site out of hand. Washen would never remain here. Not for a year, much less for several millennia. Already feeling his mind eroding, his will and heart deflating with every little breath, Pamir was quite sure that no other captain would willingly live inside this two-dimensional realm.

Two steps, and he wanted to run away.

Halting, Pamir took a deep breath, then made certain that the hub's lone doorway was locked open. Then he knelt and opened a sack of tiny scuttle-bugs and dog-noses and peregrine-eyes.

Set loose, the sensors fanned out along two dimensions.

With access to certain secure files, Pamir asked for back-ground on the leech. What was given him was sketchy, unyielding. The exophobes had lived in this intention-ally bland habitat for six hundred years, then the entire species had disembarked, their vessel carrying them off into a molecular dust cloud that had long since been left behind.

The leech were gone before the captains vanished.

'Good-bye,' he whispered. Then he lifted his head, his voice magnified by the floor and ceiling, that single word racing out in a perfect circle that ended with the distant round wall, then returned to him again, loud and deep and mutated into a stranger's voice.

'Good-bye,' the room shouted at him.

As soon as I can, he thought. The moment I am done.

THE PROBES FOUND anomalies.

They always did; nothing about their alarms was unexpected.

Pamir constructed a map of the anomalies, checked for patterns, then began walking in a sweeping pattern, examining each in turn. Nothing was large enough to see with the naked eye. Most of the oddities were dried flakes of human skin. But what struck Pamir as peculiar, even remarkable, was that barely a dozen flakes were waiting to be found. If humans had wandered into this place, wouldn't they have left a good deal more tissue? Old tissue, when he measured the decay. Abused to where their genetic markers couldn't be read. And there wasn't any bacteria clinging to the flakes, either. None of that benign, immortal stuff that had ridden humanity into space.

Cleansing agents or microchines had scrubbed this place to the brink of sterility. Which wasn't too unlikely. This was an alien home, and its human trespassers could have been mannerly.

Could have been.

One more purple light showed on the map, nestled near the wall.

It was a twist of incinerated flesh. Submerged inside the plastic floor, it must have gone unnoticed by the trespassers. But a scuttlebug hadn't any trouble finding it, and with its guidance, Pamir used a laser drill, extracting the blackened finger-sized treasure, then inserting it into his field lab.

Quietly, patiently, the gray floor started to patch its fresh hole.

Nearly a kilo of living flesh had been charred down to almost nothing. There were genetic markers, though not enough to match against any of the missing captains. But the caramelized flesh implied a homicidal violence, which offered another reason to explain why visitors might try to cover their traces.

Pamir watched the floor grow flat and slick again, then he measured the gray plastic, carefully mapping a network of fine, almost invisible scars. This tiny portion of the habitat had been damaged. Perhaps recently. The floor had scars, as did the ceiling and the thick gray wall. Some kind of machine had been destroyed *here*. Pamir found a thin taste of metals inside the smart hydrocarbons. Explosions and lasers had riddled this place. He could make out where determined hands had chiseled out anything that would constitute a clue, the floor healing and healing again, struggling to hold its seal while another force, just as relentless, struggled to erase its crime.

Pamir was sweating, thinking again of ghosts.

What now?

Sitting on an ancient pillow, he turned a full circle, noticing the scuttlebug with its face pressed against the patched wall.

'Already looked there,' Pamir told it.

But the bug refused to move.

Pamir rose, nearly bumping his head on the ceiling. Walking toward the wall, he asked, 'What is it?'

In many species, perhaps even in ancient humans, language evolved as a tool to speak with the dead. Since the living world can read your face and body, only ghosts require those simple first words.

Whose theory was it?

Pamir was trying to remember, thinking of nothing else when he knelt beside the scuttlebug and tapped into its data. Buried deep in the wall – closer to the cold vacuum than to him – was a single metal object. It was round and smooth, and as far as he could see, it couldn't be more simple.

It's nothing, thought Pamir.

Nothing.

But he used a laser, carving a narrow hole, then widening it enough for the bug to scramble in, then scramble out again.

The artifact was fashioned from dirty silver, and the laser had left it too hot to hold. Pamir set it on top of the bug and ate a small meal of dried whiskey and sweetened coelacanth. Then he examined the artifact's hinge and its crude latch, using his eyes and fingers. Whatever happened here, the object had been damaged. X-rays showed him a primitive network of gears and empty space. Removing one of the bug's limbs, he used it as a prick, finally triggering the battered latch. Then as Pamir carefully lifted the lid, the hinge shattered and the lid fell between his long feet, and he stared at the clock's face, archaic and very simple and wondrously strange.

A crude battery had run itself dry.

The elegant black hands were frozen in place. A dial showed what might be a date. 4611.330, Pamir read. And his heart paused for a long, long moment.

Was it some sort of luddite prop?

Or a child's toy?

Whatever it was, it had delicate, carefully forged metal workings. Pamir could see the wear of fingers on the bottom and edges of the silver case. As an experiment, he held the clock in his hand, trying to imagine its vanished owner. Then he turned and started toward the wall, and by accident, he kicked the broken lid across the slick gray floor.

The lid lodged beneath one of the hard pillows.

To the ghosts, Pamir said, 'It's mine.'

He knelt and reached under the pillow, pulling out that heavy piece of silver and stronger, more enduring metals, and for a moment, he stared at the top of it, the lid polished and gray as the floor, yet anything but bland. Then as an afterthought, he flipped it over and saw the scratches. No, they were too regular to be scratches. Turning the lid like the hands of a clock, he brought the marks around until they revealed themselves to be letters engraved into the silver by means that humans hadn't used for aeons.

He read the words to himself.

Then to the ghosts, he read them aloud.

'A piece of the sky. To Washen. From your devoted grandchildren.'

And for a long, long moment, it seemed to Pamir as if the vastness of the room were filled with the echoing beats of his heart.

Thirty-two

THE MASTER WHISPERED a secret command, and an armada of sensor-encrusted robots were dispatched to the leech habitat, hunting for Washen and the other missing captains along every reasonable avenue.

The robots found nothing, and Pamir realized that nothing about this search would ever be obvious or easy.

After his urging, the Master allowed various specialists to sign security pacts, then join his mission. The leech habitat was studied on site by every available means, then samples were delivered to competing laboratories and examined in nanoscopic detail. The giant fuel tank's shaped-vacuum wall was scanned for flaws and secret doorways. Bursts of sharp sound probed the vast hydrogen ocean, from its surface to its slushy middle depths, and targets that were human-sized or larger were carefully snagged and brought to the surface – a painstaking, time-rich chore made worse by the profound cold and the need for perfect secrecy. Even the mission engineers were given no clear picture of what they were hunting, their genius severely diluted as a consequence. After three hard years of bringing up sunken ships and frozen robots, they rebelled. En masse, they confronted Pamir, explaining what he already knew full well: hundreds of thousands of cubic kilometers of hydrogen remained unexplored; and worse still, the fuel had been tapped over the last few years. Some of it was burned. More cubic kilometers were split between half a hundred auxiliary fuel tanks. And worst of all, strong and highly chaotic currents had flowed through this cold ocean, if only briefly.

'We don't know what we're chasing here,' they complained. 'Give us an exact shape size and composition, and we can build some reliable models. But until you tell us something useful, we can't even make better guesses. Do you understand?'

Pamir nodded, one hand grasping the primitive clock, opening the repaired lid and staring at the slow black hands.

In principle, he was the mission's leader. But the Master demanded instantaneous briefings and made almost every decision, including the routine ones. The two of them had anticipated this very issue; Pamir knew what to tell his staff. 'As you've probably guessed,' he remarked, 'we're looking for the leech. Dead or otherwise, we think that the aliens are still nearby, and there are some good security reasons for this bit of news to go no farther than *here*.'

He hated to lie, and he did it with a discomforting skill.

'You are a species of paranoid exophobes,' Pamir continued, 'and there are several hundred of you, and you want to hide. Perhaps you're somewhere nearby. Which is the only sort of clue I can give away. Now what new ideas can you give me?'

The engineers dreamed up a secret city. Thermally and acoustically buffered, the city could be buried deep inside the fuel tank, down where the hydrogen was a rigid and pure and nearly impenetrable solid. But that kind of technology meant power, which implied fusion power, which meant a detectable stream of neutrinos. A large array of state-of-the-art detectors were built, then floated on the ocean's surface. Even though he believed that this was a very, very, very unlikely answer, Pamir was nervously hopeful, activating the detection system with the Master on his shoulder, watching the data flow, the machinery's soft, insistent alarm telling him and the Master, 'I see something. Something. *Down there*.'

But the ship was laced with fusion reactors, each producing its own radiant stream of neutrinos, and every stream was deflected and diluted whenever it passed through the megabonds of hyperfiber. Separating the important from the superfluous was hard, slow work. Six months of meticulous drudgery followed; ninety-eight-plus percent of the neutrinos were excluded from consideration, leaving a trickle that might or might not be important.

Then with a delicious abruptness, the detectors were forgotten.

Two of Pamir's engineers had gone off by themselves, wanting more than a little privacy. Like a thousand robots before, they followed an obscure fuel line, moving deeper into the ship, finally reaching a point where for no apparent reason, the hyperfiber wall looked younger. Fresher. Wrong.

Robots would have dismissed such data as unimpressive. Obviously, the fuel line had been patched. But that sort of work was common in the early days of the voyage, and much of it was accomplished without records being kept. And since there were no seams or signs of traffic – nothing here but a good strong wall – the robots had lingered for only a few microseconds, then continued their plunge.

But the lovers were intrigued.

They lingered for a full hour, making sensitive probes before returning to their cramped car for another round of clumsy sex. Then in the afterglow, one of them said, 'Wait. I know what this is.'

'What's what?' said his lover.

'It's a hatch. A nice big hatch.'

The other man said, 'And look, here's my nice big penis!'

'No, listen to me,' said the first man. Then he was laughing, adding, 'What is it, it's a secret hatch. That's why this hyperfiber looks wrong.'

'Okay. But we'd see the seams along the edge. Wouldn't we?'

'Not if the hatch itself is small. And not if the seams are perfect.'

Which left his lover with another doubt. 'How could the leech manage *that* sort of trickery?'

It would be a difficult task, yes. But they made more tests, finally sniffing out a nanoscopic flaw that intersected with approximately another twelve billion other flaws that created a hatch just large enough for a small cap-car to pass through. Perhaps. Armed with their fresh data, they returned to Pamir. The mission leader met them on the aerogel barge drifting in the middle of the hydrogen sea, surrounded by darkness and a perpetual chill, and with matching darkness, he listened to the engineers, then nodded, and quietly told both men, 'Thank you. On behalf of the Master and myself, thank you.'

The first engineer had to ask, 'But what about the leech?'

'What about them?'

'We didn't realize they had the means to build that sort of doorway, much less fool us for this long.'

'Yet fooled we were,' Pamir replied.

He stared out at the smooth, untroubled face of the hydrogen ocean, his thoughts turning back to Washen. If they had ever left her. Nobody else in his long life had been a better friend. In his gut, Pamir knew that Washen was waiting for him. She needed him, or she was dead. Either way, it was imperative that he find her, and with that thought burning inside him, he dismissed the two men and contacted the Master; and three minutes later, the engineers' mission was officially terminated, handshakes and fat bonuses given along with warnings that no one else needed to learn anything more about this strange cold business.

WHAT CAPTAINS COULD build, captains could comprehend; and if it came to that, what they could build they could also break.

Thirty Submasters and high-grade regulars, most with engineering experience, were briefed in full and assembled inside an abandoned pumping complex above the secret doorway. Special scuttlebugs and smart-dust probes examined the area, then undertook an equally exhaustive search of every similar fuel line. But there was only the one doorway, and every test confirmed that it was real, that it hadn't been opened for at least several years, and to the limits of their technology, there were no watchdog sensors or any sort of booby trap lying in wait.

The Master decided on cautious research.

But six months later, with her captains still hiding inside that pumping complex, her patience dissolved into a frustrated boldness.

'Break open the hatch,' she roared.

Pamir was in the conference room, sitting behind a row of Submasters. Quietly, but not too quietly, he said, 'Madam.' Then he sighed and added, 'Maybe we're narrowing your search a little too much.'

Faces turned.

But not the Master's face. Her dark eyes remained buried in the holomaps and equipment lists and the expanse of her own hand, one great finger pointing to a minuscule, yet suddenly vital detail.

Without looking at him, she said, 'Elaborate.'

Then she added, 'Quickly, Captain Pamir.'

'Someone or something could have fallen out of the leech habitat,' he remarked, looking at everyone but the Master. 'We should keep searching the fuel tank. And I still have that neutrino array in place. It was detecting a possible source . . . coming from somewhere below us, if the early data are true . . .'

One of the Submasters gave a rumbling cough, then reminded his superior, 'The fuel tank has been searched. Nearly exhaustively, madam. And Pamir is talking about a piss of neutrinos too thin to have any value—'

Knowing the hazards, Pamir interrupted. 'We should watch the doorway, and wait,' he argued. He was looking at the faces that were open enough to look back at him. Then he added, 'If our captains are behind that door, then we'll be showing them what we know. And like any game, you don't want to give up your turn too soon.'

The Master took a moment, allowing his words to evaporate into the tense silence. Then she said, 'Thank you.'

Pamir's opinion had been crisply dismissed.

Speaking to more trusted captains, she ordered, 'Keep yourselves and your ship safe. But as soon as physically possible, I want you to force the hatch. Please.'

Twenty-four hours later, hair charges of antimatter were set against the hidden hinges, then detonated.

The hatch shifted a nanoscopic distance, then jammed firmly in place.

The sophisticated equivalent of a prybar was deployed, and it gave a yank, then another, and that shiny gray plug of pure hyperfiber slid out slowly, then faster, tumbling down the fuel line for twenty kilometers, reaching a closed valve and slamming into an aerogel bed that caught it like a great hand, saving it for later studies.

Scuttlebugs, then high-ranking captains, descended on the gaping hole, all dressed in armor and bristling with weapons, the machines devoid of expectations while the humans assured themselves that they were ready for anything.

Behind the secret doorway, waiting for them, was nothing.

Cold iron-rich rock was mixed with splinters of hyperfiber. Which wasn't exactly nothing. But as spidery limbs and gloved hands touched the stratum, a sturdy disappointment struck, the captains asking themselves, Is the hatch a decoy? Is it just a half-clever way to keep our eyes and minds pointed in the wrong direction?

But no, analysis showed that this was the topmost portion of a vertical tunnel, and if the tunnel kept plunging straight down, it would merge with one of the crushed access tunnels – ancient, enigmatic, and utterly useless.

Eleven days after Washen's mysterious reappearance, an

antimatter charge had destroyed the tunnel. Seismic records showed a bump and creak that had gone unnoticed among the ship's usual bumps and creaks. But the damage looked obsessively thorough. The surrounding rock was pulverized, and treacherous. Rebuilding just the first few kilometers of the tunnel would take time and vast resources.

'Do it,' the Master ordered.

But they didn't need thirty captains for what three of them, plus a brigade of mining drones, could accomplish with the same ease.

Pamir asked permission to return to the fuel tank and continue his search.

'Refused,' the Master replied instantly, out of hand.

Then she told him, 'You'll remain with the digging team. And if you find a moment or two of free time, I can't stop you from doing what you want.'

'Alone?' he asked.

And her golden face smiled as she told her most difficult captain, 'I am sorry. My apologies. I thought that's exactly how you like to do everything.'

Thirty-three

NEUTRINOS AND THE slow ghosts remained, but only in the corner of the eye and the mind. The central duty in Pamir's life was to carve a simple hole, following the shattered vein wherever it led, and with the years that seemingly straightforward task evolved into what might have been the deepest, most demanding excavation in human history.

Nothing remained of the original access tunnel. A series of sharp shaped explosions had obliterated the hyperfiber walls, and worse, they had pumped fantastic amounts of heat into the surrounding rock and iron. A column of red-hot magma led down into the ship's depths. Reconstructing the tunnel wasn't impossible, but it was nearly so. What was simpler was to extract the magma like stubborn cream through a wide straw, then slather the surrounding walls with better and better grades of hyperfiber, creating a vertical shaft more than a full kilometer wide.

Thirty years of digging, and three captains stood at a point as deep as the fuel tank's deepest reaches.

In another fifty years, they were clawing their way through a wilderness of iron.

Pamir was always present. But the other captains changed faces and names every eight or ten years. Duty in the 'big hole' was by no means an honor. After the first century of work and several catastrophic collapses, the Master and most of her staff had lost hope in the project. The camouflaged hatchway had been nothing but a clever distraction. The access tunnel had been destroyed by someone, yes. But throwing antimatter bomblets down a tiny hole would be easy enough. Among the tiny circle of AIs and captains who knew about the digging, none could believe there was anything worth finding *down there*.

Even Pamir found his imagination failing him.

In his dreams, when he saw himself digging fast with a handheld shovel, he couldn't picture finding anything but another gout of hard black iron.

Yet the hole was Pamir's duty, and it was a grand, consuming obsession. When he wasn't choreographing the digging, he was badgering distant factories for improved grades of hyperfiber. When he wasn't overseeing the pouring of a thick new stretch of wall, he was personally examining the finished stretches, from bottom to top, searching for any flaw, any inadequate seam, where the brutal pressures of the great ship threatened to buckle all of his wasted work.

Those rare moments when he climbed out of the hole and into the fuel tank felt like vacations. His aerogel island still floated on the placid hydrogen sea. Alone, he would repair the neutrino detectors and comb the last year or two of data, searching for traces of that soft signal, trying to decide if it truly came from below.

After decades of growing subtly stronger, the signal was weakening now.

There were years when it seemed to vanish altogether.

The Master and her loyal AIs, privy to the same data, came to the same rigorous solution. 'It's vanishing because it never was,' they claimed. 'Anomalies have that wicked habit.'

Pamir asked permission to build new detectors, increasing his sensitivity, and he was curtly refused. When he mentioned that a second array floating inside an adjacent fuel tank would let him identify every ghost particle's birthplace, he found agreement based upon solid technical reasoning.

'But there's more to this issue,' the Master warned. 'It's a question of resources and general discomfort.'

'Discomfort?' he inquired.

'My discomfort,' she replied, her holoimage feigning a grimace. 'Floating on the hydrogen like they do, your toys are hazards. We don't dare pump out important amounts of fuel, since that might disturb them. And worse, what if they clog a line?'

Half a dozen easy solutions occurred to Pamir.

But before he offered any, the Master added, 'That's why I want your array disassembled. And soon, please. We've got a major bum coming in a little more than eighteen months — a burn and subsequent flybys — and I need my hydrogen. Free of aerogel and detectors, and all the rest of it.'

'In eighteen months,' Pamir echoed.

'No,' she said, her patience worn into the thinnest of veneers. 'Sooner than that. If you need, take a leave of absence from your hole. Is that understood?'

He nodded, bristled in secret, and decided what to do.

With the help of mining drones, Pamir dismantled exactly half of the array, packing up the sensors, then on his authority, sent them up to Port Alpha. He followed the fancy crates, and in a cramped assembly point beneath the outer hull, he met an ancient Remora who owed him more than one good favor.

Orleans had a splendid and ugly new face. Wide amber eyes rode on the ends of white worms, pressed flush against the lifesuit's faceplate, and something that might have been a mouth smiled. Or grimaced. Or it changed shape for no other reason than it could.

A sloppy voice asked, 'Where?'

Pamir gave the coordinates, then with his own easy smile added, 'This is only for us to know.'

Orleans stared through the diamond wall of a packing crate, regarding its contents with his mutated senses. Perhaps no one appreciated a good machine more than a Remora, married as they were to their own bulky suits. 'You're on a hunt for neutrinos,' he remarked. Then he added, 'I don't believe in neutrinos.'

'No?' said Pamir. 'Why's that?'

'They pass through me, but they don't touch me.' The nearly molten face managed to nod. 'I don't believe in things that mysterious.'

Both men laughed, each for his own reason.

'Okay,' said Pamir, 'but will you do this for me?'

'What about the Master below us?'

'She doesn't need to know.'

Orleans was smiling. The expression was sudden and obvious, and with the wormy green eyes staring at the captain, his smiling voice said, 'Good. I like keeping secrets from that old bitch.'

HALF OF THE original array was deployed out on the ship's hull, thousands of kilometers higher and some ninety degrees removed from the remaining half, tucked into the vastness between a pair of towering rocket nozzles.

Calibrations and synchronization took time. Even when there was reasonable data, it proved stubbornly uncompelling. The universe was awash with neutrinos, and the ship's hyperfiber hull and bracings distorted that mayhem into a pernicious fog. Removing every source of particles took time and a narrow genius. AIs did the tedious work. When they were finished, Pamir was left staring at a vague, possibly fictitious stream. Not coming from a point, no. It was a diffuse source aligned around the ship's core: a soft white sheen of particles rising from a region even deeper than the deep hole.

Pamir found excuses to leave the detectors in place, reasoning that he could acquire more data over the next months and years. But the neutrino stream stubbornly continued to weaken, as if it were willingly and maliciously working to make him appear foolish.

The Master lost her last shreds of patience.

'I see that half of your toys are gone,' she mentioned. 'To where, I haven't been told. But the point is that we have potential hazards drifting inside a fuel tank. Still. Against my better judgment.'

'Yes, madam.'

'It's a little more than thirty days to the burn, Pamir.' The Master's projection approached him, glowering. 'I want the freedom to use my hydrogen. And without even the remote prospect of getting your playthings caught in my throat.'

'Yes, madam. I'll see to it immediately.'

She wheeled in a graceful circle, then said, 'Pamir.'

'Yes, madam.'

She stared at him, admitting, 'I think it's time to quit digging. Or at least leave that work with the mining drones. They know the tricks as well as you do, don't they?'

'Nearly, madam.'

'Visit me.' She sounded almost friendly, her golden face shining down at him. 'My annual feast is in four days. Join me and the rest of your colleagues, and we'll discuss your next assignment. Is that understood?'

'Always, madam.'

The smile acquired a useful menace, and as she vanished, she warned, 'The Remoras have better things to do than look after your toys. Darling.'

OVER THE NEXT three days, detectors were dragged along-side the barge and taken off-line, and drones began to stow them for shipment. The sonar array and deep-dredges waited their turn. Where everything would end up, Pamir didn't know. Probably stored inside a warehouse, and he didn't particularly care about their fate.

Whatever happened now, he was definitely done with this place.

Because it was an order, and because it might do some good, Pamir decided to attend the Master's feast. Returning to his quarters, he let his sonic shower carve off several layers of old flesh, then he stepped into his garden, the clean new skin beneath maturing in the false sunlight. In his absence, his llano-vibra had gone wild; thousands of mouths sang badly, a chorus of wild, unlovely sounds accompanying him as he dressed in his most ornate uniform. He tied the mysterious silver clock to his mirrored sash. A mouthful of bacterial spores guaranteed that he could eat and drink anything, his belches and farts turned to perfumes. Then he boarded his personal cap-car, and once under way, Pamir realized that he wasn't simply tired, he was exhausted, better than a century of hard, thankless work suddenly grabbing him by the throat.

He slumped, and slept.

He would have slept until he pulled up beside the Grand Hall, but an AI yanked him out of a perfectly delightful sex dream.

The dream faded, as well as his erection. On a secure channel, he opened a channel to the AI. A dry, unimpressed voice reported, 'There has been, sir, a rather considerable surge in neutrino activity.'

'From where?'

'From below,' the AI replied. 'With just one array, I cannot pinpoint a source—'

'Straight below?' Pamir interrupted.

'And in a region encompassing an eight-degree dispersion, yes.'

'How big of an increase?'

'I'm witnessing activity levels approximately two hundred and eighteen thousand percent greater than our previous max—'

'Show me,' Pamir grunted.

The neutrino universe engulfed him. Suns were points of light burning in a endless gray haze. The nearest sun was a red giant orbiting a massive black hole, its fiery core and the black hole's weak accretion disk both bright. But the brightest lights belonged to the ship, tens of thousands of fusion reactors producing the ship's essential power, the power gridwork looking to his wide eyes like a beautiful and delicate orb composed of many tiny, brightly lit pearls.

Beneath the orb was a region of blackness.

In the neutrino universe, stone and iron were theories, were ghosts, and ordinary matter could rarely be seen, or felt, or believed in.

But beneath the blackness, enshrouding the ship's core, was a second orb. What Pamir didn't notice at first glance became obvious, then unmistakable. Eight degrees of the sky was covered with a neutrino-bright object. Staring hard, he heard himself asking, 'Could it be an engine firing? An early burn, maybe?'

That would at least explain the neutrinos.

With no small measure of disdain, the AI said, 'Sir, no engine is at work, and even if there was, no reaction vessel is properly aligned. Sir.'

Pamir blinked, asking, 'Is it getting brighter?'

'Since we began this conversation . . . it has brightened nine hundred and eleven percent, with no signs of a plateau, sir . . .'

Softly, to himself, Pamir said, 'Shit.'

To the AI, he demanded, 'Explanations.'

'I have none, sir.'

But it was a tech-AI, not a theory-spawner. Pamir squinted at the mysterious projection, noting that unlike the ship's bright pearls of light, this object had a diffuse glow, almost milky, and sourceless, and in its own fashion, lovely.

Then he noticed a brighter splotch.

Ninety degrees removed, which placed it . . . shit, directly beneath his own deep, deep hole . . . five hundred kilometers deeper, and what, if anything, did that mean . . . ?

Pamir excused the tech-AI, then contacted his crew.

The AI foremachine answered.

'Where are the captains?' Pamir asked.

'One is sitting with the tenth-grades. The other with the fifteenths. Sir.'

At the Master's feast, he realized.

'What do you see?' he blurted. Then, narrowing the topic, he asked, 'How's the work progressing?'

'I see everything, and all is nominal. Sir.'

'Do you sense any odd activity?'

'None.'

'Just the same,' he responded, 'put yourself and the crew on alert. Understood?'

'I don't understand, but I will do it, sir. Is that all?'

'For now.'

Pamir cleared the channel, then fought to contact the Master. But her staff were doing their reliable best to protect her on this busy day. A rubber-faced AI glared at him. 'The traditional festivities have begun,' it snapped, glass eyes filled with disdain. 'Only in the most severe emergencies—'

'I realize—'

'—will I allow you to interrupt the Great Master.'

'Just deliver a message to her security nexuses. Will you do that?'

'Always.'

Pamir squirted the latest data to the Master's station, then added a quick cautionary note. 'I don't have any idea what's happening, madam. But something is. And until someone understands it, we'd better try to be careful!'

The AI absorbed the data, the words. Then it volunteered, 'If you feel this strongly, perhaps you should deliver the message in person—'

He blanked the channel, gave his cap-car a new destination, and once that destination was registered, he overrode it, effectively masking his plans. Then he sat back, feeling a momentary sense of doubt. The feast would be a waste; he wouldn't be able to reach the Master's ears, or mind, for hours. But instead of flying down into the hole and seeing things for himself, which was his first duty, Pamir was returning to the giant fuel tank and his aerogel raft, reasoning that if he could get half a dozen of the detectors on-line, and if he could recalibrate them in the next half-day . . .

What would happen?

More and better data. And maybe some obvious explanation would take him by the head, and give him a good shake . . .

EN ROUTE, HE twice contacted the foremachine in the hole.

Both times, the familiar voice told him, 'Nothing is out of the ordinary, sir. And we are digging at the usual furious rate. Sir.'

To reach the aerogel barge required passing through the leech habitat. An elevator had been grafted into the alien structure, running from its hub down to the calm cold surface of the sea. As his car pulled to a stop in the tunnel above, a thought found him. Again, he contacted the foremachine. Again, it said, 'Nothing,' and, 'We are digging.' Then he asked the tech-AI for an update on the neutrino activity.

'The counts have tripled since our last words,' the AI replied. 'They have reached a plateau that's holding steady. Sir.'

Pamir climbed from the car and paused, taking a deep, slow breath of air.

He smelled something . . .

What?

'Is there anything else, sir?' asked the tech-AI.

Pamir began to walk, maintaining contact through his implanted nexuses. 'What we're seeing looks like a sphere of neutrinos, but it doesn't have to be. Am I right? What we're seeing could come from a single point *inside* a refractory container. Like an ancient glass bulb wrapped around an incandescent filament. But instead of light, we see neutrinos. Instead of glass, the neutrinos are emerging from an envelope of hyperfiber—'

'Sir?' the machine squeaked.

'Calculate this for me. Imagine the strongest known hyperfiber, then tell me how thick it would have to be to show what we're seeing.'

The answer came quickly, wrapped in an easy doubt. 'One hundred and ninety-seven kilometers thick, and without purpose. Sir.'

Pamir began to run, one hand and then the other rubbing against the tunnel's diamond walls. 'Assume it's real,' he barked. 'Would that much hyperfiber be strong enough to withstand the ship's own mass?'

Silence.

'It would be, wouldn't it?' He ran to his left, then down a narrow steep set of stairs, a leech grayness taking hold now. And laughing with a giddy nervousness, he told the distant machine, 'You're embarrassed, aren't you?'

He cried out, 'This big old ship still has secrets. Doesn't she?'

But the AI wasn't responding, and in that half-moment when curiosity should have turned to concern, Pamir reached the bottom of the stairs, and staring down the last few meters of the gray tunnel, he saw a stranger.

A human, and male.

The stranger had grayish skin and no hair whatsoever, and he seemed to be wearing, of all things, a captain's uniform. Clenched in his left hand was a tool or weapon, and his right hand and eyes were examining the sealed door-way to the leech habitat. He must have heard Pamir's boots on the gray plastic, but he didn't react. He waited until Pamir was close before he spun around, his face almost smiling, the left hand lifting the device — some kind of soldier-class laser — with a practiced nonchalance.

Pamir pulled to a stop and held his breath.

The stranger indeed wore a captain's uniform, but with odd embellishments. A rich golden hair was woven into a decorative braid, and there were tall leather boots and a leather belt cluttered with tools, some familiar and some not. He was a short man, but thickly built. A strong finger gripped what was obviously a mechanical trigger, and quietly, almost softly, the man said to him, 'Keep still.'

His voice had an unexpected accent.

Pamir told him, 'I'm not moving anywhere.'

'Good.'

There was no way to escape, and very little chance to attack the stranger. Wearing a dress uniform, Pamir had minimal armor. In a whisper, he said, 'Emergency channel. Now.'

The stranger shook his head, remarking, 'That won't help.'

Sure enough, no one seemed to hear him.

What was happening?

Pamir curled his toes inside his boots, then uncurled them. And he breathed deeply, twice, before saying, 'You look lost, Captain. And frankly, you smell a little odd.'

The man shrugged, then gestured with his right hand. 'Open this door for me.'

'Why?'

'I want to see the aliens' house.' Then with a controlled but palpable alarm, 'The house is still there, isn't it?'

Pamir titled his head, and smiled.

'It has to be there,' the strange captain decided. 'Don't try to confuse me!'

'I can open the door for you,' said Pamir.

The man had gray eyes that easily turned to suspicion. Some calculation was made, a decision was made. He aimed his laser at Pamir's chest, telling him, 'I don't need you. I can break your little lock myself.'

'So do it.'

'Stand still,' the stranger advised, gray eyes narrowing. 'I'll cripple you if you behave. If not, I'll have to kill you.'

Reflexively, Pamir took a half-step backward.

Then those gray eyes dropped, and quietly, with a mixture of surprise and thick awe, he asked, 'What is *that*?'

Pamir slowly unfastened the silver clock, then opened it.

'What are you doing with *that*?' he asked. 'Did my mother give it to you—?'

'Washen's your mother?' he blurted.

The stranger nodded, then asked, 'Where is she?'

'Why? Don't you know?'

The man couldn't help but glance at the sealed doorway, and that was the moment when Pamir threw the watch, aiming for the shaved back of the head, and with all of his speed and desperation, he threw himself, too.

Thirty-four

THE GRAND HALL was a hemispherical compartment more than a kilometer tall at its apex and exactly twice as wide. Its ceiling had arching bands of hyperfiber riding next to

the greenish olivine, the former lending a glittery brightness to the room's floating lights and to every echoed
sound. The original floor was simple stone, but the humans
had pulverized it, then mixed compost into the rock dust,
creating a rich deep soil in which grew ornamental trees
from a thousand worlds, and a soft green grass known as
Kentucky for no reason other than that it had always been.
For most of the year, the room was a public garden. In a
ship jammed with spectacles, this was a quiet, sober place
where frayed nerves found solace and a few despairing
souls had gone to attempt suicide. But as the captains' feast
drew near, robots set up tables and chairs in careful patterns,
and the tables were covered with intricate linen designed
for this single occasion, and ten thousand place settings
were arranged according to conventions older than anyone
could calculate. Plates whiter than bone were flanked by
heavy goldware utensils, and perfumed cloth was folded
in artful patterns, waiting to wash dirty faces and fingers.
Crystal goblets filled themselves through hidden nipples,
every liquor and molten drug grown somewhere inside
the ship, and every sip of chilled water was brought up
from the famous artesian wells next to the Alpha Sea, celebrating the first impromptu captains' feast held more than
a hundred millenia ago.

Each captain had her place, or his, marked with a handwritten placard, the Master Captain's loud script obvious
at a distance. The placement of one's chair was everything.
Rank mattered, but so did the quality of the officer's year.
Captains to be bestowed new honors sat near the Master's
own table. Captains who needed humiliation were assigned
more distant seats than expected, the worst of them set
behind a bank of walkyleen flycatchers. The meal itself was
meant to be a surprise, and in an attempt to honor their
passengers, it was usually an array of alien dishes, their

amino acids and stereochemistry left untouched – a grand tradition that made a few bellies uncomfortable, and some years, more than a few.

Today's meal was cold uncooked fish from the sunless depths of the harum-scarum sea. Vast dead eyes stared up at the hungry captains. The eating mouths were clamped shut while the gill mouths slowly opened and closed, the flesh too stubborn to stop its useless search for oxygen. Inside every fish stomach was a salad of purple vegetation and sour fruits and tenoil dressing that resembled, in texture and in odor, unrefined petroleum. Hidden elsewhere inside the corpse was a golden worm, smaller than any finger and treasured by the harum-scarum as a delicacy to be consumed one lucious segment at a time.

Every active captain had a place set for her and for him.

Even the absent captains were given a plate, a fish, and the honor of a seat. Though cynics liked to complain that the apparent honor only underscored their absence, giving their snobbish peers the opportunity to say whatever they wished about those who weren't present to defend themselves.

Centuries ago, when the captains vanished abruptly, their seats remained, and placards with their names written by one of the Master's automated hands, and their meals were prepared in the captain's galley, delivered by crew members in dress uniforms, and left there for the flies.

For years, the Master would rise to her feet, beginning the evening with a vague yet flowery toast to those missing souls, wishing them well as they fulfilled the mysterious duties of some unmentionable assignment.

Then came the inevitable dinner when she announced with a booming, yet sorrowful voice that the captains' vessel had struck a shard of comet, and they would not be seen again. Her toast was made with vinegary wine – the standard drink for such gloomy occasions – and dinner itself was the funeral feast borrowed from a species of cold deep-space aliens. The captains destroyed their mouths with a ritualistic bite of a methane-ice fruit. That was the last year when places were set for their vanished colleagues. For Miocene, and Hazz. And Washen. And for the rest of the much-honored dead.

More than forty-eight centuries had passed since the Vanishing.

One hundred and twenty-one feasts had been held since two ghosts had appeared suddenly, talking about a nonexistent world called Marrow.

Nothing had come of it. Someone's stupid and very cruel joke had thrown the Master into an unseemly panic, and she had spent the last century trying to convince everyone that the apparitions were anything but real. They had to be someone's cruel illusion. Because what other choice did she have? A Master Captain's first duties were to her chair and her ship, and what kind of Master would she be if a holoimage and a handful of vague clues were to steer her away from traditions that had served both ship and chair for more than a hundred millennia . . . ?

No, she didn't want to think about the Vanished. Not tonight, or ever again. But she seemed unable to stop herself, and trying to purge her mind, to make herself stronger and inflexible, only seemed to make the ghosts stronger, too.

The Master's long table was set on a grassy ridge, affording a view that improved when she slowly, majestically rose to her feet. Her goblet was filled with a blood-colored harum-scarum wine. Was that why she was thinking of the dead? Or was it because directly in front of her, practically mocking her, was the empty chair reserved for Pamir? Absent again. Just like last year, and the year before. What was wrong with that captain? Such a talent . . . question-able but quick instincts married to an admirable, almost transcendent tenaciousness . . . and despite his ugly temperament, a captain able to inspire his subordinates and the average passenger . . .

Yet he couldn't let himself bend for these little captainly rituals.

It was a weakness of character, and spirit, that had always, even in the best times, crippled his chance to rise into the ship's highest ranks.

'Where's Pamir?' she asked one of her security nexuses.

'Unknown,' was the instant response.

'Are there any messages from him?'

The next response was slow in coming, and odd. The nexus's sexless voice asked her, 'Where do you think that captain might be?'

In frustration, she killed that bothersome channel.

Sometimes the Master found herself thinking that she had lived too long and too narrowly, and the simple grind of work had worn away the genius that had earned her this high office. If everyone in this room were suddenly set equal, she almost certainly wouldn't be named the Master Captain. Even in her most prideful moments, she understood that others could fill her chair as well as she could, or better. Even when she felt utterly in control, like now, a wise and ageless and extremely weary part of herself wished that one of these worshipful faces would tell her, 'Sit elsewhere. Let yourself relax. I'll take the helm for you, at least for a little while.'

But the rest of the woman seethed at the idea of it.

Always.

It was the steely, self-possessed part of her that was stand-ing now, gazing across the hectares of smiling faces and mirrored uniforms and cold dead fish. For this feast, the local birds and the louder insects had been lured into cages, then taken away. Everything that could know better knew to be quiet. An unnatural silence hung over the room. With her right hand, the Master grasped the crystal goblet. She swirled the wine once, a dark red clot dislodging from the rim and turning slowly as she lifted the goblet to her face, inhaling the aroma before the hand raised the goblet higher, up over her head, as she said, 'Welcome,' in a thunderous voice. 'All of you who cared enough to be here today, welcome. And thank you!'

A self-congratulating murmur passed through the audience.

Then again, silence.

The Master opened her mouth, ready to deliver her much anticipated toast. Captains who dealt with the newest alien passengers were to be singled out this year. She would sing praises for their excellence, then demand improvements in the coming decades. The ship was entering a region thick with new species, new challenges. What better way to ready your staff than by feeding them congratulatory words, then showing them your hardest gaze?

But before the first word found its way out of her mouth, she hesitated. Her breath came up short, and some obscure sense tied to one of her security nexuses started to focus on something very distant, and small, and wrong.

Her eyes saw a slow, unexpected motion.

From behind the walkyleen flycatchers came several figures. Then dozens more. And accompanying their appearance was a growing commotion, the seated captains wheeling around to stare at these visitors.

They were captains, weren't they?

Pamir and the other rude ones were arriving, at last and together. That's what the Master told herself, but she couldn't see anyone with Pamir's build, and she noticed that most of the newcomers, no matter their color, had a smoky tint to their flesh.

For a better look, she tried to interface with the security eyes, only to learn that each of them had fallen into their diagnostic modes.

Like a clumsy person trying to hold a lump of warm grease, the Master struggled to find any working security system.

None were responding.

'What's happening?' she asked every nexus.

A thousand answers bombarded her in a senseless, unnerving roar. Then she focused on the newcomers, on their nearest faces. The ship and everything else had vanished. The Master found herself staring at the handsome woman at the lead, the tall one with her constricted face and the slick, hairless scalp, who looked rather like someone in whom she had given up all hope . . .

'Miocene,' the Master blurted. 'Is it?'

Whoever she was, the woman smiled like Miocene – a sturdy, almost amused expression leading her up to the main table. Flanking her were people who resembled the missing captains, in their faces and builds and in the confident way they carried themselves. One man in particular caught the Master's attention. He had Miocene's face and baldness, and a boyish little body, and bright eyes that seemed to relish everything he was seeing. He was the one who looked left, then right, nodding at his companions, causing them to stop next to the various tables, each of the strangers picking up the cold fishes, examining them with a peculiar astonishment, as if they had never before seen such creatures.

Miocene, or whoever she was, climbed the grassy ridge. The bright-eyed man remained at her side.

Softly, the Master asked, 'Is it you?'

The woman's smile had turned cold and furious. Her

uniform was mirrored, but too stiff, and the leather belt was totally out of place. She paused in front of the Master, and looking up and down the long table – staring at each of the Submasters – she said nothing.

Nothing.

Earwig and the other Submasters were hailing the nonexistent security systems. Demanding action. Begging for information. Then, looking at one another, a wild panic began to take hold.

Softly, the Master asked, 'How are you, darling?'

The reply came with Miocene's voice and her cold firmness. She stared across the table, saying, 'Earwig. Darling. You're in my seat.'

The Master halfway laughed, blurting, 'If I'd known you were coming—'

'Bleak,' said the bright-eyed man.

A hundred other strangers said, 'Bleak,' together, in a shared voice.

Thousands of voices, from every part of the Great Hall, screamed, 'Bleak,' in a ragged, chilling unison.

Finally, the Master's First Chair started to rise, asking, 'What are you saying? What's this "bleak" mean?'

'That's you,' the man offered with a cold smile.

Then Miocene reached out with her left hand, taking a gold carving knife from the Master's place setting, and with a quiet, hateful voice, she said, 'I waited. To be found and saved, I waited for centuries and centuries . . .'

'I couldn't find you,' the Master confessed.

'Which proves what I have always suspected.' Then she used the Master's name, the pathetically ordinary name that she hadn't heard in aeons. 'Liza,' said Miocene. 'You really don't deserve that chair of yours. Now do you, Liza?'

The Master tried to answer.

But a knife had been shoved into her throat, Miocene

grunting with the exertion. Then grasping the gold hilt with both hands, she gave it another thrust, smiling as the blood jetted across her, as the spine and cord were suddenly cut in two.

Thirty-five

WITH A BRIGHT whoosh, the laser fired.

A whiff of coherent light boiled away half of Pamir's fist.

But he kept swinging what remained, feeling nothing until his blackened flesh and the blunt ends of his bones struck the stranger's face, a dazzling sharp pain racing down his arm, jerking loose a harsh little scream.

The other man grunted softly, a look of dim surprise coming to the grayish face, to the wide gray eyes.

Even without both hands, the captain had a thirty-kilo advantage. He drove with his legs, then his right shoulder, shoving his opponent against the sealed elevator door and pinning the arm with laser flush to the body . . . a second whoosh evaporating a portion of his ear and the edge of his captain's cap . . . and Pamir screamed again, louder this time, his good hand smashing into the squirming body, punishing ribs and soft tissues while he flung the man's hairless head against the hyperfiber door.

With a heavy clatter, the laser fell to the floor.

Pamir absorbed blows to his belly, his ribs. Then with his good hand, he grabbed the other man's neck and yanked and twisted, squeezing until he was certain that not a breath of oxygen could slip down that crushed throat. Then he used his knee, driving bone into the groin, and when a look of pure misery passed across the choking face, he screamed, 'Stop,' and flung the man back up the hallway.

The laser lay beside Washen's clock.

Pamir reached with his bad hand, realized his blunder, then too late, put his good hand around the weapon's handle, the whiteness of polished bone braced with the archaic heft of forged steel.

A booted foot, hard as stone, kicked Pamir in the face, shattering both cheekbones and his nose.

He felt himself flung back against the door, and lifting his good hand, he fired, a sweeping ray of blackish-blue light cooking his opponent's other foot.

The man collapsed, and moaned quietly for a breath or two.

With his own trembling legs, Pamir pushed against the slick door, forcing himself upright, watching the stranger's face grow composed. Resigned. Then once again, a look of defiance came into the gray face.

'Kill me,' the stranger demanded.

'Who are you?' Pamir asked.

No response.

'You're a luddite, aren't you?' The captain said it with confidence, unable to envision any other explanation. 'Washen was living in one of your settlements. Is that it?'

A blank, uncomprehending expression gave him his answer.

'What's your name?' he asked again.

Gray eyes glanced at Pamir's epaulets. Then with a low croaking voice, the man announced, 'You're a first-grade.'

'Pamir. That's my name.'

The man blinked, and sighed, and said, 'I don't remember your name. You must be new to the captains' ranks.'

'You know the roster, do you?'

Silence.

'You've got a big memory,' Pamir allowed.

The silence acquired a distinct pride.

'But then,' Pamir added, 'Washen always had an excellent memory, too.'

At the sound of her name, the man blinked. Then he stared at Pamir, and with a forced calmness, he asked, 'Do you know my mother?'

'Better than anyone else, nearly.'

That statement puzzled the man, but he said nothing.

'You resemble her,' Pamir confessed. 'In your face, mostly. Although she was a lot tougher, I think.'

'My mother . . . is very strong . . .'

'Is?'

Silence.

'Is?' he asked again. Then he picked up Washen's clock, using the two surviving fingers on his battered hand. The pain was constant, and manageable. He dangled the silver machine in the air between them, saying, 'She's dead. Your mother is. I found this and nothing else. And we looked everywhere, but we didn't find a body.'

The man stared straight up, showing the ceiling his contempt.

'It happened inside the leech habitat, didn't it?' Pamir guessed he was right, then asked, 'Did you see her die?'

The man said, 'Kill me,' again, but without as much feeling.

His burnt foot was healing itself. A good luddite wouldn't possess such talents. And for the lack of any better guess, Pamir said, 'I know where you're from. From the middle of the ship somehow. Somehow.'

The man refused to blink.

But Pamir had a sense of what was true, impossible as it seemed. 'How did you climb up here? Is there a secret tunnel somewhere?'

The eyes remained open.

Under control.

'No,' the captain whispered. 'I was digging a nice wide hole toward you. Almost all the way down, and that's how you got up here. Am I right?'

But he didn't wait for a response. On a secure channel, Pamir called the foremachine working inside the hole. Quietly and confidently, the AI told him, 'Everything is nominal, sir. Everything is as it should be.'

Pamir shifted channels, as an experiment.

Again, 'Everything is nominal, sir.'

And he selected a third channel – a route and coding system that he had never used before – and the response was a perfect, seamless quiet that caused him to mutter, 'Shit,' under his breath.

His captive was flexing his growing foot.

Pamir cooked it again, with a lance of blue-black light. Then he pocketed the clock and grabbed the man by an arm, promising him, 'I'll kill you. Eventually. But we've got to look at something first.'

HE DRAGGED THE man to his cap-car.

Racing his way along a roundabout course, Pamir tried to contact the Master. An AI's voice responded. A constricted, heavily encoded image of the bridge and a rubber face appeared just past the car's window. 'Be brief,' was the response.

'I have an emergency here,' Pamir explained. 'An armed intruder—'

'One intruder?'

He nodded. 'Yes—'

'Take him to the nearest detention center. As you were instructed—'

'What instructions?'

A genuine discomfort spread across the sexless face. 'A first-degree alarm has been sounded, Captain. Did you not hear it?'

'No.'

The machine's discomfort turned to a knifing pain.

'What's going on?' Pamir demanded.

'Our alarm system has been compromised. Plainly.'

Pamir asked, 'What about the captains at the feast?'

'I've lost all contact with the Great Hall,' the machine confessed, almost embarrassed. Then it hesitated abruptly, and with a different tone, it said, 'Perhaps you should come to the Master's station, sir. I can explain what I know, if you come to me immediately.'

Pamir blanked the channel.

For a long while, he sat motionless, ignoring his prisoner, considering what he knew and what he needed to do first.

More than a century ago, after the discovery of the camouflaged hatch, the captains constructed a blind inside the local pumping station. Like any good blind, there were a dozen secret ways to slip inside it. Like anything built by captains, the facility was in perfect repair, every sensor off-line but ready to come awake with the proper codes from the approved people.

Pamir slipped into the blind without incident. But he didn't bother with sensors; his own eyes told him everything.

Rising up the fuel line were dozens, perhaps hundreds of odd cars, windowless and vast, shaped like some kind of predatory beetlelike creature and built from a bright gray metal. Steel, perhaps. Which made them exceptionally strange vehicles, and impressive. He calculated their volume and the possible numbers of bodies stuffed inside each of them. Then staring at his prisoner, Pamir said nothing. He stared and waited until the man looked back at him, then he finally asked, 'What did you want?'

'My name is Locke.'

'Locke,' he repeated. 'What do you want?'

'We're the Builders reborn,' said the strange little man. 'And you're one of the misguided souls in service of the Bleak. And we are taking the ship back from you—'

'Fine,' Pamir growled. 'It's yours.'

Then he shook his head, adding, 'But that's not what I'm asking, Mr Locke. And if you're half as smart as your mother, you know that perfectly well . . . !'

PAMIR TOOK THEM on another roundabout journey.

Inside a secondary fuel line, he pulled to a stop, then used the laser to surgically maim his prisoner. With Locke left harmless, he sprayed emergency lifesuits over their bodies, and after a few moments to let the suits cure, he unsealed the main hatch.

The cabin's atmosphere exploded into the vacuum.

Pamir scrambled into the open, removed a tool kit, then gave the car a random course and an unreachable destination. Then he dragged Locke out of the car before sealing it again, and together, they watched it accelerate into the blackness.

A valve stood beside them. Built by unknown hands, unused for billions of years, it had been left open, seemingly just for them.

Pamir dragged his prisoner after him. Then he tripped a switch that slowly, slowly closed the valve.

The tertiary line was a kilometer long, ending at a tiny, never-used auxiliary tank. And past that tank was the world-sized ocean of hydrogen.

Walking rapidly, carrying Locke on his back, Pamir started to talk, his voice percolating through the spray-on-fabric. 'She isn't dead,' he said. 'There was a fight, and I assumed that if she was there, she was obliterated, or someone recovered her body. But Washen was left behind, and you never found her. Did you? You came back to that alien house for a reason. Your first chance in more than a century, and you ran back there to look for your mother. For Washen. One of my oldest, best friends.'

Locke took a deep, pained breath.

'We searched. If anyone fell from that habitat, we should have found them. A heavy body spat out by the decompression would have had a small horizontal vector. That's why we looked directly beneath the alien house.' He was halfway running, thinking about how much time they had and what he would do if he couldn't find any help. 'Are you listening to me, Locke? I know something about how much abuse a person can take. And if we can find enough of your mother, she's alive again.'

Silence.

'You were there, Locke.' Pamir said the words twice, then added, 'The hydrogen has currents. Slow, but complex. And like I said, we were looking for a whole corpse. Because that's what was easiest. But if there was just a small piece of her, like her head, the decompression would have given her a terrific horizontal vector. Her poor head would have frozen in moments and fallen hard in the darkness, dropping straight to the icy bottoms, and if that's the case, the two of us could find her. The search equipment is still there, ready to try. It just needs to know its target—'

'She was cut into several pieces,' said the man's close, soft voice. 'Her head, with one arm still attached. We recovered the rest of her.'

Pamir waited a moment, then said, 'All right, then.'

He said, 'That helps us a lot. Thank you.'

Then after a sympathetic pause, he asked, 'Who did that
to her, Locke? Who treated your mother that way?'

A deep, brooding silence.

Then with withering, practised pain, Locke admitted,
'My father . . . Diu . . . was trying to kill her . . .'

Pamir heard a deep breath, a shallow gasp.

Then an anguished voice asked, 'Is there any method
you know, First-grade Pamir? Is there any way to kill a
memory that you can't forget . . . ?'

Thirty-six

THE RUMOR WAS sudden and spectacularly fantastic, and if
only a little bit true, its consequences would be nothing
short of momentous. The common first reaction among
passengers and crew was to laugh at the whole silly notion,
and mock it, and insult the soul who dared tell the foolish story, and perhaps beat him senseless, or piss on his
lying face, or in some other species-specific way prove
one's doubts about what was clearly, utterly impossible.

'The Master Captain is dead!' said billions of soft, nervous voices.

How could she be? She was too wily and much too
powerful to die!

'All of her captains have been murdered! At their annual
dinner! By armed strangers coming from a secret part of
the ship!'

How could any of that be true? How, how, how . . . ?

'And now these strangers have stolen control over the
Great Ship!'

Which was just absurd. Of course, of course. The ship was too strong and far too large to be conquered by any force. Certainly not in a day, and with such little fuss, too. Where were the Master's security troops? And her tough old generals? And more to the point, where were the AIs and the other elaborate machines whose only duty was to serve that giant human woman? How could such a deeply ingrained, fiercely loyal army allow an invasion to succeed in a thousand years, much less inside a single day?

For a full ship-day, that was the gist of almost every public and private conversation – abbreviated wild rumor countered with hardheaded doubt.

But the rumor had its own life, gaining breadth, depth, and a kind of robust logic.

On the second and third days, and particularly on the fourth, lowly mates and certain engineers offered new clues. What had happened wasn't an invasion. Not precisely. It more properly resembled a mutiny, the ringleaders being one-time captains. The Vanished had returned from the dead, it was said. At least some of the missing captains had rematerialized, led by that axe-faced Submaster. That Miocene woman. In the avenues and parks, along the seashores and inside dream parlors, passengers told this new story and wrestled with its consequences. Who was Miocene? In memory, she was the quiet and efficient and apparently bloodless First Chair to the now deposed Master. And that was about all she was. Every biography written about the woman was sold ten billion times, at least. Most read only the highlights. Only enough to recognize the woman's ambition and her obvious powers. If anyone could overthrow the Master Captain, it was her First Chair. That was the obvious verdict. Who else in Creation had intimate knowledge into every security array, every communication system, and the ship's wellsprings of power?

But Miocene didn't come home alone. She brought an army of loyal and tough soldiers who were deployed in the opening hours, trapping most of the ship's troops in their barracks or surprising them in the field. A few witnesses described pitched battles and soldiers killed on both sides. But even the largest stories involved small units and minimal damage. Most of the ship's weapons failed before they could be fired, sabotaged by security codes that the Master herself had set in place — codes meant to protect the public and the captains should those weapons find the wrong hands embracing them. A few units loyal to the Master managed to slip away, merging with the general population. But they were scattered and leaderless, without the tools necessary to hurt any enemy.

About the old Master and her captains, no one seemed to know.

One comforting tale was that the old leaders were still alive, in some diluted form or another. Perhaps they weren't conscious or whole, but they were still capable of being reborn again . . . should Miocene, in her wisdom, decide to consider them harmless . . .

About the new Master and her staff, even less was known.

From where did they come?

A thousand rumors told the same basic story: the Vanished must have left the ship, probably against their will. Then on a mysterious high-technology world, Miocene gathered up the tools and army and fleets of star-ships necessary to catch up again. Where her fleet was today, nobody knew. Everyone agreed that the main ports were quiet; the Great Ship had been passing through a thinly inhabited region around an active, modestly danger-ous black hole. And it was hard to imagine that little ships could have caught them without being seen. But didn't that explanation make far more sense than that silly noise about secret chambers and worlds hiding within the ship's heart?

And yet. Travelers reported seeing enormous bug-shaped cars rising through a certain basement district. On that first day, and each subsequent day, there was a relentless parade of the steel machines gaining speed as they climbed, swarming for the Master's station and every other essential hub.

'They have to be coming from somewhere,' was the sluggish verdict, delivered in spoken words and structured scents and soft flashes of dumb-founded light.

'Somewhere' meaning a place below them.

Deep inside the fuel tanks, some assumed. While others preferred more fantastical locations, including a secret chamber or chambers buried in the ship's iron heart.

On the mutiny's fourth day, this mysterious place acquired a name. *Marrow*. Suddenly, everyone was whispering that odd old word, in ship-terran and in the full multitude of other ship languages. That word appeared so suddenly and in so many places that souls with a taste for conspiracy decided that the knowledge, genuine or false, had come directly and with purpose from whoever was in charge.

There was a world hiding inside the Great Ship, voices claimed: a hidden realm, and wondrous, and undoubtedly powerful.

Tantalizing details about Marrow started to rear up into the light.

Open-minded, undisciplined species embraced the revelation. A few even celebrated it. While others, deeply conservative by nature or by choice, ignored everything said and every wild implication.

As a rule, humans were somewhere in the middle.

There were small, modestly bothersome events. Some districts went dark as key reactors failed, power rationed to the most essential systems. Communications became snarled everywhere for the next four days. It was a time of modest chaos. But generally, little changed. Ancient passengers and crew went about the rituals of their lives, habits ingrained over the millennia and not so easily dropped. Even when the public com-networks failed completely, there were still private pathways where electrons and structured light could send good wishes and viable currency and the lastest, best gossip. Then those little outages seemed to be finished, and the com-networks found their feet again, and the last rumors of armed combat turned stale and were generally forgotten. It was the mutiny's ninth day, and the public mood, as measured by twenty-three subtle means, was on the rise in every district, every major and minor city, and in most apartments and alien habitats and occupied caves.

That was the ripe, perfect moment for the Master to appear.

With ancient commands, she took control of the newly restored com-networks, and suddenly she was everywhere – a holoimage dressed in a Master's bright uniform and a bright, well-practised smile, her face even narrower than expected, and her dark gray hair cut very short, and her flesh looking changed by the centuries, as if dirty or tinged with smoke or rust; and her dark walnut-colored eyes, colder than any space, regarded each of her passengers and crew with an expression that fell just short of being comforting, her thin smart smiling mouth opening and then closing again, giving her audience a moment to adjust to her presence before she opened her mouth again, telling them in a quiet strong voice:

'I am Miocene.

'On my authority as a First Chair Submaster, I have removed the Master Captain from her office. From her duties. From her long-held chair.

'Never worry. The woman still lives. Most of her captains are alive. In coming years, you will learn about the depths and scope of their incompetence. In accordance with the ship's charter, public trials will be held, and punishments will be just and slow, and the Great Ship will continue to follow its planned course.

'I will worry for you.

'If you let me.

'Your lives need not change. Not today, or in the future. Unless of course you wish to change what has always been yours.

'As Master Captain, I make that promise to you.'

Then for a moment, unexpectedly, the eyes gained a sudden warmth – genuine and a little shocking – and the image closed by saying:

'I love this wonderful ship of ours. I have always loved and cherished it. And I want nothing but to protect the ship, and defend its passengers and good crew, today and until the end of its historic voyage.

'My son will serve as my First Chair.

'Word of other postings will follow.

'This is your Master Captain wishing you a good day, and a wonderful next hundred millennia, my darling friends . . .'

Thirty-seven

A SHINY GOLD bust of the Master Captain was perched at the end of the pearlwood table, its face suffused with a look of serene power and perfect arrogance; and beside the bust, set at a sloppy almost careless angle, was the Master's own severed head. The long hair was white and tangled. The flesh was soft and badly desiccated, and pale, no trace left of its gold pigments. Some slow anaerobic pathway, not to mention a fantastic rage, allowed the head to open its eyes while the gaping mouth moved with a slow vigor. Without lungs to supply breath, the Master couldn't so much as whisper. But what she was saying was obvious. Anyone with patience and a talent for reading lips could understand her. 'Why?' she was asking. 'Miocene, why?' Then after a long pause, she said 'Explain.' She said, 'For me.' Then she began to say, 'Please,' but she was too exhausted to finish the word, and with a soft wet sound, her eyes and mouth pulled themselves shut again, and she descended back into a deep, fitful coma.

With a cool fondness, Miocene stroked the white hair.

She gazed up and down the conference table, and after a moment's consideration, she pointed and called out a name, and one of her staff responded with a crisp, highly officious summary of what had been managed and what they were doing now and everything they intended to accomplish in the critical, wondrous near future.

'Blessing Gable,' she called next.

A small, burly woman – born Loyalist, but joining the Waywards as a child – rose from her black chair, then spoke about resistance among the last of the crew. 'They still have their stronghold at Port Alpha, and two or three armed bands are operating near Port Denali. But the first group is trapped, and the others are disorganized and short on resources.' She paused for a moment, referring to one of her security nexuses. Then she added, 'We just arrested the ones who sabotaged the reactors. Disgruntled engineers, just as you predicted, madam. The repairs, I am told, are well ahead of schedule. What the Builders create refuses to be destroyed easily.'

There were murmurs of approval, and many of her fellow officers repeated, 'The Builders,' with the habitual reverence.

Blessing was a ship's general. She paused, one hand smoothing the perpetually smooth purple-black fabric of her uniform. Like most of the grandchildren, she didn't appreciate the art of wearing clothes. It required discipline and new habits. But as Miocene had reminded everyone, time after time, the ship's passengers expected a certain wardrobe from its crew. Captains and soldiers clothed in their own hair and flesh wouldn't reassure anyone. And reassurance was an important, even critical task for these next days and centuries.

Miocene's First Chair inquired, 'How many of their captains are running loose?'

Blessing said, 'Thirty-one. At the very most, sir.'

Sitting on his mother's left, Till showed everyone a look of confident concern. Unlike most Waywards, he seemed comfortable in uniform. Splendid, even. Each time Miocene glanced at him – at the bright fabric and the shiny epaulets and the slender, sturdy shoulders ready to accept any burden – she felt a powerful love as well as a withering, almost terrifying sense of pride.

Till was the perfect First Chair.

Already knowing the answer, he asked, 'Of those thirty-one, who are the most dangerous?'

Blessing listed the important names.

She said 'Pamir,' with a dismissive tone. 'He's the high-est-ranking officer still at large. But his first-grade status can be misleading. Judging by the Master's records, the man isn't well regarded. Not by her or by the other captains. His loyalties are suspect. The Master herself made only sparing use of him.'

'I remember that one,' said Daen. Then with a quick gesture and a giddy laugh, he added, 'I wouldn't worry. Pamir's probably hiding in one of his old holes, praying for the next amnesty.'

Daen was her Second Chair – the same position he had enjoyed before Marrow. But it was a post that he had taken grudgingly, even when he finally admitted that the old Master was inept. Letting a crazy man like Diu acquire so much power, then not finding her captains after nearly five millenia . . . well, she probably deserved to be unseated. Yet even then, if it wasn't for his loyalty to Miocene, he wouldn't have taken part in this ugliness. He had made that point plain on numerous occasions. And in turn, Miocene gave him no important role or linchpin respon-sibilities. Daen and the other old captains served a single clear, vital purpose: they showed that Miocene was oper-ating legally, and morally, supported by proven souls who thought as she thought.

Miocene agreed with her Second Chair's assessment of Pamir; but as usual, Daen ignored certain key points.

'Regardless what we think of the man,' she countered, 'Pamir has talents. And more importantly, he has that first-grade rank. If there's going to be an organized counter-attack, by law and by tradition, Pamir's the leader. If only as someone's puppet, he can now be regarded as the ship's true Master.'

Her warning had a slow, inadequate impact.

Daen blinked as if flustered, then admitted, 'I just hope

it doesn't come to counterattacks and open rebellion.'

Other long-term officers agreed with him.

But Till reminded them and his Waywards, 'There isn't time to worry about one man. Or rebellions that only exist in our fears.'

Miocene nodded, then deflected the focus. She glanced at another old Submaster, saying, 'Twist.' She smiled and asked, 'How soon will you have the new nexuses ready to be implanted. In you, and in the others. And in me.'

Most importantly, *me*.

The charming Submaster tried to smile, and failed. 'Another fifteen days,' he admitted. 'Just in time for the big burn.'

Stripping away an ancient, byzantine system, full of booby traps and failed policies, then constructing a better system from the rawest ingredients . . . no, the delays weren't much of a surprise, nor even much of a disappointment . . .

'Pepsin,' said Miocene.

Aasleen's grandson nodded agreeably, then promised, 'You already have full control over the main engines, madam.'

Miocene let everyone see her smile.

Then the engineer added, 'There were some incidents of sabotage. A few. But what the Builders create is most definitely resilient . . .'

'You have enough hands to make repairs?'

The stocky man nodded, saying, 'Yes, madam. I do.'

He was lying. She sensed it as she nodded, then in the most casual way, she mentioned, 'When you come up short, contact Till or me. Every resource will be shoved your way.'

'Thank you, madam. Thank you.'

Pepsin's grandmother would have been an enormous

help here. But Miocene didn't allow herself the luxury of making wishes. Aasleen had made her choice, and now she was living a comfortable, dull existence in Hazz City. She'd lived that way since the Waywards took over the Loyalists' cities and industries. Their invasion – a proving ground for what was happening to the ship today – had come swiftly, with a minimum of blood and discomfort. By the time Miocene was reborn, the Loyalist society was dissolving into the much larger, more potent Wayward culture. By the time she was healthy and whole again, her son could present her with an empire rich in possibility.

'For you, Mother,' he had whispered into one of her new ears. 'This is for you. And I promise, this is nothing but the beginning.'

Again, Miocene felt compelled to glance at her son, and she couldn't help but feel singularly blessed. During her rebirth, her son had taught her what was possible. Every question was answered in full. Every doubt evaporated into her love for Till. Then through his love and devotion, Till offered her the ship's helm. 'The Master doesn't deserve her chair,' he had assured her. 'She doesn't serve the ship as she should, or as you will. Isn't that true, Mother? Can you argue it otherwise?'

That was a great, perfect moment.

Everything about Miocene's long ambitious life pointed at that epiphany. Her duty was obvious. Indeed, it seemed as if every hardship and wrenching pain were nothing but the careful preparation of her soul, making her ready for what was, for lack of any better word, her destiny.

'Both of us are Builders reborn,' Till had purred.

'We are,' she had mouthed, beaming at her only child.

To Miocene, the Builders were an abstraction. An idea with which she could coexist. No, she didn't believe that their souls were billions of years old. But clearly, they were the natural ones to take control over this great, wondrous machine. She looked at the hardened souls at this long table. Waywards; Loyalists. She imagined the millions of children born before, then after the merging of those two nations. And there were the captains who had proved themselves during this century-long march toward this moment. Now . . .

Till asked, 'May I stand now, madam, and have a word?'

Miocene nodded, then gladly sat in the Master's oversized chair, letting every eye focus on him.

For the next few minutes, her son spoke about duty. About the importance of these next days and weeks. He repeated what his mother had already stated emphatically, that it was crucial for the ship's burn to be made on schedule. They needed to prove to the passengers and to the galaxy that the ship was in proficient hands.

It was her speech, and it wasn't.

As always, Miocene noticed how the faces seemed to drink in her son's words. Again, she could appreciate why he was able to find followers and motivate them. Even old men like Twist and Daen would nod appreciatively, their fealty having shifted — in some abstract, convoluted fashion — a little closer to the Waywards.

Then she wasn't thinking about Till, her eyes focusing on a new captain who had just entered the conference room, bowing at his superiors and taking one of the two empty chairs at the far end of the table.

Till concluded by saying, 'Welcome, Virtue.'

The one-time traitor from the Wayward camp managed a deeper bow, then said, 'My apologies. There was a problem—'

'With the spine, again?'

Asked Till.

'With its borehole, specifically. Sir. Madam. The old

hyperfiber has been putting up a tenacious fight.' Gray-white eyes blinked as if embarrassed, then stared at Virtue's own hands. 'Within the week, I can assure you, madam . . . you will be able to rule the ship from anywhere, including Marrow . . .'

At this moment, they were nothing more than a boarding party. A few million highly motivated, thoroughly trained, and well-armed people living far from home.

'When the spine is finished, integration of command functions won't take long,' he promised. 'Another day, or two. Or perhaps three.'

Till glanced at his mother. For both of them, he said, 'Thank you, Virtue.'

Miocene barely noticed the exchange. What she was studying was the final empty chair, feeling that instinctive disquiet. When she listened again and heard nothing but patient silence, she leaned forward across the pearlwood table and said, 'Locke.'

She asked, 'Has anyone heard from him?'

No one responded.

But ever so slightly, Till's expression tightened. And he quietly admitted, 'No, there hasn't been any news.'

In the mutiny's opening moments, without warning, Locke had disappeared. It was commonly known but never discussed. The other captains and generals pretended to busy themselves with details while Miocene whispered to her son, 'Do you still think that he's off chasing his mother's soul?'

'Of course,' Till replied.

What was she hearing in his voice?

'I know the man,' he continued. 'He very much loved Washen, even though he didn't see her for centuries at a time—'

It was a love that Miocene could appreciate.

'And the poor man was wracked by guilt. For what happened, for what he had to do . . . it was very difficult for him . . .'

Locke killed his own father, trying to save his mother. Yet Washen had died regardless. The two Waywards had seen her body torn apart by explosives. Shredded flesh and the dying mind were scattered across a great ocean of liquid fuel, and lost. Every report in the Master's files documented a long, fruitless search. A solitary Wayward had no chance of finding her. None. Miocene felt certain, yet she had to ask, 'Did you send anyone to search the leech habitat? As I suggested?'

'Naturally,' Till replied.

'And what did they find?'

'It was sealed, but there were signs of a struggle,' he admitted, shaking his head with a sudden heaviness. 'It's possible, just possible, that Locke stumbled into an armed guard. The evidence is narrow, but reasonable. There was a fight, and he was killed with his own weapon.'

She waited for a moment, then asked pointedly, 'Why didn't you tell me this?'

Till blinked. He sighed. Then with a peculiar sadness, he replied, 'It didn't feel like critical news.'

'If Locke's been captured—'

'Mother,' he growled. 'Locke is not a danger. You know that.'

She sat upright in the Master's chair, staring at that pretty face with all of the coldness that she could summon.

'He knows nothing,' her son insisted. 'His place at this table is honorary. Nothing else. For a long time, I haven't given him any authority. Because, as I promised, I know him so very well.'

Do you? she thought, in secret.

Then her coldness turned inward, and she shivered in

invisible ways. After a long moment, she remarked, 'You might wish to search the fuel tank itself.'

'We already have,' Till replied.

Something about his eyes were flat. Unreadable. Even dead.

'That tank is huge,' Miocene reminded him.

'Which is why it took until today to finish our search.' The unreadable eyes wore a smile, and a smiling mouth added, 'I sent ten swarms to search—'

Ten swarms pulled from what duties?

'And all that they found were aerogel barges. Scientific instruments packed for shipment. And nothing alive or even a little bit important.'

'You're certain?' she asked.

Till calmly stepped into her trap, telling her, 'Yes, madam. I am quite sure.'

With a harsh, loud voice, Miocene cried out, 'But you've missed important things in the past. Haven't you, First Chair? Haven't you?'

Her son stiffened.

The room fell silent, waiting.

Till forced himself to relax. Then quietly and angrily, he said, 'Locke is useless.'

Ten swarms were an enormous number of soldiers, particularly if you were chasing someone who was useless.

But Till just kept shaking his head, telling everyone at the long pearlwood table, 'Even if he wanted, he couldn't hurt *us*.'

Thirty-eight

'DON'T WORRY. IT'S just my hand.'

The pressure was soft, soothing.

'Keep still now, dear. Still.'

Who was moving?

The voice said a familiar name, and with the hand pressing, it complained, 'She's fighting. Me, or something else.'

The voice is talking about me.

Another voice, deeper and more distant, said, 'Washen.'

Said, 'Just lie still. Washen. Please.'

Then a larger hand tried to smother her, pressing over her mouth and nostrils, and the deep voice drifted closer, familiarly intimate, telling her, 'We don't have much time. We're sprinting you through this regrowth.'

Regrowth?

'Sleep,' he advised, his hand lifting.

The woman's voice said, 'I think she is.'

But Washen was only keeping her eyes closed, feigning sleep, savoring the constant white pain of her new body's birth.

FRESH EYES OPENED.

Blinked.

A piercing green light was eclipsed by a man's silhouetted face, and Washen heard her own voice asking, 'Pamir? Is that you?'

'No, Mother,' he replied.

Flinching, she asked, 'This is Marrow? Are we back?'

Locke said nothing.

'Pamir!' she cried out.

'Your friend isn't here now,' said another voice. It was the same voice as before – feminine, and soft-spoken. 'He left for a little while,' the woman promised. 'How do you feel, darling?'

She moved her head, and her neck burst into flames.

'Slow, dear. Slow.'

Washen breathed deeply and found herself staring at a lovely human woman dressed in an emerald sarong. Black hair. Full lips. Smiling, and shy. She wasn't a Wayward, obviously. Or any normal Loyalist. Her clothing said as much, and the smooth, unhurried way she moved under-scored her ancient origins. This woman was a passenger. Wealthy, almost certainly. And probably unaccustomed to having a dead woman in her home.

'My name is Quee Lee.'

Washen nodded slowly, dancing with the pain. Eyes panned across the terran jungle. Wet green foliage was punctuated with riots of wild tropical flowers. Birds and painted bats darted through the sweet warm air. On the rotting stump of a tree, a troop of tailored monkeys sat in a sloppy ring, conspicuously ignoring the humans, playing some sort of game with stones and sticks and the delicate white skulls of dead owls.

'They'll be back,' said the hostess. 'Soon.'

'They?'

'My husband and your friend.'

Washen lay inside an open autodoc bed, her new body dressed in a blackish goo of silicone and dissolved oxygen and a trillion microchines. This was how a soldier was reborn – too fast and clumsily, flesh and bone made in bulk while immunological functions were kept to a mini-mum. Quee Lee sat on one side of the bed, Locke on the other. Her son was dressed in a passenger's colorful garb, his flesh darkened by UV light, his lovely thick hair grown long enough to make a golden stubble, hands and broad bare feet lashed together with standard security cord.

Quietly, anxiously, she asked, 'How long has it been?'

He didn't respond.

Quee Lee leaned forward, saying, 'One hundred and twenty-two years. Minus a few days.'

Washen remembered the explosive blows and the sensation of being yanked out of the leech habitat, tumbling and tumbling as her flesh froze and her mind pulled itself into the deepest possible coma.

When the nausea passed, she asked, 'Did you find me, Locke?'

He opened his mouth, and he closed it again.

'Pamir rescued you,' said Quee Lee. 'With your son's help.'

Again Washen glanced at the black security cords, then managed to laugh. 'I'm glad the two of you have become good friends.'

Embarrassment bled into a chilly anger. Locke straightened his back, then forced himself to explain. 'It was an accident. I went to the alien house. To see if the captains, or anyone else, had been there. And that ugly man stumbled over me.'

Pamir. Sure.

Her son shook his head in disgust, bare toes curling and uncurling in the black earth. What would a Wayward make of this rich soil? And the impossibly green trees? And the monkeys? And what about the ornate song of that little rilly bird that fell on them from the highest branches?

Finally, with a massive sadness, Locke admitted, 'I was weak.'

'Why?' asked Washen.

'I should have killed your friend.'

'Pamir's difficult to kill,' she responded. 'Believe me.'

Again, Locke clung to his silence.

Washen took a deep, thorough breath, then sat up in

bed, the black goo clinging to her baby-smooth, utterly hairless flesh. When the worst of the pain subsided, she looked at Quee Lee and said, 'One hundred and twenty-two years.' She sighed and said, 'Circumstances have changed while I was sleeping. That's my guess.'

The woman flinched, then smiled shyly.

'What's happening?' asked Washen. 'With the ship—?'

'Nothing has happened,' said her hostess. 'According to our new Master Captain, the ship needed a change of leadership. Incompetence was rife. And now, according to her, everything is the same as before, except for what's better, and we'd be fools to entertain the tiniest concern.'

Washen glared at her son.

He refused to blink or look at any face.

Then to herself, in a soft angry voice, she said, 'Miocene.'

And she turned back to Quee Lee, adding, 'That's who she sounds like.'

THE APARTMENT's AI spoke with a firm authority, announcing, 'Perri is approaching. With the other one, he is.'

It said, 'They seem to be alone.'

Then it asked, 'Do I allow them inside, Quee Lee?'

'Absolutely.'

Three more days had passed. Washen was six hours out of her bed, dressed in a simple white sarong and white sandals, and she had just eaten her first solid meal in more than a century, the endless fatigue turning into a nervous energy. She stood beside Quee Lee, waiting. The apartment door opened, its security screen in place, and out in the wide, tree-lined avenue, there was no one. What should have been a busy scene on any normal day was unnaturally quiet. Suddenly two men strode into view. The smaller man was handsome, smiling with an unconscious charm. The other man was larger and simple-faced, and Washen made the obvious mistake. Once the door was closed and locked by twenty means, she said to that larger man, 'Hello, Pamir.'

But the simple face peeled away, exposing a second face identical to the smaller man. Pretty in the same way. And charming. And most definitely not Pamir.

'Sorry,' said a laughing voice. 'Try again.'

The smaller man was Pamir. He peeled away his disguise, and the rumbling deep voice explained, 'I got an autodoc to peel away thirty kilos. What do you think?'

'You look wonderful anyway,' she allowed.

Pamir's face was rugged, like something hacked from a block of dense dark oak, an asymmetric tilt to the rough features and his dirty, badly matted hair tilting things even more. The man looked as if he couldn't remember when he last slept. Yet the bright brown eyes were clear and alert. When he looked at Washen, he smiled. Looking anywhere else, his expression grew distant, distracted. To no one in particular, he said, 'I'm famished.' Then his gaze returned to Washen, and the smile swam up from the massive fatigue, and with a familiar bite, cynical and wise, he said, 'Don't thank me. Not yet. If these grandchildren of yours find us, you'll wish that you were still at the bottom of that hydrogen sea.'

Probably so.

Yanking off the rest of his disguise, Pamir asked, 'Where's my prisoner?'

'In the garden,' Quee Lee replied.

'Has he grunted anything important?'

Both women said, 'Nothing,' in the same breath.

A bare hand pushed through the dirty hair. Then Pamir allowed himself a smile, and he confessed to Washen, 'I wanted to be with you. When you came back to us. But I had to see to this and to that first. Sorry.'

'Don't apologize.'

'Then I won't,' he grumbled.

Quee Lee asked her husband, 'What is happening out there?'

The pretty man rolled his eyes and thrust his tongue into one cheek. 'In a word?' he said. 'It's awfully and weirdly and relentlessly quiet.'

She asked, 'Where did you go, darling?'

The men glanced at each other, and Perri said, 'Darling,' as a warning.

Then Pamir shook his head, saying, 'Food first. I want my thirty kilos back.' He peeled away the false flesh on his hands, saying, 'Then we've got to go somewhere. Just us, Washen. I've got a trillion questions, and barely enough time to ask ten.'

PAMIR WAS CLEAN and wearing new clothes. He and Washen were inside a guest suite. The suite's floor diamond was inlaid with sun and holo generators. Looking between their feet, they could see into Quee Lee's garden room, and in particular, they could watch the blond-haired man who sat in the largest clearing, who never yanked at the restraining straps, and who carefully watched each motion of every bird and bug and half-tame monkey.

'Tell me,' Pamir began. 'Everything.'

Nearly five thousand years were crossed in what felt like a single breath. The false mission. Marrow. The Event. Children born; Waywards born. The rebirth of civilization. Washen and Miocene escaping from Marrow. Then Diu caught them and brought them to the leech home, and Diu explained that he was the source of everything that had happened . . . and just as she was about to finish the story, she paused to breathe, and nod, telling Pamir, 'I know what you've been doing these last days.'

'Do you?'

'You were trying to decide if I was genuine. If you could trust me.'

He took a last bite of half-cooked steak, then watching her, asked, 'How about it? Can I trust you?'

'What did you find out?' she pressed.

'Nobody mentions you. Nobody seems to care. But Miocene and your grandchildren are searching hard for *him*.' Pamir pointed at the floor. 'They nearly found him, and me, inside the fuel tank. But don't let his glowering silences fool you. Locke told me enough to narrow our search site enough . . .'

'How many captains are running loose?'

'My count is twenty-eight. Or twenty-seven. Or maybe it's down to twenty-six.'

Quietly, she said, 'Shit.'

'Not including you,' he added. 'But your commission was dissolved long ago. And if that doesn't make you crazy, listen to this. Right now, you're sitting with the ship's legal Master Captain. Isn't that a frightening thought?'

Washen did her best to digest the news. Then she bent and placed the palm of her new hand on the floor, as if trying to grasp her son's head. 'All right,' she whispered. 'Tell me everything you know. Fast.'

He told about his search for her and Miocene. About Perri's help and the mounting frustration, and how at the end, moments before he gave up, he stumbled across that archaic silver-encrusted clock—

'Do you still have it?' Washen blurted, her head lifting.

And there it was, dangling on a new silver chain. Pamir didn't have to say 'Take it' twice. Then, as Washen opened the lid and read the insignia, he told more of his story – the neutrino source; the hidden hatch; the collapsed tunnel – and he stopped where he and Locke were facing each other above the leech house.

With a soft click Washen closed the silver lid.

With a tone of apology, Pamir said, 'If I'd expanded the search radius, and chased down every small target—'

'I'm not disappointed,' she interrupted, showing a warm smile.

'I was distracted,' he continued. 'First, the neutrinos. Then we found Diu's secret hatch, and I was doing nothing but digging.'

Washen cupped her hands around her clock, concentrating.

Pamir said, 'Diu,' with a firm contempt. Then he shook his head, adding, 'I honestly can't remember the little prick.'

I loved the man, thought Washen, in astonishment.

Then she said, 'Neutrinos,' with a soft, curious voice. Looking up at him, she asked, 'What did you see? Exactly. And how big was the flux?'

Pamir told everything, in crisp detail.

When Washen didn't react, he changed topics. 'As soon as you're strong enough, we're leaving. I don't have any official ties to Perri or Quee Lee. But there might be an old security file somewhere, and Miocene'll find it. We need a fresh place to hide. Which is partly what I've been doing these last days—'

'And then?'

'Bide our time. Be patient, and make ready.' He spoke in slow, certain tones, sounding like a man who had given this issue his full attention. 'If we're going to take back our ship, and keep it, then we'll need to gather up the resources . . . the muscle and wisdom . . . to make things a little less impossible . . .'

Washen didn't speak. She didn't quite know what she was thinking. Her mind had never felt emptier or more useless. What passed for her focus drifted from her cupped hands to a long pained look at her son sitting in that beautiful jungle. Then she pried open her hands and the silver lid, staring again at the slow, relentless hands.

'We have allies,' Pamir allowed. 'That's also what I've been doing these last few days. Making contacts with likely friends . . .'

Again, she closed the clock and cupped her hands around its blood-warmed metal, and quietly, almost in a whisper, she said, 'We didn't have fusion reactors.'

Pardon?'

'When I left Marrow. Most of our energy came from geothermal sources.'

'You were gone for more than a century,' Pamir cautioned. 'A lot can change in that little bite of time.'

Perhaps. Perhaps.

'Judging by the evidence,' he continued, 'I'd guess that the Waywards had to punch a wide hole up from Marrow. Since they were coming back along the old hole, theirs met mine, making their work easier. But still. Hundreds of kilometers dug in days, or hours. That's why we didn't have any warning. And that's why they must have built all those fusion reactors, I'm guessing.'

She said, 'Perhaps,' but shook her head regardless.

Again, Washen opened her hands. But this time she dropped the clock, and it landed on its edge with a soft click, and bending over to pick it up, she found herself staring at her son as he stared at a strange green world, his soft gray eyes betraying nothing – not a whispery sense of awe, much less the tiniest concern.

'What is it, Washen?'

She opened her mouth, and said nothing.

'Tell me,' Pamir insisted.

'I think you're wrong,' she heard herself saying.

'Probably so. But where?'

Until she said it, she wasn't certain what she would say.

'About the energy source. You're mistaken. But that's not what matters most.'

'What matters?'

She said, 'Look at him.'

The ancient man stared between his feet, regarding the prisoner for a long moment. Then finally, with a measured disgust, he asked, 'What should I see?'

'Locke is a Wayward. He still believes.'

Pamir gave a low snort, then said, 'What he *is* is a fanatic. And he just doesn't know any better.'

'He and Till were in the leech house,' she countered, shaking her head. 'You know the place. Whisper anything, and your words are audible everywhere.'

Pamir waited.

'Ever since you woke me, it's been gnawing at me.' She picked up the clock and coaxed her sarong to grow a pocket that would hold it securely. Then she looked at Pamir with bright certain eyes, telling him, 'Till and Locke must have heard Diu talking. They wouldn't have had any choice. His confession was thorough, and it didn't leave room to maneuver. Everything the Waywards believe was invented by Diu. And that's enough of a revelation to cripple the most robust faith.'

With more stubbornness than reason, Pamir said, 'Your son's a fanatic. And Till's an ambitious, pernicious climber.'

Washen barely heard him.

Narrowing her eyes, she thought aloud. 'Those two Waywards heard everything, and it didn't matter. Maybe they weren't even surprised that Diu was alive. That's not so outrageous. Waywards always knew everything that was happening on Marrow. No secrets for them. And after Diu was dead, they took Miocene home. Because she was needed. Because if they are the Builders reborn, and if they were going to retake the ship . . . then they required a high-ranking captain, like Miocene . . . someone who knows how to defeat the security systems, and the old Master . . .'

Pamir took a deep breath, let it leak out between his teeth, then offered, 'Till is cynically using Diu's dreamed-up religion, and Miocene is playing along—'

'No,' said Washen. 'And maybe.' Then she pointed at Locke, saying again, 'He believes. I know my son, and I understand, I hope, his capabilities. And he's still very much a Wayward.'

Out of frustration, Pamir asked, 'So what do you believe, Washen?'

'Diu told us . . .' She closed her eyes, remembering what seemed to be only three days removed from her. 'When he was first on Marrow, alone, he had a dream. The Builders and the hated Bleak came straight out of that dream . . .'

'Which means?'

'Maybe nothing,' she confessed. Then she shook her head and rose to her feet, saying, 'If there's any answer, it's somewhere on Marrow. That's where it's waiting. And I think you're absolutely wrong about our timetable up here.'

'Do you?'

'We wait, and the Waywards only grow stronger.'

Pamir looked between his feet again, staring at their prisoner with a new intensity, as if seeing him for the first time.

'Wait too long,' she warned, 'and we'll have to tear this ship apart with a total war. Which is why I think we need to do everything now. The first instant that it's possible.'

'What we need to do,' he echoed.

Then he asked, 'Like what?'

Washen had to laugh, quietly and sadly.

'You're the Master Captain here,' she replied. 'My only duty is to serve the Great Ship, and you.'

Thirty-nine

'THERE IS A PLACE,' Miocene reminisced, inviting her son and the other high-ranking Waywards to accompany her on a little journey. 'It's very high, and quite secure, and perfect for watching the burn.'

It would be a moment rich in symbolism, and more important, a moment of pure vindication.

But Till wore a doubting expression. He looked past Miocene, then said, 'Madam,' and gave the smallest of bows. 'Is this trip absolutely necessary? Considering the risks, I mean. And the thin benefits.'

'Benefits,' she echoed. 'Did you count tradition?'

He knew better than to respond.

Miocene said, 'No, you didn't,' and laughed gently, her scorn barely showing. Then she told him, 'This is a noble tradition. The Master Captain and her loyal staff stand on the open deck, watching as their ship turns in the wind.'

'Noble,' he replied, 'and ancient, too.'

'We've done it on board this ship,' she promised. 'Many, many times.'

What could he say?

Before any answer was offered, she added, 'I appreciate what you're thinking. That we might be too exposed. Too vulnerable. Open to some celestial disaster—'

'Not on the trailing hemisphere, madam. I know that much.'

'Then you're worried about a closer, more emotional enemy.' Master or mother, her task was to lend confidence. To inspire, and hopefully, instruct. 'No one else knows about this venture. There isn't time to prepare an ambush. And believe me,' she added, a swollen hand lifting into the air between them, 'I'm strong enough to defend us from any part of the ship, and anywhere on its enormous hull, too.'

Frantic days had brought a transformation. The new Master sat on the old Master's bed. She wasn't as vast as her predecessor, but the trend was obvious. Interlocking networks of nexuses lay beneath her century-old skin, speaking to one another in dense lightspeed languages, and speaking to the ship's important systems in a tangle of frequencies and coded wisps of laser light. A newborn instinct told Miocene that the reaction chambers were being fueled and readied. She could practically taste the cold compressed hydrogen being drawn from the deep tanks. This giant burn, scheduled millennia ago, would happen without delay or embarrassment. How could anyone doubt that she was in charge? The symbolism was blatant. Nervous passengers would take comfort in the burn. The disgruntled crew would have to admit that this old woman knew what she was doing. And the Milky Way would notice, trillions of potential passengers having even more good reasons to forget the old Master and her incompetent ways.

Soon and in countless ways, Miocene would improve her ship. Efficiencies would jump. Confidence would blossom. The ship's prestige would swell as a consequence, and with her guiding hand, the knowledge of a million species would be beamed home, enriching humanity as well as the Master's personal legacy. For the last century, whenever she wanted a taste of pleasure, Miocene had imagined the glorious day when the ship would complete its circuit of the galaxy, approaching the Earth after a half-million-year absence. By then, and mostly because of her work, humanity would dominate their little portion of the universe. And with her loyal, loving son at her side, she would accept every honor and the radiant blessings from a people that would have no choice but see her as a god and savior.

'The universe,' she whispered, speaking to herself.

Till leaned closer, asking, 'What did you say, madam?'

'You need to see it for yourself,' she replied. 'The stars. The Milky Way. Everything, and in its full glory.'

A shifting expression became simple doubt. 'I have seen it,' Till reminded her. 'By holographic light, and perfectly rendered.'

'Nothing rendered is perfect,' she countered.

Then before her son could say anything else, she reminded him, 'One of us is the Master. The other is her First Chair.'

'I know that, madam.'

With a wide hand, she touched her son on the forehead, the slender nose, then with a single finger, she fondled the handsome strong chin. 'Perhaps it's too much of a risk,' she allowed. 'You can make a good argument, yes. So it will be just you and me watching the burn. Is that a worthy compromise?'

He had no choice but to say, 'Yes, madam. Yes, Mother.'

But as always, Till said the words with a convincing enthusiasm, wrapped tight in a smile that couldn't have been any brighter.

THE SHIP'S HULL was thinnest on the trailing face – a few dozen kilometers of original, nearly virginal hyperfiber laced with access tunnels and cavernous pipes and pumps vast enough to move oceans. Aesthetics as well as security issues played a role; Miocene and Till traveled inside one of the main reaction chambers. Nothing lived here, and next to nothing came here. Against the banks of perfect mirrors, there was no place to hide. And since no one but Miocene could fire these engines, they could pass untroubled, their swift little car rising into the craterlike maw of the rocket nozzle, the sky above them illuminated by a billion fires, each of them dwarfing the powers of their magnificent machine.

'The stars,' said Miocene, and she couldn't help but grin.

Till looked very young, standing with his hands holding each other behind his back, his back arched and his boot-clad feet slightly apart, his uniform and cap and the wide brown eyes reflecting the brilliance of the universe.

For a moment, he seemed to smile.

Then he closed his eyes and turned to her, and he opened his eyes again, admitting, 'They're lovely. Of course.'

Of course.

Disappointment grabbed Miocene. Had she really believed that a naked-eye look at the Milky Way would cause a revelation? That Till would throw up his arms and drop to his weak knees in a wonderstruck rapture?

She was disappointed, and worse, she was infuriated.

Perhaps sensing her mood, Till asked, 'Do you remember when, Mother? When you looked into a nanoscope and saw your first naked proton?'

She blinked, then confessed, 'No.'

'One of the essential bones of the universe,' he chided. 'As vital as the stars, and in its own way, more spectacular. But it was real to you before you saw it. Intellectually, and emotionally, you were prepared.'

Miocene nodded, saying nothing.

'From the moment that I was reborn and for every day since, people have talked about the stars. Describing their beauty. Explaining their physics. Assuring me that the simple sight of a sun will fill me with awe . . .'

What would it take to impress Till?

'Frankly, Mother. After such an enormous buildup, I think the sky looks rather thin. Almost insubstantial. Which is doubly disappointing, since we're close to one of the galaxy's big arms. Aren't we?'

If Miocene ignited the engine beneath them, Till would be impressed.

For a fiery instant, yes.

Smiling in a thin, almost mocking fashion, she looked ahead. Their car swerved abruptly, heading for the parabolic nozzle. Ancient hyperfiber had been blackened by corrosive plasmas, leaving a featureless wall that appeared close when it was distant, then remote as they slowed and suddenly passed through a camouflaged hatchway. Engineers had added this feature. The hatchway led into a small tunnel that passed through the nozzle, ending with a blister of diamond suspended a thousand kilometers above the hull.

Only an imbecile couldn't be impressed by this view.

Mother and son remained inside the armored car, and the car floated inside the blister. The Great Ship possessed fourteen giant rocket nozzles: one in the center, four ringing the one, and nine more nozzles surrounding the first five. Theirs was one of the four, and on the horizon, standing side by side, were two of the outer nozzles, fueled and waiting the command to fire. Morphing metals and lakes of hydraulic fluids had tilted the nozzles, giving them a fifteen-degree angle. The ten-hour-and-eleven-second burn would change the ship's trajectory just enough that in another two weeks it would pass near a red giant sun, then plunge even closer to the sun's companion – a massive yet essentially calm black hole.

In less than a day, the ship's course would be tweaked twice. Instead of leaving this dense region of suns and living worlds, they would continue following the galaxy's arm, moving into new and lucrative places.

There was a soft, impressed 'Hmm.'

Till wasn't staring at the stars or the giant nozzles. Instead, he was looking down, and with a slightly contemptuous voice, he remarked, 'There's certainly a lot of *them*.'

Lights were sprinkled across the hyperfiber landscape. But unlike the pleasant disorder of the stars, these lights had defining principles, connected into lines and circles and dense masses that glowed with a cumulative light. Yes, there were a lot of them. Probably more than there were five thousand years ago, and certainly more than the last time she visited that place. Miocene shook her head and said, 'Remoras,' with a growling tone. 'They build their cities on the trailing face. More cities all the time.'

Till smiled, and with a charming wink, he observed, 'You don't like Remoras. Do you, madam?'

'They're stubborn and exceptionally strange.' But she allowed, 'They do important work. We would be hard-pressed to replace them.'

Her son made no comment.

'Twenty seconds,' she announced.

Till said, 'Yes,' and politely looked up, those bright brown eyes squinting against the anticipated glare of the engines.

And with Till momentarily distracted, Miocene slipped away.

THE ROOM NEVER changed.

Sitting along each wall, wearing the symbolic bodies and white togas of wizened old scribes, were dozens of sophisticated AIs. Each was a little different from its neighbor, in abilities and aesthetic sensibilities. In this realm, differences were a blessing. The reason for their existence was a single question – a question requiring utter concentration as well as a fondness for novelty. Every day or week or month, one of the scribes would propose some new solution, or a variation on an old solution, and with a boundless youth, the machines would discuss and debate, and occasionally shout at one another. Inevitably they would find some critical flaw in the elaborate mathematics, or the logical assumptions, and the proposal would be given a quick funeral, its corpse placed on an electronic shelf next to millions of failed hypotheses – proof of their zeal, if not their genius.

In the room's center was a dense and extremely precise map of the ship. The map didn't portray the ship as it was today, but the ship as it existed when the first captains arrived: Every vast chamber and long tunnel, tiny crevice and grand ocean, was displayed in all of its abandoned glory.

Yet a substantial, perhaps critical feature was missing.

Into that ignorance, the new Master appeared.

The AI scribes regarded her with a cold scorn. They were conservative souls, by nature. They didn't approve of mutinies, even mutinies justified on legal grounds. With a machine's humor, one scribe said, 'Who are you? I don't recognize you.'

The others laughed in low, disgusted voices.

Miocene said nothing for a long second. Then her image pretended to sigh, and in a passing fashion, she mentioned, 'I can improve this map of yours. I know things that the old Master couldn't have imagined.'

Doubt bled into interest.

Then, curiosity.

But one of the scribes shook its rubber face, warning her, 'Your predecessor has to be put on trial. A fair and public trial, as mandated by the ship's own laws. Otherwise we will not work with you.'

'Haven't I promised trials?' she replied. 'Examine my life. Any profile you wish. When have I been anything but a champion of the ship's laws?'

The scribes did as Miocene advised, and just as she expected, they grew bored. Her life wasn't a puzzle. It held no interest for them. One after another, their gazes returned to their elaborate, mysterious map.

'If I give you this information,' she told them, 'you cannot share it with anyone else. Is that understood?'

'We understand everything,' the first scribe warned.

'And if you find a possible solution, tell no one but me. Me.' She stared at each set of their glass eyes. 'Can you embrace those terms?'

In a voice, they said, 'Yes.'

Into the map, Miocene inserted the newest parameters: she drew the hyperfiber shell surrounding the core, then set Marrow inside the shell, and finally she showed what was inside Marrow. Then she caused Marrow to expand and contract, a flood of data explaining how energy cycled through the iron body, how the buttresses kept it firmly in place, and anything else of potential interest that she had absorbed over the horrible centuries.

In a fraction of a second, old faces grew enthralled.

Miocene felt the faint shudder as the ship's engines began throwing plasma out into the cold, cold universe.

The physical portion of her sat beside her son, watching as he turned and showed her another good smile.

'It's lovely, yes,' he admitted.

The plasma river was a wide column moving at near lightspeed, only a tiny portion of its energies given off as visible light, but still bright enough that the stunning glare caused the stars to vanish in their blinking, tearing eyes.

'May we leave now, madam?' he asked quietly, like a bored little boy.

The other part of her, the holoimage, was equally disappointed. She was surrounded by scribes who whispered at lightspeed, able to accomplish miracles inside an instant.

Then with a calm, knowing face, one of the scribes gave
her a tentative and ridiculously simple solution to the great
puzzle.

'That?' she cried out. 'That's your answer?'

The first scribe spoke for its peer, admitting, 'That's an
artistic solution. Not a hard mathematical one. Madam.'

'Obviously.' Then as she vanished, she growled, 'Tell no
one, just the same. And keep working at it. Will you do
that for me?'

'No,' the scribe replied, speaking to empty air.

'We do it for ourselves,' said its neighbors.

And they were whispering again, using those quick
dessicated voices, their plaything-puzzle suddenly transformed, everything about their tiny universe made fasci-
nating again, and inside this stuffy room, everything was
enormous.

Forty

TO WATCHFUL EYES, they were another anonymous repair
crew: several dozen Remoras happily imprisoned inside
their bulky lifesuits, sitting shoulder to shoulder inside one
of their tough old skimmers, every face different from its
neighbors's faces, everyone telling good filthy Remoran
jokes as they made their way toward the ship's leading face.

'How many captains does it take to fuck?' one asked.

'Three,' the others shouted. 'Two to do it, while the
third captain hands out the appropriate awards and cita-
tions!'

'Where does the Master send her shit?' asked another.

Everyone pointed at the nearest of the rocket nozzles, then broke into a familiar, half-amused giggle.

Then Orleans leaned forward, asking, 'What's the difference between the new Master and the old one?'

There was an abrupt silence. Everyone knew the question, but nobody recognized the joke. Which wasn't surprising, since the old man had just dreamed it up.

His newest mouth pulled into an enormous smile, short tusklike teeth tapping against the faceplate. 'Any ideas? No?' Then he let off a big laugh, telling them, 'Our new Master came back from the dead. While the old one was never alive.'

Polite, if somewhat nervous laughter gave way to silence.

Pivoting his helmet, Orleans showed his face to the crew. On a public channel, he told them, 'It wasn't very funny. You're right.' But on a scrambled private channel, he said, 'Don't dwell on things.' He told them, 'We'll be dead soon enough. Relax.'

Nervousness mutated into a useful determination. No, they were thinking, they wouldn't die. His crew's outlook was betrayed by their straight-backed postures and defiant fists. These were mostly youngsters, and most still believed they could fool death by culturing a positive attitude along with their innate cleverness and deserved good fortune. 'Not me,' each thought. 'I won't die today.' Then one after another, they turned their faces toward the rocket's nozzle, looking at its vastness, and at the brilliant column of light – the new Master's farts – the light dwarfing everything else, splitting the universe neatly in two.

Only Orleans ignored the spectacle. He kept his amber eyes focused on the blisterlike buildings that flanked the wide roadway. In a rare mood, he found himself feeling sentimental, recalling that when he was a youngster, he thoroughly expected to be dead by now. Vaporized by an impact comet, probably. The idea that he could outlive everyone in his generation . . . well, it didn't seem like a possibility then. Such an impossibly long life would prove a Remora's cowardice, or at least a crippling sense of caution. Yet Orleans was neither a coward nor a worrier, and he had a sharp disrespect for luck, good and otherwise.

Over the centuries, then the millenia, he had seen friends die without warning or a fair chance. He had outlived children and grandchildren, then descendants who carried a tiny fraction of his unique seeds. But it wasn't luck that had carried him this far. Not good luck, or its evil mate. What was to blame, undoubtedly, was the universe's own magnificent, seamless indifference.

Orleans was too small to be noticed.

Too insignificant to send a comet plummeting his way.

His was a faith rich with logic and an ascetic's beauty, and until this moment, it seemed to be a durable, determined faith. But suddenly a second possibility had crawled into view. Perhaps, just perhaps, some great Fate had long ago taken Orleans under its protective shroud, saving him for this day and this moment, making it possible for him to make this inconspicuous journey across the ship's vast and stark and enchanting hull.

The city wasn't even a name when Orleans was born. But today it was large enough that leaving it seemed to take forever. Building after blister-shaped building streaked past. Hyperfiber homes, for the most part. Minimalist places with walls and a roof, hard vacuum and ample privacy, where couples and other mating configurations contributed their seeds, babies born inside hyperfiber wombs that expanded as needed, both child and machine developing hands and legs, and a head, and deemed 'born' during a day-long celebration that culminated when a fully functioning reactor and recycle system were strapped onto the Remora's wide back.

Between the homes were the rare shops hawking what few wares could entice citizens who had absolutely no need for food or drink, and who disapproved of most possessions. Other structures were assembled from clear diamond, and unlike buildings, they were sealed against the vacuum. Sealed and stocked with a variety of species, terran and otherwise. Every organism was nominally immortal, and under the rain of hard radiations and the force of simple time, they had mutated in chaotic fashions, yielding a wild assortment of shapes and unlikely colors, and unexpected, sometimes entertaining behaviors.

Remoran parks, in essence.

The largest park was on the city's fringe, and as they passed that blur of color and shape, Orleans told himself to go there and take a look at its inhabitants. Who knew? Perhaps he would find inspiration for his next self-induced transformation.

The skimmer streaked into the open, accelerating to its limits.

Time moved sluggishly, stubbornly. Again, then again, Orleans showed his face to his crew, and on the scrambled channel, he forced them to repeat their timetable and describe each of their critical jobs. Then for the first time, he finally looked at their target, and he allowed himself a deep quick breath, holding his personal atmosphere inside lungs that were only glancingly human – lungs built by a lifetime of carefully directing mutations that gave them and their slow black blood an efficiency bordering on perfection.

The Remoran ideal.

Like thousands of skimmers in the past, theirs was slipping close to the giant nozzle, taking them toward the ship's leading face. A slab of scrap hyperfiber lay in the open. Even at their enormous speed, the AI pilot should have had time to notice it, and react. But the AI – old and notorious for its failures – announced that it was ill, and a human would have to drive from this point on.

In those critical moments, the slab cocked itself, then sprang up.

Engulfed by the skimmer's forcefield, it spun once, then was driven into the diamond body, slicing into machinery and knocking both reactors off-line.

In less than three kilometers, the skimmer dropped to the hull and stopped.

Within moments, an automated plea was sent, and an empty skimmer began navigating its way though city traffic, making for the crippled vessel. And just to make the drama more genuine, the Remoran dispatcher laughed at the crew's misery and embarrassment, telling a favorite old joke.

'Why's the sky full of stars?'

Several dozen recorded voices replied in a carefully ragged chorus.

'To entertain Remoras!' they screamed. 'While we wait for fucking parts!'

Forty-one

WASHEN COULD TELL, even at a distance, even though they were wearing the bruise-black uniforms of security troops, and their skin was gradually losing its smoky cast as the ship's lights and new foods worked on their flesh; with all that, Washen could still see them for what they were.

Waywards.

The two-engine burn was half-finished, and five Waywards were calmly working their way down the narrow avenue. If Washen was as obvious as they, she was doomed. The next pair of staring eyes would spot her, and a narrow burst of laser light would boil away her new body, and whatever was left would be carried straight to the new Master, Washen's miseries just beginning. But she reminded herself that she didn't stand out, even a little bit. She had a name and robust identity that would absorb every scrutiny. She was wearing a mask of someone else's skin, giving her an appearance designed not to draw attention. What's more, Washen had ceased to be. The first-grade captain was thousands of years dead. The Loyalist leader died more than a century ago. If she was especially fortunate, both of these women had been forgotten, wiped into a delicious anonymity that in the fullness of time would claim everyone who happened to be sitting here today.

'Delicious,' she muttered.

'What is?' asked one of her companions.

'The ice cream,' she allowed, smiling as she dipped her spoon back into the melting brown mound. Then with an understated honesty, she said, 'It's been a little while since I enjoyed a good chocolate.'

Pamir nodded agreeably. He was wearing a handsome face, and like Washen, he wore a simple dark ochre robe that made them look like clergy members in any of several different Rationalist faiths. As clergy members, they were ready to proselytize with the slightest encouragement, which was why most of their fellow passengers tried to avoid small talk with them. It was the perfect identity for two humans who needed to hide in the bustling heart of the ship.

The third member of their little party was even more imposing. Massive and towering, he lifted a mug of something rancid and took a few long swallows down his eating hole, while his breathing hole quietly whistled a few words.

'It is a beautiful place, this place,' his translator declared.

Pamir glanced at Washen, allowing himself a knowing grin. Then he stared at the harum-scarum's face, asking, 'How's your drink?'

The alien was mostly heated plastic and hidden motors. Locke was tucked inside the long body, his legs tied back and arms bound at his sides. Everything that the harum-scarum would see, he saw. Everything it heard was piped into his ears. But his mouth was filled with a permeable plastic, and a small AI told the machine when to move and what to say. Locke was a passenger inside that automaton. He was cargo. Since the early days of the ship, devices of this ilk had smuggled things illegal and precious. According to Pamir, this was the best model on hand – considering the limits of time and their very special needs.

The false voice whistled, answering Pamir's question. 'My drink is beautiful,' said the box on the broad chest.

'And what's beauty?' asked Washen, sounding very much like a proselytizer. 'Do you remember what we told you, friend?'

'The residue of reason mixed in a sea of chaos,' their companion answered.

'Precisely,' said the humans, in a shared voice, both dipping spoons into their beautiful desserts. Then Washen stared off at the Waywards, saying, 'Chaos,' to herself, under her quickening breath.

WALKING THE AVENUE, watching aliens and strange humans going about their very strange lives, the Waywards struggled to retain a sense of total control. No, they didn't come from a backward world. No, they weren't awed by the endless cosmopolitan landscape that was the Great Ship. In their smiling faces and grim, staring eyes, they showed nothing but a cocky toughness common to police officers anywhere. And elaborate sensors automatically probed and prodded the strange bodies around them, teasing out their secrets, proving that there was nothing here to be feared.

And yet.

Behind the eyes was a nervousness, childlike and almost endearing.

As they approached the cafe, Washen studied them with nothing but her own eyes and experience. Obviously, the five Waywards had spent their short lives making ready for today. For this particular walk. They'd always known that they would board the Great Ship, reclaiming it for the Builders. They had studied their roles and practiced a thousand scenarios to exhaustion – scenarios designed by Miocene, no doubt – and like children anywhere, they couldn't help but accept this day with a rigorous lack of imagination.

Of course they were here. Of course they ruled the ship! After all, this moment had been promised to them by Till and the dead Builders. From the moment they were born, and in every spoken word . . . !

But despite simulations and every carefully entombed lesson, the reality of this place was beginning to slam down on their inexperienced heads: a whiff-Kon saluted them with its tail, and one young man jerked his hand, ready to fend off an imagined blow. A golden rilly bird landed on one of their armored shoulders, wanting to sing for food and getting nothing but a quick shove for its trouble. Then a human child, perhaps knowing a little something about Waywards, said, 'For you,' He was sitting at a nearby table, and he said, 'A gift, sir.' Then he handed up a wide, greenish-brown beetle. No, it was a cockroach. Something that the child had caught under the cafe tables, probably.

The Wayward accepted the gift and pointed sensors at its body and kicking legs. Then he glanced at his companions, and receiving no suggestions, he did what must have seemed like the polite thing.

He pushed the roach into his mouth, and chewed.

What was a quiet avenue became deathly silent. Passengers and a few off-duty crew members held their breath until the Wayward swallowed. By then, he sensed that he had guessed wrong, and for a moment, he was lost. What should he do *now*? But then some teacher's sage advice came back to him, and he said, 'What a wonderful flavor.' He said it with a humble charm. Then he laughed, working desperately to expose his embarrassment to his very tense audience.

A palpable relief came from everywhere at once.

Wrapped inside that tiny drama was a lesson. Washen glanced at Pamir, and he nodded, seeing it for himself.

The old Master and her dusty old captains weren't missed. The mutiny had been quick and virtually bloodless, and the mutineers – whatever their motives – had a simple charm, not to mention other qualities that tourists always appreciated:

These Waywards were a different sort of people, novel and new, and in the most unexpected ways, they could be entertaining.

The patrol continued with its sweep, and after another few moments, they arrived at Washen's table, a first little glance giving them no reason to linger. But the trailing officer – a strong chocolate-colored woman – seemed to notice something about the three of them, and she hesitated. She stared at Washen, and too late, Washen realized that she had been staring at one of the youngish men, his quick face and smoky gray eyes reminding her of Diu.

One of Diu's children, perhaps.

The woman said, 'Please, if you would. Your idenitities, please.'

Her fellow officers paused and looked over their shoulders, waiting with a professional impatience.

Washen, then Pamir, offered their new names and flecks of other people's skin. The harum-scarum obeyed last, its attitude perfectly in keeping with its nature — an angry tangle of sounds diluted in the translation:

'I resent you, but you have the power.'

The woman seemed to understand the species. 'I have the power,' she agreed, 'but I admire you just the same.' Then their names were checked against the ship's extensive rosters, and when everything appeared as it should, she told the three of them, 'Thank you for your gracious cooperation.'

'You're welcome,' Pamir replied, for everyone.

The Wayward seemed ready to leave, then had second thoughts. Or she pretended second thoughts, taking a half-step before pausing, a glance at Washen preceding the careful question, 'Why don't you approve of us?'

'Is that what you think?' asked Washen.

'Yes.' There was something of Aasleen in the face and manners. Perhaps it meant nothing, but the woman seemed less like a Wayward than the others. She said, 'Ignorance,' with a delicate anger. Then shaking her head as if disappointed, she added, 'You consider yourself a person of rational intelligence. As I understand your Rationalist uniform. But I don't believe you have any understanding of me. Is that true?'

Washen said, 'Probably somewhat true, yes.'

The officer was scanning her — a deep, thorough scan meant to find any abnormalities, any excuse for a deeper interrogation. Conversation was an excuse to stand too close and stare.

'About this world of yours,' Washen began. 'This Marrow place—'

'Yes?'

'It seems very mysterious. And unlikely, I think.'

These weren't points easily deflected. The woman shrugged her shoulders, and with a forced amiability quoted a Rationalist maxim. '"Good questions asked well dispel every mystery."'

'Where were you born?'

'Hazz City,' the woman replied.

'When?'

'Five hundred and five years ago.'

Washen nodded, wondering if she had ever met this woman. 'Hazz City . . . is that a Wayward place . . . ?'

'Yes.'

'Always?'

The woman nearly took the bait. Then she hesitated, and with a delicate accuracy, she told everyone in the cafe, 'Marrow isn't a large world. And as long as humans have lived there, in one flavor or another, everything on it has been Wayward.'

Washen sat motionless, and silent.

Their interrogator turned to Pamir, saying, 'Please, sir. Ask a good question.'

The false face grinned, and after a half-moment, he wondered aloud, 'When can I go down and see this world of yours?'

She was scanning Pamir, and her companions formed a half-circle around the table, their sonics and infrareds probing from different vantage points. The man with Diu's eyes laughed gently, then said, 'You can visit there now, if you want.'

As a prisoner, he meant.

The woman disapproved. She said it with a hard glance, then calmly and smoothly explained to Pamir, 'In the near future, there will be tours. Of course. It's a very lovely world, and I'm sure it will be a popular destination.'

Some of the passengers nodded agreeably, probably eager for the day.

Then the harum-scarum belched with a solid thud, and drawing everyone's attention, he promised, 'I have a better question than theirs.'

'By all means,' said the woman.

'May I join the Waywards?'

That brought a nervous little silence. Then the woman smiled with a genuine serenity, and she gave the honest answer.

'I don't know,' she told the alien. 'But when I find myself in Till's company again, I will certainly ask—'

She was interrupted by a sudden motion.

Abrupt, and small. But the motion was noticed. Patrons at other tables looked down in astonishment, watching as the faces of their drinks rippled, as the ceiling and walls and rigid stone floor trembled.

A sound followed after the motion. There was a low, low roar that came sweeping from above, racing down the avenue and passing deeper into the ship.

Washen feigned surprise.

Pamir did it better. He straightened his back and looked at the woman officer, and with a voice edging into terror, he asked, 'What the fuck was that?'

She didn't know.

For a long moment, the five Waywards were as lost as anyone. Then Washen offered the obvious explanation. 'It was an impact.' She looked at her companions, telling them, 'It was a comet. We're closing on that next star and

black hole . . . it must have been one of their comets
hitting us . . .'

Word spread through the cafe, merging with the same
explanation as it was generated up and down the long
avenue.

The Wayward was trying to believe Washen. But then
she heard a general announcement coming through an
implanted nexus, explaining enough that she winced as if
in pain, and she growled under her breath, then turned to
her companions and announced, 'One of the engines . . .
has failed . . .'

Then she seemed to realize that she shouldn't have
spoken so freely. A conjured smile framed her next words.
'But everything is very much under control,' she told everyone, her expression and tone saying the precise opposite.

Human faces looked wounded, or they laughed with a
giddy nervousness. Aliens digested the news with everything
from calmness to a pheromonal scream, the cafe's air suddenly
thick with odd stinks and piercing, indigestible sounds.

Another message was delivered on a secure channel.
The woman tilted her head, paying rapt attention. Then
to her team, she shouted, 'With me. Now!'

The five Waywards ran, pushing into a full sprint.

If anything, that made the panic worse. Patrons began
searching through official news services as well as the rumor
oceans, holo projections covering tabletops and slick granite floor and dancing in the air. One of the ship's two
firing engines had fallen into a premature sleep. Nothing
else was certain. A thousand self-labeled experts promised
that no combination of mistakes could cause a malfunc-
tion, certainly nothing this catastrophic. Again and again,
voices mentioned the pointed word, 'Sabotage.'

Within three minutes, sixty-five individuals and ghostly
organizations had claimed responsibility for this tragedy.

Washen gave Pamir a brief look.

He did nothing. Then after a few moments, he announced, 'We need to be leaving,' as he rose to his feet. Looking up the avenue, he seemed to be deciding on their route to the next hiding place. Then he said, 'This way,' and took the harum-scarum under its spiked elbow, coaxing it along.

Perpendicular to the avenue was a narrow, half-lit tunnel.

Pamir and the false alien were walking side by side, passing through a demon door into a thicker, warmer atmosphere. Where the tunnel bent to the right, a figure appeared, small and running hard, the black of the uniform making it blend into the gloom.

There wasn't space for three bodies.

The collision was abrupt and violent, and utterly one-sided. The security officer found himself on his back, gazing up at an unreadable alien face.

Pamir started to kneel, started to say, 'My apologies.'

He was offering the officer a big hand.

The Wayward gave a low, wild scream. And that's when the rest of his squad appeared, rounding the turn to find one of their own apparently being assaulted. Weapons were deployed. Curt warnings were shouted. The loudest Wayward told everyone, 'Stand back!'

The harum-scarum kept true to its nature.

'I stand here,' he rumbled. 'You stand there.'

A kinetic round entered the neck, obliterating flesh and ceramic bones, nothing vital damaged and the automation barely wavering, long hands thrust up against the ceiling while the translation box cried out:

'No no no no!'

In a wild panic, every Wayward fired on the monster.

The head dropped backward, riding a hinge of leather, and the legs were dissolved with lasers, the great body dropping hard onto its stumplike knees. Then an explosive round cut into the body itself, exposing a human tied into a secret bundle, wrapped inside a transparent silicone envelope.

Locke stared out at the armed officers. His expression was simple. A pure withering terror had taken hold of him, the surprise total and dismantling.

Standing nearby, Washen saw his enormous eyes and little else.

Every weapon was pointed at him. There was a slippery instant when everything was possible, and maybe they would set down their lasers and free him. Maybe. But then Washen threw herself toward her son, screaming, 'No—!'

They fired.

What Locke would see last was his mother trying to cover him with her inadequate body, and then a purple brilliance stretching on forever.

Forty-two

A CHAIN OF tiny, almost delicate explosions had smashed valves and pumping stations. No target was vital. The Great Ship was nothing but redundancies built on sturdy redundancies. But the cumulative effects were catastrophic: a lake of pressurized hydrogen gathered in the worst possible place, and a final sabotage caused a magnetic bottle to fail, a mirroring mass of metallic anti-hydrogen dropping into the sudden lake, the resulting blast excavating a plasma-filled wound better than twelve kilometers across.

The vast rocket coughed, then stopped firing.

Within seconds, security forces were on full alert,

gathering at predetermined disaster-management stations.

Within minutes, using lasers and hyperfiber teeth, a scuttlebug worked its way through the thinnest part of the slag, a spare head shoved out into the open, its mouth blistered by the residual plasmas and the eyes seeing a rainbow of hard radiations.

Miocene saw nothing but the rainbow. Then she closed that set of eyes and opened her own, seeing her son's hard gaze. And with a calmly low voice, she said, 'It's nothing.'

She told Till, and herself, 'It's just an inconvenience.'

Then before he could respond, she assured both of them, 'Our burn resumes in seven minutes. Using backup pumps, and at full strength. I'll extend the burn to allow for the delay, and the ship will be back on course.'

He had assumed as much. With a heavy shake of the head, he asked, 'Who?'

What she knew, she told.

He repeated the critical word. 'Remoras,' he said, a painful disappointment wrapped around it. Then, 'Which ones? Can we tell?'

Miocene fed him compressed gouts of data, including coded transmissions and visual images culled from distant security eyes. The presumption of guilt was just that. Nothing was perfectly incriminating. But the innocent break-down of the skimmer was too perfect to be believed. She admitted as much, then concluded with the cold, perfectly honest comment, 'I've never particularly trusted Remoras.'

Between them, Till showed less emotion.

'Our enemies,' he said calmly. 'Where are they now?'

A replacement skimmer had rendezvoused with the Remora crew, then continued out onto the ship's leading face. 'I've ordered its capture,' Miocene mentioned. 'But my sense is that they won't be on board.'

Her son agreed, seeing the best alternative. 'The disabled skimmer—'

'Was towed back to the city.'

Till was silent for a long moment.

Through a security nexus, Miocene felt a ripple, a tremor, and her breathing quit abruptly. 'Did you—' she began.

'Wouldn't you?' was his response.

Before Miocene could offer her opinion, he assured her, 'We'll use a minimum of five-person teams. And they'll only search for that one crew. Isn't that the reasonable course?'

'Reasonable or rash,' she answered, 'it's the Master's responsibility. Which means that it's my decision to make.'

Till sighed heavily, then forced a wide smile.

'Make it,' he coaxed.

A universe of data begged to be noticed. In a mostly thorough, near light-speed fashion, Miocene assigned degrees of importance to each bit of news, real or rumored, then absorbed and digested what seemed critical. Small protests were being held in scattered parts of the ship. Weapons had been discharged in half a dozen public venues. But mostly as warnings. With billions of passengers, there was the guarantee that a few of the fights were simply criminal. There was always a perfectly normal trickle of violence. Locke was still missing, a thousand little whiffs of evidence implying that he was killed on the first day. Then she focused on the teams that Till had dispatched to the Remoran city: their makeup; their training histories; their inadequate experience. They were as good as some units, no better than most. But wouldn't this work demand the best? Sending a few bodies into an enemy-held city seemed like such a blatant waste, and dangerous . . .

She lingered on that one telling word.

Waste.

Then again, she examined the damage through the scuttlebug's eyes. She took a deep breath of the blistering plasmas, thinking about the ancient machines that had been slaughtered for no worthy purpose, and she calculated the numbers of engineers and drones that these repairs would demand. Wayward engineers, probably. Since she still didn't yet trust her own corps. And when she was angry enough, her living mouth dropped open, remarking to her First Chair, 'I'm going to let your orders stand.'

'As you wish, madam.'

'Also,' she continued, 'I want a full weapons array positioned nearby. In case our troops are attacked. Where we were when the rockets fired . . . that would be a natural vantage point, and nicely ironic. Don't you think?'

Till's face brightened, and he said, 'All in your service, madam.'

Then he bowed.

Bowed to Miocene, she could only hope.

Forty-three

AN ARMY OF tiny bone-white toadstools stood on a carpet of something dark and wet, with warm, feathery vapors rising into the bright damp air.

For a long while, nothing happened, nothing changed.

Then a fissure opened, and a filthy hand and wrist pushed up into the light, the elbow exposed, the arm bending one way, then the other, fingers obliterating the delicate toadstools with groping motions growing more desperate by the moment.

Finally the hand retreated, vanished.

A half-instant passed.

Then with a sloppy, wet sloosh, the ground spilt wide, and a naked body sat up, spitting and gasping, then coughing with a choking vigor that after several painful minutes fell away into a string of quiet moans.

The man stared at his surroundings.

Surrounding him was a forest of thick-bodied mushrooms, each as large as a full-grown virtue tree. His face was amazed and dubious and frightened, and even when he should have recovered from his suffocation, his breathing remained elevated, and his heart rattled along with an anxious gait, and no matter how many times he wiped his eyes with the dirty heels of his hands, he couldn't make sense of what he was seeing.

Under his ragged breath, he muttered, 'Where? Where?'

At the sound of his voice, a tall man stepped from the mushroom forest. The man was wearing the uniform of a Submaster, but the mirrored fabric was wrinkled and tired, the sleeves frayed, a vertical gash exposing one of his long pale legs. He was smiling, and he wasn't. He approached to a point, then knelt and said, 'Hello.' He said, 'Relax.' He said, 'A name. We usually start with a name.'

'My name . . . ?'

'That might be best.'

'Locke.'

'Of course.'

'What happened to me?' Locke sputtered.

'You were there,' the other man remarked. 'Better than me, you would know what happened.'

Like a person suddenly cold, Locke pulled his knees out of the stinking black earth, grabbing them and holding tight for a long moment. Then he quietly, quietly asked, 'What is this place?'

'Again,' said the man, 'you would know that answer, too.'

Locke's face seemed quite simple, and for the moment, very young. After a thoughtful gasp, he said, 'All right,' and forced himself to look up with a mixture of resignation and hopefulness. 'I don't know you,' he admitted. 'What's your name?'

'Hazz.'

Locke opened his mouth, then closed it again.

'I'll take that as a sign of recognition,' the long-dead man responded. Then he stood and beckoned, telling the newcomer, 'Clean yourself. Tell me what you want for clothes, and they'll appear. Then if you wish, follow me.' The dead man smiled in a knowing fashion, saying, 'I know someone who very much wants to see you.'

LOCKE MUST HAVE been hoping for someone else.

Wearing a Wayward's leather breechcloth, he followed Hazz out of the mushroom forest, and the simple young face vanished abruptly. He was angry now. His back stiffened. His voice failed on its first attempt. Then he forced himself to say, 'Father,' with a pure, unalloyed bitterness.

Diu sat on a petrified toadstool outside a simple shelter, wearing the same gaudy clothes in which he had died. Gray eyes danced. A mischievous look came over his craggy features. Quietly, mockingly, he asked, 'So who murdered you? One of your sons, I can hope.'

Locke stopped short, his mouth grim and determined.

Diu laughed and slapped his knees, then said, 'Or it wasn't. But I bet it was some distant relative. Your own blood, almost assuredly.'

'I had to do it,' Locke grunted. 'You were killing Mother—'

'She deserved to die,' Diu replied, framing the words with big shrugs. 'Escaping from Marrow that way. Too soon, and without warning anyone. Nearly alerting the Master to our presence. How did that help the Wayward cause?'

Locke opened his mouth, and waited.

'She was dangerous,' Diu assured. 'Everything you want and deserve was at risk because of her and because of Miocene.'

A deep breath filled Locke's chest, then lay there growing stale.

'But let's forget your mother's despicable, endurable crimes,' Diu continued. 'There's another offender. Someone who's potentially far more dangerous to the Waywards, and to the Builders' great cause.'

'Who?'

Diu growled, 'Please,' and shook his head in disgust.

Then he rose to his feet, saying, 'You had an assignment. A clear duty. But instead of doing your duty, you rushed off to that alien house as soon as you had the chance. And I want to know why, son. Why was it so fucking important to go there?'

Locke turned in a quick circle, but Submaster Hazz had vanished.

'Tell me,' Diu pressed.

'Don't you know why?'

'What I know,' he replied with a rasping voice, 'is inconsequential. What I don't know, and what matters here, is your response.'

Locke said nothing.

'Were you hoping to find your mother?'

Nothing.

'Because you couldn't have. You and Till couldn't recover her body more than a century ago. What good could you accomplish by going there alone?'

'I don't need to explain—'

'Wrong!' Diu interrupted. 'You do! Because I don't think you know what you want. For this last horrible century, you've been nothing but lost.' His father shook his head, saying, 'I'm not asking these questions to soothe my arrogant soul. I'm asking for the sake of your miserable one.' Then he laughed in a large, tormenting way, adding, 'What? Did you think that being dead was easy? That the Builders would simply ignore your last-breath crimes . . . ?'

'I did nothing wrong!'

'The old Master was digging her way toward Marrow, but the Waywards never knew how she found the old hole. Chances are, a routine search had turned up that hidden doorway.' Diu closed his eyes for a long moment. Then he opened them again, acting angry to find his son still standing before him. 'You went to that leech house . . . you went to see if the old Master had been there first. Because if she had been, then she might have realized where Washen was. And maybe, just maybe, your mother had been rescued. Admit that much to your father, Locke. Go on.'

'Fine. I admit it.'

'Maybe you were afraid that nobody had found your mother, and you wanted to help her. A noble sentiment, always.'

Nothing.

'Because a long burn was coming,' Diu continued. 'The longest in many centuries. And what if her remains were piped into one of the engines, then incinerated? What if that happened before you, the dutiful son, could pull her to safety?'

Locke took a new breath, holding it close to his panicking heart.

'Tell me that's the truth,' Diu snapped.

'It's true.'

The Diu said, 'You're lying,' with a crisp, dismissive confidence. 'Don't try to fool your old father, Locke. I know a little something about telling lies.'

Trembling hands tugged at the breechcloth.

'The fuel tank is a vast ocean of hydrogen – one of several – and what are the odds that Washen would be yanked out of her grave?' Diu rose and took a step toward Locke, and with the gray eyes staring, he asked, 'What are the odds that she would ever be found? Shattered and scattered like she was . . . Washen could have lain in the depths forever, and except for you and Till, and Miocene . . . who would have known . . . ?'

Locke didn't reply.

'About your mother's little clock,' said Diu.

Locke's eyes grew large and simple, and exceptionally sad. Softly, almost too softly to be heard, he asked, 'What do you mean?'

'You and Till cleaned the leech house. It took days and you had minimal resources, but you did an exemplary job of things. Considering.' Diu smiled as if he could see everything, and he remarked, 'It's so very odd, isn't it? Such a good job of hiding your tracks, yet that one critical clue went unnoticed. Left behind, buried deep in the plastic leech wall—'

Locke gave a low, pained moan.

'It makes a person wonder,' his father continued. 'Was it overlooked by chance? Or was it purposely ignored?'

Wide shoulders slumped forward, and Locke stared at his bare toes.

'Or did someone find her clock . . . hold it in his own hands, perhaps . . . then willfully leave it where someone else would have to eventually come across it . . . ? Which is precisely what you hoped would happen, isn't it . . . ?'

'Am I right about that, son . . . ?'

'Till wasn't watching your work, because he trusted you. And you left behind a sign. A marker. Because you wanted very much for your mother to be found . . .'

Locke opened his mouth, then closed it. Then with a new defiance, he screamed, 'No. I won't tell *you*—!'

But Diu wasn't standing before him. Not anymore.

Locke blinked and felt his body sagging, hopelessness mixed with relief. Then a warm hand took him on the bare shoulder, and he turned into her, knowing it was her, crying in the soft angry way of a man who knows that he has been fooled and who discovers that really, at the heart of things, he doesn't even care . . .

'WHAT IS THIS place, and these dead men . . . ?'

'Just another corner of the ship,' Washen assured him, holding him tight around his back and the back of his head. 'Pamir found it before he found my clock. An AI lives here. With my help, it created Hazz. And your father. With its help, I watched your reactions, and parts of your nervous system.'

'You read my mind?'

She said, 'Never,' and relaxed her arms, letting him pull away and look into her face before she confessed, 'You didn't see Wayward soldiers. No one shot at us. That was a different performance, existing as false data fed straight to your eyes and ears. And you're certainly not dead now.'

Relief bled into a guilty, self-aware grimace.

'It's just us,' she promised.

'Pamir?'

'He's doing other work now.' She sat on the petrified toadstool, never taking her eyes off Locke. 'There's nobody else. Tell me what you want to tell me. Then if you wish, I'll let you go back to Till. Or just sit here.' She waited a half-moment, then added, 'And if you don't want to tell me, I'll accept that, too. All right?'

Locke sighed, glancing at his own empty hands.

Finally, quietly, he announced, 'I think I will. Explain things. Maybe.'

Washen struggled to say nothing and to choke down her excitement. Instead, she nodded, and with a gentle voice asked, 'How is our home?'

'Changed,' he blurted. Wide, astonished eyes lifted. 'You don't realize, Mother. This has been a very long century . . . !'

Locke couldn't stop talking, the words coming out under pressure.

'By the time I was home, the Loyalists were gone. Conquered. Dissolved. There were so many sympathizers and outright believers inside your borders that it was an easy invasion. Hazz City was clean and quiet, and very little had changed.' He paused, then said, 'For a while.' He raked his golden hair with both hands, explaining, 'Till and I returned, and Till had me detonate Diu's charges, closing the shaft overhead. Then Till gave a speech to everyone. Standing in your main temple, with Miocene's head at his feet, he told everyone how our societies would join, and everyone would be stronger for joining, and we were part of the Builder's ultimate plans, and soon, soon, soon everything would be explained.' He breathed quickly, deeply. Then, 'You wouldn't know Marrow. It's a very strange place now.'

Washen resisted the urge to ask, 'When wasn't it strange before?'

But Locke guessed her thoughts. He tilted his head as if to reprimand, then with a despairing gasp, he announced, 'Time's very short now.'

'Why? What do you mean?'

'I'm not sure,' Locke confessed.

With a quiet, sharp voice, Washen asked, 'Exactly what do you know?'

'There were timetables. Till wanted us to regain the ship before it changed course. Before today's burn, if possible.' He shook his head, eyes lowering. 'Since you left, our population's grown tenfold. Factories as large as cities. We've been building weapons and training soldiers, and we manufactured enormous boring machines designed to dig upward. And downward, too.'

Washen said, 'Downward,' and leaned closer.

Then with a breathless excitement, she asked, 'Where do you find the power to fuel all of this?'

Locke examined his toes.

She prompted him, saying, 'Till knew. About Diu, he knew. And probably from the earliest times.' Then because she might be completely mistaken, Washen added, 'That's the only way it makes sense to me.'

Her son gave the tiniest nod.

Washen didn't have the luxury of feeling clever. Instead, she dropped to her knees in front of Locke, forcing him to look at her eyes. 'Till knew about Diu's secret caches. Didn't he?'

'Yes.'

'How? Did he see your father using them?'

Locke hesitated, considering. 'When Till was young, just after his first visions, he found a cache. Found it and watched it, and eventually, Diu climbed out of it.'

'What else did he know?'

'That Diu was feeding him the visions. Diu was telling the stories about the Builders and the Bleak.'

She had to ask, 'But why did Till believe any of it?'

A chiding look was followed by a sharp warning. 'Father was an agent, he realized. A vessel.' Locke shook his head, adding, 'The steel bowl doesn't have to believe in the water that slakes a man's thirst.'

'Granted,' said Washen.

'The day the Waywards were born . . . ?'

'What about it?'

'That valley, that place I took you to . . . the hyperfiber cache was tucked inside one of those crevices . . . and we walked right past . . .'

Washen said nothing.

'I didn't know. Not then.' A bitter little laugh leaked out of him. 'Years before, Till asked his mother about security systems. How they worked; how they were fooled. Miocene thought it was good captainly knowledge, so she taught him. Then Till climbed inside the cache and convinced its AI that he was Diu, and he rode it into Marrow. Down beneath all that wet iron, and the heat, he found the machinery that powers the buttresses.'

Quietly, Washen said, 'All right.'

'That's where almost all our power comes from,' said her son. 'The core is a matter-antimatter reactor.'

'Have you seen it?' she asked.

'Just once,' he replied. Then he reminded Washen, or maybe himself, 'Till trusts me. After we returned to Marrow, and after Miocene was reborn, he took us down there. To show us the place. To explain what he knew, and how. All of it.' Another pause. 'Miocene was thrilled. She had a conduit built that taps the energies. She claims that the reactor, once it's fully understood, will transform the Milky Way, and humanity, and each of us.'

'Does that place offer answers?' Washen asked. 'Does it tell us anything new about the Great Ship?'

Locke shook his head, disappointment rimmed with anger.

With a pitying voice, he said, 'Mother,' and stared at her

eyes. He stared and sighed, and as if addressing a small child, he asked her, 'If Marrow hides inside the ship, and if this machinery hides inside Marrow . . . then what makes you think these mysteries ever come to an end . . . ?'

'There's something even deeper?' she sputtered.

A quick, tight nod.

'Have you seen *that*?'

Again, he looked at his toes. 'No,' he admitted. Then after a few deep breaths, he said, 'Only Till has been that deep. And maybe, I suppose, Diu.'

'Your father—?'

'He was also Till's father,' Locke blurted. 'Till always suspected it. In secret. And in secret, he had our best gene-delvers decipher the genetics. Just to be sure.'

Washen silently absorbed the newest revelation.

Then she asked, 'Is that everything you want to tell me? Till's your half brother, and the ship's full of mysteries?'

'No,' Locke replied.

He looked up at the towering mushrooms and gray hints of the hyperfiber roof, and with a weary anguish, he admitted, 'I have certain thoughts. Doubts. For the last century, since I killed Diu . . . I've listened to Till's plans, and Miocene's, and I've helped meet all the deadlines, and I've watched what they've done to Marrow, and its people . . . a place I don't even recognize anymore . . .' Locke took a deep full breath, then said it. 'When I look inside myself, I wonder.'

Down came his eyes, desperate for their mother.

But Washen refused to embrace him again. She stood and stepped back, and finally, with a slow and hard and pitiless voice, she asked, 'Are you one of the Builders?'

The gray eyes pulled shut.

'That's what you're asking yourself. Isn't it?' Then she gazed up at the sky, saying, 'Because if you're not the good souls of Builders reborn, by accident or by design . . . maybe you and Till and the rest of the Waywards . . .

'Maybe you're the Bleak reborn . . . !'

Forty-four

EVERY FACE WAS elaborate and utterly unique, and each had a sturdy, unexpected beauty that always became obvious with time.

Pamir watched the faces and listened to the watery voices.

'It was my decision. My plan. My responsibility.' Orleans's mouth smiled, and his amber eyes changed shape, creating mouth-shaped patterns that mimicked his smile. 'I accept the blame, and your punishment. Or your praise and blessings. Whichever verdict you, in your wisdom, wish to deliver.'

Most of the Remoran judges appeared uncomfortable, and it wasn't because Pamir might be misreading their expressions. One old woman – a direct descendant of Wune, their founder – quoted the Remoran codes. 'The ship is the greatest life. Injure its vitals, and you surrender your own life.' Her single eye, like a ruby floating on yellow milk, expanded until it half filled her faceplate. Then the compressed mouth added, 'You know our codes, Orleans. And I remember two occasions when you carved the life-suit off another offender . . . for crimes less serious than disabling one of the main engines . . . !'

Perhaps a hundred judges and elders shared the diamond building. There were no airlocks, and not so much as a breath of atmosphere. Two doorways opened onto public avenues where hundreds of citizens fought for the chance to see this semisecret trial. Every officious sound was a scrambled broadcast. Unlike Pamir, the audience could only measure the proceedings by watching faces.

Another elder rose to her feet, and into the angry buzz, she said, 'Another code applies. Wune's first and most essential code, as it happens.'

Together, in a shared voice, Remoras chanted, 'Our first duty is to protect the ship from harm.'

The speaker's blue face seemed to nod, and her musical voice offered, 'This could be Orleans's defense, if he chooses. Harm is harm, whether it comes from an impacting comet or a dangerous leadership.' Her helmet pivoted, and she asked the defendant, 'Is this your argument, Orleans?'

'Absolutely,' he cried out.

Then he glanced at his companion, signaling him by swirling his eyes on their stalks.

As planned, Pamir stepped forward. 'Distinguished citizens,' he proclaimed. 'I ask to address the court.'

His lifesuit contained an electronic signature. As Remoras did with each other, a glance was enough to give his name, rank, and official status.

The one-eyed elder grumbled, 'Is this appropriate? A wanted criminal defending a captured criminal?'

But a third elder – a small round fellow with a red-furred face – growled at her, saying, 'Sarcasm later. Talk, Pamir. I want to hear you.'

'There isn't time,' the captain agreed. 'Wayward squads are coming. They want Orleans, but they'll be thrilled to find me, too.'

The one-eyed woman grumbled, 'Good.'

'I wish there was time,' Pamir continued. 'For reflection. For a great debate. For a wise decision rendered by everyone. But every moment makes the Waywards stronger. Every minute, another steel ship rises up from Marrow, bringing soldiers and munitions and a set of beliefs that are laughable, and narrow, and indifferent to the wishes of every Remora.'

He paused a half-instant, checking with a security nexus, measuring the Waywards' steady progress.

Then to the beautiful faces, he said, 'I don't want to be the Master Captain. But the rightful Master is dead, or worse. And I'm the ranking officer. According to the ship's charter, I am its Master, and Miocene is a treasonous pretender. And since I'm parading the obvious here, maybe I should remind you.' He glanced at One-eye, then everywhere else. 'For more than a hundred millenia, you've served the ship and its charter, just as you've served Wune's faith. With devotion and bravery. And what I want from you now − what I am asking for, begging for − is this:

'Resist the Waywards. On my authority as the momentary Master Captain, give them nothing. Not your cooperation, or your resources, or any of your expertise. Is that too much to ask?'

An unnerving silence descended.

Then One-eye stated the obvious. 'Miocene is going to be very unhappy. And these Waywards are sure to respond—'

'Then we'll respond, too,' growled the blue-faced woman.

Every judge spoke, crowding into the same secure channel, the noise defiant and worried, angry and sad. But defiance seemed loudest, and knowing that emotions can change in the beat of any heart, Pamir chose that moment to shout out:

'Will you promise me? To give them nothing?'

A quick vote was taken.

Two of three Remoras nodded, saying, 'Agreed.'

Then Pamir made the next logical step.

He said, 'Good. And thank you.'

If he was going to escape the Waywards, he was going to have to slip away now. But instead of fleeing, Pamir stepped into the middle of the blister-shaped building, and again, quietly, he repeated the admonition, 'Give them nothing.'

Then with the heavy grace of his lifesuit, he bent his legs and dropped to the floor, sitting on the smooth gray hull of the Great Ship.

WAYWARD TEAMS WERE forcing their way through the bystanders. Pamir heard the broad-band squawk of sirens and saw bright helmets parting to let them pass. But he remained sitting, like the elderly judges and Orleans, showing a grim, determined face, spending those last moments reminding himself that he had done a few things just as stupid as what he was doing now.

But very few, and always for himself. No one else riding the risk.

Another harsh squawk caused the last civilians to scatter, and purple-black lifesuits emerged from the chaos, marching through the doorways with lasers held high and hard gray faces showing behind the faceplates – the descendants of lost captains, their strong features laid over a tough, uncompromising nature.

The soldiers' armor was light, and their weapons could have been stronger. Miocene, or someone, was showing a calculated restraint.

Pamir took a deep breath, and he held it deep.

Two of the Wayward teams blocked the open doors. A third discovered an unregistered staircase leading into the city's basement. The final two teams found Orleans, their lasers kept high but ready as they scanned him, then as they examined the other Remoras.

'On the authority of the Master Captain—' a Wayward began.

'Whose authority?' dozens of voices replied, in a sloppy chorus.

'We take this man into custody—'

A taunting laugh broke out from some, while other Remoras remained silent. And One-eye shook her head, cautioning, 'We should do as they want.'

With a blurring voice, the Wayward listed other suspected saboteurs. Then with his free hand gesturing and his urgent voice breaking, he told his soldiers to hurry their scans. 'Fast, and right!' he barked. 'Fast, and right!'

But the rest of Orleans's crew was missing. Soldier after soldier said as much, their grim faces suffused with a toxic mixture of excitement and fear and an instinctive disgust. It took two scans, then a naked-eye stare through the face-plate for someone to say, 'This isn't one. Like the others, Look, sir.'

Pamir forced a grin, and finally, he let his spent breath slip out of his mouth.

A slow, astonished expression spread across the Wayward's face. And after a little gasp, he said, 'It's that missing first-grade, sir. It's Pamir!'

The ranking Wayward turned, and said nothing.

Every soldier felt surprise, then a wild, unexpected elation that ended when the blue-faced Remora announced. '*This* is the Master Captain. Our guest, in our home. Which means—'

'Take him!' the ranking Wayward cried out.

Half of the Remoras screamed, 'No!'

The Wayward pointed his weapon, warning everyone,

'Stand out of our way, or I'll cut you out of your fucking shells! Am I understood?'

Plainly.

One-eye was sitting on a standard Remoran squirt-pack. She had volunteered for the duty, arguing that even if she didn't agree with the vote, it had been taken, and perhaps the soldiers wouldn't scan her as closely as some. The pack's safeties were dismantled. Its vents were permanently closed. When she kicked it into the center of the room, the Remoras and Pamir remained sitting, doing nothing but turning toward the rounded wall, putting their armored packs between them and the makeshift bomb.

The explosion was silent, then otherwise.

Pamir was still on the hull, head thrust between his knees, and the sudden blast smacked him across the slick grayness, bouncing him against Remoras and soldiers, and finally, one shoulder slamming into the diamond wall.

The building filled with a temporary, scorching atmosphere. Standing bodies were flung hardest, and lasers were ripped loose, and in the next seconds, in that purposeful mayhem, new hands grabbed the lasers, their safeties instantly rendering them harmless.

Pamir staggered to his feet.

His left knee was shattered, but the suit's servos made the leg carry him. He screamed, 'Orleans,' three times before the welcome figure appeared next to him, then sprinted ahead, the Remora flinging himself down the staircase.

A laser blast emerged, punching through the rounded ceiling.

Then the soldier was wrestled down, her weapon yanked free, and Orleans waved and called out, 'This way,' and sprinted along a narrow, barely lit hallway. His lifesuit was punctured. Pamir saw a white fountain of leaking vapor. Orleans's self was dissipating into the vacuum. But not too quickly, thought Pamir. More hope at work than any expertise.

The hall divided three ways.

Left, right. And straight down.

Orleans turned, and in a gesture old as humankind, he placed one of his gloved fingers to his rubbery mouth.

'Quiet,' he was saying.

Orleans dove into the black bottomless hole.

Feet first, Pamir followed.

In that perfect darkness, there was no sense of falling. The body felt nothing of its own rapid acceleration, and time seemed to slow, and Pamir was trying to relax, readying himself for a distant floor, when a voice suddenly, unexpectedly whispered into his ears.

'Pamir?' said the voice. 'Can you talk?'

Washen.

'Can you hear me, Pamir?'

He didn't dare use even a scrambled channel. Someone might hear his convoluted bark, then trace the source. But maybe Washen realized as much, because she kept talking, making it feel as if they were falling together.

'I've got news,' she reported. 'Our friend has helped, and will help us . . .'

Good.

'But I need to know,' she continued. 'Will our other friends assist? Have they agreed to fight with us?'

Just then, something powerful struck the hull.

For a screeching instant, Pamir brushed against the shaft wall. The entire hull was rippling under the impact. Then he was tumbling through space again, free of weight, momentarily functioning as a tiny, tiny starship . . . and he closed his eyes, remembering to breathe, then telling Washen, and himself, 'The Remoras will fight.'

He whispered to her, 'We've got ourselves a war.'

THE BLEAK

MY PERFECT, ETERNAL solitude shattered by a wealth of stars, and by life, boisterous and abundant life, and it felt as if this was how it had always been. Skies filled with suns and living worlds, and the life within me fat and steady, prosperous beyond need or reasonable want, and how could it be any other way? Life peaceful, more than not. Life punctuated with great loves and endurable defeats. Life conjuring children out of semen and egg, software and cold crystals, and those children racing through their fresh-scrubbed incarnations with an innocent zest that always eroded into the steady cool pleasantness that is a mark of maturity that time, under its tireless hand, forces upon each of us.

I had nearly forgotten Death.

Not as a theory, never. As a principle and occasional tragedy, I couldn't help but think of that great balancer. But as hard practicality — as the simple inevitable consequence of Life — Death seemed as left behind as my ancient, much treasured solitude.

Or perhaps I never actually knew Death.

To me, Her face appears grim and self-assured, yet unexpectedly beautiful. That beautiful face rests on a tall body growing stronger as the carnage worsens, and more lovely. A body that feeds on one soul or ten million souls, choosing her mouthfuls with a fickle maliciousness sure to leave the living wondering:

'Why not me?'

'Why am I still here, alone?'

I hear their voices. From my skin come murmurs. Shouts. Coded ticks and great white roars of EM noise, and always, lovely Death drinks in their glorious misery.

'Abandon your station . . . now . . . !'

'Attack . . . now . . . !'

'Do you see them . . . no . . . not yet, no . . . !'

'Hold—'

'Not there, you need to be . . . by the patch-and-pray shop
. . . do you see, no . . . !'

'Retreat—!'

'Casualties . . . in excess of . . . eleven million in the bombardment, and twenty million displaced into basements . . .'

'They ambushed us at the assembly point, with machine-shop
nuclears . . .'

'Kill me. If it comes to it.'

'I will. I promise.'

'Casualties eighty percent. Swarm still functioning.'

'Fall back, and dig . . . !'

'We have a reactor sabotaged. Off-line. Request engineers.'

'How about it? A quick screw?'

'Prisoners will be assembled here. Ranked according to their
likely knowledge here. By me. Then taken home for interrogation, or disposed by standard means . . .'

'Fanatics.'

'Maniacs.'

'Soulless fucks.'

'How about a really quick fuck?'

'Come see, come see! I want to show all of you. These are
cyborgs, my friends! Much as the Bleak were! Nothing but
machines with odd guts shoved inside them. Here, touch their
guts. Touch them, and smell them. Make yourselves clothes with
this odd flesh. Cut up their shells for trophies. Machines and
meat, and a great evil, and nothing else. I promise you—!'

'Casualties, ninety-two percent. Swarm effectiveness diminished.'

'Escape wherever you can, however you can . . .'

'NOTICE: WITHIN THE LAST SHIPMENT OF
PRISONERS WAS A CAMOUFLAGED FINGER OF
ANTIMATTER. ALL PRISONERS MUST BE EXAM-
INED THOROUGHLY BEFORE EMBARKING—'

'Retreat again . . . with all available skimmers . . . !'

'They're the Bleak, reborn! And this is our duty, and our honor, to chop them open and kill them slowly—!'

'Our last city . . . Wune's Hearts . . . abandoned . . .'

'NOTICE: PASSENGERS ARE NOT SUBJECT TO THE SAME TREATMENT AS REMORAS. THEY MAY NOT BE SUMMARILY EXECUTED, REGARDLESS OF BEHAVIOR. CIVIL CODES WILL REMAIN IN EFFECT. ALWAYS. FROM THE OFFICE OF THE MASTER CAPTAIN—'

'I won't tell you anything, Bleak! Ever!'

'They're calling us the Bleak now. Whatever that is. I don't know. Considering, maybe we should be insulted . . .'

'Press them! Run them!'

'I'm finished, and you promised.'

An EM crackle, then a solid whump.

'Good dreams, friend.'

'My swarm's gone. No one else alive. My family, most of them, are in Happens River. Tell them—'

'All right you shits! I'm a Bleak. We're all pretty fucking Bleak in here. Does that scare you? Does that make you want to drip your piss? Because we're going to keep holding our positions, you fucks, and if you want to take us, you've got to follow your piss down into our hole—!'

'All engines secured!'

'Reactors, on-line!'

'Waywards, they keep coming . . . new units keep coming . . . there's more Waywards than we've got stars . . .'

'Again, retreat. You know how!'

'PUBLIC ANNOUNCEMENT: FIGHTING SLOWS IN THE INSURRECTION'S LAST HOURS. THE SHIP'S TRAILING FACE IS SECURE. ESSENTIAL SHIP OPERATIONS HAVE NEVER BEEN IMPAIRED. PASSENGER DISTRICTS HAVE NEVER BEEN ENDANGERED. FOR YOUR SUPPORT AND YOUR

BLESSINGS, THANK YOU. FROM THE OFFICE OF THE MASTER CAPTAIN—'

'So we've got some time. How about a slow screw?'

'Sounds nice.'

'Doesn't it, now?'

Forty-five

ONE OF THE generals said it first, and said it badly.

'The Remoras are just about beaten,' he declared, standing over the latest strategic holomaps. When he realized that the Master had overheard his audacious words, he straightened his back and squared his shoulders, adding, 'We've destroyed every one of their cities, imprisoned or killed most of them, and pushed their refugees out onto the ship's bow. Without cover, and with only a fool's hope left to them.' Then he said, 'Madam,' with a minimal bow, smiling in the Master's direction while his pale eyes kept careful track of Till.

A reprimand was in order.

Something blunt, and powerful, and lasting.

Miocene showed a narrow grin, and in a near whisper, she assured her officer, 'There is nothing to celebrate here.'

'Of course, madam.' Again, the little bow. 'I simply meant—'

She stopped him with a crisp wave of the hand, and said nothing.

Instead of the expected words, Miocene stared at each of her generals, and Till, then conspicuously looked at no one when she said, 'When we first arrived here, I noticed a man. A human male standing outside the bridge, wearing nothing but a handwritten sign.'

Silence.

'The End Is Here,' she quoted.

The silence grew less sure of itself.

'I'm a busy person, but I still have time enough to ask simple questions.' She shook her head, telling everyone, 'He was a fool, obviously. One of those poor souls whose focus narrows too much, who can't work free of some consuming, pathetic idea. For the last six centuries, that fool wore his sign in public. Outside the Master's station. Did you know that? Did you know that he painted those words on fresh parchment every morning, careful to never repeat the curl and color of any letter. Why that was important to him, I can't say. Two days ago — the last time I left these quarters — I could have stopped for a moment and asked him those questions. I could have let him explain his passions to me. "What makes it so important, sir, that you're willing to invest hundreds of years in what looks futile to a normal soul . . . ?"'

Miocene sighed heavily, then admitted, 'Even if I wanted, I couldn't ask him any questions now. Nor could I help him, if that's what I thought was best. Because he has vanished. More than two hundred thousand mornings of rising before dawn and painting his important pronouncement according to his difficult, choking logic . . . and for some reason, the fool couldn't stand on his usual ground two mornings ago. Or yesterday morning. Or today, for that matter. I can't see him through any of my security eyes. Quite simply, he has vanished. Now don't you think that is odd?'

One of the Wayward generals — Blessing Gable — cleared her throat, squared her shoulders, and started to say, 'Madam—'

'No. Shut up.' Miocene shook her head, then warned everyone, 'I'm not interested in anyone's reasons. Not for this or for that. And frankly, the fate of one odd soul is not particularly compelling to me. What sickens me is knowing that someone made assumptions, not asking simple questions first. What worries me is my own simple question: "What else are my arrogant, inexperienced generals forgetting to ask themselves and each other?"'

Till stepped forward. This staff meeting belonged to

him. For sturdy and obvious reasons, Miocene had given her First Chair responsibility over the war. She had too many new duties of her own to embrace just now. Besides, these events were too large and much too savage to directly involve a Master. Better her son than her, yes. Not one nanogram of self-doubt gnawed at Miocene now.

'You're right, madam,' Till allowed. Then he showed the generals how to bow, saying to the foot-worn marble floor, 'It's too soon to call anything won, madam. Victory comes at a terrible cost. And of course the Remoras may only be the first of our enemies.'

She said, 'Yes. Yes. Exactly.'

Because this wasn't her meeting, she was free to leave it. A show of power was her only agenda, and she turned suddenly, strolling toward one of several hallways leading into the back of the Master's mazelike apartment . . . telling her son on a private channel, nexus to nexus, 'When you're finished here, come see me . . .'

'Yes, madam,' said a crisp voice. While the voice on the private channel promised, 'It won't be long, Mother.'

Miocene thought to glance over her shoulder. But no, that would do little good. She knew from experience that she wouldn't see unexpected emotions in those faces. Ask all the simple questions you want, she told herself. But don't waste precious energy when you know that the answers, pleasing or bitter, will simply refuse to show themselves.

THE APARTMENT HAD always been familiar terrain, and a weaker person, infected with self-doubts, might have avoided these rather small, always comfortable, and purposely ordinary rooms. But the new Master had never considered living anywhere else. If she deserved the old Master's chair, then why not the woman's home? Indeed, after these first weeks, the hallways and alcoves, potted jungles and even the old expansive bed, made Miocene feel nothing but at ease.

Her bed already had an occupant.

'The meeting—?' he began.

'Everything is fine,' she replied. But to be certain, she linked herself to security eyes and ears, the constant bark and flutter of her generals interrupted by the quieter, more forceful growl of Till. After a moment of satisfied eaves-dropping, she asked, 'Is there progress?'

'Of a slow sort,' Virtue replied. 'Yes.'

The Remoras knew how to damage the ship. It seemed that Wune's professed love for this machine didn't mean much, and they were attacking it with the same zest with which they fought her office and her authority. In an instant, Miocene consumed the latest damage reports and repair predictions, one of her nexuses failing to give her the data on her first try.

In a crisp, angry voice, Miocene said, 'That problem's surfacing again.'

'That's what I warned you about,' he replied. Virtue regarded her with bright gray eyes, too big for his face and too open to hide anything. 'What we're doing to you . . . well, it's never been done. Not to a human. Profound changes—'

'"—in a profane amount of time." I remember what you, and everyone, has told me.' She shook her head regard-less, then casually told her uniform to melt at the shoul-ders, the fabric collapsing onto the living rug, leaving her wide and deep and lovely body shining in the bedroom's false sunshine.

She sat on the edge of her bed.

Virtue moved nearer, but it took him a moment to find the strength to touch her on the bare breast. Of course he didn't like her new body, and of course she didn't care. Nexuses needed room and energy, and her body had to increase proportionally to her responsibilities. Besides, Virtue's timidity had a charm. A sweetness, even. She couldn't help but smile, eyes dropping, watching those little fingers desperately caress the brown expanse of her left nipple.

'We don't have time,' she reported. 'My First Chair will be here soon.'

Virtue was thankful for that, but he had poise enough to make his hand linger for a moment longer, fingers feeling the nipple swell with blood and newer fluids.

When his hand vanished, she told her nightgown to dress her.

Afterward, speaking with a quiet concern, Virtue reported, 'You look tired. Even more than usual, I think.'

'Don't tell me to sleep.'

'I can't tell myself to sleep,' was his reply.

Miocene began to smile again, her head turning and her mouth opening, a compliment phrased and ready to be uttered. 'I wish you were as good with my nexuses as you are with my mood.' She fully intended to say those words, but an abrupt, unexpected urge became a coherent flash inside one of her working nexuses . . . and she hesitated after saying only, 'I wish . . .'

Virtue waited, ready to smile when it was his turn.

She focused on something no one else could see.

After a long moment, her lover mustered the courage to ask, 'What's wrong?'

Miocene said, 'Nothing.'

Then she rose from the bed, looking at her nightgown with a confused expression, as if she couldn't remember asking for it.

Again, she said, 'Nothing.'

Then Miocene told Virtue, 'Wait here. Wait.' She took a step toward the room's back wall, ordered her uniform to cover her body again, and for a third time, with barely a whisper's force, she said, 'Wait,' as a doorway appeared in what looked like polished red granite.

'But,' he sputtered, 'where are you—?'

The door closed and sealed behind her.

That the Master's apartment had secret places had been no surprise. As First Chair, Miocene realized that the complex layout of rooms and hallways left spaces for privacy, or avenues of escape. The only surprise was that these secret places were at least as ordinary as the public ones. They were blandly furnished, and more than not, without clear purpose. The largest of the hidden rooms had been improved already during her tenure, then filled with severed, slowly mummifying heads. It seemed an appropriate means of storing the disposed captains, cruelty and banality perfectly joined together. But the room behind her bedroom was much smaller, and no one, not Virtue or even Till, knew that it contained a hidden hatchway that the former Master had had installed during some recent attack of paranoia, the hatchway leading to an unregistered cap-car that had been built on-site, ready for this exact instant.

Once under way, Miocene made certain that no one was searching for her. And only then did she reexamine the message that had found its way to her on one of the oldest, most secret channels employed by captains.

'Here's what I propose,' said the familiar voice, and the very familiar face, speaking to her from a holobooth inside a certain waystation deep in the ship.

A booth she already knew well, it turned out.

The woman smiled, her black hair short and downy, her features bright and smooth as if the flesh and nose and the rest of her had just been regrown. She smiled with a mixture of smug pleasure and vindictiveness, telling Miocene, 'I know what the Great Ship is. And I really think you need to know, too.'

Washen.

'Meet me,' said the dead woman. 'And come alone.'

When she first saw the face and heard those unlikely words, Miocene had nearly muttered aloud, 'I won't meet you, and certainly not alone.'

But Washen had anticipated her stubbornness, shaking her head with a genuine disappointment, telling her, 'Yes, you'll meet me. You don't have a choice.'

Miocene closed two of her eyes, letting her mind's eye focus on the recorded message, on those deep, dark, and utterly relentless eyes.

'Meet me in the Grand Temple,' said Washen.

'In Hazz City,' she said.

'On Marrow,' she said.

Then she almost laughed, and looking at the Master's imagined eyes, she asked, 'Why are you afraid? Where in all of Creation could you possibly feel as safe, you crazy old bitch of bitches?'

Forty-six

A FLEET OF old skimmers and sleeks and retrofitted capcars fled across the endless hull, dressed to resemble the battered hyperfiber beneath, their engines masked and muted, and every vehicle surrounded by false cars – holo-echos designed to be obvious, hopefully looking danger-ous or weak, the projections begging the Waywards to fire at them instead of tormenting phantoms that might or might not be.

Orleans was steering one of those phantoms.

An EM pulse had pushed its AI pilot into insanity, leaving him no choice. The same pulse had killed its main reactor, leaving them depending on an auxiliary that whispered to the driver. 'I am sick. I need maintenance. Do not depend on me.'

The Remora ignored the complaints. Instead, he looked back at the passengers, a whisper-signal carrying his minimal question:

'How soon?'

'Ninety-two,' said a white-as-milk face.

Minutes, she meant. Ninety-two minutes, according to the latest projection. Which was too long, and what could be taking so much time . . . ?

But he didn't ask the question.

Instead, he spotted a Wayward dragonfly lifting up off the horizon behind them, trying to catch them. Too late, he whispered, 'Target.' Two baby men in the back of his skimmer had seen the enemy, and they were aiming at the fly's weakest centimeter. But their ad hoc laser needed too much time to charge up, and a burst of focused light swept away holoprojection – a column of purple-white light dancing along the hull with an eerie grace, searching for something to incinerate.

Too late, the boys cried out, 'Charged. Fire—!'

But Orleans had jerked the wheel, spoiling their aim, and where they would have been was blistered with the raw energies, a trailing EM scream stunning everything electronic within a full kilometer. Every lifesuit seized up for a horrible instant. The skimmer's controls obeyed imagined orders, ignoring real ones. With his private voice, Orleans cursed, and he regained control after everyone's living juices had been jerked savagely by the gees, and he cursed again, sharing his feelings with the others.

Again, a voice said, 'Fire.'

Their weapon was tiny compared to the Wayward's, but it had sighting elements ripped out of one of the ship's main lasers – elements meant to find and strike dust motes at a fantastic range – and the soft narrow bolt reached up into the bright lavender sky, then reached inside the armored target, bringing it plunging down to the hull, where it belonged.

There was a little cheer.

Pure reflex.

A dozen new phantoms appeared beside them, but none looked convincing. Orleans saw that immediately, and he realized that their projectors were mangled now, failing fast, and he erased the phantoms before the Waywards noticed.

Better to depend on your own camouflage now. And if he could, catch up with the rest of the fleet, then get lost among their countless phantoms and deceits.

That seemed possible, for a little while.

The woman behind him, eavesdropping on a secure channel, leaned forward and shoved him on a shoulder, his suit's false neurons too fried to feel more than a slight pressure. But he appreciated the pressure, the touch. Orleans leaned back into it, and again, he asked, 'How soon?'

'Forty,' she replied.

The sabotage teams were back on schedule. And in twenty-two minutes, they would be inside the bunker.

The woman almost spoke again, but her voice was interrupted by the complaining voice of the skimmer's reactor. 'I am failing utterly,' it declared. Then with a prickly pride, it told Orleans, 'I will last another eleven minutes. I promise.'

He said, 'Fuck,' to himself.

Then with a whisper, he told the others, 'Sorry. No roof for us.' Then he asked, 'Any ideas? Anyone?'

There was no sense of surprise. What Orleans saw in the faces and could practically taste in the ether was nothing but a weary disappointment that evaporated in another moment. Two weeks of war had done it. Emotions were as flattened and slick as new hyperfiber. Then because it was expected, the gunnery boys said, 'We should turn around. Turn and charge the fuckers, and kill a few of *them*.'

They wouldn't kill anyone, except themselves.

Orleans turned in his seat, showing them his face. Hard radiations had blistered his flesh, leaving mutations and weird cancers that appeared as lumps and black blisters. Amber eyes dangled, and his tusks were misaligned. But his defiant mouth announced, 'That's not a choice.'

Dozens of faces closed a wide, splendid assortment of eyes – a sign of the purest Remoran respect.

'I know a place,' he confessed. 'Not a bunker by design. But it's got a roof.' Then he turned forward, muttering, 'At least I hope it does,' as he wrestled the skimmer into a new course.

Again, the woman touched him on the deadened shoulder.

Was she going to tell him the time?

But no, she only wanted to feel him. And as he massaged the last drops of energy out of the skimmer's dying reactor, and himself, Orleans concentrated on the dim touch of her hand, treating himself to a fantasy older than their species.

REMORAS EXISTED BECAUSE the hull needed constant repair.

What they did very well. But not perfectly. Speed was

critical when a deep blast crater needed to be filled. Hyperfiber, particularly the better grades, was sensitive to a multitude of variables. And on occasion, mistakes were made. One layer went bad before it could cure, and already one or more new layers were on top, soft as flesh and as pliable. Freed volatiles made bubbles. Bubbles weakened the patch. But to tear out the newest work and repair the damage meant time lost, and worse, it gave the universe an opportunity to strike the comet's grave with a second, perhaps larger comet.

'Better to let the flaw remain,' Wune had said, speaking about hulls and about other matters, too. 'Build around it, and preserve it. Remember: one day's flaw will be another day's treasure.'

A spacious flaw lay far out on the ship's leading face. Hidden tunnels led into a chamber large enough to hide every surviving Remora, and stockpiles of machinery and shop-made weapons had been delivered secretly over the last ten days, making a last-stand fortress out of someone's long-ago fuck-up.

Except Orleans would never reach it. His skimmer was barely able to fight its way within four kilometers of a smaller, less secure bubble. He had found it while visiting one of the tall bone-white memorials to read the names of dead friends – centuries ago, on some look-around tour. Beside the memorial was a frozen gas vent leading into the hull, into a cramped, lightless, and not particularly deep bubble.

When the skimmer died, he shouted the obvious advice: 'Run!'

Lifesuits had strength, not speed. A dreamlike slowness and a dream's sense of utter helplessness held sway, each man and woman pounding along a smooth and gray and essentially featureless plain. If not for the memorial, they would feel lost. The white spire beckoned from the first clumsy stride, and every eye that looked up could measure their progress, the minds behind the eyes thinking, 'Closer.' The mouths saying, 'Not far.' Everyone lying with a desperate earnestness, whispering to each other, 'Just a few more seconds. Steps. Centimeters.'

The sky was purposely ignored.

The lavender fire of the shields was brightening, capturing greater and greater amounts of gas and nanoscopic dusts. The giant lasers continued pummeling hazards big as fists and men and palaces. And blotting out the usual stars was a single swollen red giant sun, ancient and dying, its mass already touching the ship, starting to pull at its trajectory.

A brighter flash of light came from behind, startling everyone.

The boys said, 'Skimmer,' and nothing more.

Orleans let himself slow, looking backward long enough to see darting shapes and more bursts of light. Lasers, and in the distance, the soundless delicious flash as nuclear mines detonated themselves.

Then he was running again, falling behind everyone and thinking, 'We have time,' when he knew full well they didn't. An army of Wayward monsters were charging, and if the last timetable was right, they had barely three minutes left before . . .

Before.

Then he stopped his thinking and looked up, and again, quietly and confidently, he told himself, 'Just a few more steps.'

The memorial was too tall and close to absorb with a look, but it was still too far away to feel imposing. Orleans looked down again. He forced the servos in his legs to drain themselves fully with each stride, and he used his own muscles to lengthen the strides, and because it made him feel better, he cursed with each ragged wet breath.

The milk-faced woman said, 'Hurry.'

He looked up again, realizing that he was falling farther behind.

She said, 'Faster,' and glanced back at him, one long bright arm waving clumsily.

Orleans's suit was in desperate trouble. He knew it before its own machinery confessed to any weakness, war and bad luck having eroded the servos in both legs, both falling within three strides of each other.

'Piss away,' he cursed.

His muscles lifted his legs and dropped them again.

The suit was fantastically heavy, but their goal was finally close. Honestly, teasingly near. Orleans grunted and took another few steps, then had no choice but to stop and stand motionless, his deep perfect lungs sucking in free oxygen wrenched from his own perfect sweet piss and blood, feeding the black blood that needed a few moments to purge the muscles of toxins, bringing them back into something resembling fitness.

His people were at the spire's base, disappearing one after another into a tiny, still invisible hole.

Again, quietly, the woman told him, 'Hurry,' and turned and waved with both arms, her face just visible, something about its whiteness afraid.

Orleans staggered, stopped. And as he gasped again, he turned his head and looked back over the ground that he had covered. Armored vehicles were skittering and skidding across the grayish plain. Following some Wayward logic, each was shaped like a bug, useless wings folded back and jointed legs holding weapons, one laser firing, a blistering light sweeping over him and slashing into the memorial, then continuing on into infinity . . . the white spire melting near its base, tilting with a silent majesty, then collapsing without so much as denting the hull.

A second blast melted the memorial's raw base.

Where was the woman, and the others?

Orleans couldn't see them, or anything but a sudden pool of melted hyperfiber. Maybe they were underground, and safe. He kept telling himself it was possible, even likely . . . and after a little while he realized that he was running again, legs trying to carry him away from a swift, relentless army.

He couldn't look more pitiful.

He reached the edge of the molten goo, and because there was nothing else to do, he turned again and stared at his pursuers. They were almost on him. In the end, seeing that he was alone and defenseless, they were taking their time. Maybe he would make a valuable prisoner, the monsters were telling each other. Maybe the top monster Herself would reward them for capturing a tremendous criminal like Orleans.

He took a long exhausted step backward.

The hyperfiber was fantastically hot, and deep, and filled with bubbles of freed gases. But without an influx of energy, it was curing again. It would be sloppy, a very weak grade, and someday someone would have to wrench it off the hull and replace everything. Then build an even larger memorial, of course. But Orleans's suit was hyperfiber, too. An excellent grade, if somewhat battered. It could withstand the heat. His flesh would blister and boil, yes. But if he could keep his diamond faceplate from bursting, then maybe . . . maybe . . .

He stepped back once more.

And stumbled.

The weight of his reactors and recyke systems helped drive him partway under the surface, and the pain was vast and relentless, then in another moment, there was no pain.

Orleans's helmet and head were the only parts of him in view, and his face survived long enough to let his eyes stare up at that big glorious red sun, shrouded in the shields and the constant bursts of laser light . . . and then he was wondering if it was time, and maybe he should try to dive deeper . . .

Suddenly, without the smallest warning, the shields evaporated, and every one of the giant lasers quit firing at the coming hazards.

And one breath later, a sudden and fierce rain began to fall . . .

Forty-seven

BECAUSE THEY SAW a Wayward car — a little machine patterned after a copperwing — Washen and the others climbed up into the epiphyte forest, into a camouflaged blind, watching from above as the car set down on the graveled shoreline. Because he could have been anyone, they kept hiding when a man with Pamir's face and build jumped out, big boots kicking the gravel and a hard, tired voice calling, 'Washen,' over the constant rush of the river. Because was Pamir, and tired, he said to the forest, 'I guess you thought again and changed your mind.' He shook his head, saying, 'Good. I can't blame you. I never liked this leg of our plan.' Then he lifted his gaze, somehow knowing exactly where to stare.

Washen stood, shouldering her laser as she asked, 'Could you see me?'

'Long ago,' he replied with a crisp sense of mystery. Then he motioned at the car, telling her, 'It's stolen. Scrubbed and reregistered, if we did everything right.'

Quee Lee and Perri stood. Then finally, Locke.

A sudden dull shiver passed through the canyon. One of her newly implanted nexuses told Washen what she'd already guessed: a comet had impacted on the hull, instantly obliterating a thousand cubic kilometers of armor.

'If you're going,' said Pamir, 'you've got to go now. Everything's late as it is.'

Quee Lee touched Washen on the arm, and with a motherly concern, she said, 'Maybe he's right. You shouldn't do this.'

They were filing down onto the gravel bar. To her son, Washen said, 'Make sure you're happy with things. Quickly.'

Locke nodded grimly, leaping into the hovering car.

She reminded everyone, including herself, 'We need bait, and we need it convincing. Delicious and substantial. What else can we offer but me?'

No one spoke.

'What about Miocene?' she asked.

'She got your invitation twenty-three minutes ago,' Pamir reported. 'We still haven't seen any traffic that might be her. But it's a long trip, and unplanned, and since she's got to suspect an ambush, I don't expect her to come too fast or follow the easy routes.'

A massive shudder rumbled through the ship's body.

'The biggest yet,' was Perri's assessment.

The shields had been down for five minutes. 'What's the official explanation?' Washen asked.

'Remoras are bastards,' said Pamir. 'Officially, they're proving themselves to be enemies of the ship, and in another ten or twenty or fifty minutes, repairs will be made, the shields will be restored, and within the day, every last bastard will be dead.'

Boom, and then a sudden second boom.

From inside the car, Locke shouted, 'Everything's ready.'

Washen jumped inside, paused and took a ragged breath. She was anxious, and it took a moment for her to realize why. No, not because she was the bait. Her thundering heart had nothing to do with any danger. In a perfect peace, she would feel the same way. She was returning to Marrow after more than a century's absence. She was returning home, and that was enormous in its own right.

Washen waved to Quee Lee and her husband.

Then the steel door was yanking itself shut, and with a hurried, inadequate voice, she called to Pamir, 'Thanks for these days.'

WAYWARD SECURITY WAS thorough.

Was seamless.

And it was totally unprepared for an invasion of exactly two people: a famous dead captain and her even more famous son.

'You've been missing,' a uniformed man declared, staring at Locke with a mixture of awe and confusion. 'We've been looking for your body, sir. We thought you were killed that first day.'

'People make mistakes,' was Locke's advice.

The security man nodded, then stumbled over the first obvious question.

Locke answered it before it was asked. 'I was on a mission. At the insistence of Till himself.' He spoke with authority, and impatience. He sounded as if nothing could be more true. 'I was supposed to recover my mother. By any means, at any cost.'

The man looked small inside his dark uniform.

Glancing at their prisoner, he said, 'I should beg for instructions—'

'Beg to Till,' was Locke's sound advice.

'Now,' the man sputtered.

'I'll wait inside my car,' promised one of the greatest, most honored Waywards. 'If that's all right with you.'

He had no choice but to say, 'Yes, sir.'

The waystation was perched on the throat of the access tunnel. Traffic flowed rapidly up and down. Washen saw giant steel vehicles patterned after the familiar hammerwings. The empty ones dove into the kilometer-wide maw, while others appeared beneath them, rushing fresh units into the gaps in the Wayward lines.

The war's carnage was relentless. And perhaps worse for the ship was the swelling, unstable panic among passengers and crew.

Washen closed her eyes, letting her nexuses sip updates. Coded squirts. Images from security eyes and ears. Avenues and public plazas were filled with terrified, furious passengers. Angry voices blamed the new Master, and the old Master, too. Plus Waywards. Remoras. And that largest, most terrifying foe: simple stupidity. Then she watched dust and pebbles falling at one-third lightspeed, smashing Wayward vehicles as their terrific momentum was transformed into a brilliant light and withering heat. An army had charged into the Remora's desperate trap, and it would be dead in another few moments. But a new army was coming to replace what was lost. Washen opened her eyes and watched the steel hammerwings rising up to the fight. And in that mayhem of coded messages and orders and desperate pleas, one small question was misplaced. Then a fictional but utterly believable answer was delivered, wrapped snug inside bogus encryption seals.

The waystation's AI examined the seals, and because of

a subtle and recent failure in its cognitive skills, it proclaimed:

'From Till, it is. And it is authentic.'

With a palpable, almost giddy relief, the Wayward told Locke, 'You need to take the prisoner home. Great sir.'

'Thank you,' Locke replied.

Then he unberthed their car and dove after one of the empty hammerwings, accelerating until the rising hammerwings blurred into a single dull line — all of Marrow seemingly rising up now, eager to behold a vast and exceptionally dangerous universe.

'CHANGES,' LOCKE HAD promised.

He had thoroughly described the new Marrow, displaying a good poet's taste for sadness and Irony. Washen came with expectations. She knew that the compliant Loyalists had finished Miocene's bridge, then with Wayward resources, the bridge had been improved, making it possible for whole armies to be transported through the fading buttresses. The old captains' base camp housed the engineers who quickly rebuilt the access tunnel. Energy and every raw material had been brought from the world below. Lasers with a fantastic punch had widened the old tunnel, and the chamber's own hyperfiber was salvaged and re-purified, then slathered thick and fast on the raw iron walls above. Then the same lasers were moved, digging a second, parallel tunnel barely wide enough for power and communication conduits. That was dubbed the Spine. It linked Marrow to the ship, making them one and the same.

With a soft pride, Locke mentioned, 'From here, everything is our work.'

The tunnel suddenly became narrower, hammerwings missing them by nothing in the silent vacuum.

'How strong is it?' Washen inquired.

'Better than you would think,' he replied, his voice almost defensive.

Again, Washen closed her eyes and watched the war. But the Waywards had retreated, or died, and most of the Remoras' links were dead. There was nothing to see except the battered hull glowing red, radiating the heat of impacts and battles as well as the bloody glow of the passing sun.

She shut down all of her nexuses, and she kept her eyes closed.

Quietly, Locke identified himself to someone, then demanded, 'I need immediate passage to Marrow. I have a critical prisoner with me.'

Not for the first time, Washen asked herself:

'What if?'

Locke had offered to bring her here. On his own, without compliant, he had helped find workable ways through the security systems – a journey that had gone remarkably well. Which made her wonder if everything was a ruse. What if Till had told his old friend, 'I want you to find your mother somehow. For both of us. Find her and bring her back home, and use any means you wish. With my blessing.'

It was possible, yes.

Always.

She remembered a different day, following their son into a distant jungle. Locke was obeying Till's orders then. Unlikely as it seemed, it could be the same now. Of course, Locke hadn't warned anyone about the rebellion coming, or the Remoras' plan to scuttle the ship's shields. Unless those events had also been allowed to happen, serving some greater, harder-to-perceive purpose.

She thought about it again, and again, with a muscular conviction, she tossed the possibility aside.

The hammerwing in front of them was slowing.

Locke pulled around it, then dove for the still invisible bottom.

Perhaps he guessed his mother's thoughts. Or maybe it was the moment, the shared mood. 'I never told you,' he began. 'Did I? One of Miocene's favorites came up with an explanation for the buttresses.'

'Which favorite?'

'Virtue,' Locke replied. 'Have you met him?'

'Once,' she admitted. 'Briefly.'

Their AI took control, braking their descent as they passed thousands of empty hammerwings docked and waiting for the next belly full of troops.

'You know how it is with hyperfiber,' her son continued. 'How the bonds are strengthened by taming little quantum fluxes.'

'I've never quite understood the concept,' she confessed.

Locke nodded as if he could appreciate the sentiment. Then he smiled. He smiled and turned to his mother, his face never more sad. 'According to Virtue, these buttresses are those same fluxes, but they've been stripped of normal matter. They're naked, and as long as they have power, they're very nearly eternal.'

If true, she thought, it would be the basis of another fantastic technology.

Her mind shifted. 'What did Miocene think about his hypothesis?'

'If that's true,' he said, 'it would be an enormous tool. Once we learned how to duplicate it, of course.'

She waited for a moment, then asked, 'What about Till?'

Locke didn't seem to hear her question. Instead, he mentioned, 'Virtue was worried. After he offered his speculation, he told everyone that stealing energy from Marrow's core was the same as stealing it from the buttresses. We could weaken the machinery, and eventually, if we weren't careful, we might even destroy Marrow and the ship.'

Washen listened, and she didn't.

Their car had passed through a quick series of demon doors and slowed to a near stop, and suddenly the tunnel around her opened up, revealing the diamond blister below, the bridge thick and impressive at its center, and Marrow visible on every side. She thought she was prepared for the darkness, but it surprised her regardless. The entire world had swollen since she was last here, and it had fallen into a deeper dusk, countless lights sparkling on its iron face, each little light plainly visible through a hot, dry atmosphere.

Marrow was one vast, uninterrupted city.

And despite being warned, Washen felt a sudden sadness.

'Till listened to Virtue's worries,' Locke reported. 'Listened to every one of them, and he looked concerned throughout. But do you know what he said to that man? What he said to all of us?'

Obeying some inaudible command, their car dove toward the bridge, toward an open shaft. Toward home.

'What did Till say?' Washen muttered.

'"These buttresses are too strong to be destroyed that easily," he told us. "I'm certain of it." Then he showed his smile to each of us. You know how he smiles. "They're simply too strong," he repeated. "That would be too easy. The Builders don't work that way . . ."'

Forty-eight

FROM THE BREATHING mouth came a long whistle, hard and sharp, plainly excited.

Pamir growled, 'Quiet.'

As if it were necessary; as if anyone could possibly hear them inside here.

'She comes,' said the translator fused to the harum-scarum's chest. 'I see the false Master. One little shot, and she is forever removed.'

'No,' said Pamir. Then he announced to everyone, 'We will wait. Wait.'

He was speaking to five hundred humans, including seven of the surviving captains, and perhaps twice as many harum-scarums. But this was a mammoth facility, and most of them were busy attacking the last-moment work with their ad hoc training and a professional desperation. Booby traps had to be found and disabled. Machinery that hadn't worked in billions of years had to be awakened, in secret. And this team's actions had to be married to the actions of twenty other teams, each operating at a key note, everyone pushing to meet a timetable that looked more fanciful with each worried breath.

Again, the harum-scarum said, 'I will shoot her.'

'Shoot yourself,' Pamir snapped.

That was a savage, dangerous insult; suicide was the ultimate abomination.

But the alien had known Pamir for a long time, respecting him in a joyless fashion. He decided to absorb the insult without comment. Instead, an enormous finger pointed to a tiny knot of data moving rapidly down the fuel line, and with a slow, reflective whistle, he told the human, 'This is the false Master's vehicle. It is. And with the reigning confusion, no one will miss her until it is too late. If you allow me—'

'Expose us?'

Both mouths closed tight.

Pamir shook his head, disgust mixed with a burning fatigue. 'Miocene isn't an imbecile. Mask your scan to make it look Wayward, then examine that car as it passes. She won't be on board. Even in a hurry, she knows better.'

The alien made ready, big hands and an obstinate mind sending out a string of crisp instructions to hidden sensors.

Pamir hunkered closer to the viewing port, watching the Waywards' steel vehicles rising and falling past their hiding place. Miocene's cap-car was a tiny fleck of hyperfiber, barely visible to the naked eye and past them in a half-instant. He waited another few moments, then asked, 'What did you see?'

'A passenger.'

Pamir nearly flinched. Then he thought to ask, 'What sort of passenger?'

'Composed of shaped light,' the harum-scarum confessed. 'A holo in the false Master's likeness.'

A single nod was the only gloating that Pamir allowed himself. Miocene probably slipped inside one of the empty troop cars, telling no one her whereabouts . . . in case her enemies were waiting en route . . .

The gloating quiet was interrupted by a sudden deep rumbling.

In the distance, humans and harum-scarums called out to each other, asking, 'An attack? Or another impact?'

'An impact,' barked several knowledgeable voices.

'How big?'

'How bad?'

A fat comet had struck not far from Port Erindi, and

scanning the early data, Pamir knew it was a huge blast. A record breaker. He fought the urge to call the Remoras, to order Orleans or whoever was left to bring up the shields again. But it was still too soon. 'Keep working,' he told everyone, including himself. And he stared at images stolen from farther below, picking one of the steel machines at random, watching it plunging into the access tunnel's mouth, rushing past the waystation where Washen and her son had lingered, waiting for permission before vanishing into those impossible depths.

Suddenly, with absolutely no warning, one of the team leaders whispered into his ear. 'We're ready here. The big valve is ours.'

And in the next instant, another voice – the translated boast from a harum-scarum engineer – announced, 'We're prepared here. Against much greater odds, and unseen, and ahead of schedule.'

Pamir let himself think: It's going to happen . . . !

His heart responded, swelling and pounding hard against his throat, his voice nearly breaking when he asked the alien beside him, 'How are we?'

'Close,' the whistle promised.

A pause.

The next whistle was a curse. 'A stranger's shit,' said the harum-scarum, an instinctive rage rising, then collapsing again.

'What's wrong?' Pamir asked. 'Don't tell me it's the pumps . . .'

His companion said, 'No.'

A fat, spike-nailed thumb pointed, showing him that one of the rising vehicles was slowing in front of them, deploying antennae and sturdy lasers, armored soldiers already marshaling inside its injection airlocks.

'My scan—' the harum-scarum moaned.

'Or it's a routine patrol,' Pamir offered. 'Or someone noticed their power being funneled away.'

The alien moaned, saying, 'If it was me, I will shoot myself.'

Pamir said, 'Fine.'

He backed away from the viewing port and viewing screens, stepping out onto a gangway that he helped build just a century ago. People were specks, almost unnoticed in the darkest corners. The giant pumps looked close in the ancient gloom, and they were deceptively simple: slick balls and eggs of hyperfiber wrapped around machinery vaster than any heart, and fantastically strong, and durable enough to wait for billions of years before they took their first thunderous beat.

This was the same pumping station that the captains had used as a blind. The Waywards had searched it thoroughly, and with good captainly tricks, they had tried to secure it. On occasion, they sent patrols. But there were only so many soldiers, and there were thousands of kilometers of fuel lines begging to be guarded, and there was a war to wage, and they were always too much in a hurry to dismantle the sophisticated camouflage that Pamir had helped install.

In a whisper, he asked his team, 'How soon?'

'Ready,' said a few.

'Soon,' others promised.

Then he returned to the port and screens, estimating how soon the Waywards would be shaking his hand.

'Ready,' said another voice. And another.

The harum-scarum remarked, 'With what we have now, we can do it.'

Fewer pumps than ideal, and not every valve in their control. But yes, they could do it. What he had dreamed up in Quee Lee's apartment and what had always felt slippery as a dream . . . it was a genuine reality now . . . somehow . . .

Both of the alien's mouths opened, and the air-breather whistled, 'We must now. Remove these monsters from the universe.'

Pamir said nothing.

Again, he looked through the port, watching the bug-shaped chunk of steel aligning itself for an assault. Then he glanced at a snoop screen. A bright sparkle marked another descending car, this one dropping faster, showing not so much as a breath of caution.

Pamir told his ally, 'No.'

Then he told every team in a thousand-kilometer radius, 'Finish your preparations. Do it now.'

The alien gave out a sharp, furious whistle, the translator having the diplomatic sense not to explain what had just been said.

'We're waiting,' Pamir repeated. 'Waiting.' Then to himself, under his breath, he muttered, 'This crazy trap needs to be a little more full.'

Forty-nine

NEARLY FIVE MILLENNIA had been spent making the climb to freedom. A strong soul accomplishes what can only be considered impossible, building a society out of nothing, then gaining her destiny as her fair reward. How else could Miocene look at this epic? Yet she found herself suddenly retracing her ascent, making the desperate long fall in what felt like the jump of an eye, the throb of the heart, too quickly to suffer even the littlest doubt. And all because a dead colleague and the closest thing to a friend sent her a few words, promising to meet her and tell her a story.

Plainly, this was someone's trick.

Miocene saw the obvious instantly, and instinctively.

But even then, she left the security of her station, her decision made. Then the Remoras brought down the ship's own shields, and she began to understand what an enormous trap this could be. Yet she continued the plunge. Able to lead from anywhere, she spat out orders and directives and fierce encouragements and outright threats, helping make certain that the insurrection would be crushed shortly. Then she arrived victorious at the apex of the new bridge, stepping out of the empty hammerwing and toward the waiting car . . . and she hesitated, finding herself staring across the swollen gray face of Marrow, if only for an instant . . .

The guard on duty – a square-faced man named Golden – stepped close and smiled up at the ship's Master. Then with a proud voice, he reported, 'I sent them straight down, madam. Straight on down.'

She had to ask, 'Who's that?'

'Locke and his prisoner,' he answered, his tone asking in turn, 'Who else do you expect?'

Miocene said nothing.

Slowly, slowly, she pulled her eyes closed. But in her mind she could still see the cold lights of Marrow, and its black iron face. She saw them better with her eyes shut. And what she felt, if anything, was an infectious relief. And a jittery, infinite joy.

If this was someone's ambush, she reasoned, then Washen was the bait. And Miocene reminded herself that she wasn't without resources, and tremendous power, and oceans of experience and cleverness, and cruelty, too.

Every possibility was reviewed in succession. Then she made the same decision again, with a new resolve.

Opening her eyes, she glanced at Golden, saying, 'Good,' without focusing on his smiling and proud and exceptionally foolish face.

Miocene told the earnest man, 'Thank you for your help.'

Then she stepped into the sealed, windowless car, sat in the first chair, and with a single word, she was falling again, fast and then faster, the weary old buttresses reaching through the wall and licking at her mind, making her feel, for just those sluggish few moments, wondrously and deliciously insane.

Fifty

THE TEMPLE ADMINISTRATOR will wore the long gray robes of her office and still fought against any force that might threaten to disrupt her life or her day. She rose to her feet, staring at the newcomers with a sputtering horror, then she crossed her arms, took a fierce quick breath, and exhaling with an obvious pain, said to Washen, 'No.' She snapped, 'You died a hero. Now stay dead!'

Washen had to laugh out loud, replying, 'I've tried to be dead. I did my very best, darling.'

It was Locke who stepped forward. He moved close enough to intimidate, then spoke with a soft rapid voice that left no doubt as to who was in charge. 'We need one of the temple's chambers. We don't care which. And you will personally bring your guests to us, then leave. Is that understood?'

'Which guests—?'

'The sad souls locked inside your library.'

Washen leaked a smile.

The woman opened her mouth, framing her rebuttal.

But Locke didn't give her the chance. 'Or would you rather be reassigned, darling? Maybe to one of these heroic units heading up onto the hull.'

The mouth pulled shut.

'Is there a free chamber?' Locke asked.

'Alpha,' the administrator allowed.

'Then that's where we'll be,' he replied. And with a captain's decorum, he waited for the underling to turn and slink away.

It was a short, illuminating walk to the chamber.

Washen was prepared for changes, but the overcrowded and desiccated world outside remained outside. The hallways were nearly empty and exactly as she remembered them, complete to the potted flycatchers. And while the air was drier than before, and probably purified, it still managed to stink of Marrow: rusts and bug dusts and heavy metals, not to mention a subtle odor that could only be described as *strangeness*.

A pleasant stink, she found herself thinking.

The occasional parishioner bowed to Locke, then gawked at his mother.

She noticed how everyone seemed equally thin, as if an orchestrated famine were in effect. But at least everyone was dressed in simple clean clothes that they hadn't made from their own flesh. A leftover Loyalist tradition? Or maybe hungry people couldn't heal quickly enough to make skinning themselves worthwhile.

She didn't let herself ask.

Suddenly impatient, Washen stepped into the chamber, her simple presence causing lights to awaken. The domed ceiling was exactly as she remembered it, pretending to be the sky, and behind the polished steel railing, the diamond likeness of the bridge was much the same. But the bridge was thicker and and stronger and better shielded than Aasleen's original plans, conduits filling two shafts, then merging at the old base camp: an armored thread just visible, clinging to the curved sky for perhaps ten kilometers, then vanishing again.

The Spine.

'Is this a model?' she asked.

Locke had to look up, taking a moment to decipher the question. 'No,' he allowed. 'It's a holoprojection. Real time, and accurate.'

Good.

Then she looked at Locke, ready to thank him again. And to compliment him on everything that he had already done.

A new voice interrupted them.

'It is,' someone cried out. 'Washen!'

Manka's voice, followed by Manka. And Saluki. Zale. Kyzkee. Westfall. Aasleen. Then she stared at the siblings. Promise with Dream beside her, as always. Both were shuffling forward, feet never quite leaving the floor. The legs and faces were the same, only thinner. There was a chill to their touch, and behind the chill, a desperate warmth, and a genuine happiness, and then a reflexive concern that Washen wasn't real or might vanish any moment.

'I'm real, and I might get taken away,' she allowed.

More than a hundred old captains hugged her or each other. Close whispering voices asked, 'How's the mutiny today?'

'Which mutiny?' Washen asked.

Aasleen understood. She laughed and straightened her

back, then the folds in her badly worn uniform. 'We've heard rumors. Grumbles. Warnings.'

'New, half-trained guards have replaced our old keepers,' Manka offered. 'And the old ones didn't look very happy about their prospects, either.'

Faces turned to the diamond bridge and the distant images, and for a long while, nobody seemed able to speak.

Then Saluki asked, 'What about Miocene? Is the new Master healthy, or are we going to be happy?'

Washen almost answered.

But as her mouth drew its breath, a new voice called to them from the entranceway, telling them, 'Miocene is very healthy, darling. Very healthy. And thank you so much for your sweet, heartfelt concerns.'

THE NEW MASTER strode among the captains.

She seemed unconcerned by any threat, and to the distant eye, she would have appeared to be in total control. But Washen knew this woman. The swollen face and body hid clues, and the bright uniform gave her an instant, effortless authority. But the eyes were open and obvious. They danced and settled on Washen, then danced again. Surrounded by once loyal captain, she seemed to be deciding which one might strike her first. Then she looked past them, those cold dark eyes contemplating enemies that couldn't be seen from here.

In a voice that sounded in perfect control, she told Washen, 'I came. Alone, as you asked. But I assumed that it would be just the two of us, darling.'

For a careful moment, Washen said nothing.

Silence irritated Miocene and dragging her eyes back to Washen, with a grumbling tone, she said, 'You wanted to tell me something. You promised to "explain the ship," if I remember your words.'

'"Explain,"' Washen responded, 'is perhaps too strong. But at least I can offer a new hypothesis about the ship's origins.' Gesturing at the long virtuewood seats, she told her fellow captains, 'Sit. Everyone, please. This explanation won't take long, I hope. I hope. But considering what I want to tell you, you might appreciate being off your feet . . .'

WITH ONE HAND, Washen pulled the clock from her pocket, the lid popping open with the touch of her finger. Then without looking at its face, she closed it again, and holding it high, she said, 'The ship.'

She said, 'How old?'

Before anyone tried to answer, she said, 'We found it empty. We found it streaking toward us from what's perhaps the emptiest part of the visible universe. Of course, we uncovered clues to its age, but they're conflicting, imprecise clues. What's easiest to believe is that four or five or six billion years ago, in some precocious young galaxy, intelligent organic life arose, and it lived just long enough to build this marvel. To fashion the Great Ship. Then some horrific but imaginable tragedy destroyed its builders. Before they could claim their creation, they were dead. And we're just the lucky ones to find this ancient machine . . .'

Washen paused for a moment. Then quietly and quickly, she said, 'No. No, I think the ship is much older than six billion years.'

Miocene rose for the bait.

'Impossible,' she declared. 'How can you explain *anything* if you let yourself entertain that idiocy?'

'Trace its course backward through space and time,' Washen interrupted, 'and you see galaxies. Eventually. Empty space allows us a long view, and these are some of the oldest infrared specks of light that we can see. The universe wasn't a billion years old, and the first suns were forming and detonating, spewing out the first metals into the tiny hot and exceptionally young cosmos—'

'Too soon,' was Miocene's response. Unlike most of the audience, she was standing, and carried by a mixture of nervous energy and simple visceral anger, she approached Washen, her fists lifting, taking hard little jabs at the air. 'That's far too soon. How can you imagine that sentient life could have evolved *then*? In a universe with nothing to offer but hydrogen and helium and only thin traces of metals?'

'Except that's not what I'm proposing,' Washen replied.

The puffy face absorbed the words, and the mouth opened again. But Miocene didn't make any sound.

'Think even older,' Washen advised. Then she glanced at Aasleen, at Promise and Dream, telling them, 'Locke explained this to me. At the center of Marrow, hydrogen and antihydrogen are created. Each fuses with its own kind. And the two kinds of helium ash are fused into carbon atoms. And the process leads to both flavors of iron, which the reactor throws together, annihilating both. And the energies from this bit of wizardry power the buttresses, and the Wayward industries, and cause Marrow to expand and contract like a great heart.'

'We've heard about the buttress engine,' Aasleen offered.

Washen nodded, then said, 'Under our feet, it's like the Creation.'

A few hungry faces gave knowing nods.

Miocene bristled but said nothing.

'We've always accepted that the ship was carved out of an ordinary jupiter,' Washen continued. 'And Marrow must have been carved from that jupiter's core. But I think we're confused here. I think we've got it backward. Imagine an ancient, powerful intelligence. But it's not organic. It evolves in that rapid, dense, rich environment of the earliest universe. Using the engine beneath us, it creates hydrogen and carbon and iron. Creates every element. Our ship could have been built from scratch. From nothingness. Perhaps before the universe was cold enough and dark enough for ordinary matter to form on its own, someone constructed this place. As a lab. As a means of looking into the far, far future. Although if that's true, I wonder, why would these Builders then throw their fancy toy so very far away?'

The chamber was silent. Alert.

'Clues,' said Washen. 'They're everywhere, and they're meant to be obvious. But the mind that left them for us was strange, and I think, it was in an awful hurry.'

She glanced up at the diamond bridge, breathed deeply and said, 'Marrow.'

She looked at Aasleen, saying, 'This is a guess. Nearly. But there are good reasons to imagine that Marrow may have been the first place where organic life evolved. Under a bright, buttress-lit sky, in an environment cold and empty compared to the surrounding universe ... the first microbes were born, then evolved into a wide range of complex organisms ... this place serving as nothing but an elaborate stage where future kingdoms and phyla got their first tentative existence ...

'The engines and fuel tanks and habitats were built later. What was learned here was applied to its design. Humans found untouched stairs waiting for humanoid feet. Why? Because according to the Builders' research, organic evolution would inevitably build creatures like us. We found environmental controls ready to adjust atmospheres and temperatures according to the physiologies of our passengers. Why? Because the Builders could only guess at our specific needs, and they were eager to be helpful.

'Remember our old genetic research?' she asked Promise and Dream. 'Marrow life-forms are ancient. More genetic diversity than anything found on normal worlds. That tends to hint that this is a very, very old place—'

'What about those first humanoids?' Dream asked. 'What happened to them?'

'They went extinct,' his sister replied instantly. 'Small, highly adaptable species are what's needed here. Not big apes stomping around on big feet.'

Aasleen offered a raised hand, then her question. 'I don't understand. Why build such a big wonderful machine, then throw it away? Maybe I'm too much of an engineer, but that sounds like a miserable waste.'

Washen dangled her clock on its chain, and she said, 'Clues,' again.

Then she twirled her clock and flung it down the aisle, a dozen gaunt hands reaching out and missing it, the bright alloyed case hitting the floor with a hard click, then skidding toward the far end of the chamber, into the shadows and out of sight.

'Not only did they throw it away, but they threw it where it was certain not to hit *anything* for a long, long while.' She spoke slowly, with a certain and easy weight. 'They sent it through the expanding universe, making sure that it pierced each wall of galaxies where the wall was thinnest.' A pause. Then, 'They didn't want it found, obviously. And if the ship's motion had varied by a nanoscopic bit, it would have missed our galaxy, too. Missed us and continued on out of the Local Group and into another vacuous realm where it would go unnoticed for another half a billion years.'

She paused, then said, 'The Builders.'

She shook her head and smiled, admitting, 'I never wanted to believe in them. But they're real, or at least they were. Somehow, Diu sensed a portion of their story. And so has Till. And so have all the Waywards. Through their culture or through some preplanned epiphany, humans have the capacity to absorb and believe in a story that is probably more than fifteen billion years old . . . a story from the beginnings of our Creation, and despite the cushion of time, it is a story that I suspect is still important. Still vast. Still and always, and I think we've got to face that unlikely fact . . . !'

Miocene was staring at the floor, her face taut and startled, her fists fallen to her sides and forgotten.

A captain shuffled toward Washen, placing her broken clock into her offered hand.

Washen said, 'Thank you,' and waited for him to sit again. Then in a careful voice, she said, 'If the Builders were real, then there must have been the Bleak. Except I think the Waywards have things a little backwards. The Bleak didn't come from outside, trying to steal the Great Ship. At least not according to our sense of geometry.' She hesitated, not quite looking at the captains. Then she asked, 'Why would you build a great machine, then throw it away, and throw it as far as possible? Because the machine serves a specific, terrible purpose. A purpose that demands isolation and distance, plus the relative safety that comes with those blessings.

'I can't know this for sure, but I'm guessing that the Ship is a prison.

'Beneath us, beneath the hot iron and even underneath the buttress engine, lives at least one Bleak. I'm guessing. The buttresses are its walls. Its bars. Marrow swells and contracts to feed the buttresses and keep them in good repair. The Builders assumed that those who first boarded the ship would be careful and thorough, and Marrow would be found soon enough. Found and deciphered. But the poor Builders didn't guess, except maybe in their nightmares, that our species would come here and realize nothing, then make the Builders' prison into a passenger vessel – a place of luxury and small endless lives.'

Washen paused, breathed.

For a long moment, Miocene said nothing. Then in a low, furious voice, she asked, 'Have you spoken to my AIs?'

'Which AIs?'

'The old scholars,' she said. Then she looked up at the arching ceiling, admitting, 'One of those machines made a similar prediction. He said that the ship is a model of the universe. He claimed that Marrow's expansion is supposed to mimic the universe's inflationary period, and then comes lifeless space, and farther out are the living spaces . . .'

The woman shook her head, then dismissed everything with one word.

'Coincidence.'

Aasleen asked the obvious. 'If this a prison, then where are the guards? Wouldn't the Builders leave behind something to watch over everything, and when the time came, explain it to us?'

Locke answered.

Standing beside and a little behind his mother, he reminded the captains, 'Guards are wonderful. Until they decide to change sides.'

'The Bleak is imprisoned,' Washen offered, 'but I think it can whisper between the bars. If you know what I mean.'

Half a hundred captains muttered, 'Diu.' Muttered, 'Till.'

'Both of whom went deep inside Marrow,' Washen reminded. Then she glanced at her son, biting her lower lip before adding her last speculation.

'The Bleak,' she said, 'isn't some Builder who turned evil.'

She said, 'It has to be something else entirely.'

With a booming voice, she said, 'The Builders couldn't reform the entity, or destroy it. All they could do was put it away for the time being. And now the Builders have vanished. Have died. But the thing beneath us still lives. Is still dangerous and powerful. Which pushes me toward the opinion that what we have here − what our stupid ambition has forced us to claim − is an entity even older than the Builders. Even tougher. And after it's been locked away for so long, I think it's safe to guess what it wants . . . and that it will do anything to achieve its ends . . . !'

Fifty-one

THE INJECTION AIRLOCKS hit the wall with a soft, sudden thump, shaped nukes piercing the hyperfiber, the roar muted by the wild keening of the pumps. Then came the abrupt purple-white flash of lasers, absolutely soundless, and Pamir hunkered down, shouting at the harum-scarum, shouting, 'Shoot the car . . . !'

But the little car braked suddenly, slipping behind one of the empty troopships, letting the ship's lasers intercept the spray of baby nukes while its bug-shaped body absorbed the furies of every retrofitted laser and microwave shout that the harum-scarum could aim. Steel turned to slag, and the slag exploded into a fierce white-hot rain . . . and the car accelerated again, dashing past the pumping station . . . gone . . .

The harum-scarum said nothing about his lousy aim.

Pamir growled, 'Shit,' and turned to his companion,

finding no one. Where the alien should have been standing, a cloud of incandescent gas and ash drifted with a deceptive peacefulness. The gangway had melted. A random blast from below, or they would have killed him, too. Pamir wheeled and sprinted for the nearest lift-tube, his laser panning for him, his most secure nexus awakened, his quick command wrapped deep in code and squirted to every team and every AI.

'Flood the bastards,' Pamir roared.

Then he leaped inside the tube, and a lift-glove grabbed him and accelerated him upward, moving too fast for him to keep his feet under him. As if suffering from a savage beating, Pamir dropped to his knees, then his aching belly, and as he lay motionless against the padded floor, it occurred to him that the pumps' keening had changed. A deep, powerful throb rose up to him as liquid hydrogen passed through the greedy mouths, gaining a terrific velocity, a swift river born in an instant, vaster than any Amazon and fabulously, righteously furious.

A TEAM OF harum-scarums had closed the giant valve.

A column of frigid, pressurized hydrogen struck the valve, and the enormous fuel line shuddered, shivered and held.

Hydrogen pooled and swirled, and half a hundred hammerwings – manned and empty – were swept down in the maelstrom. Slammed against the walls and valve, the abrupt cold shattered their alloyed hulls, splinters and anonymous gore swirling, then slowing as the pool grew deeper, settling on the bottom as a thin, uncomplaining sediment.

At the waystation, duty threw a yoke on the panic. The ranking officer – the same officer who had allowed Washen to pass – called to Till. To Miocene. Both were below somewhere, at risk. He estimated flow rates and offered computer simulations of the impending flood, and with a dry, scared, sorry voice, he mentioned, 'Maybe sir, madam, you should close the tunnel. Save Marrow.' Preset charges would crack the new hyperfiber walls, and the collapse would seal everything. Would save the Waywards for another day . . .

At first, Miocene didn't reply.

Till did. With a calm, almost indifferent voice, he told everyone in his command, 'The tunnel remains open. Now, and always.'

'Now, but not always,' the officer grumbled.

'If you can,' Till advised, 'save yourself. And if you cannot, I will kiss your soul when you are reborn again . . . !'

The officer straightened his back, and unable to imagine any solution, he stood beside the nearest window, and waited.

A falling hammerwing appeared.

It was the same ship that had attacked the enemy stronghold, airlocks deployed, then shattered, its gray carapace thrown against the opposite wall and plunging into one of the waystation's buildings. There was a momentary vibration, then a high-pitched crash. Surprised, the officer realized that an atmosphere had formed outside, hydrogen fuel evaporating, forming a thick sudden wind that he could almost feel, one hand now pressed against the diamond window as the wind rose into a hurricane, then something much worse.

'But if nobody closes the tunnel,' he whispered to himself, 'and if this flood reaches my house . . .'

Obviously, Till didn't understand the problem.

On a different channel, the man called to Miocene. And hoping that she was listening, he explained everything again, letting the panic creep into his voice.

Outside, the torrent was worsening. The hydrogen had filled the fuel line level to the waystation, the first fingers of liquid racing between the buildings, then quickly rising into a wall that swept over and down, tugging and wrenching at the armored structures and at the scared little souls inside.

To himself, staring out into that roaring blackness, the officer said, 'Shit.'

He said, 'It's not supposed to be this way.'

Then another voice joined him, close and familiar. Respected, if not loved. The voice asked, 'What are you doing?'

'Miocene?' the man whispered. Then he explained, 'Nothing. I am waiting.'

'I don't understand . . . what . . . !'

He said, 'Madam,' and turned, confused enough to think that perhaps the Master was standing beside him. But she wasn't there. It was just a familiar voice on his nexus, angrier than he had ever heard it before.

Miocene screamed, 'What, what, what are you doing!'

'Nothing at all,' the man promised.

And again, he touched the window, feeling the brutal chill slipping through it . . . and there was a soft, almost inconsequential creak from somewhere close . . . and the man's last act was to pull his eyes shut, something in that very simple, very ancient reflex lending him the strength to keep standing his ground . . .

Fifty-two

'WHAT, WHAT, WHAT are you doing?!'

The question roared out of every one of Miocene's mouths and through every nexus, and it exploded from the flesh and spit and ceramic-toothed mouth inside the Great Temple. Her words were carried up the newly made Spine, then amplified, passengers and crew listening in a horrified amazement as the ship's new Master seemed to be asking each of the cowering fools to explain what they were doing.

Billions answered.

In whispers, grunts, and farts, songs and violent shouts, they told the Master that they were scared and sick of feeling this way, and when would she get the shields to work again, and when could their lives be their own again . . . ?

Miocene heard none of them.

Wild dark eyes stared at the watchful captains, and at Washen, and at Washen's betrayer son. But the only face Miocene could see was streaking down the access tunnel, approaching the bridge now. That pretty face was smug, then hopelessly distracted, then it was enraged by something that it saw in the distance, then smug again when the problem resolved itself. And finally, with a strange, almost embarrassed smile, Till met his mother's stare, looking up at one of the car's security eyes, remarking to his companion, 'I think she understands . . . finally, finally . . .'

Virtue shrank as if expecting to be beaten. Then with a low, desperate squawk, he said, 'I had no choice, madam. My love. No choice, ever—'

Miocene fled the falling car.

Returning to the Temple, rejoining the captains, her

oldest mouth took a deep, useless breath before declaring, 'I've been an idiot.'

Washen nearly spoke, then seemed to think better of it.

Aasleen tried to comfort the Master. 'We couldn't have imagined it, much less believed it,' she remarked, thin black fingers caressing her own astonished mouth. 'Assuming that there really is such a thing as the Bleak, and the ship's its prison . . .'

Miocene put her arms around herself and squeezed hard, and sobbing, said, 'No. No, I don't believe this. No.'

How long had tears been running on her face?

Washen looked at the other captains, and quietly, with a comforting matter-of-factness, she explained, 'This was a trap. Maybe there is a Bleak under us, and maybe not. But there are creatures called Waywards, and they've taken charge of my ship, and I want that to end. Now.'

In crisp, clear terms, she described the hydrogen river falling toward them, and she estimated when gravity would bring the river this far. Of course the base camp overhead would be obliterated. And the diamond blister. And the bridge. Then the cold fluid would turn into a horrific rain, static electricity or someone's forgotten candle starting a great fire. Marrow's oxygen would try to consume the flood, transforming hydrogen into sweet water and a fierce heat. But the fuel tank was vast, and eventually, there would be no more oxygen. Eventually the frigid rain would fall unencumbered onto the ash and iron, and the dead, and the Wayward civilization would be dead . . . and after a moment's pause, Washen added, 'There's only one other choice. Or two.' She was staring at Miocene again, feeling enough confidence to bristle. 'Your total surrender,' she offered. 'Or I suppose, if you can, you could kick the wall of the access tunnel, kick it good and hard, collapsing it and destroying the Spine and plugging everything before the flood reaches us.'

A perverse pleasure took hold of Miocene.

She was still weeping, still miserable. But even as she pushed the tears across her swollen, unfamiliar face, she felt a smile forming. With a cold horrible joy, she told Washen, 'You're clever, yes. I see how you stole those pumps and valves. I couldn't steal them back again. Not in time, probably. But when I look up at those pumps, do you know what else I see? Do you know what's happening up there?'

Washen gathered herself, then asked, 'What?'

Miocene linked with the chamber's holoprojection, and she showed them. In an instant, after a silent command, the captains found themselves inside an observation blister on the ship's backside, surrounded by towering rocket nozzles that were doing nothing. Except for the steep, almost lazy tilt to each of them, they seemed perfectly ordinary. But even as a dozen voices begged for explanations, fires large enough to broil worlds rose up out of them, plumes of gas and light racing for the stars.

Every nozzle was firing.

No captain could remember a day when every engine was needed, and with a confused amazement, they asked for explanations.

'It's my son,' Miocene confessed.

Again, she grabbed hold of herself, and she squeezed, angry hands jerking at her swollen, useless flesh, yanking until vessels burst and blood flowed from beneath her hard fingernails.

'When we made the last little burn, I thought I was the one controlling the engines,' she muttered. 'And Till let me believe whatever I wanted to believe . . .'

Washen stepped close enough to touch her. And with

a crisp voice, she said, 'I don't care about Till. I want to know . . . why he is firing the engines *now*!'

Miocene laughed, and sobbed, and laughed harder.

Then Washen swept her long hands through her dark hair, and in the words of every pilot about to crash, she whispered, 'Oh, shit.'

Fifty-three

A BRUTAL CHILL took Washen by the throat and by the belly, and for a slippery instant she found herself waiting for the panic. Hers, and everyone's. But the enormity was too much, and it hit them too suddenly. Among the captains, only Miocene seemed able to grieve with the proper anguish, collapsing to the steel floor, hands clawing at her thick neck as she sobbed, incoherently at first, then muttering to herself with a robust, unexpected confidence, 'This is my catastrophe. Mine. The universe will never forget me, or forgive me. Ever.'

'That's enough,' Washen growled.

The captains whispered to one another and moaned under their breath.

Washen yanked at the woman's hands and hair, forcing the anguished eyes to look up at her. Then with the sturdiest voice she could manage, Washen said, 'Show us. Exactly what's happening. Show us now.'

Miocene closed her eyes.

The captains found themselves standing on the ship's leading face, staring up at a senile red sun that seemed large and frighteningly close. But they had several billions of kilometers left to cross. At one-third lightspeed, the journey would take fifteen hours, and according to exacting plans drawn up centuries ago, they would miss that sun's hot atmosphere by a comfortable fifty million kilometers.

With each passing second, their course was being changed. Was being mutated, and in dangerous ways.

'If the engines keep burning,' said Miocene, eyes still clamped shut.

The image leaped ahead fifteen hours. The ship dipped into the sun's outer fringe — a warm plasma, thinner than most worthy vacuums. The hull could absorb both heat and trillions of little impacts. But simple friction had to alter the ship's velocity even more, and in another blink, the captains were falling toward the dying sun's tiny, infinitely dense partner, its mammoth gravity twisting the hull until it shattered, the ship's ancient guts strewn into a hot accretion disk, every lump and particle destined to fall into that great black nothingness, leaving the universe entirely.

'No, no, no!' Locke cried out.

'What about the Bleak?' asked dozens of voices.

With a doubting voice, Aasleen suggested, 'It'd be destroyed, maybe.'

But black holes existed in the earliest universe, created in the swirls and eddies of hyperdense plasmas. Washen reminded everyone, 'The Builders could have done this. But they knew best, and what they did instead, whatever the reason, was throw the ship out where there were very few, if any, black holes.'

The overhead image dissolved, the Temple surrounded them again.

Washen glanced at the high ceiling and base camp. Then she stared at Miocene, and she quietly asked, 'Are you sure you can't stop the engines?'

With a vivid anger, Miocene said, 'What the fuck do you think I'm doing? I'm trying to stop them now. But the engines don't know me, and I can't cut Till's hold on them!'

'Then why is he coming here?'

Silence.

'If there's nothing we can accomplish,' Washen continued, 'why doesn't Till just huddle close to the engines, and wait?'

The crying woman's face grew calm.

Reflective.

After a long moment, astonishment took her. 'Because it isn't my son,' she sputtered. 'Of course. He isn't the one who's controlling the engines.'

The Bleak, Washen realized. Fifteen billion years as a prisoner, and of course you'd want the helm at this pivotal, perfect moment!

Miocene gazed up at the diamond bridge, at the blister and the Spine. The Spine was allowing something in the depths of Marrow to give captainly commands, and as she accepted that impossibility, she asked, 'If I can bring down the bridge, Washen – cut the connection with Marrow – do you think you and your allies could sabotage enough machinery quickly enough to save us . . . ?'

Washen started to say, 'I don't know.'

An abrupt, almost gentle whump was heard, and felt, and the steel floor moved just enough to make people look at their feet.

'What did you do?' Locke asked.

Miocene rose with a tired majesty, her reddened eyes blinked a few times, and with an exhausted voice, she said. 'The array that controls the quakes. It's an old system, and it's always been mine. They couldn't steal it from me without my feeling the thief's damp fingers.'

A second tremor passed through the Temple.

Smiling at her own wicked, nearly infinite cleverness, Miocene announced, 'The iron's tired of sleeping, I think. And I don't believe we have that much time.'

A WORD AND glare gave the captains every available lift-car, and every car on the bridge, empty or filled, immediately began falling toward the Temple.

'Did you know the array has failed?' the administrator squeaked. 'That's the city's plate had already shifted five meters?'

Miocene considered, then said, 'I know. Yes.'

'Do I put key staff on the cars? To save them?'

The woman meant herself, naturally. And with a quiet indifference, Miocene told her, 'Yes. Of course. But remain here until the others can assemble. Understood?'

'Yes, madam. Yes—'

They boarded the largest car. Washen sat between Miocene and Locke, and she took a half-breath before the car jumped skyward, the air squeezed out of her. Then the entire bridge jerked sideways. The car's walls scraped against the tube. Someone gave a shout, and Washen realized that it was her own voice. She had cried out. And Locke reached up against the acceleration, finding the strength to lay a massive hand on her hand, a sad sturdy voice telling her, 'Even if we die, we might win.'

'Not good enough,' she replied. 'Not nearly.'

Again, the bridge bucked and rolled around them. Miocene made a sound, a low voice whispering to someone.

Washen let her head fall sideways. But no, the old bitch wasn't speaking to her. She was muttering to someone only she could see, her face simple and composed, and in a strange, chilling way, happy.

Washen started to ask, 'What are you doing—?'

But then they were inside the buttresses, and insane, and the car was yanked and kicked, and an unreal screech dwarfed every holler and curse, the tube surrounding the car twisted by the shaking, and slowing, nearly stopping entirely before some auxiliary system found the muscle to carry them to the top.

Doors opened with a soft, anticlimactic hiss.

Captains vomited bile and unfastened themselves, then vomited bile-scented air when they stood. Then everyone staggered out onto the open diamond platform, into the dim gray light of the nearly deserted base camp.

Two men stood waiting. Virtue wept without dignity or the smallest composure. Till, in perfect contrast, was staring at Miocene, his cold expression growing colder as he quietly remarked, 'You don't have any appreciation for what you have done, Mother. None.'

'What I'm doing,' Miocene replied, 'is saving the ship. My ship. That's all that matters here. My ship!'

The boyish face stiffened.

Then, softened.

The bridge screamed beneath them, and it pulled, and the platform plunged a full meter, then caught itself.

Washen looked down. What resembled rain clouds at first glance were billowing columns of smoke, countless fires started by the brutal, endless quakes that were tearing through the thick crust, shattering the iron plate along every weakness.

She looked up again.

A comforting hand fell on Virtue's shoulder, and Till said, 'Into the car.' He gave a soft shove, then added, 'If you wish, Locke. You can return with us, too.'

Locke straightened his back. He didn't reply.

'Then die here,' was Till's pronouncement. 'With the rest—'

Miocene lifted a hand.

Stuck into that swollen mass of flesh and nexus and bone was a small laser. It looked insubstantial. Worse than useless. Almost pathetic. But Washen knew that it could incinerate a man with a shaped flash, leaving nothing. And she knew from Miocene's face that she meant to kill her son.

The shot was never fired.

Another bolt of light came from above, evaporating her weapon and her hand. But instead of shock or pain, Miocene seemed filled with a wild, indestructible power. Bending forward, she screamed and drove with her legs, with her new bulk, slamming into her son exactly as the bridge twisted again, a seering of purple light obliterating her trailing leg.

Washen dropped down.

Then looked overhead.

She saw the Wayward soldier. Golden, was it? She saw him standing on a high catwalk, aiming the big laser with a professional calm. Quick bursts, too fast to count. Then she looked back at Miocene, watching as the woman wailed, vanishing in whiffs of boiled blood and white-hot ash.

Dying, she clung to her son.

Near death, she still managed to mutter, 'Till,' with a desperate voice. Soft, in the end. Doomed, and sorry. 'Please,' her boiling mouth whispered. And then, nothing.

A last surgical burst of light obliterated the head and the Master's mirrored cap, and late by a half-moment, her son turned to see the car and its sole occupant drop away without the slightest warning.

The bridge's machinery was failing. A safe-mode took Virtue racing downward, trying to save the precious car.

Miocene had delayed her son just enough.

Washen stared at Till, watching an impossible thought play itself out on that appealing face. How could this happen? What great purpose did it serve? In a voice meant for someone else, Till asked, 'Now what do I do?'

If there was a reply, Washen didn't hear it.

But something must have been heard, or at least thought. Because without hesitation, Till flung himself into the open door, and a moment later, the door closed and the bridge jerked sideways one last time, it and the Spine shattering just beneath the camp's diamond blister, plunging sideways toward the burning face of Marrow.

Eventually the liquid hydrogen would fall.

Captain spoke about making plans. About taking cover, or perhaps finding a car that might survive the storm. But Washen didn't take part in the plan-making, occupying herself by sitting with her legs crossed, watching nothing but the slow patient turning of her clock's little hands.

Asaleen thought she was crazy.

Again, to himself, Locke spoke comfortably about death's embrace.

Promise, then Dream, tried to thank Washen for pulling them off Marrow. 'We never thought we'd be anywhere else again,' they confessed. 'And you did your best.'

Even Golden joined them, offering his weapon in surrender, then spending the next few minutes watching Marrow boil and explode.

Finally, Washen closed her clock.

And with a nonchalant importance, she rose.

Everyone watched as she stepped out into the open and looked up. But wasn't it too soon for the cold rain? Then they saw her waving at something overhead, and every captain and both of the Waywards looked up together, watching in stunned silence while a fleet of whale-shaped vessels began to slow, making ready for a hard landing.

Pamir was first to step out.

Perri and ten armed harum-scarums followed.

Aasleen immediately recognized Pamir's craggy face, and she laughed, and she said, 'What is this? Don't you know there's a flood coming?'

Pamir lifted his eyebrows, grinning. Then he took his first good look at Marrow.

'Oh, I turned off that flood,' he remarked in a casual voice. 'Long ago,' he said. 'A lake of hydrogen inside that big long tube of vacuum . . . well, it evaporates as it falls. Believe me, we swam through what's left of it, and we probably won't get two drops here.'

Sounding insulted, Dream asked Washen, 'What about your threat? About sending down that killing flood?'

'I'm not that cruel,' Washen replied. 'I don't murder helpless worlds.'

Pamir shook his head and threw a long arm around Washen, pulling her close. 'You wouldn't have?'

'I just like to tease worlds now and again,' she added, smiling and weeping in the same instant, thinking that never in her long, strange life had she ever felt so tired . . .

THE BUILDERS

EACH OF MY engines screams and spits fire, and those titanic, withering energies translate into the gentlest of nudges. I hear nothing but a quiet coaxing voice trying to whisper me nearer to that swollen, dying sun. And I obey the voice. I obey even when I foresee a collision with its tenuous atmosphere. Even as I feel pricks and little deaths within my body, I obey the simple laws of motion and force and inertia, dipping nearer to the sun, and nearer . . . a bracing, wondrous fear taking hold of me . . .

An engine dies.

Then, two others.

Deep inside me, a series of hard bright explosions collapse fuel lines and fuse screaming pumps. The surviving engines continue to burn, but softer now. The gentle nudge has diminished to a gentle breath from behind and beside me.

But still, I fall toward the sun.

My fear loses its wonder.

Gradually and thoroughly, a wild panic seizes me.

With a sudden clarity, I watch the great war against my engines. Every act of violence is too small to matter, or slightly misplaced, or simply ill-timed. The cumulative effects are slow to gather, hard to perceive. Finally, in agony, I rally myself, trying to come to the aid of my companions.

Perhaps in tiny ways, I am felt. Heard. Believed.

A Remora considers a thousand valves, and as I whisper my advice, she closes the only valve that does lasting good.

A magnetic bottle, billions of years old and never ill, fails abruptly, at the best possible moment, spewing shards of antiiron into a spiking facility working at full throttle.

Human engineers assassinate AIs who won't listen to reason, then replace the machines at their posts.

Debris clogs a minor fuel line.

Harum-scarums attack my engines as if their brilliant fire and light are personal affronts to them.

One stubborn engine is tilted in the opposite direction, then fed all of the fuel that it can possibly consume.

And finally, the leech habitat is torn from the fuel tank's ceiling, then shoved crosswise into the gaping throat of an enormous fuel line . . .

Two more engines sputter, good as dead.

But still I can nearly taste the sun, feeling its heat and breath against my great skin . . . and a moon-sized lump of iron and nickel plunges into my side, cutting deep but leaving me intact . . . lending just enough momentum to keep me out here . . . to make me miss the sun by what, when I consider the vast distances that I have covered, is nothing . . .

I miss by nothing.

And a little later, still celebrating my very good fortune, I pass near a tiny and black and enormously massive something . . . and again, my trajectory changes . . . and peering past the curtain of stars and whirling planets. I can see where I will be going next . . .

Blackness, again.

The sunless nothing, again.

And in a strange, almost unexpected fashion, I realize this is where I want to be . . . feeling as though I am happily falling toward home again . . .

Epilogue

'TRY TALKING.'

'Hello?' said a sloppy, slow voice.

'Sorry. It's still too early, madam. I'm well aware. But you deserve to know what's happened, and what's happening now, and what you can expect when you get legs again. And a real voice. Not sounds made by a mechanical box.'

'Pamir?' she squeaked.

'Yes, madam.'

'Am I . . . alive, still . . . ?'

'We found your remains, and the other captains', too. Most of them, at least.' Pamir nodded, even though the patient couldn't see him. 'Your heads were stacked inside one of your little rooms. Waiting for trial, I suppose. If Miocene had had her way . . .'

'Where's Miocene?'

'Your best friend? Your favorite and most trusted colleague?' He allowed himself a harsh laugh, then admitted, 'Miocene died. And let's just leave it there for now. Explanations can wait a few days.'

'My ship?'

'Battered, but recovering. Madam.'

Silence.

'Her mutiny managed to fail,' he promised. 'There are pockets of resistance. Gangs and loners, and that's about it. There's no way to bring up reinforcements now.'

'Who . . . who do I thank . . . ?'

Pamir offered silence.

'You?' she asked.

Again, silence.

Finally, betraying a stew of emotions, she said, 'Thank you, Pamir.'

'And Washen, too.'

A confused sound rose up from the box. Then the Master muttered, 'I guess I don't understand very much. Do I?'

'Barely anything. Madam.'

A pause. Then, 'Who else do I thank?'

'The Remoras,' he said. 'And the harum-scarums. With help from another hundred species, plus a few million machine intelligences, too.'

Silence.

Pamir continued, admitting to the Master, 'I found lots of cooperation. But to keep it, I had to make promises. Fat ones.'

A pause. Then, 'Yes?'

'We've got holes to fill among the captains' ranks, and elsewhere. I assured our new allies that they would be our first candidates—'

'Remoras?' she interrupted.

'"Everything that can think, can serve." That's been my little motto for the last few weeks. I thought it was best.'

'Harum-scarums? As captains?'

'If they want to stay on board. Yes, madam. Naturally.'

'But why would they leave? Because a few sick officers tried to take my ship—?'

'Well, that's not really what's happening.' Pamir laughed again, adding, 'Everything is complicated, and most of the answers would take too long. But what you need to know, before anything . . . we aren't following our planned course, I'm afraid—'

'What?'

'In fact, in another few millennia, we'll be passing out of the galaxy entirely. Moving in the general direction of the Virgo cluster, it seems.'

A glowering silence.

Then the mechanical voice asked, 'What about me?'

'What about you, madam?'

'Will I remain the Master?'

'Personally, I'm split on this issue.' Pamir took a dark satisfaction, each word delivered with a practiced care. 'You surrounded yourself, madam, with competent achievers, and you cultivated their ambition, and when a few captains turned on you, you were surprised. Unprepared, and incompetent, and flabbergasted.'

Angry silence.

'Miocene wanted to put you on trial. And I could do that. As acting Master, I have the authority, in principle, and with the general mood around here, I think you'd lose your precious chair. In a fair trial, or even if you were allowed every advantage.'

A pause. Then, 'All right, Pamir. What are your intentions?'

'We can't lose you. Not in the wake of any mutiny, and not with so many changes coming this quickly.' He sighed, then added, 'Our ship needs continuity and a familiar face, and if you don't agree to reclaiming your chair – with some provisions – I will contrive some way to put your face and your big windy voice in front of the passengers and crew. Am I understood?'

She said, 'Yes.'

After a contemplative moment, she said, 'Fine.'

After a long, painful wait, she said, 'Of course you want to be my First Chair. Isn't that right, Pamir?'

'Me? No.' He laughed for a long moment. A deep, honest laugh. Then he told her, 'But I know someone more qualified. By a long ways.'

The Master might be battered and disoriented. But she was sharp enough to make a good guess, asking, 'Where's Washen? May I speak with her?'

'Eventually,' Pamir allowed.

Then he rose to his feet and set the mirrored cap on his head, at the customary angle, and he mentioned, 'Your First Chair is setting things right around the ship. Believe me, you wouldn't trust anyone else with this assignment.'

Quietly, almost submissively, the Master said, 'Thank you again, Pamir.'

'Yeah. You're welcome.'

Then with a whispering laugh, she added, 'I knew you'd bring sweet luck someday. Didn't I tell you that I had a feeling? Didn't I?'

But the Master was alone now. Pamir had slipped away without begging for permission, and nobody was there to hear the raspy voice from the little box saying, 'Thank you, thank you.' With a giddy joy, she cried out, 'To everyone who helped save me and the ship . . . a trillion sweet thanks . . . !'

AT FIRST GLANCE, they looked like lovers and nothing more.

The woman was human, tall for her species and quite lovely, and the human male sharing her table was just as tall and not nearly so pretty. The woman smiled and spoke quietly, and the man grinned and laughed, then with a word or two, he caused the woman to laugh hard and long. Then they held hands like lovers. It was a simple, natural gesture that their fingers and palms managed with a practiced perfection. Passerby barely gave them a glance. Why should they? Lovers were common along this particular avenue, and these passengers were far too busy with their own important lives to notice two humans who happened to be out of uniform, wearing faces that changed their appearance just enough to lend them a well-earned anonymity.

These were exciting times. Perhaps even wondrous

times. After aeons of utter, unruffled sameness, everything on board the Great Ship was changed. There had been a mutiny and a war, and even with that finished now, there were new changes bearing down on everyone. A new course for the ship! Talk of new captains being hired from among the passengers, and new opportunities for every species! And at the center of this great old vessel were mysteries too incredible to describe, much less comprehend in a matter of days and weeks!

Everyone wanted to see this Marrow place, if only from a safe distance. And since they couldn't actually see the world, they talked about it in loud, excited voices, or in chemical shouts, or with complicated touches that asked obvious questions for which nobody seemed to have answers.

What was locked at the center of Marrow?

What, really, was this thing they kept calling the Bleak . . . ?

And what about the Great Ship? It was on a course to leave the galaxy, which was more than a little complication for most passengers. There were only so many taxis and so many living worlds between here and the intergalactic beyond . . . and it seemed unlikely that even a fraction of those who wanted to embark would be able to do so . . .

Which left the passengers where?

Trapped, in one sense. Or in a different sense, infinitely blessed. How many souls had ever taken a voyage of this scope? Hundreds of millions of years from now, with luck, the Great Ship would slice its way through the Virgo cluster . . . and beyond those wild ports was more emptiness, and black reaches of time, and marvels that undoubtedly would astonish all of those who could endure that long, long wait . . .

And what about the Waywards? the voices asked each other, with fear and with grave respect.

Rumor stated that billions of Waywards still lived on Marrow, keeping close to the ancient Bleak. While other wise, apparently knowing voices claimed that Waywards were still running at large among the ship's well-lit, apparently peaceful avenues. They had vanished during the chaos, and now they were hiding in the most remote, empty places, gathering themselves for their next awful assault.

Unless, of course, they were nearer than that.

A few voices suggested that maybe the Waywards were among them now. Perhaps there was a chosen, well-trained cadre of priests who only pretended to be wealthy human passengers. But how would you recognize them? In what subtle, accidental way would they betray their identity, letting a simple passenger have the danger and the honor of capturing them in the middle of a brightly lit avenue?

Those two lovers were Waywards. It was their meal that gave them away. Someone noticed that the tall, pretty woman had ordered a platter filled with some monstrous thing called a hammerwing, and when it arrived at her table, she cut it open with a casual expertise, dishing out a portion to her man, then kissing the back of his hand before she let him have the first little bite.

Someone shouted, 'Waywards! There!'

Individuals from various species heard the warning translated, then responded by pushing up to the little table, leveling arms and jointed legs at the diners, and with scared voices and farts, they repeated their accusation.

'Look there! Waywards!'

'Stop them!'

'Someone, arrest them!'

The lovers couldn't have been more calm. Unhurried,

they set down their eating utensils and reached across the table one last time, fingers knotted together in that same comfortable fashion . . . and after a moment of blistering suspense, they decided to let their disguises fall away, and they stood up tall, and their touristy clothes changed back into the brilliant and lovely uniforms that captains were always supposed to wear.

To her lover, the woman asked, 'What do you think?'

'You ate this bug for how long?' the man growled.

'Nearly five thousand years,' she confessed.

'And did it ever taste good?'

'What do you think?' she asked.

Then they were laughing, and they were hugging each other . . . and it was as if there weren't crowd gathered close around them . . . as if it were just them, and they were perfectly alone . . .

'I THOUGHT YOU needed to see this for yourselves,' Washen told them. 'Sitting in the same room for an eternity can't help the creative process.'

The AI scribes stared down at the face of Marrow, saying nothing.

'Does it inspire? Are you finding any new ideas?'

Speaking for all, one of the scribes said, 'No,' with a disgusted tone. Implied were the words, 'Of course this doesn't help!'

There was little to see, in truth. Sweeping fires and the pent-up energies of countless volcanoes had filled the atmosphere below with clouds, black and opaque to almost every wavelength. But as awful as things looked from here, most of Marrow was neither burning nor boiling. Long-range sensors and every AI simulation gave the same sturdy answer: the old Wayward lands hadn't been touched by the conflagration. What was happening to the world wasn't much worse than what a million other disasters had wrought in the past. In fact, the ecosystem would probably be revitalized by the chaos, while some or most of the Waywards could hunker down, lick their wounds, and wait for the skies to clear.

The scribes continued to stare politely at the boiling black clouds.

Washen motioned. Locke walked out onto the diamond platform, knelt beside the scribes, and with a quiet reverence said, 'Maybe I can offer you a new idea. Are you interested, machines?'

One after another, the rubber faces turned toward him. Polite expressions were left frozen in place, while the rapid minds behind them ignored everything but the one vast problem worthy of their considerable trouble.

Locke said, 'This ship.'

He asked, 'What if you don't know its real dimensions?'

There was a momentary flicker of interest.

Locke licked his lips, then explained, 'When I was a child, I had a toy. A model of the ship. It fit in my hand, it was that small. But I was a boy, too young to appreciate the ship's real dimensions.'

Eyes widened, imagining his long-ago toy.

'My mother tried to explain the size of things. She told me about protons and kilometers and light-seconds, and light-years, and she promised me that the ship was huge. But light-years are huge, aren't they? So when I was five or six, I believed that the ship must be that big. Millions of light-years across, I thought. Which was silly, of course. She teased me, I remember. Oh, I was stupid in ways that none of you have ever been, I bet.'

The eyes began to drift off again.

But then Locke asked, 'What if? When they were fabricating the ship . . . what if the Builders didn't stop with the hull? Marrow surrounds the Bleak, whatever that is, and what we call the Great Ship sourrounds Marrow. But what if the hull isn't the end of their work? What if their project reaches out a lot farther, and now, after all this time, it has reached as far as we can see, or imagine . . . ?'

Without exception, the scribes leaned forward.

'You're looking into the ship's structures and exact proportions, hunting for some hidden message,' Locke concluded. 'But what if the message isn't written just in this stone and iron and hyperfiber? What if the Builders' ship is the universe, too . . . the trillions of stars and the whirling galaxies, and every unmapped mote of dust, and everything else that we can see or suppose throughout the entire visible creation . . . ?'

None of the AIs moved.

To the human ear, none made even the tiniest sound.

Washen laid a hand on Locke's shoulder, telling him, 'They're interested. They're considering it now.'

He said, 'Good.'

Mother and son walked out onto the gangway, look-ing between their feet at the dim black face of Marrow. Every available engineer was waiting above them, ready to begin pouring hyperfiber into the base camp, then the access tunnel. This wouldn't be a catastrophic collapse. They would take their time, slowly and thoroughly plug-ging this gaping hole in the chamber's otherwise perfect wall. Plainly, the Builders had reasons for what they did. As far as Washen or Pamir could see, the only sensible course was to seal the prison again, making things much as they were before and doing it as permanently as possi-ble . . . the only change being a few small, impossible-to-find security eyes stuck to the chamber's slick silver wall, watching over her millions of grandchildren . . .

For a moment, as she stood on that gangway thinking

about her grandchildren, Washen felt the sudden strange urge to throw herself at Marrow.

But she took a breath and the feeling passed, and with a practiced motion of her hand, she looked at the time. Then to Locke and the AI scribes, she announced, 'We need to be leaving. Now.'

The machines stood and gathered in a neat line.

'Have you thought about what I told you?' Locke asked them.

One of the machines replied, 'Naturally.'

'Will you have answers soon?' he pressed.

The rubber face merely smiled, and with an appealing haughtiness, it said, 'Soon. In a century or a million years. Yes. Soon.'

Washen barely heard the voice or her son's hearty laugh.

Kneeling on the gangway, where the new hyperfiber would be poured first, she set out her mechanical clock with its silver lid opened, and she left it there. It was the hardest thing in the world. But she managed to stand and walk away, muttering to herself, 'For later. I'll leave it here for now and come back to get it later . . .'

LOOK TO WINDWARD

Iain M. Banks

It was one of the less glorious incidents of a long-ago war. It led to the destruction of two suns and the billions of lives they supported. Now, eight hundred years later, the light from the first of those ancient deaths has reached the Culture's Orbital called Masaq'. For the Hub Mind, Overseer of the massive bracelet world, its arrival is particularly poignant. But it may still be eclipsed by events from the Culture's more recent past.

When the Chelgrian Ziller, a composer of galactic renown living in self-imposed exile on Masaq', learns that an emissary from his home world is being sent to the Orbital, he fears what he assumes to be the worst: that the Chelgrians want him to return.

But the composer is far from being the only thing on the Chelgrian emissary's mind. His mission has another purpose; one so secret he does not know it himself at first. Discovering its nature will take him on a journey into his past and the haunting memories of another terrible war whose legacy threatens to be much more than just an unfortunate diplomatic incident.

ENDER'S SHADOW

Orson Scott Card

Ender Wiggin was not the only young general
trained to defend Earth from a terrifying alien
threat. Many others had a part to play. But
for one of them, it was to prove crucial.

No one knew his real name, but they called him
Bean. His early life was a fight just to survive.
Even living on the streets, however, his extraordinary
talents did not escape the attention of the Battle
School recruiters. For in him they recognised a
master strategist. Someone who could become
Ender's right hand. This is the story of the boy
who became Ender's Shadow.

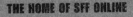